a
TOUCH
of
RUIN

SCARLETT ST. CLAIR

Bloom *books*

Published by Bloom Books, an imprint of Sourcebooks
P.O. Box 4410, Naperville, Illinois 60567-4410
(630) 961-3900
sourcebooks.com

Originally self-published in 2020 by Scarlett St. Clair.

Library of Congress Cataloging-in-Publication Data is on file with the publisher.

Printed and bound in the United States of America.
MA 30

also by
SCARLETT ST. CLAIR

When Stars Come Out

HADES X PERSEPHONE
A Touch of Darkness
A Touch of Ruin
A Touch of Malice

HADES SAGA
A Game of Fate

ADRIAN X ISOLDE
King of Battle and Blood

To the readers of A Touch of Darkness.
*Thank you for your enthusiasm
and your love of Hades x Persephone.*

PART I

"Fate's arrow, when expected, travels slow."
—DANTE ALIGHIERI, *PARADISO*

CHAPTER I
A Touch of Doubt

Persephone walked along the bank of the river Styx. Jagged waves broke the dark surface, and her skin tightened as she recalled her first visit to the Underworld. She'd attempted to traverse the wide body of water, unaware of the dead inhabiting the depths below. They'd taken her under, their fleshless fingers cutting into her skin, their wish to destroy life provoking their attack.

She thought she would drown—and then Hermes had come to her rescue.

Hades had not been pleased about any of it, but he'd taken her to his palace and healed her wounds. Later, she learned the dead in the river were ancient corpses who had come to the Underworld without coin to pay Charon's toll. Sentenced to an eternity in the river, they were just one of many ways Hades protected the borders of his realm from the living who wished to enter and the dead who wished to escape.

Despite Persephone's unease near the waterway, the

landscape was beautiful. The Styx stretched for miles, soldering to a horizon shadowed by sable mountains. White narcissus grew in clusters along its banks, ignited like white fire against the dark surface. Opposite the mountains, Hades's palace haunted the horizon, rising like the jagged edges of his obsidian crown.

Yuri, a young soul with a thick mane of cascading curls and olive skin, walked beside her. She wore pink robes and leather sandals—an ensemble that stood out against the shadowy mountains and black water. The soul and Persephone had become fast friends and often went on walks together in the Asphodel Valley, but today Persephone had convinced Yuri to stray from their usual path.

She glanced at her companion now, whose arm was looped through hers, and asked, "How long have you been here, Yuri?"

Persephone guessed that the soul had been in the Underworld for a while based on the traditional peplos she wore.

Yuri's delicate brows drew together over her gray eyes. "I do not know. A long time."

"Do you remember what the Underworld was like when you arrived?"

Persephone had a lot of questions about the Underworld from antiquity. It was that version that still had its claws in Hades, that made him feel ashamed, that made him feel unworthy of his people's worship and praise.

"Yes. I don't know that I'll ever forget." Yuri offered an awkward laugh. "It was not as it is now."

"Tell me more," Persephone encouraged. Despite

being curious about Hades's past and the history of the Underworld, she couldn't deny that part of her feared uncovering the truth.

What if she didn't like what she found?

"The Underworld was...bleak. There was *nothing*. We were all colorless and crowded. There were no days and no nights, just a monotone of gray, and we existed in it."

So they really had been *shades*—shadows of themselves.

When Persephone had first visited the Underworld, Hades had taken her into his garden. She'd been so angry with him. He had challenged her to create life in the Underworld after she'd lost to him in a game of poker. She hadn't even realized the consequences of inviting him to play, had not realized he agreed to join her with the intention of roping her into a contract. The resulting challenge was even more infuriating after she had seen his garden—a beautiful and lush oasis, full of colorful flowers and lively willows. Then he had revealed it was all an illusion. Beneath the glamour he maintained was a land of ash and fire.

"That sounds like punishment," Persephone said, thinking it terrifying to exist without purpose.

Yuri offered a faint smile and shrugged. "It was our sentence for living mundane lives."

Persephone frowned. She knew that in ancient times, heroes were usually the only ones who could expect a euphoric existence in the Underworld.

"What changed?"

"I do not know for sure. There were rumors, of course. Some said that a mortal whom Lord Hades loved died and came to exist here."

Persephone knit her brows. She wondered if there was some truth to that, considering Hades had a similar change in perspective after she'd written about his ineffective bargains with mortals. He'd been so motivated by her critique, he started the Halcyon Project, a plan that included the construction of a state-of-the-art rehabilitation center specializing in free care for mortals suffering from addiction of all kinds.

An ugly feeling crept up her spine and through her body, spreading like a plague. Maybe she hadn't been the only lover who'd inspired Hades.

Yuri continued, "Of course, I tend to think he just… decided to change. Lord Hades watches the world. As it became less chaotic, so did the Underworld."

Persephone didn't think it was that simple. She had tried to make Hades talk about this, but he avoided the subject. Now she wondered if his silence was less about shame and more about keeping the details of his past lovers a secret. She spiraled quickly, her thoughts becoming turbulent, a whirlwind picking up uncertainty and doubt. How many women had Hades loved? Did he still have feelings for any of them? Had he brought them to the bed he now shared with her?

The thought soured her stomach. Luckily, she was pulled from her thoughts when she spotted a group of souls standing on a pier near the river.

Persephone halted and nodded toward the crowd. "Who are they, Yuri?"

"New souls."

"Why do they cower on the banks of the Styx?"

Of all the souls Persephone had encountered, these looked the most…*dead*. Their faces were drawn and their skin ashy and pale. They clustered together, backs bent, arms crossed over their chests, shivering.

"Because they are afraid," Yuri said, her tone implying that their fear should be obvious.

"I don't understand."

"Most have been told the Underworld and its King are dreadful, so when they die, they do so in fear."

Persephone hated that for a lot of reasons—mainly because the Underworld wasn't a place to be feared, but she also found that she was frustrated with Hades, who did nothing to change the perception of his realm or himself.

"No one comforts them once they reach the gates?"

Yuri gave her a strange look, as if she didn't understand why someone would attempt to ease or welcome newly arrived souls.

"Charon takes them across the Styx, and now they must walk the road to judgment," Yuri said. "After that, they are deposited in a place of rest or eternal torture. It is how it has always been."

Persephone pressed her lips together, her jaw tightening with irritation. It amazed her that in one breath, they could talk about how much the Underworld had evolved and yet still witness archaic practices. There was no reason to leave these souls without welcome or comfort. She broke free of Yuri's hold and strolled toward the waiting group, hesitating when they continued to tremble and shrink away from her.

She smiled, hoping it might ease their anxiety.

"Hello. My name is Persephone."

Still, the souls quaked. She should have known her name would bring no comfort—it was meaningless. Her mother, Demeter, the Olympian Goddess of Harvest, had ensured that. Out of fear, she had kept Persephone locked in a glass prison most of her life, barring her from worship and, inevitably, from her powers.

A jumble of emotions tangled in her stomach— frustration that she could not help, sadness that she was weak, and anger that her mother had tried defying fate.

"You should show them your divinity," Yuri suggested. She had followed Persephone as she approached the souls.

"Why?"

"It would comfort them. Right now, you are no different from any soul in the Underworld. As a goddess, you are someone they hold in high regard."

Persephone started to protest. These people did not know her name—how would her Divine form ease their fears?

Then Yuri added, "We worship the Divine. You will bring them hope."

Persephone did not like her Divine form. She'd had a hard time feeling like a goddess before she had powers, and that hadn't changed even when her magic flared to life, encouraged by Hades's worship. She quickly learned it was one thing to have magic, another to use it properly. Still, it was important to her that these new souls felt welcomed in the Underworld, that they see Hades's realm as another beginning, and most of all, she wanted to ensure they knew their king cared.

Persephone released the hold she had on her human glamour. The magic felt like silk slipping from her skin, and she stood in an ethereal glow before the souls. The weight of her white kudu horns somehow felt heavier now that she was exposed in her true form. Her curly hair was brightened from a brassy gold to a pale yellow and her eyes burned an unearthly bottle green.

She smiled at the souls again. "I am Persephone, Goddess of Spring. I am so pleased you are here."

Their reaction to her radiance was immediate. They moved from trembling to worshipping on their knees at her feet. Persephone's stomach hardened, and her heartbeat quickened as she shot forward.

"Oh no, please." She knelt before one of the souls—an older woman with short, white hair and paper-thin skin. She touched her cheek, and watery blue eyes met hers. "Please, stand with me," she said and helped the woman to her feet.

The other souls remained on the ground, heads lifted, eyes transfixed.

"What is your name?"

"Elenor," the woman rasped.

"Elenor." Persephone said the name with a smile. "I hope you will find the Underworld as peaceful as I do."

Her words were like a string, straightening the woman's sagging shoulders. Persephone moved to the next soul and the next until she had spoken to each one, and they all stood on their feet again.

"Perhaps we should all walk to the Field of Judgment," she suggested.

"Oh, that won't be necessary," Yuri interrupted. "Thanatos!"

The winged God of Death appeared instantly. He was beautiful in a dark way, with pale skin, bloodred lips, and white-blond hair that fell over his shoulders. His blue eyes were as striking as a flash of lightning in the night sky. His presence inspired a sense of calm that

Persephone felt deep in her chest. It was almost as if she were weightless.

"My lady," he said as he bowed, his voice melodic and rich.

"Thanatos." Persephone couldn't help the wide smile that crossed her face.

Thanatos had been the first to offer her insight into Hades's precarious role as the God of the Dead during a tour of Elysium. It was his perspective that helped her understand the Underworld a little better and, if she were being honest, provided what she needed to fully give herself to Hades.

She gestured to the souls gathered and introduced them to the god.

His smile was slight but sincere as he said, "We've met."

"Oh." Her cheeks flushed. "I'm so sorry. I forgot."

As the reaper of souls, Thanatos was the last face mortals saw before they landed on the shores of the Styx.

"I was just about to escort the new souls to the Field of Judgment," Persephone said.

She noted that Thanatos's eyes widened slightly, and he looked at Yuri, who spoke quickly. "Lady Persephone is needed back at the palace. Could you take them for her, Thanatos?"

"Of course," he replied, bringing his hand to his chest. "I would be delighted."

Persephone waved goodbye to the souls as Thanatos turned toward the crowd, stretched his wings wide, and vanished with the souls.

Yuri wound her arm through Persephone's, tugging her away from the banks of the Styx, but Persephone didn't budge.

"Why did you do that?" she asked.

"Do what?"

"I am not needed at the palace, Yuri. I could have taken the souls to the field."

"I am sorry, Persephone. I feared they would make requests."

"Requests?" Her brows drew together. "What might they request?"

"Favors," Yuri explained.

Persephone giggled at the thought. "I am hardly in a position to grant favors."

"They don't know that," Yuri said. "All they see is a goddess who might help them get an audience with Hades or return to the living world."

Persephone frowned. "Why do you think that?"

"Because I was one of them."

Yuri tugged on her arm again, and this time, Persephone followed. Strained silence filled the space between them, and Persephone frowned.

"I'm sorry, Yuri. Sometimes I forget—"

"That I'm dead?" She smiled, but Persephone felt small and silly. "It's okay. That's one of the reasons I like you so much." She paused a moment and added, "Hades chose his consort well."

"His consort?" Persephone's brows rose.

"Isn't it obvious that Hades intends to marry you?"

Persephone laughed. "You are being very presumptive, Yuri."

Except that Hades *had* made his intentions clear. *You will be my queen. I do not need the Fates to tell me that.* Her chest tightened, the words forming knots in her stomach.

Those words should have made her heart melt, and

the fact that they didn't disturbed her. Maybe it had something to do with their recent breakup. Why did she feel such apprehension when Hades seemed so certain about their future?

Yuri, oblivious to Persephone's internal war, said, "Why wouldn't Lord Hades choose you as queen? You are an unwed goddess, and you haven't taken a vow of chastity."

The soul gave her a knowing look that made Persephone blush.

"Being a goddess does not qualify me to be Queen of the Underworld."

"No, but it's a start. Hades would never choose a mortal or a nymph as his queen. Trust me, he has had *plenty* of opportunities."

A shock of jealousy shot down Persephone's spine like a match landing in a pool of kerosene. Her magic surged, demanding an exit. It was a defense mechanism, and it took her a moment to tamp it down.

Get a hold of yourself, she commanded.

She wasn't ignorant to the fact that Hades had other lovers throughout his lifetime—one being the redheaded nymph Minthe, whom she'd transformed into a mint plant. Still, she had never considered that Hades's interest in her might be, in part, due to her Divine blood. Something dark wound its way around her heart. How could she let herself think this way about Hades? He encouraged her to embrace her divinity, worshipped her so that she might claim her freedom and power, and he'd told her he loved her. If he was to make her his queen, it would be because he cared for her, not because she was a goddess.

Right?

Persephone was soon distracted from her thoughts as she and Yuri returned to the Asphodel Valley where she was swarmed by children who begged her to play. After a short game of hide-and-seek, she was dragged away by Ophelia, Elara, and Anastasia, who wanted her opinion on wines, cakes, and flowers for the upcoming summer solstice celebration.

The solstice marked the beginning of the new year and signified the one-month countdown to the Panhellenic Games—the excitement for which even death couldn't quell among the souls. With such an important celebration at hand, Persephone had asked Hades if they could host a party at the palace, to which he had agreed. She was looking forward to having the souls in the halls again just as much as they were looking forward to being there.

By the time Persephone returned to the palace, she still felt unsettled. The darkness of her doubt swelled, pressing against her skull, and her magic pulsed beneath her skin, making her feel achy and exhausted. She rang for tea and wandered into the library, hoping that reading would take her mind off her conversation with Yuri.

Curling into one of the large chairs near the fireplace, Persephone leafed through Hecate's copy of *Witchcraft and Mayhem*. It was one of several assignments from the Goddess of Magic, who was helping her learn to control her erratic power.

It wasn't working as fast as she hoped.

Persephone had waited a long time for her powers to manifest, and when they did, it had been during a heated argument with Hades. Since then, she had managed to make flowers bloom but had trouble channeling the appropriate amount of magic. She had also discovered her ability to teleport was glitchy, which meant she didn't always end up where she intended. Hecate said it was just a matter of practice, but it still made Persephone feel like a failure. For these reasons, she'd decided not to use magic in the Upperworld.

Not until she got it under control.

So in preparation for her first lesson with Hecate, she studied, learning the history of magic, alchemy, and the diverse and terrifying powers of the gods, yearning for the day when she could use her power as easily as she breathed.

Suddenly, warmth spread across her skin, raising the hair on the back of her neck and arms. Despite the heat, she shivered, her breath growing shallow.

Hades was near, and her body knew it.

She wanted to groan as an ache began low in her stomach.

Gods. She was insatiable.

"I thought I would find you here." Hades's voice came from above, and she looked up to find him standing behind her. His smoky eyes met hers as he bent to kiss her, his hand cupping her jaw. It was a possessive hold and a passionate kiss that left her lips raw when he pulled away.

"How was your day, darling?" His endearment stole her breath.

"Good."

The corners of Hades's mouth lifted, and as he spoke, his eyes dropped to her lips.

"I hope I'm not disturbing you. You appear quite entranced by your book."

"No," she said quickly, then cleared her throat. "I mean…it's just something Hecate assigned."

"May I?" he asked, releasing her from his grip and holding his hand out for the book.

Wordlessly, she gave it to him and watched as the God of the Dead rounded her chair and thumbed through the book. There was something incredibly devilish about the way he looked, a storm of darkness dressed head to toe in black.

"When do you begin training with Hecate?" he asked.

"This week," she said. "She gave me homework."

"Hmm." He fell silent for a beat, keeping his eyes on the book as he spoke. "I heard you greeted new souls today."

Persephone straightened, unable to tell if he was irritated with her.

"I was walking with Yuri when I saw them waiting on the bank of the Styx."

Hades looked up, eyes like firelight.

"You took a soul outside Asphodel?" There was a hint of surprise in his voice.

"It's Yuri, Hades. Besides, I do not know why you keep them isolated."

"So they do not cause trouble."

Persephone giggled but stopped when she saw the look in Hades's eyes. He stood between her and the fireplace, illuminated like an angel. He really was magnificent with his high cheekbones, well-manicured beard, and full lips. His long, black hair was pulled into a knot at the back of his head. She liked it that way because she liked taking it down, liked running her fingers through it, liked seizing it when he was inside her.

At that thought, the air became heavier, and she noticed Hades's chest rose with a sharp inhale as if he could sense the change in her thoughts. She licked her lips and forced herself to focus on the conversation at hand.

"The souls in Asphodel never cause trouble," Persephone said.

"You think I am wrong." It wasn't a question but a statement, and he didn't seem at all surprised. Their whole relationship had started because Persephone thought he was wrong.

"I think you do not give yourself enough credit for having changed and therefore do not give the souls enough credit for recognizing it."

The god was silent for a long moment. "Why did you greet the souls?"

"Because they were afraid, and I didn't like it."

Hades's mouth twitched. "Some of them should be afraid, Persephone."

"Those who should will be, no matter the greeting they have from me."

Mortals know what leads to eternal imprisonment in Tartarus, she thought.

"The Underworld is beautiful, and you care about your people's existence, Hades. Why should the good fear such a place? Why should they fear you?"

"As it were, they still fear me. *You* were the one who greeted them."

"You could greet them with me," she offered.

Hades's smirk remained, and his expression softened. "As much as you find disfavor with the title of queen, you are quick to act as one."

16

Persephone froze for a moment, caught between the fear of Hades's anger and the anxiety of being called queen.

"Does…that displease you?"

"Why would it displease me?"

"I am not queen," she said, rising from her seat and approaching him, plucking the book from his hands. "I also cannot figure out how you feel about my actions."

"You will be my queen," Hades said fiercely, almost like he was trying to convince himself it was true. "The Fates have declared it."

Persephone bristled, her earlier thoughts returning in a rush. How was she supposed to ask Hades why he wanted her as his queen? Worse, why did she feel like she needed him to answer that question? She turned and disappeared into the stacks to hide her reaction.

"Does that displease you?" Hades asked again, appearing in front of her, blocking her path like a mountain.

Persephone startled but recovered quickly.

"No," she replied, pushing past him.

Hades followed close.

As she returned the book to its place on the shelf, she spoke. "Although, I would rather you want me as queen because you love me, not because the Fates have decreed it."

Hades waited until she faced him to speak. He was frowning. "You doubt my love?"

"No!" Her eyes widened at the conclusion he'd come to, then her shoulders fell. "But…I suppose we cannot avoid what others may perceive about our relationship."

"And what do others say, exactly?" He stood so close, she could smell spice and smoke and a touch of winter air. It was the scent of his magic.

A shoulder rose and fell as she said, "That we are only together because of the Fates. That you have only chosen me because I am a goddess."

"Have I given you reason to think such things?"

She stared, unable to answer. She didn't want to say that Yuri had planted the idea in her head. The thought had been there before—a seed planted early on. Yuri had merely watered it and now it was growing, as wild as the black vines that sprouted from her magic.

Hades spoke faster, demanding. "Who has given you doubts?"

"I have only just started to consider—"

"My motives?"

"No—"

He narrowed his eyes. "It seems that way."

Persephone took a step away, the bookcase pressing into her back. "I am sorry I said anything."

"It is too late for that."

Persephone glared. "Will you punish me for speaking my mind?"

"Punish?" Hades tilted his head to the side, and he moved closer, hips leaning into hips, leaving no space between them. "I am interested to hear how you think I might punish you."

Those words wound her tight, and despite the heat they inspired, she managed to glare at him.

"I am interested in having my questions answered."

Hades's jaw tightened. "Remind me again of your question."

She blinked. Was she asking him if he had only chosen her because she was a goddess? Was she asking him if he loved her?

She took a deep breath and peered up at him through her lashes. "If there were no Fates, would you still want me?"

She couldn't place the look on Hades's face. His eyes were a laser, melting her chest and her heart and her lungs. She couldn't breathe as she waited for him to speak—and he didn't. Instead, he reached for her with one hand and clasped her jaw. His body vibrated. She could feel the violence beneath, and for a moment, she wondered what the King of the Underworld intended to unleash.

Then his grip softened, and his fingers splayed across her cheek, eyes lowering to her lips.

"Do you know how I knew the Fates made you for me?" His voice was a hoarse whisper, a tone he used in the darkness of their room after they made love.

Persephone shook her head slowly, ensnared by his gaze.

"I could taste it on your skin, and the only thing I regret is that I have lived so long without you."

His lips trailed along her jaw and across her cheek. She held her breath, leaning into his touch, seeking his mouth, but instead of kissing her, he stepped away.

His sudden distance left her unsteady, and she leaned against the bookshelf for support.

"What was that?" she demanded, glaring at him.

He offered a dark chuckle, the corners of his mouth lifting. "Foreplay."

Then he reached forward, swept her into his arms and over his shoulder. Persephone gave a small yelp of surprise and demanded, "What are you doing?"

"Proving that I want you."

He strolled out of the library and into the hall.

"Put me down, Hades!"

"No."

She had a feeling he was grinning. His hand crept up between her thighs, parting her flesh, and diving inside her. She gripped the fabric of his jacket so she wouldn't fall off his shoulder.

"*Hades!*" she moaned.

He chuckled, and she hated him for it. She moved her hands to his hair and yanked, pulling his head back, seeking his lips. Hades was obliging and braced her against the nearest wall, offering a vicious kiss before pulling away to growl in her ear.

"I will punish you until you scream, until you come so hard around my cock, you are left in no doubt of my affection."

His words stole her breath and her magic awakened, warming her skin.

"Make good on your promises, Lord Hades," she said against his mouth.

Then the wall beneath Persephone gave way, and she gave a cry as Hades stumbled forward. He managed to prevent them both from landing on the floor, and once they were steady, he guided her to her feet. She recognized the way he held her—protectively, an arm wrapped high on her shoulders. She craned her neck and discovered they were in the dining room. The banquet table was crowded with Hades's staff, including Thanatos, Hecate, and Charon.

The wall they'd been pressed against was a door.

Hades cleared his throat, and Persephone buried her head in Hades's chest.

"Good evening," Hades said.

She was surprised by how calm he sounded when he spoke. He wasn't even breathless, though she could feel his heart beating hard against her ear.

She thought Hades would excuse himself and vanish, but instead he said, "The Lady Persephone and I are famished, and we wish to be alone."

She froze and jabbed him in the side.

What is he doing?

All at once, people started to move, clearing away plates, silverware, and huge platters of untouched food.

"Good evening, my lady, my lord."

They filed out of the dining room with glittering eyes and wide smiles. Persephone kept her gaze lowered, a perpetual blush on her cheeks as Hades's residents paraded into the hall to dine elsewhere.

When they were alone, Hades wasted no time leaning into her, guiding her back until her legs hit the table.

"You cannot be serious."

"As the dead," he answered.

"The…dining room?"

"I'm quite hungry, aren't you?"

Yes.

But she had no time to respond. Hades lifted her onto the table, stepped between her legs, and knelt as a servant would kneel to their queen. Her dress rose as his hands trailed up her calves. He teased, lips skimming the inside of her thighs before his mouth found her core.

Persephone arched off the table and her breath hitched as Hades worked, his tongue ruthless in its assault, his short beard creating a delicious friction against her sensitive flesh. She reached for him, tangling her fingers into his hair, writhing beneath his touch.

Hades held her tighter, his fingers digging into her flesh to hold her in place. A guttural sound escaped her when his lips fastened around her cleft and his fingers replaced his thrusting tongue, filling and stretching until pleasure exploded throughout her body.

She was sure she was glowing.

This was rapture, euphoria, ecstasy.

And it was all interrupted by a knock at the door.

Persephone froze and tried to sit up, but Hades held her in place and growled, looking up at her from his place between her legs.

"Ignore it." It was spoken like a command, his eyes ignited like embers.

He continued ruthlessly, moving deeper, harder, faster. Persephone could barely stay on the table. She could barely breathe, feeling as though she were clawing her way to the surface of the Styx again, desperate for air but content in the knowledge that this death would be a happy one.

But the knock continued, and a hesitant voice called out, "Lord Hades?"

Persephone couldn't tell who was on the other side of the door, but they sounded nervous and they had reason to be, because the look on Hades's face was murderous.

This is how he looks when he faces souls in Tartarus, she thought.

Hades sat back on his heels.

"*Go away,*" he snapped.

There was a beat of silence. Then the voice said, "It's important, Hades."

Even Persephone noted heightened alarm in the person's tone. Hades sighed and stood, taking her face between his hands.

"A moment, my darling."

"You won't hurt him, will you?"

"Not too terribly."

He didn't smile as he stepped into the hallway.

Persephone felt ridiculous sitting on the edge of the table, so she slipped off, adjusted her skirts, and started to pace the extravagant dining room. Her first impression of this room had been that it was over the top. The ceiling boasted several unnecessary crystal chandeliers, the walls were adorned in gold, and Hades's chair looked like a throne at the head of the table. To top it off, he rarely dined in this room, often preferring to take his meals elsewhere in the palace. That was one reason she'd decided to use it during the solstice celebration—all this beauty would not go to waste.

Hades returned. He seemed frustrated, his jaw flexed, and his eyes glittered with a different kind of intensity. He stopped a few inches from her, hands in his pockets.

"Is everything okay?" she asked.

"Yes," he said. "And no. Ilias has made me aware of a problem better dealt with sooner than later."

She stared at him, waiting, but he didn't explain.

"When will you be back?"

"An hour. Maybe two."

She frowned, and Hades touched her chin so that her eyes were level with his. "Trust me, my darling, leaving you is the hardest decision I make each day."

"Then don't," she said, placing her hands around his waist. "I'll go with you."

"That is not wise." His voice was gruff, and Persephone's brows knit together.

"Why not?"

"Persephone—"

"It's a simple question," she interrupted.

"It isn't," he snapped and then sighed, running his fingers through his loose hair.

She stared. He had never lost his temper quite like this. What had him so agitated? She thought about pushing for an answer but knew she would get nowhere, so instead, she relented.

"Fine." She took a step away, creating distance between them. "I'll be here when you return."

Hades frowned. "I will make it up to you."

She arched a brow and commanded, "Swear it."

Hades's eyes simmered beneath the glow of the crystal lights.

"Oh, darling. You don't need to extract an oath. Nothing will keep me from fucking you."

CHAPTER II
A Touch of Duplicity

Persephone's body vibrated, warmed from the spark Hades had ignited. Without supervision, the flame had spread, consuming her whole body. She sought a distraction and wandered outside where she walked through the garden, consumed by the smell of damp soil and sweet blossoms. She caressed petals and leaves as she passed until she came to the edge of the plot where a wild field of yellowing grass danced, encouraged by a whispered breeze.

She took off at a run, orange flowers blooming at her feet as she sailed across the field. She didn't have to focus on using her magic. It radiated from her, unfiltered and uncontrolled. Hades's Dobermans joined her, chasing each other until she came to a halt at the edge of Hecate's meadow.

The goddess sat cross-legged outside her cottage with her eyes closed. Persephone wasn't sure if she was meditating or casting a spell. If Persephone had to guess, she'd say the Goddess of Witchcraft was probably cursing some mortal in the Upperworld for some heinous deed against women.

Cerberus, Typhon, and Orthrus did not follow Persephone as she approached the goddess.

"Sated already?" Hecate asked, her eyes still closed.

Persephone would never forgive Hades for what had gone down in front of his staff.

"Does it look like it?" she grumbled.

Sexual frustration was making her sullen.

Hecate opened one eye and then the other.

"Ah," she said. "Care to train instead?"

"Only if I get to blow something up."

A small smile tugged at Hecate's berry lips. "*You* get to meditate."

"*Meditate?*"

The last thing Persephone wanted to do was be alone with her raging thoughts. Hecate patted the ground beside her, and Persephone sighed, taking a seat. Her body felt rigid, her hands warm and sweaty.

"Your first lesson, Goddess. Control your emotions."

"How is that a lesson?" Persephone asked.

Hecate gave her a knowing look. "Do you want to talk about earlier? Those doors came down because of *your* magic. They weren't opened by anyone on the inside."

Persephone pursed her lips and looked away. She had assumed someone had opened the doors, not that her magic had blown them open. Somehow, that felt even more humiliating.

"Don't be embarrassed, my dear. It happens to the best of us."

That intrigued Persephone. "Including you?"

Hecate laughed. "No, dear, I don't like people."

26

Persephone frowned.

She knew her emotions were tied to her powers. Flowers sprouted when she was angry, and vines curled around Hades in moments of passion without warning. Then there was Minthe, whose insulting words had resulted in her transformation into a mint plant, and Adonis, whom she'd threatened in the Garden of the Gods by turning his limbs into vines. Not to mention the destruction of her mother's greenhouse.

"Okay, so I have a problem," Persephone admitted. "How do I control it?"

"With practice," Hecate said. "And lots of meditation. The more often you do it, the more you—and your magic—will benefit."

Persephone frowned. "I *hate* meditating."

"Have you ever tried it?"

"Yes, and it's *boring*. All you do is…*sit*."

The corner of Hecate's mouth lifted.

"Your perspective is wrong. The point of meditation is to gain control. Are you not hungry for control, Persephone?"

Hecate's voice dipped low, tinged with seduction. Persephone couldn't deny that she was eager for what the goddess was offering. She wanted control over everything—her magic, her life, her future.

"I'm listening," Persephone said.

Hecate's smile was impish, and she continued. "Meditation means focusing your attention moment by moment rather than getting caught up in the things that plague you—the things that drown you, the things that cause your magic to create a shield around you."

Hecate led her through several meditations, guiding

27

her to focus on her breathing. Persephone imagined this might be peaceful if she could keep her mind from wandering to Hades. She swore on two occasions he was behind her. She could feel his breath on her neck, the soft scrape of his beard against her cheek as he whispered words against her skin.

I have thought of you all day.

A thrill shivered through her, and her core tightened.

The way you taste, the feel of my cock slipping inside you, the way you moan when I fuck you.

Persephone bit her lip, and heat gushed between her legs.

I want to fuck you so hard your screams reach the ears of the living.

Her breath escaped in a harsh gasp, and she opened her eyes. When she looked at Hecate, the goddess arched a knowing brow and rose to her feet.

"On second thought," she said. "Let's blow some things up."

———

"I'm going to be late!" Persephone threw off her covers and jumped from bed.

Hades groaned, stretching his arm across the sheets, reaching for her.

"Come back to bed," he said sleepily.

She ignored him, running around his bedroom in search of her things. She found her purse on a chair, her shoes under the bed, and her clothes wrapped up in the bedsheets. She untangled them, and once they were free, Hades snatched them from her hands.

"Hades—" she growled, lunging for him.

His hands clamped down on her waist, and he rolled, pinning her beneath him.

She laughed, squirming.

"Hades, stop! I'm going to be late and it's already your fault."

He had made good on his promise, returning to the Underworld around three in the morning. When he slipped into bed behind her, he'd kissed her good night and hadn't stopped. After, she'd fallen into a deep sleep, hitting the snooze button when her phone alarm went off to wake her.

"I'll take you," he said, bending to kiss her neck. "I can get you there in seconds."

"Hmm," she said, pressing her palms against his chest. "Thanks, but I prefer taking the long way."

He arched a brow and gave her a menacing look before rolling off. She got to her feet again, holding up her wrinkled clothes, and frowned.

"Allow me to help," Hades said and snapped his fingers, manifesting a tailored black dress and heels.

She looked down, smoothing her hands over the fabric, which had a faint shimmer.

"Black isn't my usual color choice," she said.

Hades smirked. "Humor me," he said.

Once she was ready, he insisted she accept a ride from his driver, which was how she ended up in the back of Hades's black Lexus. Antoni, a cyclops and a servant to the God of the Dead, was in the driver's seat whistling a song Persephone recognized from Apollo's *White Raven* album. Despite not being a fan of the god's music, she'd spent Friday night celebrating her best friend Lexa Sideris's birthday at the god's club where his songs were on a constant rotation. She now felt she knew them all by heart, which only made her distaste for them stronger.

She did her best to ignore Apollo's incessant falsetto and was soon distracted by a series of messages from Lexa. The first one read:

You're officially famous.

A tidal wave of anxiety gripped her as her best friend sent several links to "breaking news" from outlets all over New Greece, and they were all about her and Hades.

She clicked on the first link, then the next, and the next. Most of the articles rehashed details of her public reunion with Hades, including incriminating photos. She blushed seeing reminders of that day. She hadn't expected the King of the Dead to appear in the Upperworld, and when she'd seen him, she thought her heart would explode. She'd run to him, jumped into his arms, and coiled around him like she belonged there. Hades's hands pressed into her bottom, and their lips locked in a kiss she could still feel.

She should have seen the media storm coming, but after Lexa's birthday party, she'd spent the weekend in the Underworld, sequestered in Hades's bedchamber, exploring, teasing, submitting. She hadn't thought twice about the state of the Upperworld once she'd left. With images like these, it was hard to deny speculation about their relationship.

The last message she received scared her the most:

EVERYTHING YOU NEED TO KNOW ABOUT HADES'S LOVER

30

It was her worst nightmare.

She scanned the article, relieved to discover there wasn't any information that would reveal her as the daughter of Demeter or a goddess, but it was still creepy. It said that she was from Olympia, that she had started attending New Athens University four years ago, began with a major in botany and ended with a major in journalism. There were a few quotes from students who claimed to "know her"—gems like, "*You could tell she was really smart*" and "*She was always really quiet*" and "*She read a lot.*"

The article also detailed a timeline of her life that included her internship at *New Athens News,* her articles about Hades, and their reconciliation outside the Coffee House.

> Onlookers say they weren't sure of Hades's motives when he materialized in the Upperworld, but it appeared he was there to make amends with the journalist, Persephone Rosi, which begs the question: When did their romance begin?

Persephone recognized the irony of her situation. She was an investigative journalist. She loved research. She loved getting to the bottom of an issue, exposing facts, and saving mortals from the wrath of gods, demigods, and themselves.

But this was different.

This was her personal life.

She knew how the media worked—she was now a mystery to be solved, and those who investigated her background were a threat to everything she'd worked so hard for.

A threat to her freedom.

I know you're freaking out right now, Lexa texted. *Don't.*

That's easy for you to say. Your name isn't plastered across headlines.

Her friend responded, *Technically, it isn't your name—it's Hades's.*

Persephone rolled her eyes. She didn't want to be someone's possession. She wanted her own identity, to be credited for her hard work, but dating a god took that away.

Another thought occurred to her—*what would her boss say?*

Demetri Aetos was a great supervisor. He believed in the truth and reporting on it no matter the consequences. He'd fired Adonis for calling Persephone a bitch and stealing her work. He'd recognized the stress she was under when it came to writing about Hades, and he'd told her she didn't have to keep writing about him if she didn't want to…but that was before he knew she was dating the God of the Dead.

Would there be consequences?

Gods, she had to stop thinking about this.

She focused on her phone and texted Lexa back.

Stop trying to avoid the BEST news of the day. Congrats on your first day!

Lexa had been hired to plan events for the Cypress Foundation, Hades's nonprofit organization. Persephone had learned about it shortly after the announcement of the Halcyon Project.

Lexa had been offered the job on her birthday.

"She would have gotten the job anyway," Hades had said when Persephone asked if he'd made it happen. "She is a great fit."

Thanks, my love! I'm so excited! Lexa texted.

"We're here, my lady."

Antoni's words drew her attention to the Acropolis.

Persephone's eyes widened, and her stomach knotted when she looked out the window

A crowd had gathered outside the one-hundred-and-one-story building. Security had stepped in to control it, erecting barriers. Several confused employees made their way inside amid the screaming crowd. Persephone knew they were there for her, and she was glad the windows of Hades's car were virtually black, making it impossible for anyone to see inside. Still, she slid lower in her seat, groaning.

"Oh no."

Antoni raised a brow at her in the rearview mirror.

"Is something wrong, my lady?"

She met his gaze, almost confused by the question.

Of course something is wrong!

The media, that crowd, they were threatening everything for which she'd worked so hard.

"Can you drop me off around the block?" Persephone asked.

Antoni frowned. "Lord Hades instructed you were to be dropped off at the Acropolis."

"Lord Hades isn't here, and as you can see, that is not ideal," she said, grinding her teeth. Then she took a breath to calm herself. "Please?"

The cyclops relented and did as she instructed. In the time it took them to get there, Persephone glamoured up a pair of sunglasses and pulled her hair into a bun. It wasn't much of a disguise, but it would get her farther than flashing her face to passersby.

Antoni glanced at her again and offered, "I can walk you to the door."

"No, that's okay, Antoni. Thank you."

The cyclops shifted in his seat, clearly uncomfortable. "Hades won't like this."

She met Antoni's gaze in the mirror. "You won't tell him, will you?"

"It would be best, my lady. Lord Hades would provide you with a driver to take you to work and pick you up and an aegis for protection."

She didn't need a driver, and she didn't need a guard.

"Please?" she begged Antoni. "Don't tell Hades."

She needed him to understand. She would only feel like a prisoner, something she'd been trying to escape for over eighteen years.

It took the cyclops some time to cave, but eventually, he nodded. "If you wish, my lady, but the first time something goes wrong, I'm calling the boss."

Fine. She could work with that. She patted Antoni on the shoulder. "Thank you, Antoni."

She left the safety of the car and kept her head down as she walked in the direction of the Acropolis. The roar of the crowd amplified as she neared, and she paused when she was within view—it had grown.

"Gods," she moaned.

"You really got yourself into a pickle," a voice said from over her shoulder. She spun and found a handsome, blue-eyed god standing behind her.

Hermes.

Over the last few months, he had become one of her favorite gods. He was handsome, funny, and encouraging. Today, he was dressed like a mortal. Well, for the most part. He still looked unnaturally beautiful with his golden curls and glowing, bronzed skin. His outfit of choice was a pink polo and dark jeans.

"A…pickle?" she asked, confused.

"It's an expression the mortals use when they find themselves in trouble. You haven't heard of it?"

"No," she answered, but that wasn't surprising. She'd spent eighteen years in a glass prison. She hadn't learned a lot of things. "What are you doing here?"

"Saw the news," he said, grinning. "You and your boy toy are official."

Persephone glared.

"Man toy?" he offered.

She still glared.

"Okay, fine. God toy then."

She gave up and sighed, burying her face in her hands. "I'll never be able to go anywhere again."

"That's not true," Hermes said. "You just won't be able to go anywhere without being mobbed."

"Has anyone ever told you're not helpful?"

"No, not really. I mean, I am the Messenger of the Gods and all."

"Weren't you replaced by email?"

Hermes pouted. "Now who's not being helpful?"

Persephone peered around the corner of the building again. She felt Hermes's chin rest atop her head as he followed her gaze.

"Why don't you just teleport inside?" he asked.

"I'm trying to maintain my mortal facade, which means no magic on Earth."

She didn't really feel like explaining that she was training to control her magic.

"That's ridiculous. Why wouldn't you want to walk down that enticing runway?"

"What about normal, mortal life don't you understand?"

"All of it?"

Of course he didn't. Unlike her, Hermes had always existed as an Olympian. In fact, he'd begun his life the same way he lived it now—mischievously.

"Look, if you aren't going to help—"

"Help? Are you asking?"

"Not if it means I owe you a favor," Persephone said quickly.

Gods had everything: wealth, power, immortality. Their currency was the currency of favors, which were, essentially, a contract, the details to be decided at a future time, and unavoidable.

She'd rather die.

"Not a favor then," he said. "A date."

She offered the god an annoyed look. "Do you want Hades to gut you?"

"I want to party with my friend," Hermes countered, folding his arms over his chest. "So gut me."

She stared at him, feigning suspicion, before smiling, "Deal."

The god gave a dazzling smile. "How's Friday?"

"Get me into that building, and I'll check my schedule."

He grinned. "On it, Sephy."

Hermes teleported into the middle of the crowd, and his fans screamed like they were dying. Hermes ate it up, signing autographs and posing for pictures. All the while, Persephone crept along the walkway and entered the Acropolis unseen. She bolted for the elevators, keeping her head down as she waited with a group of people. She knew they were staring, but it didn't matter. She was inside, she had avoided the crowd, and now she could get to work.

When she arrived on her floor, the new receptionist, Helen, greeted her. She had replaced Valerie, who had moved up a few floors to work for Oak & Eagle Creative, Zeus's marketing company. Helen was younger than Valerie and still in school, which meant she was eager to please and cheery. She was also very beautiful with eyes as blue as sapphires, cascading blond hair, and perfect pink lips. Mostly, though, she was just really nice. Persephone liked her.

"Good morning, Persephone!" Helen said in a singsong voice. "I hope getting here wasn't too difficult for you."

"No, not difficult at all." Persephone managed to keep her voice even. That was probably the second-worst lie she had ever told, next to the one where she promised her mother she'd stay away from Hades. "Thank you, Helen."

"You have already received several calls this morning. If they were about a story I thought you'd be interested in, I transferred them to voicemail, but if they called to interview you, I took a message." She held up a ridiculous stack of colorful sticky notes. "Do you want any of these?"

Persephone stared at the stack of notes. "No, thank you, Helen. You really are the best."

She grinned.

Just as Persephone started toward her desk, Helen

called to her, "Oh, and before you go, Demetri has asked to see you."

Dread grew heavy and hard in her stomach, as if someone had dropped a stone straight down her throat. She swallowed, managing to smile at the girl.

"Thank you, Helen."

Persephone crossed the workroom floor, flanked by perfectly lined desks, stowed her things, and grabbed a cup of coffee before approaching Demetri's office. She stood in the doorway, not ready to call attention to herself. Her boss sat behind his desk looking at his tablet. Demetri was a handsome, middle-aged man with salt-and-pepper hair and a perpetual five-o'clock shadow. He liked colorful clothing and patterned neckties. Today, he wore a bright red shirt and a blue bow tie with white polka dots.

A stack of newspapers lay on the desk in front of him, bearing headlines like:

IS LORD HADES IN A RELATIONSHIP WITH A MORTAL?

JOURNALIST CAUGHT KISSING GOD OF THE DEAD

MORTAL WHO SLANDERED KING OF THE UNDERWORLD IN LOVE?

Demetri must have felt her staring, because he finally looked up from his tablet. The article he was reading reflected off his black-framed glasses. She noted the title. It was another piece about her.

"Persephone. Please, come in. Close the door."

That stone in her stomach felt suddenly heavier. Shutting herself in Demetri's office was like walking right back into her mother's greenhouse. Anxiety built, and she felt fear at the thought of being punished. Her skin grew hot and uncomfortable, her throat constricted, her tongue thickened…she was going to suffocate.

This is it, she thought. *He is going to fire me.*

She found herself frustrated that he was drawing it out. Why invite her to sit? Act like it had to be a conversation?

She took a deep breath and sat on the edge of her chair.

"What did you do?" she asked, glancing at the pile of newspapers. "Pick one up on every block?"

"Couldn't help it," he said, smirking. "The story was fascinating."

Persephone glared.

"Did you need something?" she asked finally, hoping to change the subject—hoping that the reason he'd called her into his office had nothing to do with this morning's headlines.

"Persephone," Demetri said, and she cringed at the gentle tone his voice had taken. Whatever was coming, it wasn't good. "You have a lot of potential and you have proven you're willing to fight for the truth, which I appreciate."

He paused and her body stayed tense, preparing for the blow he was about to deliver.

"But," she said, guessing the direction of this conversation.

Demetri looked even more sympathetic.

39

"You know I wouldn't ask if I didn't have to," he said.

She blinked, brows furrowing. "Ask what?"

"For an exclusive. On your relationship with Hades."

The dread crawled up her stomach and spread, sizzling in her chest and lungs, and she felt the heat abruptly leave her face.

"Why do you have to ask?" Her voice was tight, and she tried to stay calm, but her hands were already shaking and squeezing her coffee cup.

"Per—"

"You said you wouldn't ask if you didn't have to," she stopped him. She was tired of him saying her name. Tired of how *long* it was taking him to get to the point. "So why are you asking?"

"It came from the top," he answered. "It was very clear that you either offer us your story or you don't have a job here anymore."

"The top?" she echoed and paused for a moment, searching for a name. After a moment, it came to her. "Kal Stavros?"

Kal Stavros was a mortal. He was the CEO of Epik Communications—which owned *New Athens News*. Persephone didn't know much about him except that he was a tabloid favorite. Mostly because he was beautiful— his name literally meant *crowned the most beautiful*.

"Why would the CEO request an exclusive?"

"It's not every day the girlfriend of the God of the Dead works for you," Demetri said. "Everything you touch will turn to gold."

"Then let me write something else," she said. "I have a voicemail and an inbox full of leads."

It was true. The messages had started pouring in the

moment she published her first article on Hades. She'd slowly been sorting through them, organizing them into folders based on the god they criticized. She could write about any Olympian, even her mother.

"You can write something else," Demetri said. "But I'm afraid we'll still need that exclusive."

"You can't be serious," was all she could think to say, but Demetri's expression told her otherwise. She tried again. "This is my personal life."

Her boss's eyes dropped to the stack of papers on his desk.

"And it became public."

"I thought you said you would understand if I wanted to cease writing about Hades."

She noted that Demetri's shoulders fell, and it made her feel better that he was at least a little defeated by this too.

"My hands are tied, Persephone," he answered.

There was a stretch of silence, and then she asked, "That's it? I have no say in this?"

"You have your choices. I need the article by next Friday."

That was it—she was dismissed.

She stood and made her way back to her desk and sat. Her head spun as she thought of ways to get out of this situation, other than writing the article or quitting. Working for *New Athens News* had been her dream since she'd decided to go into journalism her freshman year of college. She believed completely in their mantra of telling the truth and exposing injustice.

Now she wondered if all that was meaningless.

She wondered what Hades would say if she told him

41

the CEO of Epik Communications had demanded a story on them, but she also recognized that she didn't want Hades to fight her battles. She despised the fact that she knew they would listen to Hades because of his status as an ancient Olympian and not to her—someone they presumed was a mortal woman.

No, she would figure this out on her own, and she was certain of one thing—Kal would regret his threat.

Persephone didn't look up from her computer after leaving Demetri's office. Despite how focused she appeared, she was aware of the office's curious stares. They felt like spiders skittering across her skin. She focused harder, combing through hundreds of messages in her inbox and listening to voicemails from people who "had a story for her." Most were about how Zeus and Poseidon had turned their mother/sister/aunt into a wolf/swan/cow for nefarious reasons, and Persephone found herself wondering how Hades could be related to the two.

Lexa checked in during lunch, sending a text.

You doing okay?

No, things got worse. Persephone texted back.

????

I'll tell you later. Too much to text.

Wanna get drunk? Lexa asked.

Persephone laughed. *We have to work tomorrow, Lex.*

I'm just trying to be a good friend.

Persephone smiled and admitted, *Maybe a little drunk, then. Plus, we need to celebrate YOUR first day with the Cypress Foundation. How's it going?*

Amazing, Lexa replied. *There is a lot to learn, but it's going to be amazing.*

Persephone managed to avoid Demetri for the rest of the day. Helen was the only one who engaged her in conversation, and that was to tell her she had mail, which included a pink envelope. When Persephone opened it, she found it full of crudely cut paper hearts.

"Did you see who put this in my mailbox?" she asked Helen. There was no return address and no stamp. Whoever sent it hadn't mailed it.

The girl shook her head. "It was there this morning."

Weird, she thought, tossing the mess into the garbage.

At the end of the day, Persephone took the elevator to the first floor and found the crowd still outside. She considered her options. She could just exit through the front and brave the mob. Security would give her an escort but only as far as the pavement, unless she called Antoni for a ride. She knew the cyclops was willing enough, but his loyalty to her would wane if he saw these people were still waiting for her to leave work, and she really, *really* didn't want an aegis. There was also the slight chance that her magic would respond if challenged, and she wasn't willing to risk exposing herself, which ruled out teleportation. That left her with only one other option—finding another way out of the building.

There were other exits; it was just a matter of finding one that wasn't being stalked by rabid fans. She sounded paranoid, but she was informed. Admirers of gods would do anything for a glimpse, a touch, a taste of the Divine, and that included their significant others.

She turned and set off down the hallway, away from the masses, in search of another exit.

She considered leaving through the parking garage but didn't like the possibility of being cornered by a bunch of strangers in a place that was dark and smelled like oil and piss.

Maybe a fire exit, she thought, even if it set off an alarm. The doors weren't accessible from the outside, so it was unlikely anyone would wait by one.

Excited by the idea of getting home and spending the evening with Lexa after this stressful day, she quickened her pace. Rounding a corner, she slammed into a body. She didn't look up to see who it was, fearing they might recognize her.

"Sorry," she muttered, pushing away and hurrying for the exit ahead.

"I wouldn't go out that door if I were you." A voice stopped her just as her palms touched the metal handle. She turned, meeting a pair of gray eyes. They were housed in the thin, handsome face of a man with a mop of unruly hair, sharp cheekbones, and full lips. He was dressed in a gray janitor's jumpsuit. She had never seen him before.

"Because the door has an alarm?" she asked.

"No," he answered. "Because I just came in that door, and if you're the woman that's been in the news the last three days, I think the people outside are there for you."

She sighed, frustrated, and added in a desolate tone, "Thanks for the warning."

She'd started down the adjoining hallway when the man called to her.

"If you need help, I can get you out of here."

Persephone was skeptical. "How, exactly?"

The corners of his lips lifted, but it was like he had forgotten how to smile.

"You're not going to like it."

44

CHAPTER III
A Touch of Injustice

He was right. She hated it.

"I'm not getting in that thing."

That thing was a tilt truck full of garbage.

She was wrong when she said she didn't want the smell of oil and piss. She'd take it, so long as it didn't mean bathing in rancid trash.

The janitor led her to the basement, a trek that had her feeling uneasy and clutching her apartment keys tight. *This is how people are murdered,* she thought and then quickly reminded herself that she watched too much true crime.

The basement was full of various things—extra furniture and artwork, a laundry room, an industrial kitchen, and a maintenance room where she stood now, staring at her "getaway vehicle," as the man had started to refer to it.

He seemed pretty amused now.

"It's either this or you walk out the door," he said. "Your choice."

"How do I know you won't wheel me into that waiting crowd?"

"Look, you don't have to get in the cart. I just thought you might like to go home sometime tonight. As for me outing you, I'm not really interested in seeing anyone get hurt for their association with the gods."

There was something in the way he spoke that made her think he'd been wronged by them, but she didn't press. She stared at him for a moment, biting her lip.

"Okay fine," she grumbled finally.

The man helped her into the cart, and she settled into the space he'd created for her.

Holding a bag of trash aloft, he looked at her questioningly.

"Ready?"

"As ready as I'll ever be," Persephone said.

He arranged the bags over her, and suddenly she was in the dark and the cart was moving. The rustle of plastic grated against her ears, and she held her breath so she didn't have to smell rot and mold. The contents of the bags dug into her back, and each time the wheels hit a crack in the floor, the cart jostled, and the plastic grazed her like snake's skin. She wanted to vomit but held it together.

"This is your stop," she heard the janitor say, lifting the bags he'd used to hide her. Persephone was greeted by a blast of fresh air as she rose from the dark pit.

The man helped her out, awkwardly grasping her waist to set her on her feet. The contact made her cringe, and she stepped away, unsteady.

He had taken her to the end of an alleyway that let out onto Pegasus Street. From here, she could get to her apartment in about twenty minutes.

"Thank you..." she said. "Um...what was your name?"

"Pirithous," he supplied and held out his hand.

"Pirithous." She took his hand. "I'm Persephone...I guess you already knew that."

He ignored her comment and just said, "It's nice to meet you, Persephone."

"I owe you, for the getaway car."

"No, you don't," he said quickly. "I'm not a god. I don't extract a favor for a favor."

He definitely has a history with the Divine, she thought, frowning. "I just meant that I would bring you cookies."

The man offered a dazzling smile, and in that moment, beneath the exhaustion and the sadness, she thought she could see the person he used to be.

"See you tomorrow?" she asked.

He gave her the strangest look, chuckling a little, and said, "Yeah, Persephone. I'll see you tomorrow."

———

By the time Persephone arrived home, the apartment smelled like popcorn and Lexa's music blared throughout the house. It wasn't the kind you could dance to—it was the kind that could summon clouds and rain and darkness. The music cast its own spell, drawing on darker thoughts, like revenge against Kal Stavros.

Lexa was waiting in the kitchen. She had already changed into her pajamas—a set that showed off her tattoos: the phases of the moon on her bicep, a key wrapped in hemlock on her left forearm, an exquisite dagger on her right hip, and Hecate's wheel on her left upper arm. Her thick, black hair was piled on top of her head. She had a bottle of wine in hand and two empty glasses waiting.

"There you are," Lexa said, pinning Persephone with those piercing blue eyes. She indicated the bottle of wine. "I got your favorite."

Persephone smiled. "You're the best."

"I thought I was going to have to file a missing persons report."

Persephone rolled her eyes. "I'm only thirty minutes late."

"And not answering your phone," Lexa pointed out.

Persephone had been so distracted trying to get out of the Acropolis and make it home unnoticed, she hadn't even bothered to retrieve her phone from her purse. She did so now and found four missed calls and several texts from Lexa. Her best friend had started by asking if she was on her way, if she was okay, and then resorted to sending random emojis just to get her attention.

"If you really thought I was in trouble, I doubt you'd have sent me a million emojis."

Lexa smirked as she uncorked the wine. "Or I cleverly thought to annoy your kidnapper."

Persephone took a seat opposite Lexa at the kitchen bar and sipped her wine. It was a rich and flavorful cabernet, and it instantly took the edge off her nerves.

"Seriously though, you can't be too careful. You're famous now."

"I'm not famous, Lex."

"Uh, did you read any of the news articles I sent you? People are obsessed."

"*Hades* is famous, not me."

"And you by association," Lexa argued. "You're all anyone at work wanted to talk about today—who you were, where you were from."

Persephone groaned. "You didn't *say* anything about me, did you?"

It was no secret that Lexa was Persephone's best friend.

"You mean that I've known you've been sleeping with Hades for about six months and that you're a goddess masquerading as a mortal?"

Lexa's tone was light.

"I haven't been sleeping with Hades for six months." Persephone felt the need to defend herself.

It was Lexa's turn to narrow her eyes. "Okay, five months, then."

Persephone glared.

"Look, I'm not blaming you. There are few women who wouldn't jump at the chance to sleep with Hades."

"Thanks for the reminder," Persephone shot back, rolling her eyes.

"It's not like he ever would. It's his fault your relationship is such big news anyway. As far as the media is concerned, you are his first serious partner."

Except the reality was much different, and while Persephone knew there had been other women in Hades's life, she didn't know the details. She wasn't sure she wanted to. She thought of Minthe and shuddered.

Persephone took a sip of her wine. "I want to talk about *you*. How was your first day?"

"Oh, Persephone," Lexa gushed. "It really is a dream. Did you know the Halcyon Project is expected to treat five thousand people in its first year?"

49

She didn't, but that was amazing.

"And Hades gave me a tour and introduced me to everyone."

Persephone couldn't really explain how that made her feel, but it didn't feel good. The best way to explain it was…she felt embarrassed. She felt like she should have known Hades was going to be there on Lexa's first day, but the God of the Dead hadn't said anything about that this morning when he helped her get ready.

"That was nice of him," she commented distractedly.

"Apparently he does it for every new employee. I mean, I knew Hades wasn't like other gods, but to greet his staff the way he did?" Lexa shook her head. "It's just…so evident he loves you."

Persephone's gaze rose to meet hers. "Why do you say that?"

"Everywhere I looked today, I could see how he was inspired by you."

Persephone knitted her brows. "What do you mean?"

Lexa shrugged. "It's…a little hard to explain. He just…uses some of the words you use when he talks about helping people. He talks about hope and forgiveness and second chances."

The more Lexa talked, the more pressure Persephone felt in her chest—a familiar tinge of jealousy squeezing her lungs.

Her best friend giggled. "Then there are the…physical things."

Persephone raised a brow, and Lexa burst into laughter.

"No, not *that!* Physical things like…pictures."

"Pictures?"

It was Lexa's turn to look confused. "Yeah. He has pictures of you in his office. Didn't you know that?"

No, she didn't know Hades had an office at the Cypress Foundation, much less pictures of her.

Where had he gotten pictures of her? She didn't have pictures of him. Suddenly, Persephone wasn't interested in talking about this anymore.

"Can I ask you something?" Lexa said.

Persephone waited and sort of dreaded the question.

"You've always wanted notoriety for your work, so what's the problem with all this attention?"

Persephone sighed.

"I want to be respected in my field," she said. "Now I just feel like a possession of Hades. Every article is Hades this and Hades that. Hardly anyone even uses my name. They call me *mortal*."

"They would use your name if they knew you were a goddess," Lexa supplied.

"And I would have recognition for my divinity and not my work."

"What's so wrong about that?" Lexa asked. "You might be known for your divinity initially, but it could lead to being known for your work."

Persephone couldn't explain why it was important for her to be known for writing; it just was. She'd spent her whole life being horrible at the one thing she was born to be, and despite that not being her fault, she'd worked really hard in college. She wanted someone to see that hard work, and not just because she wrote about and dated Hades.

"If I were you, I'd leave this life without a second thought," Lexa said.

Persephone blanched, surprised. "It's way more complicated than that, Lex."

"What's so complicated about immortality and wealth and power?"

Everything, Persephone wanted to say. Instead, she asked, "Is it really so wrong to want to live an unassuming, mortal life?"

"No, except that you also want to date Hades," Lexa pointed out.

"I can have both," Persephone argued. She'd *had* both until a few days ago.

"That was when Hades was your secret," Lexa said.

And even though Persephone and Hades had neither confirmed nor denied media speculation, she was going to have to reveal her relationship if she wanted to keep her job.

Persephone frowned.

"Hey," Lexa said, pouring more wine into Persephone's glass. "Don't worry about it too much. Pretty soon they'll become obsessed with some other god and some other mortal. Maybe Sybil will decide she actually loves Apollo."

Persephone wasn't so sure about that. The last time they'd talked about it, Sybil had expressed that she wasn't interested in a relationship with the God of Music.

"I'm going to shower," Persephone said.

The thought of scalding hot water sounded better and better. She didn't want to feel this day on her skin any longer, not to mention she still felt like she was surrounded by trash, the smell still lodged in her nose.

"When you're finished, we'll watch a movie," Lexa said.

Persephone took her wine and purse into the bedroom. Dropping her bag on the bed, she moved into the bathroom and turned on the shower. As the water heated, she stepped back into her bedroom, sipping her wine before setting the glass aside so she could unzip her dress.

She paused when she felt Hades's magic surround her. It was a distinct feeling—a tinge of winter on the air. She closed her eyes and prepared to vanish. It wouldn't be the first time Hades had taken her to the Underworld without any notice, but instead, a hand touched beneath her chin and lips closed over hers. He kissed her like they hadn't made love into the early hours of the morning, and when he pulled away, Persephone was breathless, the stress of her day forgotten.

Hades's palm was warm against her cheek, and he brushed her lips with his thumb, dark eyes searching.

"Troubled, darling?"

She opened her eyes to narrow her gaze, suspicious.

"You followed me today, didn't you?"

Hades didn't even blink. "Why would you think that?"

"You insisted Antoni take me to work this morning, most likely because you already knew what the media was reporting."

Hades shrugged. "I didn't want to worry you."

"So you let me walk into a mob?"

He raised a knowing brow. "*Did* you walk into that mob?"

"You *were* there!" she accused. "I thought we agreed. No invisibility."

"I wasn't," he answered. "Hermes was."

Damn you, Hermes.

53

She'd forgotten to extract a promise from the God of Mischief not to tell Hades about the crowd. He'd probably waltzed into Nevernight with a smile on his face to report what happened.

"You could always teleport," Hades offered. "Or I can provide an aeg—"

"I don't want an aegis," she stopped him. "And I'd rather not use magic, not…in the Upperworld."

"Unless you're exacting revenge?"

"That's not fair. You know my magic has become more and more unpredictable. And I'm not eager to be exposed as a goddess."

"Goddess or not, you are my lover."

She didn't mean to stiffen, but she wasn't a fan of that word. She knew by the way Hades's eyes narrowed, he had noticed.

He continued, "It is only a matter of time before someone with a vendetta against me tries to harm you. I *will* keep you safe."

Persephone shivered. She hadn't thought about that.

"You really think someone would try to harm me?"

"Darling, I have judged human nature for a millennium. Yes."

"Can't you, I don't know, erase people's memories? Make them forget about all this." She waved her hand between them.

"It is too late for that." He paused a moment and then asked, "What is so terrible about being known as my lover?"

"Nothing," she said quickly. "It's just that *word*."

"What's wrong with lover?"

"It sounds so fleeting. Like I am nothing but your sex slave."

One corner of his lips curled. "What am I to call you, then? You have forbidden the use of *my queen* and *my lady.*"

"Titles make me *uncomfortable,*" she said.

She wasn't sure how else to explain why she'd asked him not to call her my queen or my lady, but it added up to the fact that they were two labels she could get used to, and that meant she was setting herself up for potential disappointment. The thoughts made her feel guilty, but the echoes of the heartbreak she'd experienced while they were separated made her cautious.

"It's not that I don't want to be known as your lover…but there has to be a better word."

"Girlfriend?" Hades supplied.

She couldn't suppress the laugh that tore from her throat.

"What's wrong with girlfriend?" he asked, glowering.

"Nothing," she said quickly. "It just seems so insignificant."

Their relationship was too intense, too passionate, too ancient for her to merely be his girlfriend.

But maybe that was just how she felt.

The tension eased from Hades's features, and he drew his finger under her chin.

"Nothing is ever insignificant when it comes to you," he said.

They stared at each other, and the air was heavy. Persephone itched to reach for him—to bring his lips to hers, to taste him. All she had to do was close the gap between them and they would ignite—fall so deep in their passion, nothing would exist beyond their skin.

A knock at her door tore her from her thoughts and sent her heart into a frenzy.

"Persephone! I'm ordering pizza. Any requests?" Lexa called.

She cleared her throat. "N-no. Whatever you order is fine," she replied through the door.

"So pineapple and anchovies. Got it."

Persephone's heart was still hammering in her chest. There was a long pause on the other side of the door, and for a moment, Persephone thought Lexa had left, until she asked, "Are you okay?"

Hades chuckled and leaned in, pressing his lips against her skin. Persephone exhaled, her head rolling back. "Yes."

Another long pause. "Did you even hear what I'm going to order?"

"Just get cheese, Lexa!"

"Okay, okay, I'm on it." Persephone could tell by the tone of her voice, Lexa was smiling.

Persephone pushed against Hades's chest and met his gaze.

"You shouldn't laugh."

"Why not? I can hear your heart beating. Are you afraid to be caught with your boyfriend?"

Persephone rolled her eyes. "I think I preferred lover."

His laugh was a deep rumble. "You are not easy to please."

It was her turn to smile. "I would give you the chance, but I'm afraid I don't have time."

Hades's eyes darkened, and his hold on her tightened.

"I don't need long," he said, hands twining in her dress as if he wished to rip it from her body. "I could make you come in seconds. You won't even have to get undressed."

She almost took the bait and challenged him to prove it, but then she remembered how he'd left her in the dining room the day before, and despite returning and making up for it, she wanted to punish him.

"I'm afraid seconds will not do," she said. "I'm owed pleasure—hours of it."

"Allow me to give you a preview, then." He held her close, his arousal pressing into her softness, but she kept him at a distance, palms pressed against his hard chest.

"Perhaps later," she offered.

He smiled. "I'll take that as a promise."

With that, he vanished.

Persephone showered and changed. When she left the room, Lexa was curled up on the couch. Persephone sat beside her, sharing Lexa's blanket and the popcorn.

"What movie are we watching?"

"*Pyramus and Thisbe,*" Lexa answered.

It was a movie the pair had watched over and over, an ancient tale about forbidden love retold in modern times.

"I'm just glad you didn't say *Titans After Dark.*"

"Hey! I like that show."

"The way they portray the gods is totally inaccurate."

"*We know,*" Lexa said. "They don't do Hades justice, but if he has a problem with it, tell him it's his own fault. He's the one who's refused to be photographed…well, until recently."

They started the movie, and it opened by introducing the feuding families, locked in a war for territory. Pyramus and Thisbe were young and eager for fun. They met at a club, and under those fierce and hypnotic lights, they fell in love, later learning they were sworn enemies.

The movie was in the middle of a tense scene between the families, the one where Thisbe's brother dies, shot and killed by Pyramus, when the doorbell rang, surprising Persephone and Lexa. They exchanged a look.

"It's probably the pizza guy," Lexa said.

"I'll get it." Persephone was already throwing off the blanket. "Pause the movie!"

"You've seen this a hundred times!"

"Pause it!" she threatened playfully. "Or I'll turn you into basil."

Lexa cackled but paused the movie. "That actually might be cool."

Persephone opened the door.

"Sybil!" She smiled wide, but excitement quickly gave way to suspicion.

Something was wrong.

Even dressed in pajamas and sporting a top knot, the blond was a beauty. Sybil stood under the pallid porch light, looking exhausted and like she'd been crying, mascara streaked down her face.

"Can I come in?" It sounded like she had something stuck in her throat.

"Yeah, of course."

"Is it the pizza?" Lexa called, walking into view. "Sybil!"

That was when the girl burst into tears.

Lexa and Persephone exchanged a look and quickly wrapped their arms around her as she sobbed.

"It's okay," Persephone whispered, attempting to soothe her.

She thought she could sense Sybil's pain and confusion, though she had never perceived emotions in another person before. They were like shadows grazing

58

her skin, flutters of sadness, strikes of jealousy, and an endless cold.

Strange, Persephone thought. She pushed the feelings down, quashing them to focus on Sybil.

The three stood like that for a while, embracing one another in a tight circle until Sybil began to collect herself. Lexa was the first to break form and poured Sybil a glass of wine while Persephone directed her to the living room and gave her a box of tissues.

"I'm so sorry," Sybil finally managed to say, accepting the wine with shaking hands. "I had no other place to go."

"You're always welcome," Persephone said.

"What happened?" Lexa asked.

Sybil's mouth quivered, and it took her a few moments to speak. "I'm…I'm not an oracle anymore."

"What?" Lexa asked. "How can you not be an oracle anymore?"

Sybil had been born with certain prophetic gifts, including divination and prophecy. Persephone also knew that Sybil could see the threads of Fate, which she had referred to as "colors" when she'd told Persephone she and Hades were meant to be together.

Sybil cleared her throat and took a deep breath, but even as she spoke, her voice broke. "I told myself I wouldn't cry over this anymore."

"Sybil." Persephone reached for her hand.

"Apollo fired me and took my gift of prophecy away," she explained. She laughed humorlessly, wiping her eyes as more tears slid down her cheeks. "Turns out you can't continue to reject a god without consequences."

Persephone couldn't believe what she was hearing. She recalled Sybil's comments about her relationship with Apollo. Everyone, even her close friends Xerxes and Aro, had assumed they were lovers, but Sybil had told her and Lexa that she wasn't interested in a relationship with the God of Music.

"He wanted more from me than friendship, and I refused. I'd heard about his previous relationships; all of them ended in disaster. Daphne, Cassandra, Hyakinthos…"

"Let me get this straight," Persephone said. "This… *god-child* got a little pissy because you wouldn't date him and took away your power?"

"Shh!" Sybil looked around, clearly afraid Apollo would appear and smite them. "You can't say things like that, Persephone!"

She shrugged. "Let him try to take revenge."

"You are fearless because you have Hades," Sybil said. "But you forget, gods have a habit of punishing those you care for most."

Sybil's words made her frown, and she suddenly felt less confident.

"So you don't have a job anymore?" Lexa asked.

Because of her gifts, Sybil had been enrolled at the College of the Divine. There, she'd learned to hone her power and had been chosen by Apollo specifically to become his public relations manager. Without her gift, the job Sybil had spent the last four years training for was not attainable. Even if she had retained her powers, Persephone wasn't sure anyone would hire a disgraced oracle, especially one Apollo had fired. Apollo was the golden god. He'd been named *Delphi Divine*'s God of the Year seven years in a row, only losing the title once after Zeus struck the magazine's building with lightning in protest.

"He can't do that!" Persephone exploded. She didn't care how beloved the God of Music was. He didn't deserve that respect if he punished people just because they didn't want to date him.

"He can do anything," Sybil said. "He's a god."

"That doesn't make it right," Persephone argued.

"Right, wrong, fair, unfair—it's not really the world we live in, Persephone. The gods punish."

Those words made Persephone shudder, and the worst part was, she knew it was true. The gods used mortals as their playthings and cast them aside when they got angry or bored. Life was nothing to them because they had eternity.

"I wouldn't even mind being fired, but who will hire me now?" Sybil said, her voice desolate. "I just don't know what to do. I can't go home. My mother and father disowned me when I applied for the College of the Divine."

"You can work with me," Lexa offered, looking at Persephone as if to say, *can't she?*

"I'll ask Hades," Persephone promised. "I'm sure they can use more help at the foundation."

"And you can stay with us," Lexa added. "Until you are on your feet again."

Sybil looked skeptical. "I don't want to inconvenience you."

Lexa scoffed. "You would not be an inconvenience. You can keep me company while Persephone's in the Underworld. Hell, you can probably have her room. It's not like she's here most nights anyway."

Persephone gave Lexa a playful push, and Sybil laughed. "I don't want your room."

"You might as well crash there. Lexa's not wrong."

"Of course I'm not wrong. If I was sleeping with Hades, I wouldn't be in my room either."

Persephone reached for a pillow and smacked Lexa.

It was the wrong thing to do.

Lexa shrieked like a banshee and reached for a cushion, swinging wildly. Persephone dodged the blow, which left Sybil to take the brunt of it.

Lexa dropped the pillow.

"Oh my gods, Sybil, I am so sorry—"

But Sybil took up a pillow too and smashed it into the side of Lexa's face.

It wasn't long before the three were locked in battle, chasing one another around the living room, delivering and taking hits until they collapsed in a heap on the couch, breathless and giggling.

Even Sybil seemed to be enjoying herself, the last few hours of her life momentarily forgotten. She sighed and said, "I wish all days were this happy."

"They will be," said Lexa. "You live with us now."

By the time the pillows were returned to their place, the pizza had arrived. The delivery guy apologized profusely and explained that traffic had been backed up due to protests.

"Protests?" Persephone asked.

"It's the Impious," he said. "Protesting the upcoming Panhellenic Games."

"Oh."

The Impious were a group of mortals who rejected the gods, choosing fairness, free will, and freedom over worship and sacrifice. Persephone wasn't all that surprised that they'd showed up to protest the games, but it was kind of unexpected, given that the Impious had kept a low profile for the last few years. She really hoped they stuck to peaceful protesting and didn't escalate. A lot of people would be out and about for the festivities, Persephone, Lexa, and Sybil included.

The girls settled down to finish their movie, ate pizza, and kept their distance from topics that involved Apollo, though that didn't keep Persephone from trying to figure out how to help Sybil.

Apollo's actions were unacceptable, and didn't she have an obligation to her readers to expose injustice? Especially when it came to the gods? And maybe, if the story was good enough, she wouldn't need to write that exclusive.

Hours later, Persephone was still awake and unable to move. Sybil's head rested in her lap, and Lexa snored, fast asleep on the couch opposite them.

After a moment, Sybil shifted and spoke in a sleepy whisper.

"Persephone, I want you to promise me you won't write about Apollo."

Persephone froze for a moment, holding her breath. "Why not?"

"Because Apollo isn't Hades," Sybil answered. "Hades didn't care what people thought and was willing to listen to you. That's not Apollo. Apollo covets his reputation. It's as important to him as music."

"Then he shouldn't have punished you," Persephone answered.

She felt Sybil's hands curl into the blanket around them. "I'm asking you not to fight in my name. Promise."

Persephone didn't respond. The problem was she

was asking for a promise, and when a god promised, it was binding, unbreakable.

It didn't matter that Sybil didn't know of Persephone's divinity.

She couldn't do it.

After a moment, Sybil looked up, meeting her gaze. "Persephone?"

"I don't make promises, Sybil."

Sybil frowned. "I was afraid you'd say that."

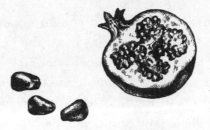

CHAPTER IV
A Touch of Warning

Persephone lay awake, listening to Lexa's shallow snoring and Sybil's wheezing breath. It was three in the morning; she had to be up in four hours, but she couldn't stop thinking about everything that had happened today. She considered the pros and cons of writing the exclusive Demetri and Kal wanted. She supposed it was one way to control the information she released, except that she was being forced to offer up details of her personal life. Worse, they'd taken the choice away from her, and she hated that.

But could she give up her dream job? She'd come to New Athens with dreams of freedom, success, and adventure. She'd had a taste of each, and just when she'd shaken the chains of her mother's custody, she found herself shackled with another restraint.

Would the cycle never end?

Then there was Sybil.

Persephone couldn't let Apollo get away with his

treatment of her friend. She couldn't understand why Sybil didn't want her to write about the God of Music. He needed to answer for his behavior.

Persephone sighed. Her head was so full of thoughts—words piled up so high, it felt like they were pushing against her skull. She stood quietly and teleported to the Underworld, slipping into Hades's bedchamber. If anyone was going to ease the tension in her head, it was the God of the Dead.

She hadn't expected to find him asleep. She'd begun to suspect he rarely slept, except when she was around. He lay partially covered by silk sheets, his muscled chest contoured from the firelight of the hearth. His arms were over his head, as if he'd fallen asleep stretching. She reached to touch his face and was surprised when his hand bit down on her wrist.

She yelped, more from fear than pain. Hades opened his eyes.

"Fuck," he cursed. Sitting up lightning fast, he lessened his hold on her wrist and drew her to him. "Did I hurt you?"

She would have answered, but he was pressing kisses to her skin, and each one sent a shock through her body.

"Persephone?" He stared up at her, a myriad of emotions clouding his eyes. It was almost like he was despondent; his breath was shallow and his brows drawn together.

She smiled, brushing a piece of hair from his face. "I'm fine, Hades. You only scared me."

He kissed her palm and held her tight against him as he lay down.

"I did not think you would come to me tonight."

She rested her head on his chest. He was warm and solid and right.

"I can't sleep without you," she admitted, feeling completely ridiculous, but it was true.

Hades's palms soothed, running up and down her back. Now and then, he paused to squeeze her bottom. She wiggled against him, his erection growing harder between them.

"That is because I keep you up so late."

She sat up, straddling him, and laced her fingers through his.

"Not everything is about sex, Hades."

"No one said anything about sex, Persephone," he pointed out.

She raised a brow and rolled her hips. "I don't need words to know you're thinking about sex."

He chuckled, and his hands moved to her breasts. Her breath caught in her throat, and her fingers curled around his wrists like shackles.

"I want to talk, Hades."

He arched a perfect brow. "Talk," he said. "I can multitask…or have you forgotten?"

He rose into a sitting position and captured a nipple between his teeth, teasing her through her shirt. She wanted to give in and let him explore. Her hands—*traitorous hands*—slid around his neck and tangled into his hair. He smelled like warm spice, and she could practically taste his tongue, flavored with whiskey.

"I don't think you can multitask this time," she said. "I know that look."

Hades pulled away long enough to ask, "What look?"

She took his head between her hands. She thought

67

to keep him from distracting her with his mouth, but his hands were moving under her shirt, over her skin, making her shiver.

"That *look*," she said, as if it explained everything. "The one you have now. Your eyes are dark but there's something…alive behind them. Sometimes I think it's passion. Sometimes I think it's violence. Sometimes I think it's all your lifetimes."

His eyes glittered, and his hands fell to her thighs.

"*Hades*," she hissed his name, and he covered her mouth with his, shifting so that she was beneath him. His tongue slipped into her mouth. She'd been right about how he would taste, smoky and sweet. She wanted more and twined her arms around his shoulders and her legs around his waist. His lips left hers to explore the contours of her neck and breasts.

Persephone tightened her hold around his waist to keep him from shifting lower.

"Hades," she breathed. "I said I wanted to talk."

"Talk," he said again.

"About Apollo," she breathed.

Hades froze and he growled—it was an unnatural sound, and it sent a shiver down her spine. He pulled away completely, no longer touching her.

"Tell me why the name of my nephew is upon your lips?"

"He's my next project."

Hades blinked, and she was certain she saw violence in his eyes.

She hurried to continue. "He fired Sybil, Hades. For refusing to be his lover."

He stared, and his silence was angry. His lips were set

68

tight, and a vein pulsed in his forehead. He left the bed completely naked. For a moment, she watched him walk away—well-muscled ass and all.

"Where are you going?" she demanded.

"I can't stay in our bed while you talk about Apollo."

She didn't miss that he had called *his* bed *our bed*. That made her feel warm inside, except that she'd fucked it up by mentioning Apollo.

She scrambled after him.

"I'm only talking about him because I want to help Sybil!"

Hades poured himself a drink.

"What he's doing is wrong, Hades. Apollo can't punish Sybil because she rejected him."

"Apparently he can," Hades said, taking a slow sip from his glass.

"He has taken away her livelihood! She has nothing and will have nothing unless Apollo is exposed!"

Hades drained his glass and poured another. After a stretch of tense silence, he said, "You cannot write about Apollo, Persephone."

"I've told you before, you can't tell me who to write about, Hades."

The God of the Underworld set his glass down with an audible click.

"Then you should not have told me your plans," he said.

She guessed his next thought: *You shouldn't have mentioned Apollo in my bedchamber either.*

His words fueled her anger, and she felt her power moving in her veins.

"He won't get away with this, Hades!"

She didn't add that she really needed this story—that it would provide a diversion for what her boss really wanted. Hades must have sensed the change in her power, because when he spoke again, his words were careful and calm.

"I'm not disagreeing with you, but you aren't going to be the one to serve justice, Persephone."

"Who, if not me? No one else is willing to challenge him. The public adores him."

She didn't understand how they could love Apollo and fear Hades.

"All the more reason for you to be strategic," Hades reasoned. "There are other ways to have your justice."

Persephone wasn't sure she liked what Hades was insinuating.

She glared at him. "What are you so afraid of? I wrote about you, and look at the good that came out of it."

"I am a reasonable god," he said. "Not to mention you intrigued me. I do not want Apollo intrigued by you."

Persephone didn't care if Apollo became intrigued by her or not—the God of Music wouldn't get anywhere with her.

"You know I'll be careful," she said. "Besides, would Apollo really mess with what's yours?"

Hades's lips thinned, and he held out his hand for her to take.

"Come," he said, sitting in a chair before the fire.

She approached as if his words were magnetic and she were steel. Hades's fingers wrapped around hers and he pulled her to him, her knees on either side of his thighs. Every curve melded to his hard frame. She kept his dark gaze as he spoke.

70

"You do not understand the Divine. I cannot protect you from another god. It is a fight you would have to win on your own."

Persephone's confidence wavered. There were a lot of rules that bound gods—promises and contracts and favors—and they all had one thing in common.

They were unbreakable.

"Are you saying you wouldn't fight for me?"

Hades sighed and brushed his finger along her cheek. "Darling, I would burn this world for you."

He kissed her fiercely, violently, leaving her lips raw. When he broke away, she was breathless, and his hands were pressed so firmly into her skin, it was like he was holding her bones.

"I am *begging* you—do not write about the God of Music."

She found herself nodding, transfixed by the vulnerable look in Hades's dark eyes. He hadn't been near as desperate to stop her from writing about himself.

"But what about Sybil?" she asked. "If I do not expose him, who will help her?"

Hades's eyes softened. "You cannot save everyone, my darling."

"I'm not trying to save everyone, just the ones who are wronged by the gods."

He studied her for a moment and then brushed a piece of her hair from her face.

"This world does not deserve you."

"Yes, they do," she answered. "Everyone deserves compassion, Hades. Even in death."

"But you are not talking about compassion," he said, his thumb brushing her cheek. "You are hoping to

71

rescue mortals from the punishment of gods. It is as vain as promising to bring the dead back to life."

"Because you have deemed it so," she argued.

Hades looked away, clenching his jaw. She had obviously struck a chord. Guilt made her stomach turn. She knew she was being unfair. The Underworld had rules and a balance of power she didn't completely understand.

She hadn't meant to upset him, but she really wanted change. She reached for him, guiding his eyes back to hers.

"I won't write about Apollo," she said.

He relaxed a little, but his face was still hard.

"I know you wish for justice, but trust me on this, Persephone."

"I trust you."

His expression was blank, and it felt a little like he didn't believe her. That thought was fleeting as he lifted her into his arms, holding her gaze and moving toward the bed.

He sat her on the edge, helped her out of her clothes, and guided her to her back. He knelt between her legs, and his mouth descended, lapping at the tight bundle of nerves at the apex of her thighs. Persephone arched off the bed, her head digging into the mattress, her hands tangling in the sea of sheets around her. She struggled to catch her breath.

"Hades!"

Her cries seemed to have no effect on him as he kept his languorous, torturous pace. Soon his fingers parted her hot flesh, joining his tongue. He stroked and stretched her, moving in tandem with her breathing until she found release.

When he was finished, he sat back on his heels, brought his fingers to his lips, and sucked them clean.

"You are my favorite flavor," he said. "I could drink from you all day."

Hades gripped her hips and pulled her toward him, sliding into her in one slick thrust. She felt him in her blood and bones and soul.

The friction built inside her, and soon her moans turned to screams.

"Say my name," Hades growled.

Persephone clutched the silk beneath her. The sheets stuck to her skin, her body warm with perspiration.

"Say it!" he commanded.

"Hades!" she gasped.

"Again."

"Hades."

"Pray to me," he commanded. "Beg me to make you come."

"Hades." She was out of breath—her words barely formed. "Please."

He thrust.

"Please what?"

Thrust.

"Make me come."

Thrust.

"Do it!" she screamed.

They came together, and Hades collapsed on top of her, kissing her deeply, the taste of her still upon his lips. After a moment, he gathered her into his arms and teleported to the baths where they showered and worshipped one another again.

With an hour to spare before she had to be up,

Persephone lay down to rest. Hades stretched out beside her, holding her close.

"Persephone?" Hades spoke, the scruff of his beard tickling her ear.

"Hmm?" She was too tired to use words, eyes heavy with sleep.

"Speak another's name in this bed again and know you have assigned their soul to Tartarus."

She opened her eyes. She wanted to look at him, to see the violence in his gaze and chase it—*why had this upset him so much?* Did the God of the Underworld, Rich One, Receiver of Many, fear Apollo?

After his warning, Hades relaxed, his breath growing even and calm. Reluctant to disturb his peace, she snuggled close and fell asleep.

CHAPTER V
Royal Treatment

Persephone relayed the disastrous conversation she'd had with Hades to Lexa at lunch the next day. They'd chosen a booth at the back of their favorite café, the Yellow Daffodil, that gave them relative privacy. Despite the roar of the restaurant, Persephone felt paranoid talking about Hades in public. She leaned over the table toward Lexa, whispering.

"I've never seen him so…"

Unyielding. So obstinate. He was usually willing to at least hear her out, but from the moment Apollo's name had left her mouth, Hades had been finished with the conversation.

"Hades has a point," Lexa said, leaning back in her chair, crossing her legs.

Persephone looked at her best friend, surprised she would side with the God of the Dead.

"I mean, do you really think you can touch Apollo's reputation? He's the golden boy of New Athens."

"An honor he doesn't deserve considering how he treats the men and women he 'loves.'"

"But…what if people don't believe you, Persephone?"

"I can't worry about whether or not people will believe me, Lex."

The thought that Apollo's victims would be ignored because of his popularity infuriated her, but what enraged her more was that she knew Lexa was right. There was a chance no one would believe her.

"I know. I'm just saying…it might not play out like you think."

Persephone frowned, confused by her friend's words. "And what do I think?"

Lexa twisted her fingers together on the table in front of her and shrugged, finally lifting her gaze to Persephone's. Her eyes looked more vivid today, probably due to the smoky shadow she wore.

"I don't know. I mean, you are literally hoping for reason from a god who can't take rejection. It's like you think you can magically change Apollo's behavior with some words."

Persephone flinched and noticed that Lexa's eyes shifted to Persephone's shoulder. In her peripheral, she saw green, and when she looked, a thread of vines had sprouted out of her skin. Persephone clapped a hand over them. Of all the times her magic had responded to her emotions, it had never manifested liked this. She pulled the vines free with a stinging pain, and blood spilled down her arm.

"Oh my gods!" Lexa shoved a wad of napkins into her hands, and Persephone pressed them against her shoulder. "Are you okay?"

"I'm fine."

"Has this ever happened before?"

"No," she said, peeling back the napkins to look at the wound the vines left behind. The gash was small, like she'd been scratched by a thorn, and the bleeding minimal.

She really needed to continue her lessons with Hecate.

"Is that a goddess thing?" Lexa asked.

"I don't know."

Persephone had never seen her mother's powers manifest this way, or Hades's for that matter. Maybe it was just another example of how terrible she was at being a goddess.

"Will you tell Hades?"

The question surprised Persephone, and her gaze shot to Lexa's. "Why would I tell him?"

She listed the reasons. "Because it's never happened to you before, because it looks painful, because it might have something to do with being the Goddess of Spring?"

"Or it's nothing," Persephone said quickly. "Don't worry about it, Lex."

A beat of silence passed between them before Lexa reached a hand across the table to draw Persephone's attention.

"You know I'm just worried about you, right?"

The Goddess of Spring sighed. "I know. Thank you."

There was more silence, and then Lexa shrugged. "I guess none of this really matters. You already promised Hades you wouldn't write about Apollo...right?"

Persephone was reluctant to meet Lexa's gaze.

"Persephone—"

77

"What about Sybil? Are we just supposed to let her suffer?" Persephone asked.

"No, we're supposed to be her friends," Lexa said.

"Which means I should do everything in my power to ensure Apollo is exposed."

"It means you should do what Sybil wants you to do."

Persephone frowned. Sybil wanted Persephone to leave this situation alone, but silence was part of the problem. How many people had been hurt by Apollo and not spoken up?

"Are all the Divine wired for revenge?" Lexa posed the question offhandedly, as if she were asking it rhetorically, but it didn't sit well with Persephone.

"What do you mean?"

Lexa shrugged. "You all want to *punish*. Apollo wants to punish his lovers so you want to punish him, and he will probably punish you for that. It's insanity."

"I don't want to punish him," Persephone said defensively.

Lexa raised a brow.

"I don't! I want people to know they shouldn't trust him."

"Just like you wanted people to know not to trust Hades?"

"That's different."

It was true Persephone had started her series on Hades with the intention of exposing his unfair bargains with mortals. Over time, however, she'd learned his intentions were far more honorable than she'd originally assumed.

Lexa sighed. "Maybe, but isn't that what Hades was telling you? Apollo is willing to punish without a second thought."

Persephone averted her gaze, frustrated, and Lexa's outstretched hand covered her own.

"I just want you to be careful. I know Hades will protect you as much as he can, but I also know how hard it is for you to ask for help."

Persephone managed a small smile. She knew Lexa was only speaking out of concern for her, but her best friend didn't know the whole story. She still hadn't told her about her boss's ultimatum. She felt like she was in a bargain with Hades again, faced with losing two things she valued most. Perhaps if she explained, Lexa would understand, but as Persephone started to speak, they were interrupted by a stranger.

"You're Hades's girlfriend, aren't you?"

The voice startled them, and the question made Persephone cringe. A young woman had appeared beside their table. She wore a long shirt, tights, and boots. Her phone was in her hand, and she was pulling at the elastic holding her hair in a top knot.

"Can I get a picture?" the girl asked as she fluffed her hair and smoothed it over her shoulder.

"Sorry, no," Persephone said. "I'm having lunch."

"It'll just take a second." The girl leaned in to take a selfie, her camera on. Persephone shifted away, holding out her hands to stop the girl.

"I said no."

"Just one," the girl attempted to bargain.

"What about no don't you understand?" Persephone asked.

The girl straightened and blinked at Persephone. Then her eyes narrowed. "You don't have to be a bitch. It's just a picture."

The girl lifted her phone and snapped a photo. Her outburst had drawn attention, and as Persephone watched her storm off, she noticed several customers had their phones pointed in her direction. She covered her face with her hand.

Lexa leaned across the table. "This would be a great time to use your powers for nefarious reasons."

"Didn't you just criticize my use of magic for punishment?"

"Yeah but…she deserves it. She was an asshole."

"I think it's time to go," Persephone said, reaching for her purse.

They left money on the table to cover their bill. Lexa looped her arm through Persephone's as they exited the cafe. The sidewalks were teeming with employees returning to work, tourists, and street vendors. It was a hot but cloudy day, and the air smelled like roasting chestnuts, cigarettes, and coffee.

"Do you have time to stop by the office?" Lexa asked. "I can give you a tour and tell you all about the project I'm working on!"

Persephone checked her watch. She still had thirty minutes before she had to be back at the Acropolis.

"I'd love that."

She wanted to see where Lexa worked and, if she were being honest, explore. She'd felt embarrassed when Lexa had listed off facts about the Halcyon Project, none of which she knew.

Lexa officed out of a building called Alexandria Tower. It was the opposite of Nevernight with an all glass and white marble exterior. Lexa held the door open for Persephone. Like every place Hades occupied, the interior was luxurious. The floors were veined marble, the receptionist desk a pool of black obsidian, and the dark furniture accented in gold. Persephone felt right at home.

A nymph seated behind the receptionist desk stood quickly. Like all her kind, she was beautiful—all sharp angles and wide eyes. She was a woodland nymph—a dryad, evident by her almond-colored hair, mossy eyes, and the faint green tinge to her skin. These were the nymphs Persephone had spent the most time with growing up in the greenhouse. She'd never considered it before, but now she wondered if they were just as much prisoners of her mother as she had been.

"Lady Persephone," the woman at the desk said as she bowed. "You honor us with your presence."

Lexa giggled, and Persephone blushed.

"I've brought Persephone for a tour, Ivy."

The dryad's eyes widened, and Persephone got the impression she didn't like being surprised.

"Oh, of course, Lady Persephone. First…can I get you anything? A glass of champagne or wine, perhaps?"

"Oh, no, thank you, Ivy. I have to return to work after this."

"Let me make a few calls," Ivy said. "I'd prefer everything to be perfect before you go up."

"It's alright, Ivy," Lexa said with a playful laugh. "Persephone doesn't care."

The dryad paled. Several months ago, this behavior would have made Persephone uncomfortable. It still gave her anxiety, but she recognized it for what it was—a servant of Hades wishing to please—and Persephone didn't want to keep her from that, so she stepped in.

"Take your time, Ivy," Persephone said. "In the interim, a water would be nice."

The dryad smiled. "Right away, my lady."

Persephone took a few steps away from the desk and swept the room. She loved the character of the building. It wasn't as modern as Nevernight, boasting antique accents like glass doorknobs, gold heating grates, and a radiator. A formal seating area was arranged in front of a set of large windows that overlooked the street. Persephone paused in front of it, admiring the busy cityscape on the other side.

"I thought you weren't thirsty," said Lexa as she joined her by the window.

Persephone smiled and said, "You can never have enough water."

"Really, what was that? I could have had this tour underway."

The goddess sighed. "I've learned a few things since being in the Underworld, Lex. You see me as your best friend, so bringing me here means nothing but a bit of fun for you, but these people—they see me...differently."

"You mean they see you as the Queen of the Underworld?"

She shrugged. That was definitely true of the residents of the Underworld. "They serve Hades, and no matter how much I argue, they seem to think they serve me by association."

More than likely because they were ordered to, she thought.

"Being of service pleases them. The more I fight it, the more I offend, I think."

"Hmm," Lexa said after a moment, and when Persephone looked at her friend, she found her smiling mischievously.

"What?" Persephone asked, skeptical.

"Nothing, Queen Persephone."

Persephone rolled her eyes and Lexa laughed, turning away from the window.

Ivy intercepted them carrying a silver tray with two glasses of water.

"Today's flavor is cucumber and ginger."

Persephone took the glass and a napkin. She knew the dryad would be eager to know if she liked the drink, so she sipped it immediately.

"Hmm, very refreshing, Ivy. Thank you."

The nymph beamed and then handed Lexa a glass. Ivy disappeared once more, and when she returned, she was still smiling, as if she were on a high.

"They're ready for you, Lady Persephone, Lexa."

Persephone's stomach was suddenly in knots. She'd been able to handle this one interaction well, but would she do as well with more?

"Finally!" Lexa said unceremoniously.

As they ascended the stairs to the second floor, Persephone turned back to Ivy.

"Thank you, Ivy. I appreciate everything."

She didn't look long enough to register the nymph's reaction as she followed Lexa up the stairs.

What they found when they got there stopped them in their tracks. The hall was lined on either side with employees who had stepped out of their glass offices to greet Persephone. There was also a man taking photos.

"Lady Persephone, it is an honor." A woman approached. She was mortal and had a crown of black curls. She shook Persephone's hand. "I'm Katerina, director of the Cypress Foundation."

"It's a pleasure to meet you," Persephone said.

"Please allow me to tell you a few things about our progress. I'm sure you will be pleased."

Persephone exchanged a look with Lexa. Her lips were pinched together and her jaw clenched. This wasn't what her friend had imagined when she'd suggested a tour. Persephone tried to ignore the sudden guilt that came with this whole experience. All Lexa had wanted to do was show off her new workplace, neither of them expecting to be treated this way. They'd have been better off coming here after hours.

Katerina narrated their walk, quoting some facts that Lexa had already shared. It was clear she had an elevator speech prepared for all situations.

"We were very excited when the Halcyon Project was announced," Katerina said. "We've worked on several initiatives with Lord Hades, but never something quite like this."

"Other projects?" Persephone asked. This was news to her.

Katerina smiled. She seemed genuinely excited to have communicated something Persephone was unaware of and explained, "The Halcyon Project is just one of many initiatives under the Cypress Foundation."

"Tell me more."

"Well, there's Cerberus House, a nonprofit for animals. The organization has founded fourteen no-kill animal shelters in New Greece and pays for pet adoption fees. We're very excited to be opening a fifteenth location in Argos. There's also the Safe Haven Project which helps families pay for funeral and burial costs. So far, we've aided over three hundred families in their time of need."

Persephone was speechless, and yet the woman kept going.

"Lord Hades's longest-running charity is Chariot, a fund that provides training for therapy dogs for children in need."

Persephone swallowed a lump in her throat.

"Th-that's amazing."

Her feelings were all over the place. She felt awe that Hades had started so many wonderful organizations but frustrated and embarrassed that she didn't know about any of them. Why hadn't he told her? Why hadn't she stumbled across any of this during her research on the God of the Dead?

Gods, she looked like such a jerk, having written such *slander* about him. Perhaps that was why so many of these people were eager to tell her about all his accomplishments, to further prove her wrong.

Damn his humility.

The tour continued a little while longer, and several introductions were made. Persephone met the people behind each of Hades's charity initiatives. At the end, Katerina turned and said, "If there's nothing else, I'd be happy to escort you downstairs, my lady."

What about Hades's office?

Luckily, Lexa intervened.

"I'll take it from here, Katerina. Persephone and I need to finalize some plans anyway."

"Oh…"

"Thank you so much, Katerina," Persephone said before the woman could protest. "I'm very excited to tell Hades how wonderful you've been."

That worked like a charm. Katerina smiled and

gave a very flustered, "Why, thank you so much, Lady Persephone."

When they were alone, Lexa leaned forward. "You wanna see Hades's office?"

"You know it."

They giggled like schoolgirls as Lexa led her up another flight of stairs. This floor was all dedicated office space, and Persephone and Lexa wound their way through a set of cubicles before reaching a row of offices at the back of the building.

"Here it is!" Lexa said, gesturing to the space with her arms spread wide as she stepped inside.

It was a glass box.

Persephone hesitated at the door. It reminded her of her mother's home, and for a moment, she had the strange feeling that this was all a well-orchestrated trap. Hades's desk sat before a lead-detailed window that made it appear like he was sitting upon a throne while he was at his desk. It was over-the-top and intimidating, and she would bet money he used this desk less than the one in his office at Nevernight.

She stepped inside just as someone called for Lexa.

"Crap." She looked at Persephone. "I'll be right back."

Persephone nodded as her best friend disappeared. Her eyes dropped to Hades's desk. There were only two things on it: a vase of white narcissus and a picture of her. It was snapped in the Underworld, in one of Hades's gardens. She picked it up, wondering when he had taken it.

"Curious?"

Persephone jumped, dropping the frame. Before it could hit the ground, Hades caught it and returned it to its place. The goddess twisted toward him, bracing a hand on the desk.

How did someone with such mass move so quickly, she thought. He stood close, his scent hitting her hard, and she was reminded of last night when he'd taken her to bed, claimed her, marked her, possessed her. She hadn't expected a simple conversation about Apollo to set him off, but it had in ways she'd never imagined.

"How long have you been here?" she breathed.

One of Hades's powers was invisibility. It was possible he'd been in this office the whole time, even more likely that he'd followed along on the tour without any of them knowing.

"Always suspicious," he said.

"Hades—" she warned.

"Not long," he said. "I received a frantic call from Ivy, who chastised me for not letting her know you were stopping by."

Persephone's first reaction was to laugh at the fact that one of Hades's employees would berate him, but her attention was diverted by the fact that Ivy had *called* Hades.

Her brows drew together. "You have a phone?"

"For work, yes," he said.

"Why didn't I know that?"

He shrugged. "If I want you, I will find you."

"And what if I want you?"

"Then you have only to say my name," he said.

Still, Persephone didn't feel like that was a good enough reason for her to not know he had a phone...or the million other things she didn't know about her lover.

"You are displeased," Hades said, and it wasn't a question.

Persephone's gaze lifted to his again.

"You embarrassed me."

It was Hades's turn to frown, and his eyes softened. "Explain."

"I should not have to learn about all your charities through someone else," she said. "I feel like everyone around me knows more about you than I do."

"You never asked," he said.

"Some things can be brought up casually, Hades. At dinner, for instance—hi, honey. How was your day? Mine was good. The billion-dollar charities I own help kids and dogs and *humanity*!"

Hades was trying not to smile.

"Don't you dare." She pressed a finger to his lips. "I am serious about this. If you wish for me to be seen as more than a lover, then I need more from you. A… history…an inventory of your life. *Something.*"

Hades's eyes darkened, and he closed his fingers around Persephone's wrist. He kissed her fingers.

"I'm sorry," he said. "It did not occur to me to tell you. I have existed so long alone, made every decision alone. I am not used to sharing anything with anyone."

Persephone's expression turned tender, and she pressed her palm to his face.

"Hades, you were never alone, and you certainly aren't alone now." She pulled her hand away. "Now, what else do you own?"

"Lots of morgues," he said.

Persephone's eyes widened. "You're serious?"

"I am the God of the Dead," he said.

She couldn't help it; she smiled. Their gazes held for a moment, and then Hades prompted in a deep, sultry voice, "Tell me, what else can I share with you now?"

Persephone glanced at the picture on his desk.

"Where did you get this?"

His eyes followed, and she knew it wasn't because he had to be reminded about the picture. He was taking his time answering.

"I took it."

"When?"

"Obviously when you weren't looking," he said, and she rolled her eyes at his humor.

"Why do you have pictures of me and I do not have pictures of you?"

His eyes glittered.

"I did not know you wanted pictures of me."

She scoffed. "Of course I want pictures of you."

"I may be able to oblige. What kind of pictures do you want?"

She swatted his shoulder. "You are insatiable."

"And you are to blame, my queen," he said, and his lips traveled down her neck and along her shoulder. "I'm glad you are here."

"I couldn't tell," she replied, shivering.

"I've wanted to pleasure you in this room, on this desk, since I met you. It will be the most productive thing that happens here."

His words were flames, and they ignited her. She swallowed thickly.

"You have glass walls, Hades."

"Are you trying to deter me?"

She narrowed her eyes and teased. "Exhibitionist?"

"Hardly." He leaned a little closer, and she felt his breath on her lips. "Do you really think I would let them see you? I am too selfish. Smoke and mirrors, Persephone."

She leaned into his heat. "Then take me," she whispered.

Hades growled and snaked an arm around her waist when someone cleared their throat. They turned to find Lexa standing in the doorway.

"Hey, Hades," she said with a smile on her face. "Hope you don't mind. I brought Persephone for a tour."

"Hi, Lexa," he said, smirking. "No, I don't mind at all."

Persephone gave a small laugh and stepped away from Hades's warmth.

"I have to get back to work," she said, meeting Lexa at the door of Hades's office. She turned to look at him. He was power, standing behind that desk, silhouetted by that beautiful glass. "I'll see you tonight?"

He nodded once.

As they returned to the first floor, Lexa said, "I know you'll go to the Underworld on Friday for the weekend, but don't forget we're helping Sybil move Friday."

"Wouldn't miss it for the world," Persephone said.

The two hugged at the door.

"Thanks for everything, Lex. I'm sorry you couldn't give me the tour yourself."

"I won't lie. It was weird seeing people fall all over themselves in your presence."

The two laughed together at that. It was strange, even to Persephone, but then Lexa said something that made Persephone's blood run cold.

"Imagine when they find out you're a goddess."

Persephone walked back to the Acropolis. This time, she begrudgingly made her way to the entrance between screaming fans who were kept at bay by a makeshift security barrier.

"Persephone! Persephone, look over here!"

"How long have you been dating Hades?"

"Will you write about other gods?"

She kept her head down and didn't answer any questions. By the time she made it inside, her body was vibrating, her magic awakened from the surge of anxiety she'd felt being at the center of the crowd. She made a beeline for the elevators, all the while thinking about Lexa's last words before they'd parted at Alexandria Tower.

Imagine when they find out you're a goddess.

She knew what that really meant:

Imagine when you can no longer exist as you once did.

Suddenly, the elevator seemed too small, and just when she thought she couldn't take another breath, the doors opened. Helen popped up from behind her desk, smiling, oblivious to Persephone's internal battle.

"Welcome back, Persephone."

"Thanks, Helen," she said without much of a look in her direction. Despite this, Helen followed Persephone to her desk. As she stored her things, she found a white rose sitting on her laptop. Persephone picked it up, careful to avoid the thorns.

"Where did this come from?" she asked.

"I don't know," Helen said, frowning. "I didn't accept anything for you this morning."

Persephone's brows knitted together. A red ribbon was tied around the stem, but there was no card attached. *Maybe Hades left it for me,* she reasoned and set it aside.

"Do I have any messages?"

Persephone assumed that was why Helen had escorted her back to her desk.

"No," Helen said.

That was unlikely. Persephone waited.

"They can wait," Helen added. "Besides, they're all leads for other stories, and I know you're working on that exclusive—"

Persephone's eyes must have flashed, because Helen stopped speaking.

"How do you know about that?" Persephone's mood dampened.

"I…"

She'd never seen Helen stumble over her words before, but all of a sudden, the girl couldn't speak, and she looked close to tears.

"Who else knows?" Persephone asked.

"N-no one," Helen finally managed. "I overheard. I'm sorry. I thought it was exciting. I didn't realize—"

"If you overheard, you'd know it wasn't exciting. Not for me."

There was silence, and Persephone looked at Helen.

"I'm sorry, Persephone."

She sighed and sat in her chair. "It's okay, Helen. Just…don't tell anyone, okay? It…might not happen."

She hoped.

Helen looked panicked. So she *had* heard a lot more than she was letting on.

"But…you'll be fired!" she whispered fiercely.

Persephone sighed. "Helen, I really need to get to work, and I think you do too."

Helen paled. "Of course. I'm so—"

"Stop apologizing, Helen," Persephone said and then added as gently as she could, "You didn't do anything wrong."

The blond smiled. "I hope things get better, Persephone. I really do."

After Helen returned to her desk, Persephone started research on Apollo and his many lovers. She realized she'd told Hades she wouldn't write about the God of Music, but that didn't mean she couldn't start a file on him, and there was no lack of information, especially from antiquity.

Almost all the stories about Apollo and his relationships ended tragically for the other person involved. Of all his lovers, the stories of Daphne and Cassandra seemed to best illustrate his heinous behavior.

Daphne was a nymph and swore to remain pure her whole life. Despite this, Apollo pursued her relentlessly, declaring his love for her as if that might sway her to change her mind. Left with no other options and fearing Apollo, she asked her father, the river god Peneus, to free her from Apollo's relentless pursuit. Her father granted her request and turned her into a laurel tree.

Laurel was one of Apollo's symbols, and now Persephone realized why.

Gross.

Cassandra, a princess of Troy, was given the power to see the future by Apollo, who hoped the gift would persuade her to fall in love with him, but Cassandra wasn't interested. Enraged, Apollo cursed her, allowing her to retain the power to see the future but making it so that no one would believe her predictions. Later, Cassandra foresaw the fall of her people, but no one would listen.

There were other ancient lovers—Coronis, Okyrrhoe, Sinope, Amphissa, and Sibylla, and newer, modern lovers—Acacia, Chara, Io, Lamia, Tessa, and

Zita. The research wasn't easy. From what Persephone understood, many of these women had tried to speak out against Apollo via social media and blogs, even going so far as to tell their stories to journalists. The problem was no one was listening.

She was so consumed by her research, a knock on her desk made her jump. Persephone found Demetri standing in front of her.

"How's the article coming?" he asked.

She glared and answered in a crisp tone, "Coming."

Her boss frowned. "You know if I had a choice——"

"You have a choice," she said, cutting him off. "You just tell him no."

"Your job isn't the only one on the line."

"Then maybe that's a sign you should quit."

Demetri shook his head. "You don't quit *New Athens News* without consequences, Persephone."

"I didn't know you were such a coward."

"Not everyone has a god to defend them."

Persephone flinched but recovered quickly. She was really starting to hate people who assumed she would ask Hades to fight for her.

"I fight my own battles, Demetri. Trust me, this will not end well. People like Kal, they have secrets, and I'll dismantle him from the inside out."

A glimmer of admiration sparked within Demetri's eyes, but the words he spoke next were a threat to her foundation.

"I admire your determination, but there are some powers journalism cannot fight, and one of those is money."

CHAPTER VI
Lovers' Quarrel

*On Friday, Persephone and Lexa found themselves stand-*ing outside an upscale penthouse in the Crysos District of New Athens where Sybil had lived with Apollo since graduation. They'd rented a giant moving truck that Lexa had managed to park crookedly on the sidewalk and street.

"This isn't what I had in mind when I said I wanted to party, Persephone," Hermes pouted beside them. The god dazzled in gold, looking very much out of place beside Lexa and Persephone, who wore yoga pants and sweatshirts.

Persephone had penciled him in for Friday after he'd helped her get into the Acropolis, but that was before Apollo had fired Sybil and taken away her powers.

"No one said you had to come," Persephone countered.

The God of Trickery had shown up at her apartment just as they were heading out to get the moving truck. He tried to argue that they had an agreement—a contract—and she couldn't back out, but Persephone shut that down.

"One of my best friends was in an abusive relationship. She's getting out and I'm going to be there for her. Now, you can either come with us or you can leave. Your choice."

Hermes had chosen to come.

"We wouldn't be here if it wasn't for your brother," Lexa said. "Blame him."

"I'm not responsible for Apollo's choices," Hermes argued. "And don't pretend like this wouldn't be more fun with alcohol."

"You're right," Lexa said. "Good thing I brought this."

She withdrew a bottle of wine from inside her backpack.

"Give me that." Hermes snatched the bottle from her hands.

Persephone's eyes widened. "Excuse me, aren't you *driving* tonight?"

"Well, yeah, but that's for after."

Except that somehow, Hermes had already managed to open the bottle.

"I hope you have more in that bag," the god replied. "Because this one's for the present."

Lexa snorted, and the door in front of them finally clicked. Sybil's voice echoed through the intercom.

"It's open. Come on up."

Hermes started forward, but Persephone put her hand out to stop him. "You can get the dolly."

"Why do I have to get the dolly? I'm carrying the wine."

Persephone took the bottle. "Now I'm carrying the wine. Dolly. *Now.*"

Hermes's shoulders slumped as he relented and trudged toward the moving truck. He returned wheeling the dolly.

Lexa giggled. "You look awfully mortal, Hermes."

The god's eyes darkened. "Careful, mortal. I'm not above turning you into a goat for my own enjoyment."

"*Your* enjoyment?" Lexa cackled. "That would be the best thing that ever happened to me."

The three went up the elevator and were let out in the middle of Apollo's living room.

Persephone wasn't sure how to feel at seeing the luxury Sybil had been living in the last few months since graduation. There was no denying being employed as an oracle was a lucrative job, and the goddess felt that seeing all this made Sybil's situation even worse. It made it tangible. She would be going from living in a high-rise penthouse with floor-to-ceiling windows, wood floors, stainless steel appliances, and the fanciest coffee machine Persephone had ever seen to occupying her and Lexa's small apartment from now until the foreseeable future.

Despite the extreme change in lifestyle, Sybil seemed in good spirits, almost as if moving out of this space was lifting a burden from her shoulders. She popped her head out of an adjoining room. Her blond hair spilled over her shoulder in loose waves, her pretty, makeup-free face aglow.

"In here, guys."

They filed into her room. Persephone expected to find that it had more personality than the rest of the house, but she'd been wrong. Sybil's room was just as colorless.

97

"Why is everything *gray?*"

"Oh, well, Apollo doesn't like color," Sybil said.

"Who doesn't like color?" Lexa asked, plopping down on Sybil's bed.

"Apollo, apparently," said Hermes, falling on the bed beside Lexa. "We should trash the place before we leave. That would really piss him off."

Sybil paled, eyes widening.

Persephone placed her hands on her hips. "You're the only one who would think that was funny and the only one who would survive his wrath."

"You would too, Sephy. Hades would cut off Apollo's balls before he got within an inch of you. I'm tempted to do it just so I can watch."

"*Hermes,*" Persephone said pointedly. "You are really not being helpful."

The god pouted. "I brought the dolly, didn't I?"

"And now you need to use it. Up! Take these boxes down."

Hermes grumbled but rolled off the bed, and Lexa followed.

They stacked boxes on the dolly, and while Hermes took them down, Persephone and Lexa helped Sybil pack the rest of her life. Persephone enjoyed the task. Each box was a new challenge, and she liked to see just how much she could place in one box. When she was finished, she wrote a quick inventory on the side of the box to make unpacking easier.

When Hermes realized what she was doing, he snorted, shaking his head.

"What?" Persephone demanded.

"You're just as regimented as Apollo."

98

Persephone didn't like being compared to the god. "What do you mean?"

"Haven't you been paying attention to this place?" He looked around. "Everything in this place is arranged by type and color."

"I'm organized, Hermes, not neurotic."

"Apollo is disciplined. Ever since I've known him, he's been that way."

"If he's so disciplined, why is he so…emotional?"

"Because Apollo takes pride in his routine—in the things he can create and execute, which means when he loses control, it's personal." Hermes glanced at Sybil. "Same goes for how he handles humans."

Once they were finished, Sybil left her key on the shiny granite countertop in Apollo's state-of-the-art kitchen, and the four piled into the moving van and left for the apartment.

"You're not staying in the lines," Persephone said, holding onto the grab handle as Lexa drove down the street.

"I can't see," Lexa complained, sitting up higher in the driver's seat.

"Maybe you shouldn't be driving," Hermes commented.

"Does someone else want to drive?" Lexa asked.

Everyone in the cabin was silent because none of them could drive.

"Just keep a lookout for pedestrians," Persephone said.

"I'll give you ten points if you hit someone," Hermes offered.

"Is that supposed to entice me?" Lexa asked.

"Uh, yeah, they're *Divine* points."

"What do *Divine* points get me?" Lexa asked, as if she were seriously considering his offer.

"A chance to be a goat," he answered.

Persephone exchanged a look with Sybil and said, "If you are wondering if I regret introducing them to each other, the answer is yes."

Unloading Sybil's things took less than thirty minutes. Finding a place to put them was another story. They lined up boxes in the hallway, part of the living room, and Persephone's room, since she would probably spend most of her time in the Underworld.

Once they had everything moved, Hermes opened a bottle of champagne, grinning.

"Time to celebrate!"

"Oops," Lexa said, snatching up the keys to the moving truck. "Before we start, I have to return this rental."

"I'll come with you," Persephone said.

"You just want me to drop you off at Nevernight."

Persephone's cheeks turned crimson.

"You're leaving us?" Hermes asked. "What happened to sisters before misters?"

Persephone rolled her eyes. "Hermes, in case you haven't noticed, you're a mister."

"I can be a sister!" he argued, more vehemently than she expected. "If you don't come back, can I sleep in your bed?" he called as she and Lexa left the apartment.

Sybil's voice followed quickly. "No, you don't! It's mine!"

"I'll share."

"Sorry, Hermes, but I've had one too many gods try to sleep with me."

Lexa's driving was a little smoother on the way to Nevernight until she parked, pressing on the brake so hard, Persephone's body strained against the seat belt. Outside, Persephone saw Mekonnen, an ogre Hades kept employed as a bouncer for Nevernight, engaged in an argument with a woman, which was nothing out of the ordinary. People often argued with Mekonnen and the other bouncers, hoping for a chance to enter the club.

"That doesn't look good," Lexa commented, nodding toward the two.

"No, it doesn't."

The girl had her finger pointed at the creature's chest. That was one of Mekonnen's biggest pet peeves and a good way to get banned from the club forever.

Persephone sighed and reached over the console of the truck to hug Lexa. "I'll see you tomorrow. Thanks for the ride."

She climbed out of the moving van. As soon as her feet touched the sidewalk, a chorus of voices called her name and a couple of people broke from the line, ducking under red velvet ropes to approach her. Two ogres appeared from the shadowy entrance of Nevernight, flanking Persephone and creating a barrier between her and the crowd. She smiled at them.

"Hi, Adrian, Ezio."

Their expressions were serious as they peered down at her and said, "Good evening, my lady."

She realized she should have thought this through better or at least called ahead to notify Hades's staff that she would be arriving soon. She could just see tomorrow's headline: *Hades's Lover Arrives at Nevernight in Rental Truck Dressed in Sweats!*

As she approached the entrance of the club, she overheard the woman.

"I demand to see him this instant!"

Persephone remembered saying something very similar to another ogre when she'd first come to Nevernight. It did not go well—for the ogre, mostly. He'd put his hands on Persephone, an offense Hades could not overlook, and she never saw him again.

"My lady," Mekonnen said, moving forward to block the woman arguing with him, but she pushed her way around him.

"*My lady?*" she demanded with her hands on her hips.

It was then Persephone noticed that the woman was a nymph. She had pale, milky skin, long white hair, and bright blue eyes that made her look ethereal. Even her lashes were white.

A naiad, Persephone thought, which was a nymph associated with water. She was beautiful, but she also looked severe, angry, and exhausted.

"Who are you?" the nymph demanded.

Persephone was surprised, but mostly because there were few people who didn't know who she was.

"You dare speak to Lady Persephone in such a manner?" Mekonnen's hands tightened into fists.

"It's alright, Mekonnen." Persephone held up her hand to calm the ogre who looked like he might just grind this woman's bones into paste at any moment.

"I am Persephone," she said. "Am I correct in understanding that you wish to speak to Lord Hades?"

"I demand it!"

Persephone's brow rose a little.

"What are your grievances?"

"My grievances? You want to hear my grievances? Where do I start? First, the apartment he put me in is a shithole."

Now she was confused.

"Second, I won't work another minute at that hellhole of a fucking nightclub—"

Persephone held up her hand to stop the nymph from talking. "I'm sorry. Who are you again?"

The woman lifted her chin, and her chest rose as she spoke with misplaced pride. "I am Leuce, Hades's lover."

Persephone felt the color drain from her face, and shock settled deep in her belly.

"Excuse me?"

The nymph chuckled like she had said something funny. Persephone's fingers curled into fists.

"Sorry, *ex*-lover, but it's all the same."

"*Ex*...lover?" Persephone said through her teeth, tilting her head to the side.

"You have nothing to worry about," Leuce said. "It was so long ago."

"So long ago that you forgot and introduced yourself as Hades's lover?" Persephone asked.

"Honest mistake."

"You'll forgive me if I believe there was nothing honest about it." She twisted toward Mekonnen. "Please show *Leuce* to Hades's office. I'll see that he's along shortly."

"Yes, my lady." Mekonnen bowed and added, "He's in the lounge."

"Thank you," she replied warmly, though her whole body felt like ice.

Persephone made her way into Nevernight. She

103

went right up the stairs to the lounge where Hades made wagers with mortals seeking more from life—love, money, health. It was these bargains that had both appalled and intrigued her. It led her to writing about the God of the Dead and eventually landed her in a contract with him.

Euryale, a gorgon who stood guard at the entrance of the lounge, waited outside. Persephone's first interaction with the woman had been hostile, as she had correctly identified her as a goddess based on smell.

"Is Lord Hades in trouble?" Euryale asked. There was amusement in her voice but also a hint of excitement as the goddess approached.

"More than you could ever know," Persephone answered.

Euryale smiled, showing a set of blackened teeth. She opened the door without pause and bowed to Persephone as she passed.

"He is in the sapphire suite, my lady."

Persephone stalked around the crowded card tables. The room was dark despite a large chandelier overhead and several intricate sconces lining the walls. Persephone's first visit to the suite sealed her fate. She'd been enamored of the people and games, she'd reveled in watching the cards fly across the table, the ease with which men and women interacted and teased, and then she'd come to a poker table where she'd sat and met the King of the Underworld.

Even now, recalling how he'd looked up close for the first time made her stomach clench tight. He was a tangible shadow, built like a fortress, and he'd crashed into her life like a force of nature. She couldn't shake him and, in truth, hadn't wanted to. From the moment she'd laid eyes on him, he'd ignited something inside her. It felt like fire, but it was his darkness calling to hers.

She knew that now—felt it in her blood and bones—as she melded with the darkness in the room and found the passage that led to a series of suites where mortals waited to bargain with Hades. They were all named after precious stones—sapphire, emerald, and diamond—each one decorated in the associated colors. They were beautiful rooms, offering a sense of grandeur, communicating to all who entered that if they played their cards right—literally—perhaps they too could obtain something just as extravagant.

Persephone found the sapphire lounge, and when she entered, a man sat opposite Hades. The mortal looked to be in his early twenties. Persephone used to wonder how people so young could end up across from the God of the Dead, but disease of any kind did not discriminate. Whatever he was here for made him defensive, because he turned in his chair to see who had interrupted his game and said, "If it's him you want, you'll have to wait your turn. Took me three years to get this appointment."

Hades's gaze melded to her. Despite his elegant appearance, he was predatory. He sat with his back straight, fingers clasped around a glass of whiskey. To the untrained eye, he probably looked relaxed, but Persephone knew by his expression that he was on edge. Probably because of her. She didn't have to say anything for him to understand she was angry. Her glamour was failing; she could feel it melting away, revealing holes in her mortal facade.

"Leave, mortal," she said. The command must have

shaken the man, because he wasted no time racing out of the suite. Persephone slammed the door.

"I'll have to erase his memory. Your eyes are glowing," he said and smirked. "Who angered you?"

"Can you not guess?" she asked.

Hades raised a brow.

"I just had the pleasure of meeting your lover."

Hades didn't react, and that made her angrier. She felt more of her glamour slipping away. She imagined how ridiculous she looked—a goddess who stood before one so ancient, unable to hold on to her magic.

"I see."

Persephone's voice shook as she spoke. "You have seconds to explain before I turn her into a weed."

She knew Hades would have laughed if he believed she were any less serious.

"Her name is Leuce," he answered. "She *was* my lover a long time ago."

She hated that she was relieved he hadn't named someone else.

"What is a long time?"

He stared at her for a moment, and there was something behind his eyes—a living thing full of rage and ruin and strife.

"Millennia, Persephone."

"Then why did she introduce herself to me as your lover *today?*"

"Because to her, I was her lover up until Sunday."

Persephone's fists clenched, and suddenly, vines erupted from the floor and covered the walls. Hades didn't even flinch.

"And why is that?"

"Because she's been a poplar tree for over *two thousand years.*"

Persephone's brows rose. She hadn't expected that.

"Why was she a poplar tree?"

Hades's hands rested on the tabletop, and they curled into fists as he answered, "She betrayed me."

"*You* turned her into a tree?" Persephone gasped, stunned by the revelation.

Sometimes she forgot the extent of Hades's powers. He was one of the three most powerful gods in existence, and while each brother became king of a respective realm—Zeus the sky, Poseidon the sea, and Hades the dead—they shared power over the earthly realm, which meant there was the potential that she and Hades had similar powers.

Apparently, one was turning people into plants.

"Why?"

"I caught her fucking someone else. I was blind with anger. I turned her into a poplar tree."

"She must not remember that, or she wouldn't introduce herself as your lover."

Hades stared at her for a moment. He hadn't moved from his spot at the table.

"It is possible she has repressed the memory."

Persephone started to pace.

"How many lovers have you taken?"

"Persephone." Hades's voice was gentle, but there was an undercurrent that said *that's not a path you want to go down.*

"I just want to be prepared in case they start coming out of the woodwork."

Hades was silent, staring. After a moment, he said, "I won't apologize for living before you existed."

"I'm not asking you to, but I'd like to know when I'm about to meet a woman who *fucked* you."

"I was hoping you'd never meet Leuce," Hades said. "She wasn't supposed to be around this long. I agreed to help her get on her feet in the modern world. Normally, I'd pass the responsibility on to Minthe, but seeing as how she's indisposed—" He glanced at the ivy on the walls. "It's taken me longer to find someone suitable to mentor her."

Persephone stopped pacing and faced Hades. "You weren't planning to tell me about her?"

Hades shrugged. "I saw no need until now."

"No *need*?" Persephone echoed, and the ivy on the walls thickened and bloomed. The room felt infinitely smaller. "You gave this woman a place to stay, you gave her a job, and you used to *fuck* her—"

"Stop saying that," Hades said through his teeth.

"I deserved to know about her, Hades!"

"Do you doubt my loyalty?"

"You're supposed to say you're sorry," she snapped.

"You're supposed to trust me."

"And you're supposed to communicate with me." That was what he had asked of her. Why shouldn't he be held to the same standard?

There was silence, and Persephone took a breath, feeling the need to brace herself for this question.

"Do you still love her?"

"No, Persephone." Hades's response was immediate, but he sounded annoyed that she would even ask.

Persephone wasn't sure where to go from here. She was angry, and she didn't understand why Hades had chosen to hide his previous lover from her. It wasn't that she believed he had been unfaithful; it was that this was just one of several things that had taken her off guard this week when it came to Hades's life.

She was starting to feel like she truly knew nothing about him.

After another minute of tense silence, Hades sighed and suddenly looked exhausted. He came around the table and reached for her, his fingers twined into her hair at the base of her head.

"I hoped to keep all this from you," he said. "Not to protect Leuce but to protect you from my past."

"I don't want to be protected from you," Persephone whispered, the air between them growing thick with a different kind of tension. "I want to know you—all of you, from the inside out."

He offered a small smile and cupped her face, the pad of his thumb brushing her lips.

"Let's start with the inside," he said, and their mouths collided, his tongue twined with hers. He tasted like smoke and ice. His hands moved down her back and over her bottom, and he drew her to him so that she was cradled between his legs as he leaned against the table. Each flick of his tongue hypnotized her. The hard press of his erection against her stomach made her dizzy with lust. She held on to him, fingers digging into his tight muscles. She would be lying if she said she didn't need this. Not only had he left her aching and empty nights ago, but the stress of work was putting her on edge. She needed release, but she also needed Hades to understand, so she pressed her hands against his chest and pulled away.

"Hades, I am serious. I want to know your

greatest weakness, your deepest fear, your most treasured possession."

His expression grew serious then, and he stared at her with an intensity that made her insides shudder.

"You," he answered, his fingers teasing her kiss-swollen lips.

"Me?" For a moment, she was confused, and then she realized what he was saying. "I cannot be all those things."

"You are my weakness, losing you is my greatest fear, and your love is my most treasured possession."

"Hades," she said gently. "I am a second in your vast life. How can I be all those things?"

"You doubt me?"

She pressed her palm to his cheek. "No, but I believe you have other weaknesses, fears, and treasures. Your people, for one. Your realm for another."

"See," he said very quietly. "You know me already—inside and out."

His response made her sad because she knew it wasn't true.

I don't know you at all.

He went in for another kiss, but she stopped him.

"I just have one more question," she said. "When you left Sunday night, where did you go?"

"Persephone—"

She took a step away. She knew. He didn't even need to answer.

"That's when she returned, wasn't it?"

Her anger was once again renewed. He had wound her so tight, she hadn't been able to breathe, and instead of releasing the tension he'd built inside her, he'd chosen to leave—to help a former lover.

"You chose her over me."

"It isn't like that at all, Persephone." He reached for her.

"Don't touch me!" Persephone stepped away, lifting her hands. Hades's jaw tightened, but he didn't approach. "You had your chance. You fucked it up."

His reasons for keeping Leuce a secret didn't matter right now. The fact was, he hadn't told her. He'd done the opposite of what he'd asked of her—*communicate*—so the words she used against him next seemed more than fitting.

"Actions speak louder than words, Hades."

She vanished from the lounge.

CHAPTER VII
Truce

Hades's Lover Arrives at Nevernight in Rental Truck, Dressed in Sweats

Persephone sat behind her desk at work on Monday, glaring at the article on her computer screen. She could be an oracle with the way she was able to predict headlines. If only she'd been able to predict meeting Hades's ex-lover too.

Her mood hadn't improved over the weekend. Maybe that was due to the fact that she had yet to hear from Hades. She wasn't even sure she wanted to talk to him, but she had expected him to try to contact her—either manifest in her bedroom in the middle of the night to apologize or send Hecate, the peacekeeper.

As the hours turned into days, the more Persephone grew frustrated with Hades and the more she wanted to write about Apollo just to piss him off.

The God of Music was in the news today, having been

selected as the chancellor for the upcoming Panhellenic Games. His christening was no surprise, as he had been given the title for the last ten years. It was basically a designation Apollo paid for, since his money funded the entertainment, uniforms, and construction on a new stadium. No one would want to believe that the god who gave them sports was also an abusive asshole.

Persephone sighed and closed her browser, opening a blank document. She had another week to write the exclusive Demetri and Kal had ordered. This was probably not the best time to begin, because every word she thought of to describe Hades was something angry and unkind.

Frustrating, thoughtless, jerk.

After a moment, she sighed and checked her mug. She needed more coffee if she was going to attempt this article. She left her desk and went into the break room. As her coffee brewed, Helen found her.

"Persephone...there's a woman here to see you. She says her name is Leuce."

Persephone froze and looked at Helen.

"Did you just say *Leuce*?"

The girl nodded, her blue eyes wide. Persephone's frustration burned, and she clenched her fists to keep a handle on her magic. All she needed was to sprout vines in front of her coworker. What was Hades's ex-lover doing here?

"Should I tell her you're busy?" Helen asked. "I'll tell her you're busy."

Helen started to leave.

"No." Persephone stopped her. "I'll see her. Show her to an interview room."

Helen nodded and returned shortly after she disappeared.

"She's in there."

"Thank you, Helen."

The girl hovered, and Persephone took a breath.

"Yes, Helen?"

"Are you sure you're alright?"

"Just peachy," she answered.

What else was there to say? She was being forced to write about her love life—a love life that was being threatened by a woman who'd just showed up at her job.

Things were complicated.

Persephone kept Leuce waiting. It was the woman's fault for showing up unannounced. When she finally entered the interview room, Leuce was standing by the window, and when she turned to face Persephone, the goddess was surprised to see that she looked worse than the night they had met.

Then, she'd been exhausted.

Today, she looked filthy. Her string-straight hair was matted, and she was wearing the same clothes that she'd had on at Nevernight. Persephone also noted the tear stains on her cheeks, visible because of the dirt on her face.

"What are you doing here?" Persephone asked.

"I came to apologize," Leuce said.

Persephone startled. That was the last thing she expected Leuce to say. "Excuse me?"

"I shouldn't have introduced myself the way I did." The words poured out of Leuce's mouth quickly, almost like she was berating herself. "I was angry with Hades. I mean, I am sure you understand—"

"Leuce," Persephone interrupted her. "You will

forgive me if I don't wish to be reminded about how well you know Hades. Why are you here?"

The nymph pressed her lips together tightly. "Hades kicked me out and fired me last night."

Persephone just stared.

"I know I don't deserve your kindness, but please. I have nowhere to go."

Persephone shook her head. "What exactly are you asking of me?"

"Can't you…talk to him…for me?" Leuce seemed to struggle saying those words.

"Why aren't *you* talking to him?"

"You don't think I tried? He told me I had to go. He wasn't going to risk losing you."

"If he really meant that, he would apologize," Persephone muttered under her breath.

"Look, I know you don't want to hear this but… Hades is an idiot. He's probably thinking you want space, and the more he gives you, the better."

"You're just saying that because you want me to ask him for your job back."

"And my home," Leuce said shamelessly.

Persephone lifted a brow. "Didn't you call it a shithole?"

"It is a shithole, but it was *my* shithole and it had a bed," Leuce said. "Which was far better than the park bench I found last night."

Hindsight is twenty-twenty.

The two stared at each other for a long moment before Persephone asked, "Why I should help you? You weren't even thankful for what Hades gave you."

Plus, you cheated on him.

"Because I'm an idiot too. I guess I thought I had more…leverage. Turns out I have nothing. I don't even understand this world. I barely made it here because crossing your streets is almost impossible." Leuce paused and looked away, and when she spoke again, her voice quivered. "Imagine waking up in a world that doesn't even resemble the one you left. It's…frightening. It's… the worst punishment."

Leuce's shoulders fell, and Persephone suddenly realized she could relate to her more than she had wanted to admit. She'd been in a similar situation four years ago. She sighed and checked her watch. She couldn't believe what she was about to say.

"Look, I have a few more hours of work left. You can hang out in the lounge until I'm off. I can't *promise* I'll talk to Hades today, but…eventually. Until then… you can stay with me."

Leuce's eyes widened. "A–are you sure?"

No, Persephone thought, but Lexa was spending the night at Jaison's this week, which freed up her room for Sybil and meant Leuce could have the couch.

"Thank you. Thank you, Persephone."

The goddess stiffened as the nymph threw her arms around her. After a moment, she pulled away.

"You won't regret this, I promise."

She sure hoped not.

Persephone didn't return to working on the exclusive. Instead, she continued to research Apollo. At the end of the day, she copied everything she found into a Word document and emailed it to herself before gathering her things and retrieving Leuce from the lounge. Together, they left the Acropolis through the front, braving the waiting crowd to find Antoni waiting outside Hades's black Lexus. He opened the door as they approached, smiling.

"My lady," he said.

Antoni's eye became menacing as his gaze fell upon Leuce.

"What's *she* doing with you?"

Persephone's brows rose, and she looked from the cyclops to the nymph. "You know Leuce?"

"Yes," he hissed. "Once a traitor, always a traitor."

Leuce rolled her eyes. "Don't be dramatic."

"It's alright, Antoni," Persephone interrupted. "I'm helping her."

The cyclops pressed his lips tight and said nothing as the two women slid into the back seat. Once the door was shut, Leuce looked at Persephone.

"Does that crowd wait for you every day?"

"Yes."

"All because of Hades?"

"Yes."

The nymph looked out the window. "That's insane."

"It is insane," Persephone agreed. "I hate it."

"When I was…alive," Leuce said, "in ancient times, the gods were feared and revered. Their worshippers were serious about honoring their gods. It wasn't this… false obsession."

Persephone grimaced. "Welcome to the modern world."

Antoni dropped them off at Persephone's apartment. Before he left, the cyclops took Persephone aside. "I'll have to tell him Leuce is with you. He will want to know."

She shrugged. "Tell him."

Antoni frowned. "You'll talk to him soon, won't you, my lady?"

Persephone was surprised by his question. She wondered how much Antoni knew about her fight with Hades.

Her frown matched his. "I don't know," she said. "Probably. Right now, I am angry."

He nodded. "I'll see you tomorrow, my lady."

She didn't say anything and turned to lead Leuce into the apartment, finding Sybil at the kitchen bar, wiping at her face as soon as they entered.

"Sybil, what's wrong?"

"Nothing. Everything's fine."

But it was obvious she was lying. Her voice was thick, and her eyes were red. Persephone peered over her shoulder to find a rejection email for a job.

"Sybil," Persephone said gently, placing a hand on her arm.

"I knew it would be hard, but I don't think I realized how difficult. No one wants a god's discarded...*plaything.*"

"You are no such thing, Sybil," Persephone said quickly.

"That's not how the world sees it," Sybil said. "My worth is equal to the desire a god had for me. It has been since my powers manifested. Now I don't even have those."

Sybil turned to Persephone and sobbed against her chest. The goddess stood there, soothing her friend.

"It's going to be okay," Persephone said. "I'll help in any way I can. Let me talk to Hades. I'm sure they need more help at the Cypress Foundation."

She'd been so angry about Leuce, she'd forgotten to ask about openings.

"I can't ask that of you, Persephone," Sybil said, pulling away.

"You're not asking." Persephone offered what she hoped was a comforting smile.

Persephone introduced Leuce to Sybil and poured three glasses of wine. Persephone was starting to feel like she was running a home for displaced women. They sat in the living room, watching *Titans After Dark* and talking about life. At some point, the inevitable topic of Apollo made its way into their conversation, and the longer they spoke, the angrier they became.

"He's as horrible as I remember," Leuce commented.

"Oh, girl, you don't even know," Sybil said, then took a drink from her glass. "He is so *controlling*. He punishes his lovers for being independent! It's pathetic!"

"Can you believe Hades told me I couldn't write about him?" Persephone said.

"If you want to write about Apollo, you write about Apollo!" Leuce said.

They were all on their fourth glass of wine. Despite this, Persephone expected Sybil to protest. Instead, she said, "Get the laptop, Seph!"

Persephone grinned and ran into her room to grab her computer. When she came back, she sat cross-legged on the sofa.

"Write this down," Sybil directed. "*Apollo, known for his charm and beauty, has a secret—he cannot stand rejection.*"

"Oh, that's good!" Leuce encouraged.

"Oh, oh! Hold on," Persephone said, typing quickly, the words coming faster than her fingers would move. When she was finished, she read the piece aloud:

"The evidence is overwhelming. I would have his many ex-lovers vouch for me, but they either begged to be saved from his wily pursuits and were turned into trees or died horrible deaths as a result of his punishment."

"Yes!" Leuce cried.

Persephone continued, adding the stories of Daphne, the nymph who was turned into a tree, and Princess Cassandra, whose accurate predictions were dismissed.

"Cassandra cried that Greeks were hidden in the Trojan Horse but was ignored. Which begs the question, how noble can Apollo truly be when he fought on the side of Troy yet compromised their victory, all because he was given the cold shoulder?"

"Gods, he's so terrible," Sybil said. "I don't know why I didn't see it before."

"He's abusive," Persephone said. "Don't blame yourself."

"You should say that in the article!" Leuce said. "*Apollo is an abuser—he has a need to control and dominate. It's not about communication or listening; it's about winning.*"

They continued like that for hours until Sybil and Leuce could no longer keep their eyes open. With the two asleep on the couch, Persephone was pinned against the armrest. The pallid glow from her computer hurt her eyes, but she continued to revise what they'd written together. The result was a critical and hostile article about the God of Music. Persephone excluded Sybil's story, even though she'd contributed a few lines illustrating her own experiences with the god. She didn't want Apollo to retaliate against the oracle.

The more Persephone read and reread the piece, the angrier she got, and before she could think it through, she composed an email to Demetri and sent the article. She felt triumphant for all of two seconds—before she scrambled from the couch, ran into the bathroom, and threw up in the toilet.

You are in so much trouble, she thought as she sagged against the bathroom wall. Her stomach felt like it was boiling, a combination of too much wine and guilt.

Apollo did this to himself, she thought, reminding herself why she'd sent the article. *He deserves this. This is about justice, about giving a voice to his victims.*

What about Hades?

Her stomach lurched, and Persephone got to her knees just as bile rose to the back of her throat. She vomited again. Her nose and throat burned, and all she could taste was bitter, acidic wine. She knelt for a while, breathing through her mouth until she felt steady enough to rise to her feet.

When she looked in the mirror, she didn't recognize herself. She looked like a soul that had just arrived in the Underworld, pale and shivering.

"Hades kept secrets," she said aloud, as if that explained why she'd gone back on her word.

You kept secrets, she reminded herself as she rinsed her mouth and brushed her teeth. *You didn't tell him about Demetri's ultimatum.*

"That's different." She met her gaze in the mirror.

How?

121

It was different because it was her battle. She hadn't wanted Hades's help fighting it.

"It's different because that secret won't hurt him," she said.

But the secret he'd kept about Leuce? It hurt.

She didn't like the words that followed. They grew like menacing clouds, a storm of tormenting words in her mind: *This will hurt Hades.*

She turned out the lights.

CHAPTER VIII
Abduction

When Persephone arrived at work the next day, the crowd outside the Acropolis had grown to include members of Apollo's cult—worshippers and die-hard fans. They were obvious because they wore wreaths of laurel in their hair and gold dust like war paint. Even from inside Hades's Lexus, Persephone heard angry shouts.

"Liar!"

"Apologize to Apollo!"

"You're just jealous!"

"Bitch!"

Clearly her article had been published.

Antoni looked in the rearview mirror at her.

"Would you like me to walk you to the door, my lady?"

Persephone stared out the window. Security guards were approaching the car and prepared to escort her.

Gods. What had she done?

"No, Antoni. That's alright."

He nodded once. "I'll return for you this afternoon."

When she left the car, she was thrust into hostility. Everything was so loud, and she felt everyone's emotions—anger and hate, anxiety and fear. They weighed upon her chest, smothering her.

"Come, my lady," one of the security guards said. He stuck out his arm as if to corral her but didn't touch her. She looked at him, blinking.

"Did you call me 'my lady'?" she asked.

The guard blushed.

"It's not safe out here. Hurry!"

She knew it wasn't safe. She could feel the violence of the crowd growing, and by the time she reached the entrance, part of the group had broken out into a fight. She was ushered inside and turned to watch as the officers took charge, dividing the throng and defusing the situation.

I don't understand. All this over a few words I wrote.

No one had gotten this angry when she had written about Hades, but she knew why—the God of the Underworld was hardly beloved, just intriguing. Apollo was the literal God of Light. He was a God of Music and Poetry. He represented all the things in life mortals wanted.

Including the darkness they never wanted to acknowledge.

When she turned to head up the elevator, she found she was being watched by everyone on the first floor—the front desk receptionist, security, random employees.

They stared at her, wide-eyed, and kept their distance. Maybe they were afraid Apollo would appear and strike her down. Whatever the case, she was glad to have an elevator to herself. The reprieve was short-lived, however, because the stares continued as she made her way to her desk.

Helen was her usual chipper self, greeting Persephone and following her to her desk. The only indication she gave of the backlash outside was when she informed Persephone that she hadn't forwarded any calls to her voicemail.

"I could take over your email if you'd like. Just for the day."

"No, that's okay, Helen."

"Do you need anything? Coffee or a snack?"

Persephone thought for a moment. "Tylenol," she answered. "And some water."

"I'll be right back!"

Helen returned a short time later. Persephone took the medicine and tried to concentrate on her work, which consisted of reading hate mail and staring at a blank document that was supposed to contain her exclusive.

If she was being honest, she was on edge, waiting for Hades to slam his way through the doors of her workplace, gather her up, and carry her off to the Underworld to be punished for her decision to betray him.

At first, she was anxious about his potential arrival, but as time passed, she became more and more frustrated with the God of the Dead.

What would it take to get his attention?

She got up and walked to the break room to make coffee. While there, she looked out the window. A crowd was still gathered outside the Acropolis.

"Your article is causing quite a stir." Demetri joined

her. He turned on the television in the corner. The news was streaming, and the headline read:

Hades's Lover Attacks Beloved God

She squeezed her coffee cup so hard, the lid came off, sloshing hot liquid all over her hands. She gasped and Demetri took it from her, handing her some napkins.

"You think they could at least use my name?"

"You might not want them to," he said. "It's probably best they remember who you belong to."

Persephone glared at her boss. "I don't *belong* to anyone."

"Fair," he said. "Poor word choice. I just meant that… you'll want people to remember that you're with Hades, because they aren't happy that you went after Apollo."

That was obvious—and no wonder. The news was particularly critical of her article.

"She mentions eight mortal women who apparently experienced abuse from Lord Apollo, but where are they?"

"She's only doing this because of her association with Hades. No other mortal would dare write this… trash about a god."

"Guess she didn't gain enough fame by sleeping with Hades. She had to go after Apollo too. Is this the kind of fame you wanted, Persephone Rosi?"

She felt sick and frustrated and a little hopeless.

"This isn't fair. They aren't even trying to fact-check," she said.

He shrugged. "They're probably too afraid."

"That's no reason to avoid it."

Demetri sighed. "No, but it's the way of our world. The vengeance of the gods is a real and feared thing."

The news continued bashing Persephone for her critique of Apollo. For the fact that she'd used two stories from antiquity to illustrate his horrid behavior, claiming that all gods in antiquity were different from who they were now, that change was possible, and that Apollo should be forgiven.

Persephone snatched the remote from Demetri and turned off the television.

"They weren't eager to come to Hades's defense when I wrote about him," she said.

"That's because Hades is supposed to be feared. He's supposed to be bad. Apollo, he's…the God of Music. The God of Light. He's…revelry and beauty. He's not supposed to be an asshole."

"Well, he is!"

"You don't have to convince me, Persephone. You have to convince the world."

She shouldn't have to convince anyone, but instead of a world recognizing a psychopathic god, they saw one that had just fallen deeply in love. They equated his relentless pursuit of men and women as romantic and those who rejected him as unworthy.

It was fucked up.

"Look, if you want my advice—"

"I don't," she snapped.

"Persephone." Demetri seemed desperate. "Look, I know…things haven't been good between us this week, but I don't want to watch you get bashed on national television for the next year."

"Then why did you choose to publish my article?"

127

When Demetri didn't answer, she thought she knew. "It's because of money, isn't it?"

It did not matter that people hated what she had written. They would buy it to bash her.

Demetri glared at her.

"It's not about money," he said. "You want respect in this industry, and the reality is that you just lost a huge chunk of it. You want to climb that ladder? You can do one of two things—apologize…" She glared at him so hard, she thought she might melt him with her eyes. "Or write another article about Apollo. Find someone he's hurt recently. Tell their story."

Persephone frowned. "I…can't."

Demetri didn't respond immediately. "Maybe you can't," he said. "And if not, you know what you have to do."

"Your advice is shit," she told him.

Her boss seemed genuinely hurt by her response, nearly flinching when the words left her mouth, but she didn't really care. He had gone from advocating for and defending her to opposing and discouraging her.

She thought he was a fighter, but when the going got tough, he rolled over.

There was no way she was going to apologize to Apollo when he'd hurt one of her closest friends. There was also no way she would ask Sybil for an interview. That would mean exposing her to the scrutiny Persephone was now experiencing.

She couldn't do that to the oracle. She was rebuilding her life.

Gods, this is such a mess.

At lunch, Persephone broke one of her rules and

chanced teleportation to the rooftop of the Acropolis for some much-needed air.

She manifested herself on the edge of the roof. Her heartbeat pounded in her chest as she stumbled away. Once she recovered from almost falling off the side of the high-rise, she stared down at the vast city of New Athens. It was beautiful and terrifying up here. She could see the darkness of Hades's tower, a shadow that split the city in half. The glimmering glass of Aphrodite's La Rose, the beautiful and unique facade of Hera's many hotels: the Olympian, the Pegasus, the Emerald Peacock. There were other monuments too—marble statues of gods all over the city and beautiful temples arranged on hilltops and mountainside cliffs.

She'd been so enchanted with the city when she'd first moved here. She'd fallen in love with everything it promised—endless possibilities, adventure, and freedom. It was what kept her going when things got difficult, when she felt confused and lost and unwelcomed—all the things she felt now.

She searched for those promises amid the sprawling landscape, beyond the Acropolis and the angry crowd far below.

"Persephone?" a voice asked.

She whirled to find Pirithous, the janitor who had helped her leave in the tilt cart, standing behind her.

"How did you get up here?" he asked.

She opened her mouth to answer but realized she didn't even know how this roof was accessed from the inside.

"Carefully," she managed to answer with a small smile, which Pirithous matched.

"What are you doing up here?" she asked.

"Sometimes I like to eat lunch up here." It was then she noticed he was holding a lunch box. "Wanna share?" he asked.

She shook her head. "I'm not all that hungry, but I'll sit with you."

His smile widened. "I'd like that. Come on. I know of a better place to sit away from the wind."

Pirithous led her to another part of the roof, blocked by a partition, where there was a set of chairs. The space overlooked the coast of New Athens, a line of pure white sand that met a foamy ocean of the deepest emerald.

It was a breathtaking view.

"Go ahead and sit," he said. Pirithous opened his lunch and took out a sandwich and a bag of chips. "You sure you don't want any?"

"Yes, thank you."

He took a bite, and they looked out over the city. After a moment of silence, Pirithous prompted, "So what are you doing up here?"

She sighed and chose not to look at him when she said, "I'm guessing you haven't seen the news."

"Can't say that I have," he answered.

He was the only mortal she knew who didn't seem at all obsessed with the gods.

"Well, I messed up."

"I'm sure it's not that bad."

She took a deep breath. "I kinda...chose to do something I promised Hades I wouldn't do because I was angry with him, and now...I can't take it back."

"Ah." Pirithous offered a little laugh. He took a bite of his sandwich, talking as he chewed. "What did he do?"

"Something stupid," she muttered. "I don't think he sees the problem with what he did."

Pirithous smiled in his sad way. She got the sense that he understood her situation more than he wanted to admit.

"They often don't," he commented.

"I don't understand."

He shrugged. "Men just don't think."

"That is really a horrible excuse."

"It's not an excuse, really. Just a reality. All you can do is keep fighting for what you want. If he wants you, he will work to understand you."

She pursed her lips, feeling ridiculous. She knew now that she'd overreacted, but she hadn't been able to stop herself. She wanted Hades to feel as betrayed as she felt when she'd learned about Leuce. She wanted him to feel the frustration she'd felt with each passing hour that she hadn't heard from him. She'd wanted to defy him, just to see if she could get a reaction.

"Am I being irrational?"

He shrugged. "Maybe, but emotions are emotions," he said. "I have been the stupid boy before. I wish I had worked harder."

Persephone felt she understood the sadness that clung to this man. She wondered what Hades would see if he looked at his soul.

"What stupid thing did you do?"

He took a deep breath. "You will be surprised, I think, given your history."

Persephone's brows drew together, but before she could ask what he meant, Pirithous explained.

"I gambled a lot—not the kind of gambling your boyfriend does. I used to bet on the Panhellenic Games.

I was good—lucky, I guess. Until I wasn't. I thought I was doing what was best for my girl, and I believed that so much, I ignored what was important—her wish that I stop. She didn't care about the money or the status. She just wanted me."

He paused to offer a small laugh.

"Gods, I'd give anything for a woman who just wanted me now."

"What happened to her?"

"She is happily married. Expecting her first child. It's strange to watch someone you love move on and assume a life that could have been yours."

Persephone hoped she would never have to do that.

"I am sorry," she said and covered his hand with hers for a moment.

He shrugged.

"I thought I was protecting her." He paused. "Maybe that's what Hades thought he was doing for you."

She had no doubt.

"I wish he would stop. I don't need protection."

"Everyone needs protecting," he said. "Life's hard."

Persephone frowned. She'd said something similar to Hades once when she'd argued with him about why it was important to forgive mortals. She'd never considered she required the same grace.

After lunch, the day just got worse. Helen was dealing with an influx of angry phone calls, and Persephone's inbox continued to fill with hate mail. She couldn't escape the judgment, even in her text messages.

I can't believe you wrote about Apollo! Lexa texted.

She wasn't sure if that was her best friend expressing her excitement or her frustration.

Have you talked to Sybil? Persephone asked.

No. I am betting she'll lie low. If she was still Apollo's oracle, you know she'd be dealing with this mess.

If she was still his oracle, he wouldn't be in this mess.

Um, girl, I meant YOU. You're the mess

I just told the truth. So sue me.

I'm thinking Apollo will resort to more archaic means. Lexa paused. *Has Hades said anything yet?*

Nope.

There had been no apology, no lecture, and her emotions were all over the place. She had never felt like this before, torn between anger, a desperate wish to be confronted by him, and fear of his disappointment.

When Persephone left the Acropolis, Antoni met her at the doors and walked her through the aggressive crowd. He waited until they were safely in the car to ask, "Are you okay, my lady?"

She wasn't sure why, but the question made her eyes burn. All of a sudden, she was holding back tears. She would not cry over this—not yet.

She took a deep breath.

"Is he angry?"

She knew she didn't have to say Hades's name. Antoni would know who she was talking about.

"I haven't seen him," the cyclops admitted. "But I can imagine he won't be happy."

She knew that, which was why there was no way she was going to the Underworld tonight. She was thankful that the cyclops didn't elaborate or berate her for writing about Apollo. Most of the drive was spent in silence, except for when she asked Antoni to stop so she could grab takeout before heading home.

By the time she made it to the apartment, all she wanted to do was take a hot bath and go to sleep. She bid Antoni good night and headed inside. Lexa had texted her to let her know she would be out with Jaison. Sybil and Leuce were sitting at the bar, working on resumes. When Persephone walked through the door, Sybil left her seat and folded Persephone into her arms.

Persephone dropped her purse and the takeout to the floor and hugged the oracle back. Leuce turned in her seat and offered a sympathetic smile.

"I guess we got a little carried away last night," Leuce said.

Persephone offered a humorless laugh. She needed to stop working and drinking.

"I'm sorry," Persephone said to Sybil. "I didn't listen to you."

"It's okay," Sybil said. "I don't blame you for wanting to tell their stories. I just hate that no one believes you."

"I know that's why you told me not to do it," Persephone said, and she smiled a little as she pulled away to look at Sybil. "Apollo might have taken away your powers, but your instincts are on point."

Sybil shrugged. "I know how history treats women."

Sybil picked up Persephone's purse and the food she'd brought, setting it on the counter.

"It's moussaka, if you all want some," Persephone said, nodding to the bag of food. "I also got baklava because…you know…it's been a hard day."

Sybil laughed softly. "Of course."

"I think I'm going to take a bath."

Sybil nodded.

"We'll be here if you want to talk," Leuce said.

"Thanks."

Persephone navigated to her bedside table in the dark, familiar with the layout of her room, and turned on the lamp. She stepped into the bathroom, removed her jewelry, and started the bathwater. As it was running, she moved back into her room and began to undress when she noticed something shifting in the corner of her eye. She turned, startled by Hades's presence in her room.

How had she not felt him?

Because he didn't want you to, she thought immediately.

"Please continue," he said, leaning casually against the wall in partial darkness. He looked at home, born of the shadow. His hands were in the pockets of his slacks, and he'd removed his jacket. The sleeves of his black shirt were rolled up and the top two buttons undone, exposing his well-muscled forearms and chest.

Her breath caught in her throat. Would she always think of how beautiful he looked every time she saw him?

His burning eyes ran the length of her, and she suddenly remembered she was angry with him for so many things. She pulled her dress back up, and Hades offered an unamused laugh.

"Come now, darling. We are beyond that, are we not? I have seen every inch of you—touched every part of you."

She shivered because no matter how angry she was with him, she couldn't help the thoughts that surfaced in her mind at his words.

"That doesn't mean you will tonight," she said, and Hades scowled. "What are you doing here?"

"You are avoiding me," he said.

"*I'm* avoiding *you?*" she scoffed. "It's a two-way street, Hades. You've been just as absent."

"I gave you space," he said, and she rolled her eyes. "Clearly that was a bad idea."

"You know what you should have given me?" she said. "An apology."

She headed into the bathroom. Hades wasn't going to keep her from her bath. Stripping down, she stepped into the water. It was almost too hot, stinging as she submerged herself. Normally, she would stretch out, but she felt oddly subconscious and drew her knees to her chest.

Hades followed, leaning against the counter, arms crossed over his chest, mouth tight.

"I told you I loved you."

"That's not an apology."

"Are you telling me those words mean nothing to you?"

She glared. "Actions, Hades. You weren't going to tell me about Leuce."

"If we are going to speak of actions, then let us speak of yours."

Despite the heat of the water, Persephone suddenly felt chilled.

"Did you not promise me you wouldn't write about Apollo?"

There was more to her actions—they'd been fueled by Sybil and Leuce and wine—but she couldn't say that, because the results were the same. She had broken her promise.

"I had to do it—"

"Had to?" he interrupted. "Were you offered an ultimatum?"

Yes, I was offered an ultimatum, you idiot!

She didn't respond and averted her eyes, glaring at the water. If she looked at Hades for too long, she would burst into tears. There was too much emotion building inside her.

"Were you threatened?"

Again, she was silent.

"Did any of it have *anything* to do with you?"

She hated the way his voice grated against her ears. She stood from her bath, water sloshing everywhere, and snatched a towel from the bar, holding it to her chest.

"Sybil is my friend and her life was *ruined* by Apollo. His behavior *had* to be exposed."

Hades tilted his head to the side, his eyes flashing. He uncrossed his arms and stepped toward her. Persephone's heart raced as he leaned close.

"Do you know what I think?" he whispered furiously. She wanted to take a step away—she didn't want to face what she'd done. How she'd retaliated against him. "I think this is all a game to you. I pissed you off, so you wanted to piss me off, is that it? One for one—now we're even."

"Not everything's about you, Hades."

His hands clasped her waist, drawing her close. "You promised me you wouldn't write about Apollo."

Persephone cringed.

"Is your word worth nothing?"

Those words stung. She swallowed something thick in her throat and glared at him through watery eyes. "Fuck you."

Hades was ruthless. The bastard smiled.

"I'd rather fuck you, darling, but if I did right now, you wouldn't walk for a week."

He snapped his fingers, and the world around her shifted. He'd teleported to the Underworld. They were in the suite she used to get ready for the Ascension Ball—it was the suite Hades had built for his future queen. The fact that he'd brought her here and not to his own bedroom spoke volumes.

She pushed away from him. Her towel was the only thing between them.

"Did you just abduct me?"

"Yes," he answered, already turning his back on her. "Apollo will come after you, and the only way he will have an audience with you is if I am present."

"I can take care of this, Hades."

She didn't know how, but she would. Demetri had given her two options—apologizing or interviewing a recent victim. Those might be shit options, but maybe the other seven would be willing to talk to her.

Hades shut her down.

"You can't and you won't."

Persephone lifted her chin, glaring at the King of the Dead. She attempted to teleport, but nothing happened. Her rage bubbled under the surface of her skin.

"You can't keep me here."

A carpet of vines spread from her feet toward Hades. He offered a dark laugh, and the corner of his mouth lifted in an arrogant smirk.

"Darling, you are in my realm. You're here until I say otherwise."

"I have to work, Hades. I have a life up there."

He said nothing.

"Hades!"

He kept walking, and she wanted him to hurt because she really didn't think he felt anything in this. Her anger boiled over, and it felt like she had fire in her veins as black thorns burst from the tile floor, moving for Hades like venomous snakes.

But the God of the Underworld just waved his hand and the thorns turned to ash.

He'd done it so easily, so quickly.

Which meant all those times she'd used her magic against him, he'd just...let her. The reality of her weakness was harsh in the face of his indifference, and she suddenly felt unsteady on her feet.

As he went to close the door behind him, she called out in a cracked voice, "You will regret this!"

"I already do," he said, and there was a note to his voice that sounded like grief.

CHAPTER IX
A Touch of Poison

Persephone sat up in bed, knees pulled to her chest, unable to sleep. She had so much to fix and she wasn't sure she was ready—or really knew what to do. The Upperworld raged against her and Hades was hurt.

Is your word worth nothing?

She realized he'd said the words in anger, but they pierced her chest each time she recalled them, a blade slamming into the same incision.

Did he really believe that? Had she lost his trust?

She didn't know the time, but the darkness outside her windows seemed endless. Persephone rose from bed, pulled on her robe, and wandered outside into the garden. The stone path was cool against her bare feet, and the perfumed scent of flowers followed her as she walked. She paused now and then, touching velvet roses and weeping wisteria.

She wasn't outside long when she suddenly felt as if she were being watched and turned to see Hades outside his room. He stood, arms braced against the balcony. Even from this distance, she knew he tracked her every movement, her every breath. She hoped he was in agony. She hoped he ached for her. There were few places she could go in the Underworld where there were no memories of time spent with Hades. Not long ago, he had chased her through this garden, pinned her against the wall, and made love to her.

She hoped he was thinking about that now. She hoped he thought of how hot her mouth had been around his cock in the grove. She hoped he remembered how he'd praised her for tasting sweet as his mouth consumed her flesh. She hoped he thought of all these things while he slept alone in his cold bed.

Part of her wanted him to come after her, materialize out of the darkness and consume her, but this time, things were different. It wasn't that Hades was angry. Anger meant punishment, and that usually led to pleasure.

Hurt meant time. It meant distance.

She wrapped her arms tighter around herself and turned from him, continuing down the path, farther into the garden.

At some point, she returned to her room. She didn't remember falling asleep, but the next thing she knew, she was roused by a knock at the door, and Hecate entered in sweeping, crimson robes.

"Good morning, my sweet!"

A nymph followed her into the room carrying a covered tray.

"I brought breakfast. Let's eat."

Persephone joined Hecate on the balcony. She had brought an array of fruit, breads, jams, and coffee.

141

"Anything else, my lady?" the nymph asked.

"Uh, no," Persephone replied, and the nymph bowed, leaving them alone.

"It is a divine morning," Hecate said, taking a deep breath. "I thought we might practice early this morning—"

"Did you know Leuce had returned?"

"Oh no, Hades isn't going to get me in trouble. I knew she was back and advised him to tell you. What he chose to do or not isn't my fault."

"Tell me about her," Persephone said.

Hecate froze, her mug halfway to her lips. Finally, she took a sip before asking, "What do you want to know?"

"Did Hades love her?"

"Not like he loves you," she said without hesitation.

"Don't try to make me feel better, Hecate."

"Truly, I am not. Or at least, I wouldn't say something that isn't true. Hades cared for her, yes. I think he believed he loved her. I also think he knows differently now."

"I was completely blindsided."

"As I am sure your mother hoped you would be."

"My mother?" Persephone hadn't heard or spoken to Demeter since she'd destroyed her greenhouse, and she had to admit, she didn't really miss her.

"Oh yes, this reeks of Demeter," Hecate said, wrinkling her nose. "Who else has the power to turn a tree back into a nymph?"

Hades, she wanted to point out but knew that the god hadn't been the one to restore Leuce to her natural form.

"Why would my mother do Hades's lover a favor?"

Hecate laughed. "You didn't think you'd get the last word in, did you? Demeter attempted to defy the Fates to keep you from Hades. She will try anything to pry you away from him. You know that."

Persephone was quiet. She hadn't even considered that her mother might be involved in this, but now that Hecate had said something, she was shocked it wasn't her first thought.

After a moment, she put her head in her hands.

"I don't understand why he didn't tell me."

"The first rule of men, Persephone, is that they're all idiots."

She started to protest, but Hecate interrupted her.

"And don't start thinking that just because Hades is ancient and wise in other matters of life means he's above idiocy. He's not. Trust me. I have existed alongside him to see it all."

"He is an idiot," Persephone agreed. "But...so am I."

Hecate's eyes softened. "You are."

The two shared a laugh.

"Are you going to turn me into a polecat?" Persephone asked, and though she meant it as a joke, she felt tears prick her eyes.

The goddess smiled. "No, dear, I already have one."

Persephone wiped at her face fiercely. "Oh, Hecate. What do I do? I hurt Hades. I didn't think...well, I didn't think at all. I was so—"

"Hurt," Hecate said. "Hades hurt you too. You hurt each other. The answer is simple. You apologize."

"It doesn't seem like enough."

"It is enough. It's enough because you love each other."

Persephone took a breath. *Apologize.* She could do that.

"Okay," she said, standing. "Where is he?"

Hecate rose from her seat. "Just wait a little longer. You'll want him angry for when Apollo arrives," she said and winked. "Now, let's channel some of this pain into a lesson."

The two made their way to one of Hades's many orchards. Persephone was still learning the Underworld and its vast landscape, but one of the things she'd discovered was that Hades had a network of vegetation—grapes, olives, figs, dates, and pomegranates. The Goddess of Magic chose a clearing where a particularly large pomegranate tree had grown. Its emerald leaves contrasted darkly with the crimson fruit hanging heavy from its branches.

For a moment, Persephone was enchanted by the clearing.

And then came the bees.

"Where the hell did these come from?" Persephone asked, dodging another winged demon as it charged for her face. These were not nice bees.

"I summoned them," Hecate said cheerily.

"You—what?"

"Using magic under stressful situations is a valuable skill, Persephone."

"Don't you think I am under enough stress?"

"In your mind," Hecate answered. "Good practitioners of magic must learn to work under both mental and physical stress."

Not today, Persephone wanted to say.

"Well, I am not a good practitioner of magic."

"If you keep saying that, it will become the truth."

"*It is the truth.* You're the only one who can't see it. Even Hades knows. He's only been letting me think I am powerful enough to use magic against him."

Hecate's brows came together. "What do you mean?"

Persephone told her what happened last night with the thorns.

"It was effortless for him."

"My love. You must remember that Hades is in his realm. Here, he is all-powerful."

That didn't help, because all the times she'd used her magic with him, she'd been here in the Underworld. She wasn't sure why it bothered her so much. She guessed because she had used that as a measure of improvement— and just as easily as he'd used his magic to turn hers into ash, he'd taken her fragile confidence with it.

Hecate sighed. "Perhaps I have overstepped. I am sorry for the bees."

Once Hecate dismissed the bees, they focused on practice.

"Remember what I told you," the goddess said, positioning Persephone in front of the pomegranate tree. "Magic is malleable."

Persephone did remember. They were words Hecate had spoken shortly after she started to feel life in the plants, flowers, and trees around her.

Practicing magic with Hecate was nothing like practicing on her own. The goddess was dedicated to the craft and meticulous in her instruction. Persephone was told to ripen the pomegranates on the tree in the middle of the grove. They weighed down branches of the tree; their skin was a greenish-yellow, bruising with a crimson red. It meant that she was going to have to demonstrate control in gathering and channeling her power.

Hecate's words rose to the surface of her mind as Persephone called up her magic.

*Imagine it as clay. Mold it into what you desire and then...
give it life.*

It was easier said than done.

Persephone felt the heat of magic pulse through her veins. It pooled into her palms like water warmed beneath the sun, and as she closed her eyes, she imagined herself manipulating the glamour into a ripe, red pomegranate.

"Perfect," she heard Hecate say encouragingly.

Persephone took a deep breath and opened her eyes. She couldn't see the magic she held in her hands, but she could feel it. It was energy, and it charged the air surrounding her, raising the hair on her arms and the back of her neck.

"Now, direct the magic at your target."

Persephone did as Hecate instructed, pushing her hands out as the magic pulsed from her palms, leaving them covered in a cold sweat. The magic reached the tree, and the pomegranates began to swell and darken.

"Yes!" Persephone jumped, excited by her success.

But the fruit kept growing.

And growing.

And growing.

Oh no.

"Take cover!" Hecate grabbed Persephone's hand and dragged her behind a nearby tree.

A second later, she heard a loud pop as several pomegranates exploded. Persephone didn't want to look, but she peered around the tree anyway. The whole grove was covered in red. It looked like a bloodbath.

Her shoulders sagged with defeat.

"You just used too much power," Hecate said.

"I think that's more than obvious, Hecate," Persephone snapped, frustrated with herself.

The Goddess of Witchcraft didn't seem fazed by Persephone's outburst and just smiled. "Do not see this as defeat, my dear. It's only through a failure to control your power that we will learn how strong you truly are."

But Persephone didn't feel powerful, and she said as much. "I can grow plants and kill them. To gods, those are parlor tricks."

"Right now," Hecate agreed. "But that does not mean other powers won't manifest."

Persephone pursed her lips. She thought about how she'd been sensing emotions off and on since Sybil had come to her apartment.

"My dear, there's darkness inside you, and we have only touched the surface."

A shiver slithered up her spine. It wasn't the first time she'd heard those words.

Let me coax the darkness from you—I will help you shape it.

They were words Hades had spoken against her skin right before he explored her body for the first time, inside and out. She hadn't known what he meant then, she didn't know what Hecate meant now, and she decided she didn't want to ask.

"Can you fix this mess?" Persephone asked Hecate. Thick pulp dripped from tree limbs onto the flowers below. It looked like a battlefield.

"I could," Hecate said. "But then I wouldn't have a lesson for later."

"You want *me* to fix this?" Persephone knew she didn't have to, but she threw her arms out, gesturing to the disaster in front of them. "What makes you think I can mend this when I couldn't stop it from happening?"

"If I thought you could do it on your own, it wouldn't be a lesson," the goddess replied.

Persephone seethed.

One day, she would turn her mother into a carrion flower for keeping her magic from manifesting.

"Do not worry, my love. You will learn your power as you learn yourself," Hecate promised.

The two made their way back to the palace. For a while, they were able to stay away from the topic of Hades and Apollo, mostly because Hecate used the walk as a teaching moment after they'd happened upon a grove of hemlock.

"At some point, I will instruct you in the art of poison," Hecate said. "It's a useful skill for any lady to possess."

Persephone gave Hecate an uncertain look.

"I don't think poisoning is a useful skill, Hecate."

"It is when you must kill discreetly."

"And when do you need to kill discreetly?"

Hecate shrugged. "There are all sorts of instances— abusers of women and children, sex traffickers, rapists… the list goes on."

Huh, perhaps Hecate is onto something.

They walked along in silence for a little while, Persephone contemplating the usefulness of poison against one god in particular when she asked, "What does Hades have against Apollo?"

She knew why *she* disliked him, of course, but Hades's fury seemed to surpass her own.

She added, "And don't tell me to ask him."

Hecate offered a small smile. "It's what all gods have against each other, I suppose—the knowledge of their history and deeds."

Hecate paused and faced Persephone.

"Hades isn't trying to be difficult. He fears for you. Apollo…his vengeance is cruel."

"I know."

"You *don't*," Hecate argued, and Persephone was a little surprised by her tone. "In antiquity, he and his sister murdered fourteen children. The children themselves were innocents. It was their mother, Niobe, who had offended them after she claimed to be superior to the gods' own mother, Leto."

Fourteen children? How was the world not appalled by these two gods?

"Needless to say, Apollo is unpredictable, and rather than take a chance, Hades has brought you here to the Underworld—his realm—where any action Apollo takes will be considered making war upon the God of the Dead. Apollo might be rash, but he isn't stupid. He does not want Hades as an enemy."

Despite feeling a new kind of terror, Persephone was glad she'd asked.

They returned to the palace where they had dinner and discussed the finer details of the summer solstice celebration.

"I have commissioned a new crown," Hecate said just as Persephone was about to take a drink from her wine. She spit it back into the cup.

"I'm sorry. What?"

"Ian is very excited."

Persephone glared. Of course she'd bring Ian into this.

The soul was a master blacksmith. Before he died, he'd made armor and weapons and was favored by Artemis. It was that favor that got him killed. The soul now used his skill in the Underworld to craft beautiful, intricate things—lampposts and gates and the occasional crown.

"I don't need another crown, Hecate. The one Ian made for me is very beautiful. I can wear it to the solstice celebration."

She didn't say what she was really thinking. A crown was presumptuous. Hades wasn't speaking to her right now; how could she be sure he still wanted her as his queen?

"You could, but why would you when you'll have a new one?"

Persephone sighed. "I wish you had asked me."

"I'd really rather not," Hecate said. "Now, about the dress. I was thinking black…"

Hecate continued explaining her vision for what she called Persephone's grand ensemble. The goddess only half listened, her mind wandering to the story of Apollo, his sister, and Hades. During her research of the God of Music, she hadn't considered checking into other stories from his past. The god's offenses were indeed endless and violent, and she found herself wondering if even Hades could prevent his retaliation.

After dinner, Persephone returned to her suite alone. She started to curse Hades for building it. Who puts their wife in a whole other part of their palace? It was so…antiquated!

You aren't his wife, she corrected herself. *You are his… girlfriend.*

Maybe.

She couldn't be sure. She hadn't seen Hades since he'd watched her from the balcony last night. She had attempted to go in search of him earlier and hadn't found him anywhere in the palace. More than likely, he was avoiding her. She had questions and demands. What was she supposed to do about her job? Had he let Demetri know where she was? What about Lexa and Sybil and Leuce?

Her mood darkened further, and she found herself outside again, exploring the Underworld in the fading light. Her frustration caused the surrounding flowers to bloom and the grass to grow taller. She hated it. She was literally leaving a path for anyone to follow.

She traveled far, over rocky hills and mossy valleys, until she found herself on the edge of a cliff, face-to-face with a gray ocean.

The wind whipped her hair, cooling her heated face. Her insides were still raging. She felt so angry—angry with Apollo and with Hades and being stuck in that gods-forsaken suite. Was this his form of punishment? Leaving her in the Underworld and avoiding her at all costs? He didn't seem at all sorry for his part in this.

She decided she needed to calm down when a rose sprouted from her arm. The bud was painful as it grew, and when she pulled it free, she screamed from the burn, and blood poured from the wound.

This is torture, she thought.

She tore off a piece of her gown and wrapped it around her arm as tight as she could before settling on the ground. First, she focused on the sound of the sea rushing the shore below, the feel of the wind against her face, the smell of ash and salt in the air. Then she closed her eyes and breathed deep—filling her lungs with the same smells, with the same wind, with the same sounds until she felt like she was in the ocean herself, rocking back and forth, cradled in warm waves.

The anger and tension and pain broke apart.

For the first time today, she felt calm, collected, clearheaded.

When she opened her eyes, it was dark, and she knew she should head back to the palace before anyone started worrying, but as she got up to leave, she found the path her magic had created was gone.

Still, she thought she could manage on her own and started in the direction she thought she'd come. She walked for a while before she realized she was lost. Exhausted and unable to teleport, she found a spot beneath a tree and sat, sliding to the ground, where she fell asleep.

She was roused by Hades's warmth. His scent filled her nose as he cradled her close to his chest. She knew when they teleported because the air changed. If she wasn't so exhausted—so groggy—she would have opened her eyes to see his expression. In fact, she wanted to open her eyes, because her heart needed to see how he was looking at her, but she found she couldn't.

She was so damn tired.

Why was she so tired?

Hades held her close for a long time before shifting and settling her in a heap of blankets. He pressed a kiss to her forehead, and warmth seeped into her skin.

She remembered nothing else.

CHAPTER X
God of Music

When Persephone opened her eyes, the first thing she noticed were black silk sheets. She caressed them, brows knitting together. How had she gotten into Hades's room? She rolled over, thinking she might find him beside her, but the bed was empty. Then she heard the clink of a glass, and her eyes shifted to Hades's bar.

Hermes was standing in front of it, and he had frozen at the sound, looking to see if he'd woken her.

"Hermes?" she asked.

The God of Trickery turned fully, holding a decanter of amber liquid and a glass. "Sorry, Sephy. I needed a drink."

"What are you doing here?" she asked, sitting up in bed.

"What am I doing here? What were you doing last night?"

Persephone's brows drew together. "What do you mean?"

Hermes cocked his head to the side. "You really don't remember?"

"I went for a walk," she said and shrugged.

"That was some walk," Hermes scoffed. "Hades freaked the fuck out. He couldn't find you or sense you anywhere. I've never seen him so…"

"Angry?"

Hermes looked at her like she was crazy.

"No, distraught. This is the Underworld. His territory. He thought something bad had happened. He summoned every deity in the Underworld—and me—to look for you."

"I just…got lost. I wanted to clear my head. I meditated for a little while like Hecate told me to do, and when I was finished, it was dark. I couldn't find my way back. I didn't mean to make anyone worry. I just wanted to be alone."

"Well, enjoy that, because I don't think Hades will let you out of his sight for the foreseeable future."

She raised a brow. "You mean like now?"

"I'm babysitting," he said, almost proudly, and Persephone rolled her eyes.

"And why are you babysitting?"

"Because Apollo's here."

Persephone froze, and Hermes's face drained of color as the god realized his mistake.

"What?"

"Did I say Apollo was here? I meant that he's on his way. He's most definitely not here. Hades is not meeting with Apollo in the throne room without you…fuck."

Persephone was already out of bed.

"Persephone!" Hermes called as she left the room. "Sephy! Get back here! No one will take you seriously with that hair!"

She ignored him, taking off toward the throne room, her feet slipping on the marble as she went. She burst inside, where she found Hades and Apollo standing opposite each other. They really were quite the pair—shadow and light meeting on a marble battlefield.

Apollo was beautiful in his mortal form. He was boyish, athletic, and smaller than Hades. He had a crown of dark curls, a square jaw, and dimples that added to what might have been youthful charm if he didn't appear so angry.

Hades, on the other hand, was raw, primal masculinity. He towered over Apollo, his hair a halo of darkness. There was a maturity to Hades's features that had nothing to do with his well-manicured beard or tailored suit. It was in his eyes—black, endless eyes that had seen lifetimes of strife.

When she entered, the two gods turned to her.

"So the mortal has come to play," Apollo remarked.

Hades glared over Persephone's shoulder at Hermes, who had followed her. The god held up his hands to stave off Hades's anger.

"What? She guessed!"

Hades turned back to Apollo. "The deal is done. You will not touch her."

"What deal?" Persephone demanded.

The two gods looked at her again, Apollo amused, Hades angry, but she didn't care. While she understood Hades wanted to keep her safe from Apollo, he couldn't just exclude her from this conversation. She had started it, she had things to say, and Apollo would hear her out.

"Your lover has struck a deal," Apollo said. The way he said lover slithered across her skin in all the wrong ways.

It made her dislike it more, but maybe that was because she felt there was a certain amount of disrespect associated with it—that she was fleeting, temporary. She felt that way now with this meeting occurring without her.

"I have agreed not to punish you for your…slanderous article…and in turn, Hades has offered me a favor to be collected at a future time."

Hermes whistled. "Damn. He really does love you, Sephy."

They all glared at Hermes.

Hades offering Apollo a favor was huge. The god could literally ask for anything, and Hades would have to grant it. A knot settled in the pit of her stomach, but it wasn't guilt—it was dread. Why would Hades offer something so precious without telling her first?

Because he thought it was the only way to protect you, she thought. *And you wouldn't have let him do it.*

"I will not agree to this," Persephone said, looking at Apollo.

"You don't have a choice, mortal."

Persephone's eyes burned, and she felt Hades's magic rising to subdue her own, for which she was thankful. If Apollo knew she was a goddess, he would have leverage against her, and the god would use it, given his vengeful past.

"I'm the one who wrote the article," she said. "Your deal should be with me."

"Persephone."

Her name slipped from between Hades's teeth, and Apollo threw his head back, laughing.

"What could you possibly offer me?"

Persephone's fists curled, her nails digging into her palms. "You hurt my friend," she hissed.

"Whatever your friend did must have warranted punishment or she would not be in the situation she is in."

It enraged her that he didn't even seem to know which friend he'd hurt.

"You mean to tell me her refusal to be your lover warrants punishment?"

Apollo froze, though his expression remained passive.

Persephone continued, "You took away her livelihood because she declined to sleep with you. That is insane and pathetic."

"Persephone," Hades warned.

"You be quiet!" she snapped. She never thought she'd get tired of hearing her name on Hades's lips, but right now, she wanted him to shut up. "You chose not to include me in this conversation. I will speak my mind."

The god's lips thinned, and his eyes burned. She could feel the frustration brewing under his skin. It made her own tingle.

Hermes was laughing. She ignored him and turned toward Apollo.

"I only wrote about your past lovers. I didn't even touch on what you have done to Sybil. If you don't undo her punishment, I will dismantle you."

There was silence, and Apollo chuckled, narrowing his eyes. "You are a fiery little mortal. I could use someone like you."

"Speak further, Nephew, and you will have no reason to fear her threat, because I will tear you to pieces."

Apollo offered Hades an unsavory glance, his eyes returning to Persephone quickly, who promoted him.

"Well?"

Apollo stared at her for a long moment, and with a small smile on his lips that made her stomach knot, he said, "Fine. I will return your little friend's powers and I'll take Hades's favor as well, but you will not write another word about me—no matter what. Understand?"

Persephone lifted her chin. "Words are binding, and I do not trust you enough to agree."

Apollo chuckled. "You have taught her well, Hades."

The God of Music dared take a step toward her. She sensed both Hades and Hermes straighten. The tension was so thick, Persephone couldn't breathe. Apollo bent, his face close to hers and—despite his eyes being the most beautiful shade of blue she'd ever seen—there was something sinister behind them. It made her want to vomit.

"Let me put it this way—you write another word about me and I'll destroy everything you love. And before you consider the fact that you love another god, remember that I have his favor. If I want to keep you apart forever, I can."

That sent a chill of fear down Persephone's spine. She glanced at Hades, wondering if the threat was real. Her lover's expression told her it was.

"Noted," she said from between her teeth. The god straightened.

"I will warn you now, Apollo." There was an edge of fury to Hades's voice—a promise of violence Persephone felt in her soul. "If any harm comes to Persephone, favor or not, I will bury you and everything you love in ash."

Apollo offered a cold smile. "You'll only have me to bury, Hades. Nothing I love exists anymore."

Apollo left, vanishing in a blinding ray of light. The throne room was silent, and Persephone found that she was hesitant to face Hades. She had ruined his plans and deliberately disobeyed him in front of another god.

"Well, that could have gone better," Hermes said, clearly amused. Persephone cringed at his tone, knowing Hades wouldn't be pleased.

"Why are you still here?" Hades asked through gritted teeth.

"He was babysitting me," Persephone snapped, glaring at him. "Or did you forget?"

Hades might be angry about how all this played out, but she blamed him for that. He'd spent the last few days ignoring her instead of talking through the conversation with Apollo—and didn't he always insist that they talk? How could he think she wouldn't want to fight for her friend if given the chance?

"How can you say you wish for me to be your queen when, given the opportunity to treat me as your equal, you fuck it up completely? Does your word mean nothing?"

Hades's eyes widened, surprised by her words. It was the blow she wanted to land. She turned from him, looped her arm through Hermes's, and strolled out of the throne room.

"That took some real lady balls, Sephy," Hermes said.

The goddess frowned. It might have taken balls, but it didn't make her feel any better.

"At this rate, we'll never reconcile," she said, frowning.

"Oh, I really doubt that," Hermes said. "I don't think Hades is willing to go that long without fucking you."

Persephone glared at the god. "Not everything is about sex, Hermes."

"Yes, it is. I'm not saying that to be vulgar." He

paused and chuckled a little. "Well, kinda. What I'm really trying to say is Hades loves you. You didn't see him last night. I did. He won't go long without talking to you. He's too afraid he'll lose you."

She hoped Hermes was right. Despite her final words to Hades, she hadn't wanted to leave his presence, and doing so made her heart hurt.

Hermes stayed for most of the afternoon and joined her and Hecate for a picnic in Asphodel. The gods played with Cerberus, Typhon, and Orthrus and chatted with the souls. When they were finished, Persephone found solace alone in the grove Hades had gifted her.

She marveled at his work.

Here in her forest, the ground was covered in a sea of purple and white flowers. The canopy overhead was a harbor of silver leaves so thick, none of Hades's strange daylight filtered inside.

It was beautiful and ethereal.

And it was all an illusion.

She had witnessed Hades lift his magic from the Underworld, revealing desolate and deserted land. The sight had shocked her but left her in awe of his skills. How was he able to wield magic like thread, weaving ash and smoke and fire into sweet scents, vibrant colors, and gorgeous landscape?

She found a spot in her grove with periwinkle and white phlox and sat near a withered patch of ground. She took a breath, closed her eyes, and meditated. She focused on her breath like Hecate had directed, and then the flow of her blood in her body, and then the flow of power in her veins and the press of life against her skin. She tried to imagine the bald patch in front of her teeming with life, but when she opened her eyes, there was nothing. Her shoulders fell, and she felt the weight of her failure heavy on her back.

Hades's scent stirred the air, and suddenly, he was around her—his chest to her back, his arms against hers, his legs cradling her body. His warmth was like the darkness, dense and lulling. She wanted it to consume her.

"You are practicing your magic?" he asked.

"More like failing," she answered.

He laughed as he exhaled. "You aren't failing. You have so much power." His voice made her shiver, and she wanted to believe him. She wanted to believe anything he said in that sensuous voice.

"Then why can't I use it?"

"You are using it," he answered.

"Not…correctly."

"Is there a correct way to use your magic?"

Persephone didn't answer, not because she didn't have one but because she was frustrated with Hades's question. Of course there was a correct way to use magic.

The god chuckled, and his fingers clasped her wrists lightly. "You use your magic all the time—when you are angry, when you are aroused…" Hades's lips were a breath away from her skin. She wanted desperately to turn and kiss him, but she resisted.

"That's not magic," she answered quietly.

"Then what is magic?" he asked.

"Magic is…" She searched for words on a shuddering breath. "Control."

Hades chuckled. "Magic is not controlled. It is passionate, expressive. It reacts to emotions, no matter your level of expertise."

His hands shifted, cupping her own.

Persephone swallowed.

"Close your eyes," he whispered.

She did.

"Tell me what you feel."

Aroused, she thought.

"I feel…warm," she said instead.

She knew Hades was amused by the tone of her voice.

"Focus on it," he said. "Where does it start?"

"Low," she answered and shivered despite the heat. "In my stomach."

"Feed it," he breathed.

She did—with thoughts of pushing him into the flowers and pleasuring him. He would be surprised at first, but his eyes would take on that dark smolder, and he would attempt to take control.

Except that she wouldn't let him. She would take him into her mouth until he bucked against her and then lick the come from his cock. When he kissed her, he would taste himself.

Those thoughts filled her with fire, and Hades demanded, "Now, where are you warm?"

"Everywhere," she answered.

"Imagine all that warmth in your hands," he spoke faster. "Imagine it glowing. Imagine it so bright you can barely look at it."

She did as he instructed, focusing intently on the heat rushing to her palms. It was easier because she could feel the weight of Hades's hands on hers. They grounded her.

"Now imagine the light has dimmed, and in the shadow, you see the life you have created." Hades's lips touched her ear as he whispered, "Open your eyes, Persephone."

When she did, a shimmering white image of the periwinkle and phlox she had envisioned manifested between her hands.

It was beautiful.

Hades guided her hands to the barren earth, and as the magic touched the ground, it transformed into flowers.

Persephone touched one of the silky petals, just to be sure it was real.

"Magic is balance—a little control, a little passion. It is the way of the world."

She tilted her head toward him but could not see him fully. His beard scraped her cheek. The silence stretched between them, and every bit of her skin felt like an exposed nerve. Finally, she twisted, coming to her knees. His eyes were fierce, and his nostrils flared.

"I love you. I should have reminded you when I brought you here and each day since," Hades said. "Please forgive me."

Tears burned the backs of her eyes. "I forgive you—but only if you'll forgive me. I was angry about Leuce but angrier that you left me that evening to go to her," she said. The words hurt, like she couldn't take in enough air to speak them. "And I feel so…ridiculous. I know your reasons and I know you didn't want to leave me that evening, but I can't help how I feel about it. When I think about it, I feel…hurt."

Maybe it had something to do with all the emotion she had invested in that moment in the dining room. It was all so…intense, and the aftermath left her feeling unfulfilled, neglected.

"It pains me to know I hurt you. What can I do?"

She was surprised by that question. "I…don't know. I suppose what I have done must make up for it. I told you I wouldn't write about Apollo—I promised you—and broke that promise."

Hades shook his head. "We do not make up for hurt with hurt, Persephone. That is a god's game. We are lovers."

"Then how do we make up for hurt?" she asked.

"With time," he answered. "If we can be comfortable being angry with one another for a little while."

Persephone frowned, and the tears she thought had all dried up came again as she whispered, "I don't want to be angry with you."

"Nor I with you," he said, reaching to brush the tears away. "But it doesn't change feelings, and it doesn't mean we can't care for each other while we heal."

Persephone stared at Hades and started to shake her head. "How is it that I was meant for you?"

Hades's brows drew together. "We've discussed this."

He didn't sound angry, but she also knew this discussion had come up before and it hadn't gone all that well, so she explained.

"I just feel so…inexperienced. I am young and rash. How could you want me?"

She choked on the words and covered her mouth to smother the emotion.

"Persephone," Hades said gently, covering her hand with his. "First, I will always want you. Always. I failed you here too. I was angry. I didn't take care of you. I didn't include you. Don't put me on a pedestal because you feel guilty for your decisions. Just…forgive yourself so you can forgive me. Please."

She took a breath and bit her lip. Hades's eyes fell to her mouth. Everything inside her was suddenly on fire.

He was right. He hadn't taken care of her, and that was what she'd craved. Despite their shared anger, she'd wanted him—his heat, his violence, his love.

She closed the distance between them, straddling him as they sat on the ground beneath the silver trees. Hades's hands settled on her hips.

"I'm sorry," she whispered. Her gaze was level with his, and his dark eyes reached deep. She knew he could see clear to her soul. "I love you. You can trust me, my word. I—"

"Shh, my darling," he said. His mouth was inches from hers; his hands trailed up her thighs and beneath her dress. Her stomach tightened with anticipation. "I will forever regret my anger. How could I ever question your love? Your trust? Your word? When you have my heart."

She kissed him. Her tongue demanded entrance, and Hades gave it. Persephone's hands tangled into his hair. Pulling hard, she climbed up his body, kissing harder and deeper, bruising him as she bit his lips and sucked his tongue.

She was ruthless, but so was Hades.

"Where are you burning?" he asked.

"Everywhere," she answered.

She pushed his jacket off his shoulders, and Hades took over, shoving it aside as she unbuttoned his shirt, exposing his chest. She pulled away to admire him. He tried to reach for her, but she stopped him.

"Let me pleasure you."

He didn't speak, but his eyes burned, and that was enough of an answer. She guided him to his back and kissed his lips before working her way down the planes of his muscled chest, following the line of hair from his stomach until it disappeared beneath his slacks, where his cock strained against the fabric. She unbuttoned them and wrapped her fingers around his warm, velvet flesh. As she stroked him, she bit down on her lip, ready to taste him.

Hades growled.

"Keep looking at me that way, darling. I won't let you have control for long."

She raised a challenging brow and then took him into her mouth. Hades hissed as she circled the head of his cock with her tongue and took him deeper into her mouth. He groaned when he hit the back of her throat, his fingers twisting tightly into her hair. He seemed to grow larger, filling her mouth more as she moved him in and out.

"Fuck!" Hades's curse encouraged her, and she moved faster, using her hands and her tongue. He came with a roar, and his come filled her mouth—salty and sweet. His smell filled her nose, a mixture of spice and chlorine. She took her time savoring him, licking every part of him clean until he dragged her up his body and brought her lips to his, rolling so that she was beneath him.

"Such a gift," he said, inches from her mouth. "How shall I repay you?"

"Gifts don't require payment, Hades."

"Another gift, then," he offered and took her mouth in a searing kiss. He laid her bare beneath the trees and worshipped her body until the sky was full of stars, glowing full and bright with Hades's magic.

CHAPTER XI
Unraveling

Persephone draped herself over Hades's naked body and rested her head on his chest. She reveled in the feel of him against her. It was like coming home after all those nights she'd spent alone. They'd just come from the baths after making love in the grove. Her body felt warm and limber, and her eyes were heavy with sleep. She should have succumbed, lulled by the smell of salt on Hades's skin and the soft circles he was tracing on her back.

Instead, she chose to speak.

"I'll mentor Leuce," she said, peeking at him when the silence stretched too long, wondering what he was thinking.

"I'm not sure how I feel about this."

"Me either," she admitted, but she felt like it was the right thing to do. "And I need you to give her a place to stay and her job back. Please."

Hades continued to trace shapes against her skin. "Why do you wish to mentor her?"

Persephone shrugged. "Because I think I know how she feels."

Hades raised a brow. "Explain."

"She's been a tree for thousands of years. Suddenly, she's normal again and the whole world has changed. It's…scary…and I know how that feels."

Hades was quiet for a long moment, and then he said again, as if to make sure, "You want to mentor my former lover?"

Persephone sighed loudly and rolled her eyes. "Don't make me regret this, Hades."

"I don't want you to, but are you sure?"

"It's weird, I admit, but…she's a victim. I want to help her."

It was a hard thing to say to him, given that he was the reason she'd been a poplar tree. Granted, what Leuce had done was wrong, but was it worth losing out on thousands of years?

Hades touched her chin.

"You amaze me," he said.

She giggled. "I am not amazing. I wanted to punish her at first."

"But you didn't," he said. "There are no other gods like you."

"I haven't lived long enough to be jaded like the rest of you," she said. "Perhaps I'll end up like the others before long."

"Or perhaps you will change the rest of us."

They stared at one another, bodies pressed together, until Persephone sat up, straddling Hades. The god beneath her had one hand behind his head. He looked arrogant, and she supposed he had reason to be—he had made her come over and over and he had been ruthless in his pursuit.

"Eager for more, my lady?" he asked, growing harder and thicker under her.

She smiled. That wasn't why she had sat up. She had something to say, and she wanted to say it now before she forgot, but at his question, she realized she *was* eager for more—eager to take control of his body, to use him as an instrument.

"Actually, I'm afraid I must make a few demands," she said, and she slid onto his shaft, filling herself completely. She let out a breath, sore from their previous coupling. Hades's hands went to her thighs, squeezing.

"Yes?" he said from between his teeth.

"I don't want to be placed in a suite on the other side of the palace, ever," she said, rolling her hips, feeling him everywhere. "Not to get ready for balls. Not when you are angry with me. Not *ever*."

She punctuated each of her statements by slamming into him.

Hades's fingers dug into her skin.

"I thought you would want privacy," he said.

She paused in her movements and bent over him. His eyes burned into hers.

"Fuck privacy. I needed you, needed to know you still wanted me despite…everything."

He drew his arm around her neck and brought her lips to his. She started to move again when Hades rolled, taking control, except that once she was beneath him,

169

he didn't move. She glared at him and lifted her hips, but he remained still.

"I will always want you, and I would have welcomed you to my bed any night."

"I didn't know," she said.

He pressed a thumb to her swollen lips.

"Now you do."

He gave her a bruising kiss, and they came together again, working through their anger and their pain until all they felt was their hearts beating together as one.

————

Persephone rose hours later in search of Hecate. She found the Goddess of Witchcraft in her cabin, bundling sage.

"Good evening, my sweet. You look well."

Persephone smiled. "I am well, Hecate, thank you."

"You are here to ask for a favor?"

Persephone twisted her fingers together.

"How did you know?"

Hecate smirked. "I don't imagine you were eager to leave Hades's company. Something brought you to my doorstep, and it isn't training."

Persephone snorted and explained. "I need to speak to my mother, but under…controlled circumstances."

"You wish to summon her so you can also dismiss her?"

Persephone nodded. "Can you help me?"

Hecate wrapped the last of the sage. When she was finished, she turned toward Persephone, meeting her gaze.

"My dear, I would love nothing more than to help you stand up to your mother."

Persephone grinned, and they teleported to her room in the Upperworld. Hecate got to work, instructing Persephone in the art of summoning spells.

"First, we must cleanse this area," she said, burning sage and carrying the smoking bundle around the room. Once she was finished, Hecate used her magic to draw a triple circle on Persephone's floor.

"Conjuring the living is no different from conjuring the dead," Hecate explained. "In both cases, you are summoning the soul, so the spell is the same."

Hecate gave Persephone a piece of obsidian and a piece of quartz.

"Obsidian for protection," she said. "And quartz for power."

After that, she produced a black candle, which she placed in the center of the triple circle. She hovered over it, her eyes lifting to meet Persephone's.

"When I light this candle, the spell is complete. Your mother will hear the call."

"Are you sure she will come?"

The goddess shrugged. "There is a chance she may resist, but I doubt your mother will give up the chance to see you."

"You don't know how angry she was when we last spoke."

"You are still her daughter," Hecate said. "She will come."

Hecate bent, cupping her hand over the wick of the candle. Persephone saw the goddess's lips move, and when she pulled away, a black flame flickered.

"Shall I leave you now?"

Persephone nodded. "Yes, thank you, Hecate."

She smiled. "Just blow out the candle when you are ready for her to leave."

Persephone bit her lip. "You are sure she won't be able to stay?"

Or hurt me?

"Only if she is invited," Hecate promised before vanishing.

Persephone was alone for only a few minutes when the smell of sage and burning wax was cut with the scent of wildflowers and a sharp chill.

Strange.

Demeter's magic usually felt warm, like a pale spring sun.

Persephone turned and found her mother standing in the shadow of her room. Demeter hadn't changed, except for looking far more severe than Persephone remembered. She wore blue robes, and her gold hair lay straight, parted at the center, framing her beautiful and cold face. Her antlers were both elegant and dreadful. They filled space, making Persephone's room more cramped. She was perfection, and her presence sucked the air out of Persephone's lungs.

"Daughter," she said coldly.

"Mother," Persephone acknowledged.

The Goddess of Harvest studied Persephone, probably picking apart her appearance. Demeter hated Persephone's curly hair and freckles, and when given the chance, she'd cover them up with her glamour. Whatever she saw there didn't change her severe expression, and after a moment, her gaze swept the room.

"Am I too hopeful? Have you summoned me to beg my forgiveness?"

Persephone wanted to laugh. If anyone should beg forgiveness, it was Demeter. She was the one who had kept Persephone a prisoner most of her life, and even when she'd released her, it had been on a long leash.

"No, I have summoned you to tell you to stop interfering with my life."

Demeter's frigid gaze returned to Persephone, her hazel eyes turning yellow in the candlelight.

"Are you accusing me of something, Daughter?"

Persephone felt a little uneasy. It occurred to her that her mother might be responsible for more than Leuce's release from the poplar tree. What other plans did she have to force Persephone away from Hades?

"You released Hades's former lover from her prison," Persephone said.

"Why would I bother with something so trivial?" Demeter sounded bored, but Persephone wasn't convinced.

"Good question, Mother."

Demeter turned from her daughter and began snooping around her room, inspecting, judging. She pulled open Persephone's nightstand drawers and opened anything with a lid, wrinkling her nose.

"This place smells like Hades," she said, and then she straightened, eyes narrowing upon Persephone. "*You* smell like him."

Persephone crossed her arms over her chest and glared at her mother.

"I hope you're using protection," Demeter said. "That's all you need—to be tied to the God of the Dead for the rest of your life."

"That's a given," Persephone said. "You're the only one who seems to think it isn't."

"You don't know Hades," Demeter said. "You're just now learning that for yourself. I know it bothers you. You fear what you don't know."

Persephone hated her mother for being right.

"I could say the same about you, Mother. What don't I know about you? What evils do you hide under your perfect facade?"

"Do not make this about me. You jumped into his arms as soon as he said he loved you. It is embarrassing that your judgment extends to his skin. I raised you better."

"You didn't raise me at all—"

"*I imprisoned you*," Demeter interrupted, rolling her eyes. "Gods, you are a broken record. I gave you everything. A home, friends, love. It wasn't enough for you."

"It *wasn't* enough," Persephone snapped. "And it would never have been enough! Did you really think you could challenge the Fates and win? You criticize other gods for their arrogance, yet you are the worst."

Demeter smiled cruelly. "The Fates may have given you what you wanted—a taste of freedom, a taste of forbidden love—but do not mistake their offer with kindness. The Fates punish, even gods."

"They punished you," Persephone said. "Not me."

Demeter offered a small smile. "That remains to be seen, my flower. Do you know the Fates named you? *Persephone*. I didn't understand then how my precious, *sweet* flower could be given such a name. *Destroyer*. But that is what you are—a destroyer of dreams, of happiness, of lives."

Persephone's eyes glazed with tears as her mother spoke.

"Oh yes, my love. Enjoy what the Fates have offered you, because they have woven your destiny, and you are a disgrace."

Persephone kicked the candle, spilling wax and extinguishing the flame. Her mother's form vanished, yet her scent lingered, choking Persephone. She fell to her knees, breathing hard, when her door opened. Lexa, Sybil, and Leuce were gathered there.

"Persephone, are you okay?" Lexa rushed to her side. Sybil picked up the candle, looking perplexed. Leuce was the only one who seemed to know what was going on.

"Summoning spell?" she asked.

Persephone met the woman's gaze and, through her tears, she said, "We need to talk."

Lexa helped Persephone to her feet, and Sybil cleaned the wax from the floor. Once they were finished, Persephone closed the door to her room. Leuce sat on the edge of her bed, eyes wide, twisting her fingers together in her lap. She probably thought Persephone was going to kick her out.

"I've asked Hades to give you an apartment and your job back," Persephone said.

Leuce's breath caught in her throat. "Th-thank you, Persephone."

"I've also agreed to help you learn this world," she said. "There is one more thing you should know—my mother is Demeter, Goddess of Harvest."

Persephone didn't think Leuce's eyes could get any bigger.

"You—You're a goddess?"

Persephone nodded once. "It's important you keep my secret, Leuce. Do you understand?"

"Of course…but…why tell me?"

"Because I need you to be honest with me. Who freed you from the poplar tree?"

"I swear I don't know," Leuce said. Her pale brows were drawn together over her pretty ice-blue eyes. "I just remember waking up alone."

Leuce shivered, rubbing her arms, as if the memory scared her. Persephone studied the nymph for a moment and then sighed.

"I believe you." Still, that didn't mean Demeter wasn't responsible. "Will you tell me if my mother contacts you?"

Leuce nodded and then swallowed. When she spoke, her voice trembled. "Persephone…what if she was the one to free me? Will she come for me? What if she turns me back into a tree?"

Persephone hadn't thought of that, but her answer was immediate. "If she does, I'll find you."

"She could burn me to a crisp," Leuce said and then offered a humorless laugh. "It's strange, the things you fear when you're a tree."

Persephone frowned. The sad part was, she knew her mother was capable of that kind of malice. The goddess placed a hand on the nymph's arm. "I'll do my best to protect you, Leuce. I promise."

The woman smiled. "You're really not like the rest of them, Persephone."

———

Persephone wasn't sure what magic Hades used, but upon returning to the Upperworld, it was as if she'd never left. Lexa, Sybil, and Leuce did not ask any questions about where she had been, there were no missed calls on her phone from work, and the crowd still gathered outside the Acropolis to get a glimpse of her and protest her article about Apollo.

While she was not excited to see that they remained, she felt more prepared for them than she had ever been. Perhaps it had something to do with her encounter with Apollo in the Underworld, but she had decided rather than entering the building with her head down, she would face them head-on, maybe even answer a few of the questions. It wasn't exactly her idea of freedom, but it was a way to take control over the situation, and it was better than feeling trapped.

"Thank you, Antoni," Persephone said when he opened her door. "See you after work?"

"Yes, my lady."

She smiled at him and started down the aisle.

"Good morning," she chimed as she passed the gathering.

"Persephone! Persephone! Can I get an autograph?"

She stopped, meeting the gaze of a mortal man. He held out a marker and a booklet. She took it and signed her name, his eyes lighting up.

"Th-thank you," he stuttered out.

"Persephone, how long have you and Hades been together?" another person asked.

"Not long," she replied.

"What made you fall in love with him?" someone yelled.

"Well, he is charming," she said with a small laugh.

The walk continued like that—answering questions, signing articles and pictures, and taking photos with fans.

She was almost to the doors when the shouting took on a different tone.

"Why did you write about Apollo?" someone yelled.

"Do you hate the God of the Sun?" another called.

"Apollo-hater! Impious!" several roared.

The questions about Apollo seemed to incense the crowd, and then something shattered on the ground behind her. She turned to see a bottle in pieces at her feet. Security rushed the crowd, while another officer took her by the arm and ushered her inside.

"Are you alright, Miss Rosi?" the officer, an older man with a buzz cut and mustache, asked.

Persephone blinked up at him. She hadn't had time to process what had just happened. Someone tried to hurt her, she realized. She took a deep breath and let it out slow, then nodded.

"Yes."

The officer didn't look so certain, frowning down at her.

Persephone's eyes fell to his gold nameplate, and she smiled. "Thank you, Officer Woods."

The guard smirked and his face reddened. "It...it was nothing."

She broke free of the officer and headed for the elevators in a daze. Her thoughts turned to Hades's words: *It is only a matter of time before someone with a vendetta against me tries to harm you.* How would the god react once he found out about this incident?

When she made it to her floor, Helen was waiting, a concerned look on her face.

"Oh my gods, Persephone! Are you okay? I heard what happened."

"How?" Persephone asked. She'd literally just left the first floor.

"It's on the news," she said. "There was a crew filming live as you arrived. They caught everything on camera."

Persephone groaned. So much for keeping this from Hades.

"Did they show the person who threw the bottle?"

"Yes, his face is plastered all over the news."

Oh no.

Persephone hurried to her desk. She needed to get ahold of Hades before he acted. She knew the God of the Dead would seek his own revenge against the mortal who'd tried to hurt her, and as much as she wanted him to face some sort of punishment for his rash actions, torture in Tartarus seemed a bit extreme.

The only person she could think to call was Ilias. The satyr had taken over managing Hades's schedule in Minthe's…absence.

The phone rang once before he answered.

"Ilias, where is Hades?"

"Indisposed, my lady," he answered, pausing a moment before asking, "Are you well?"

"Ilias, I'm fine. Tell Hades not to hurt the mortal—"

She was interrupted when another call came through on her phone. She looked at the screen and saw Lexa was calling. She'd probably seen the news and wanted to make sure she was okay.

She sighed. "Ilias, let me call you back. Tell Hades not to hurt that mortal!"

Persephone hung up on the satyr and answered Lexa's call.

"Yes, Lex. I'm fine—"

Except it wasn't Lexa on the other end.

"Persephone, it's Jaison."

The hysteria in his voice made her heart race.

"Jaison, why—"

"You need to come to the hospital *now*."

"Okay. Okay. What happened?"

"It's Lexa. *They aren't sure she'll make it*."

Air was sucked from Persephone's lungs, and her heart stuttered, irregular and sick, poisoned by a terror so acute, she thought it might have stopped.

Lexa's in the hospital. They aren't sure she'll make it.

Suddenly she wondered if this was the start of Apollo's revenge.

PART II

"The descent into Hell is easy."
—VIRGIL, *THE AENEID*

CHAPTER XII
The Descent into Hell

Persephone stayed calm and collected despite the anxiety eating away at the bottom of her stomach. Jaison's voice echoed in her head, and the words he'd spoken felt distant and untrue.

Lexa's been in an accident. They aren't sure she will make it.

He had to be mistaken. There was no way their Lexa—*her Lexa*—was fighting for her life.

"Persephone." Jaison's voice shook as he said her name, rooting her in the reality of what he'd just told her.

She shook her head and said into the receiver, "That can't be true. I just saw her this morning."

His voice sounded strangled, as if someone were pushing on his throat, stealing his air.

"It happened in front of the Alexandria Tower. She was on her way to work. They said she was crossing the street and someone hit her."

She felt unsteady. Her body shook uncontrollably.

"I'll be there as soon as possible."

She was out of her chair before she hung up the phone, racing from the Acropolis.

Asclepius Community Hospital was a modern building made of mirrored glass, blending with the azure sky and dense, white clouds. Inside, the hospital looked more like a hotel than a medical facility. It was bright, clean, and beautiful, but nothing could hide the smell. It was what Persephone always thought of as the smell of sickness—it was the tang of chemicals, the metallic scent of stale water, and the bitter odor of latex. It filled her head and made her dizzy.

She found Jaison on the second floor in the waiting room. He sat in one of the stiff, wooden chairs, leaning forward with his head cradled in his hands, his face shielded by his hair.

"Jaison." She said his name as she approached. He looked up, eyes wide. Persephone understood his expression because she shared it—they were shocked, helpless, confused.

"Persephone."

Jaison stood and embraced her. She held him as tight as she could, like she thought he might disappear too.

"Is she okay?"

It seemed like a ridiculous question given his earlier report, but Persephone wasn't willing to imagine a world without Lexa, so she asked anyway.

He pulled away, face drawn.

"She's in surgery. That's all they'll tell me. Her parents are on their way. We'll know more then."

"How did this happen?"

"She was crossing the street. The driver claims he

didn't see her. Guess he didn't see that fucking red light either. He was probably texting."

He sat down then, as if he could no longer stand under the weight of what happened to Lexa, and Persephone joined him. She wasn't sure what to say because she couldn't think straight. It was like her mind couldn't decide how to assess the situation. Part of her wanted to prepare herself for the worst.

If she dies, then it will be your fault. You'll have manifested it, she scolded herself quickly. *She can't die. She won't. She's too young. She has too much to live for.*

Except that Persephone knew death personally. It did not discriminate, and anyone could be prey. It all depended on a thread and sometimes a gamble.

"What if...we lose her? What will we do?" Jaison's question stole Persephone's breath, and she looked at him.

He leaned forward in his chair again like he might get sick. Instead, he scrubbed his face with his hands. She thought he might be trying to keep his tears at bay, and she could see his eyes were growing red, and his face was splotchy and pink.

She reached for his hand. It was clammy and cold, and hers were shaking. "We won't lose her."

Her voice was fierce, and as she spoke, she understood all those desperate pleas mortals made to Hades— she was making one now. *Don't take her from me. I will give you anything.*

She closed her eyes against her thoughts and spoke again, more uncertain than she'd ever been. "We won't. We can't."

Torturous hours ticked by with no updates. Persephone stepped outside to call Sybil and let her know what happened. The oracle made it to the hospital within thirty minutes. Between the three of them, they'd walked the entire hospital and been to the cafeteria close to ten times for coffee and water. It was about the only thing any of them could stomach.

When Lexa's parents arrived, Jaison hurried outside to meet them and show them the way. During his absence, Persephone turned to Sybil.

"Have your powers returned?" she asked.

"Yes," the oracle whispered, giving Persephone a knowing look. They still hadn't had a chance to talk about Persephone's agreement with Apollo.

Persephone only had one question for the oracle. "Do you know if she will live?"

"I do not know. The gods are merciful that way. I do not carry the burden of knowing my friends' fates."

Persephone frowned. "Do you think Apollo had something to do with this?"

She gestured around her.

Wasn't that what Sybil had said? That Apollo would punish by hurting those closest to her?

Sybil shook her head. "No, Persephone. I think this is exactly what it looks like...a mortal accident."

Persephone wasn't sure why, but that wasn't what she wanted to hear.

Then Sybil asked, "Maybe you can ask Hades if... she will survive."

The goddess swallowed thickly. She could, but what if the answer was no? She tried to imagine going to the Underworld every day and finding Lexa walking the streets of Asphodel, arm in arm with Yuri.

She couldn't do it.

She couldn't explain why it was such a terrifying thought either. It was just that…if Lexa was in the Underworld, it meant that she was dead. It meant that she wasn't in the Upperworld anymore. That her existence had ceased, and Persephone couldn't stomach that.

When Lexa's parents, Eliska and Adam, arrived, they were given more information on the status of her injuries. The doctor wore a white lab coat and kept his hands in his pockets as he spoke.

He was older, his eyelids shielded his drooping eyes, his nose was wide, and his lips were thin and formed a permanent frown. He sounded tired, but it was just his voice, a low, raspy baritone.

"She has two broken legs and a broken elbow. Lacerations to her kidneys, bruised lungs, and blood on her brain."

Hearing the trauma Lexa's body had sustained brought Persephone to tears.

He continued, "She is in critical condition and in a coma. We have her on a ventilator."

"What does critical condition mean?" Jaison asked.

"It means that her vitals are unstable and abnormal," the doctor answered. "The next twenty-four to forty-eight hours will be very important for Lexa's recovery."

The words broke down Persephone's hope.

Lexa's parents were let in to see her first. Persephone, Sybil, and Jaison waited.

"She'll fight. She'll pull through," Jaison said aloud as if he was trying to convince them and himself.

It was Eliska who returned to get them and show them to Lexa's room. As they followed her, Persephone couldn't stop staring. Lexa looked a lot like her mother.

They had the same thick, black hair and blue eyes and sometimes the same expressions.

When Persephone entered, her gaze went straight to Lexa. It was hard to describe how she felt seeing her best friend under all that equipment. It was a little like having an out-of-body experience. Lexa was still as stone and barely visible under layers of tubes and cords running into her like the threads of Fate. They bound her in place, and right now, they bound her to life. A thick white cloth lay across her forehead, and a neck brace propped her chin up high. Her ventilator sounded like a constant exhale, and the heart monitor pulsed a steady beat. These were things that even this room—made up with colorful walls, monochrome flooring, and modern touches—couldn't disguise. This was a place where people came because they were sick or hurt or dying.

Persephone reached for Lexa's hand. She was cold, and for some reason, that surprised her. She noted all the ways her best friend didn't quite look like herself: her swollen face, her bruised skin, her colorless lips.

While they were gathered around her, a nurse entered the room, checking monitors and tubes and entering information into a computer.

"There's nothing else they can do," she heard Lexa's mother saying. "It's really up to her now."

Persephone squeezed Lexa's hand. She didn't squeeze back.

Persephone wasn't sure how long she stood there watching Lexa, but there was a point when she realized she needed to leave. The room was too small, and Lexa's parents needed privacy.

Once outside the room, Sybil turned to Persephone.

"Are you going to see Hades?"

She nodded.

"Will you ask him to save her?"

It was like someone had stabbed her in the stomach and twisted the blade.

"I will do what I can," she answered.

Once Persephone was out of view, she risked teleportation and ended up in the alley beside Nevernight. It was dark and wet and smelled rancid. She rushed to the entrance where Mekonnen stood guard. When he saw her, he smiled, showing crooked and yellow teeth, but he quickly realized something was wrong. His grin vanished, and he set his shoulders, seeming to grow larger, as if preparing to fight.

"My lady, is everything okay?" His words were rough, a hint of the monster he kept at bay.

"Hades," she said, her breath short. "I need him. Quickly!"

Mekonnen fumbled and opened the door. She rushed inside, immediately suffocated by the hot air and loud music.

She paused as she entered the club. She didn't know where Hades was—he could be in the lounge betting with mortals, or in his office behind that pristine desk, or in the Underworld playing catch with Cerberus.

She hurried down the stairs and cut across the crowded floor. She felt frantic, like she was running out of time, but that was the problem. She didn't know how much time she had. She nearly slammed into a waitress holding a massive tray of drinks. If it had been another day, she would have apologized, but she was on a mission. Instead, she continued through the crowd, pushing people aside and ramming into shoulders. One

189

man turned, scowling, and grabbed her arm, jerking her around to face him. "What the hell?"

When he saw her face, he let her go as if she were venomous.

"*Oh, fuck!*"

A second later, an ogre materialized beside him, and he was dragged from his table and into the dark of the club.

Persephone took the steps two at a time and decided to check Hades's office first. When she threw open the doors, Hades was already across the room, as if he'd felt her distress and headed straight for it.

"Persephone."

"Hades! You have to help! Please—"

She choked on a sob. She had thought she was okay, that she could at least get through this. It was the most important part, asking Hades for help. Except it wasn't, and just as she started to speak, her emotions burst from her like a dam, raw and painful and untamed.

Hades caught her in his arms, holding her close as her whole body shook. His hands tangled into her hair, fitting against the base of her head. She'd have liked to stay there, sobbing in his arms, comforted by his strength and his heat. She was exhausted, but it was then she realized they weren't alone.

There was a man bound to a chair in the middle of Hades's office. He was gagged, his eyes were wide, and she got the impression he was trying to get her attention by screaming as loud as he could.

"Hades—"

"Ignore him." Hades lifted his hand, and Persephone knew he was about to send the mortal away. She stopped him.

"Is that—is that the mortal who threw the bottle at me today?"

Hades's jaw tightened.

"Why are you torturing him in your office and not in Tartarus?"

The mortal's muffled cries increased.

"Because he's not dead," Hades responded and then glared at the man. "Yet."

"Hades, you cannot kill him."

"*I* won't kill him," the god promised. "But I will make him wish he were dead."

"Hades. *Let. Him. Go.*"

The god's dark eyes studied hers, and it seemed like the longer he looked, the calmer he became. After a moment, he sighed and gritted out, "Fine."

The mortal vanished. She would have to remember to follow up about where he actually sent the man. Persephone didn't believe for a moment that Hades had given in so easily.

Hades sat and guided her onto his lap, his hand moving in soothing circles over her back.

"What happened?" He wasn't demanding, but there was an edge to his voice that Persephone recognized as fear. She couldn't blame him. She had burst into his office without warning, on the heels of a day when she'd been in the news after being attacked. She took a long time to answer, so long that Hades tilted her head back so he could search her eyes, a frown pulling at his lips.

Does he already know what happened to Lexa? she wondered.

She tried to tell him, but her mouth quivered so badly, she had to pause and take several deep breaths.

After a few minutes of this, Hades summoned wine. She gulped it like water. The bitter drink coated her tongue but helped her nerves.

"Start again," Hades said. "What happened?"

The words came easier this time.

As she spoke, his expression melted from concern into a mask of indifference. It was a strategic move in poker—a way to deceive another player by concealing feelings. But this wasn't a game, and Persephone knew deep down that it was just Hades's way of preparing to tell her he couldn't help.

"She doesn't look like Lexa anymore, Hades."

A loud sob escaped her throat. She covered her mouth, as if that might keep all her feelings inside.

"I'm so sorry, my darling."

She twisted to face him in the plush chair.

"Hades." His name was a shaky breath. "*Please.*"

He looked away, his jaw working to quell his frustration.

"Persephone, I can't." His tone was harder this time. She stood, needing distance. The god remained seated.

"I won't lose her."

"You haven't," Hades pointed out. "Lexa still lives."

She wanted to argue, but Hades didn't let her.

"You must give her soul time to decide."

"Decide? What do you mean?"

Hades sighed, and he pinched the bridge of his nose, as if he dreaded the coming conversation.

"Lexa's in limbo."

"Then you can bring her back."

Persephone had heard of limbo before. Hades had brought a soul back from there for a grieving mother. Hope blossomed in her chest, and it was like Hades could sense it, because he dashed it quickly.

"*I can't.*"

"You did it before. You said when a soul is in limbo, you can bargain with the Fates to bring it back."

"In exchange for the life of another," Hades reminded. "A soul for a soul, Persephone."

"You can't say you won't save her, Hades."

"I'm not saying I don't *want* to, Persephone. It is best that I do not interfere with this. Trust me. If you care for Lexa at all—if you care for me at all—you will drop this."

"I'm doing this *because* I care!" she argued.

Hades scoffed. "That's what all mortals think—but who are you really trying to save? Lexa or yourself?"

"I don't need a philosophy lesson, Hades," she gritted out.

"No, but apparently you need a reality check."

He stood, shoving off his jacket, and started to unbutton his shirt.

Persephone scowled.

"I'm not having sex with you right now."

Hades glared at her but continued to unbutton his shirt. Then she saw black markings surfacing on his skin—they were all fine lines, tattoos that wrapped around his body like a delicate thread.

"What are they?" She started to reach out, but Hades stopped her with a firm hand clamped around her wrist. She met his gaze.

"It's the price I pay for every life I've taken by bargaining with the Fates," he said. "I carry them with me. These are their life threads, burned into my skin. Is this what you want on your conscience, Persephone?"

Slowly, she pried her hand from his and brought it back to her chest, eyes following the lines on his golden skin. She remembered wondering how many bargains he'd made when they'd entered their own. She had no idea they were written into his skin. Still, she found this frustrating. Hades had spoken of balance before, but this had him chained. He was one of the most powerful Olympian gods, and yet his power was limited.

"What good is being the God of the Dead if you can't *do* anything?" The words spilled out of her mouth before she could catch them. She took a deep breath. "I'm sorry. I didn't mean that."

Hades offered a gruff laugh. "You meant it," he said and placed his hand on the side of her face, forcing her gaze back to his. When she looked into his eyes, her heart felt like it was going to break into pieces. How was it this immortal god seemed to understand her sorrow? "I know you don't want to understand why I can't help, and that's okay."

"I just…don't know what to do," she said, and her shoulders sagged. She felt defeated.

"Lexa isn't gone yet," Hades said. "And yet you mourn her. She may recover."

"Do you know that for certain? That she will recover?"

"No."

His eyes were searching, and she wondered what he was looking for. Persephone had come here for hope, for comfort in the knowledge that Lexa would be okay no matter what, and yet Hades wasn't giving it. She let her head fall against his chest. She was so tired.

After a moment, Hades scooped her into his arms and teleported to the Underworld.

"Do not fill your thoughts with the possibilities of tomorrow," he said as he placed her in bed. He pressed a kiss to her forehead, and everything went dark.

CHAPTER XIII
A Touch of Panic

Persephone woke the next morning with sticky eyes and a headache. Her sleep had been fitful. The events of the day ebbed and flowed, hitting her hard, evoking a burst of sadness and raw emotion, then receding into a kind of numb stupor.

As she sat up, there was a knock at her door, and Hecate poked her head in.

"Good morning, my sweet," she said. "I've brought you some breakfast."

Something thick had settled at the back of Persephone's throat, and she thought she might vomit. There was no way she could eat right now, not with the way her stomach churned.

"No, thank you, Hecate. I'm not hungry."

The goddess frowned. "Sit with me for a little while, then. Perhaps you will change your mind."

"I'm sorry, Hecate. I can't," Persephone said, already on her feet. "I need to get to the hospital."

She checked her phone, but there were no texts from

Lexa's mother or Jaison. She hoped that was a good sign. She hurried into the adjoining bathroom and scrubbed her face. The cold water felt good against her flushed skin.

"You really should eat something," Hecate said. "It would please Hades."

It might please Hades, but Persephone was sure she would be sick if she ate.

"Where *is* Hades?" she asked, exiting the bathroom. He'd been beside her through most of the night, waking up each time she rose from bed to blow her nose or wash her face.

The goddess shrugged. "I do not know. He summoned me early this morning. He did not wish to disturb you."

She wasn't sure why, but not knowing where Hades was at this moment made her uneasy. She couldn't help where her mind wandered—was he sorting things out with Leuce? She had asked him to give Leuce a place to live and her job back, but she had not seen the nymph. She supposed she could ask today as she was scheduled to meet Leuce later. It was part of the deal she'd made to mentor the nymph.

"I am sorry about Lexa, Persephone," Hecate said at last.

The sentiment made Persephone shiver, and her eyes watered.

"It shouldn't have been her," Persephone whispered.

Hecate said nothing, and Persephone cleared her throat. After she was dressed, she grabbed her phone and her purse.

"I'll take coffee if you have it," she told Hecate as she prepared to head out.

"That is not sustenance."

"Yes, it is—it's caffeine."

Hecate frowned but obliged, summoning a steaming cup of coffee.

"Thank you, Hecate," Persephone said. "When you see Hades, tell him I had breakfast."

"That would be a lie," Hecate argued.

"No, it's not. He knows what breakfast means for me."

Hecate shook her head, grimacing, but didn't argue.

Persephone left Nevernight on foot. It was already hot, and it wasn't even noon. The heat coiled around her skin as she walked, dampening her clothes and causing her hair to stick to her neck and face. She probably should have taken the bus or asked Hecate to arrange for a ride, but she really wanted to be alone.

"Persephone!"

She glanced up. Someone on the other side of the street had called her name. She didn't recognize the figure, but they were now looking up and down the road in an attempt to cross. She quickened her pace.

"Persephone!"

She glanced behind her again. The person had made it across the street and was now running toward her.

"Persephone Rosi, wait!"

She cringed, hearing her name called so loudly, drawing stares from curious onlookers.

"Persephone?" Another voice joined in. "Hey, it's Persephone Rosi! Hades's lover!"

A man stepped in front of her and asked, "Can I get a picture?"

He was already holding up his phone.

"Sorry, no. I'm in a hurry." Persephone sidestepped the man and continued down the sidewalk.

"What's Hades like?" someone called.

"Was he angry about the article you wrote?"

"How did you meet?"

The words crowded her like the people outside the Acropolis. She kept her arms close to her body and her head down so they couldn't get pictures of her face. Did they think less space would force answers out of her? Maybe they thought fear would do the trick.

"Stop following me!" she finally yelled, feeling claustrophobic and a little terrified.

Persephone broke into a run, trying to escape the crowd that had formed around her. They yelled her name and questions and horrible things. She cut across the street and slipped down an alleyway. Just as she exited, she was caught by the shoulder and hauled around. She twisted and punched her assailant in the face.

Her knuckles met the hard-as-stone face of Hermes.

"Fuck!" she cursed, shaking her fingers out. "*Hermes!*"

His brows rose to meet his hairline. "I have to say, women are usually more agreeably engaged with me when those two words come out of their mouth."

"She went this way!" someone yelled.

Persephone met Hermes's gaze and snapped, "Get me out of here!"

He grinned. "As you wish, Goddess of Profanity."

Hermes teleported, and once they arrived safely on the rooftop garden of the hospital, she gave a frustrated cry.

"I can't go anywhere! How are you a god, Hermes?"

The god shrugged, a smirk on his face. "It isn't so bad. We are revered and worshipped."

"And *hated*," Persephone finished.

"Speak for yourself," Hermes replied.

Persephone glared at him and then sighed, running

her fingers through her hair. She had to admit, she was a little shaken by what had happened on the street.

"Sephy, if you don't mind me saying…at some point, you're going to have to accept that your life has changed."

She looked at the god, confused. "What are you saying?"

"I'm saying you probably can't just walk down the street like you want. I'm saying you're going to have to start acting like a goddess…or at least a god's lover."

"Don't tell me what to do, Hermes!" She didn't mean to sound so frustrated, but this was not the time to have this discussion.

"Okay, okay," he said, holding up his hands. "Just trying to be helpful."

"Well, you're not."

He offered her a dull look, not seeming at all frustrated by how much of a brat she was being. "Was that really necessary?"

She sighed. "No…I'm sorry, Hermes. Things are just really…awful right now."

"It's okay, Sephy. Let me know if you need a lift."

He winked and left her alone on the roof.

Before she went into the hospital, Persephone called into work. With each ring, anxiety pooled in her stomach. She'd gone from enjoying Demetri's company to dreading the sight—or sound—of him.

"Persephone," Demetri answered. "How is your friend?"

"She's…not good," Persephone said. "I won't be in today."

"Of course," he said. "Take all the time you need."

The sympathy in his voice made her grind her teeth. This man gave her whiplash. He could be considerate when he wanted to and vengeful when he had to.

"I'm going to need an extension on the exclusive," she said. She held her breath as she waited for him to speak.

Finally, he said, "I'll see what I can do, but Persephone...I can't make any promises."

That wasn't the response she was looking for, and there was an unsettling twist in her stomach.

"If you want me as your employee, Demetri, then you won't push me on this."

He sighed, and she imagined him rubbing his fingers between his brows as if he had a headache. She'd seen him do it on multiple occasions, especially when he'd been looking at his computer screen too long.

"I'll deal with it," he said. "Just...take care of your friend...and yourself."

She hung up without saying thank you.

When she arrived on the second floor of the hospital, she learned from Lexa's mother that the doctor had visited that morning. He said Lexa's vital signs were improving. Persephone felt her chest swell with hope.

"That's good news, right?"

"It's positive," she responded. "Their real worry is her brain."

Eliska went on to explain that Lexa had brain contusions and that the extent of her injuries was unknown, but it could range from minor to severe.

Persephone didn't like those odds.

The hope she'd felt a moment ago shattered.

There wasn't much to do at the hospital, so Persephone perched in a window and pulled out her laptop. She intended to catch up on the news, but her mind got tangled up in Hermes's words.

You're going to have to start acting like a goddess.

"What does that even mean?" she mumbled to herself. Was he trying to tell her she needed to be like Aphrodite or Hera? Persephone wasn't interested in giving up the things that tied her to the mortal world. They were what she'd formed her identity around when she'd come to New Athens, and now it seemed like all that was being taken away.

Everyone wanted her to be someone she wasn't.

Persephone distracted herself by reading up on Apollo.

As it turned out, others were now coming forward with stories like the ones Persephone had published in *New Athens News*—instances where Apollo had threatened to dismantle the careers of his lovers if they left him.

She wondered if that was why she had yet to hear from Apollo.

These new allegations emerged just days after Hades's lover, Persephone Rosi, published a scathing article about the god.

Still, the article refused to lay blame on the God of Music, stating,

The allegations have yet to be confirmed. Divine Entertainment has reached out to Apollo's representatives, though they have declined to issue a statement at this time.

Probably because Apollo needs a new oracle, she thought. Persephone noticed something green in her periphery and turned to find vines sprouting from the windowsill and climbing up the glass. Fueled by her anger, they were growing fast. She slammed her hand against them, as if she were smashing an insect, and tore them down.

Gods, I am a disaster.

"You okay?"

Persephone jumped and twisted toward Jaison.

He looked awful.

"Have you slept?" she asked.

He offered a weary smile. "Here and there."

"You should rest," she encouraged. "You can go to our apartment. It's closer than yours."

"I don't...what if something happens while I'm gone? Or asleep? What if I miss..."

Persephone knew what he was going to say—what if he missed saying goodbye? She had no response to that because she wondered the same thing.

"The doctors said her vitals were better today."

Jaison just nodded. Something else was on his mind. He toed the ground, hands in his pockets, and then sat down on the already-cramped windowsill. Persephone shifted, watching him intently.

"Did Hades say he could help?" He spoke fast, like he wanted to get the words out so this conversation could be over.

Persephone didn't think that question would hurt so much, but it stole her breath. She pressed her lips tight, and her eyes watered.

"He said...we haven't lost her yet."

Jaison nodded. "I figured."

Persephone's brows drew together. "What do you mean?"

He shrugged, choosing not to look at her. "He's

the God of the Dead, not the God of the Living. Why would he save a life when he can gain another resident?"

"Hades isn't like that," Persephone said. "There's more to it than you think. The Fates—"

"So he says," Jaison replied. "But…how do you really know that's true?"

"*Jaison.*" Her voice shook as she spoke. She believed Hades because she'd seen the threads on his skin, one for each life he'd bargained.

"You defend him, but what does it say about him? That he will not even help you when you need him most?"

Because I don't need him the most right now. Lexa does, she thought.

"That's not fair, Jaison."

"Maybe you're right," the mortal replied. "Sorry, Seph."

She didn't tell him it was okay because it wasn't. Jaison's words were unkind, and worse, they burrowed under her skin.

Did Hades's refusal to help her mean he did not love her as much as she thought?

That's ridiculous, she scolded herself.

And yet, she wondered, how could he watch her suffer like this?

With no changes in Lexa's health, Persephone decided to keep her appointment with Leuce. She was going to meet the nymph at the Pearl, a boutique owned by Aphrodite located in the fashion district of New Athens.

Ilias had managed to schedule a private shopping event for her and the nymph. He also arranged for Antoni to give her a ride, something for which she was thankful after this morning's disastrous walk to the hospital.

Persephone entered the shop as soon as she arrived.

The boutique smelled like roses and was exactly what she expected from the Goddess of Love. The carpeting at her feet was furry and white, the chairs were plush and jeweled, and every accent shimmered.

Persephone wandered throughout the store, fingers brushing soft fabric and inspecting fine gems.

"Lexa would love this place," she said aloud.

"I'm sure she would," a voice replied.

Persephone spun. Aphrodite lounged on a chaise in her own boutique. She was dressed in something that resembled lingerie—a pink bodysuit and a sheer, pink robe. The outfit showed off her soft curves. Her bright blond locks splayed around her head. Persephone wondered if she'd just fallen on the chair like that or if she'd posed herself.

She wouldn't put the posing past Aphrodite.

"Aphrodite," Persephone said, surprised to see the goddess.

"Persephone."

"I didn't know you would be here."

"Oh, I just came to check up on you," Aphrodite said. "Saw the news."

"You and everyone else," Persephone mumbled. "I am fine, as you can see."

The blond goddess raised a brow.

"I see your sex life is vibrant."

Persephone stiffened and then narrowed her eyes. "How do you know that?"

"I can smell it," Aphrodite said. "Hades is all over you. Must have been a wild night. Makeup sex?"

"That's a horrific power," Persephone said, and Aphrodite shrugged. "And you?" Persephone asked. "How are you?"

The goddess seemed surprised by her question, as if no one had ever asked.

She frowned, and her pretty pale brows drew together over her sharp eyes. Persephone noted the change in her expression—she seemed confused, as if she was unsure why the question had elicited emotion. Finally, the goddess answered.

"I don't know."

It was the most honest Aphrodite had ever been, and Persephone would have liked to explore the pain she sensed beneath those words, but the door chimed and Leuce entered the store.

Aphrodite cleared her throat, smiling up at Persephone. "Well, it's time for me to go."

"Wait. Aphrodite." Persephone stopped her. "I'm… sorry. If you ever need to talk—"

"I don't," the goddess said quickly, and then she offered a lopsided smile. "I mean…*thanks,* Persephone."

With that, she was gone.

"Persephone?" Leuce asked. The pale nymph looked washed out beneath Aphrodite's sparkling lights. She relaxed when she found Persephone in the adjoining room. "Oh good. You're here."

"Did you not expect me to be here?"

The nymph shrugged awkwardly and then admitted, "I wouldn't blame you if you decided you didn't want to do this."

Persephone's gaze hardened a little. "I keep my word, Leuce."

"I know," she said. "I'm just…used to disappointment is all. I'm sorry."

Persephone frowned, feeling sympathy for the nymph.

Two attendants appeared and took Persephone's and Leuce's coats and purses and gave them glasses of champagne.

"The store is yours," one of the attendants said. "We are here to serve."

It took Persephone and Leuce time to warm up to shopping, but soon Leuce was handing over armfuls of clothing to the attendants.

"Are you planning to replace your wardrobe?" Persephone asked.

"No...but I figure why not try on everything? It's not likely we'll have another chance like this."

Persephone smiled a little. She sounded like Lexa.

"Aren't you going to try anything on?" Leuce asked.

"I don't think so. I don't need anything."

"It's not about *needing,*" Leuce said. "It's for fun."

"You go ahead," Persephone encouraged. "I am content to sit here and drink."

Leuce frowned a little but disappeared into the changing room.

Persephone really wished Lexa were here. This was her thing. When they'd first met in college, Lexa had taken her to this very boutique. They'd laughed and tried on dresses and drank sparkling grape juice. It was the first time she'd been told her "colors" were red, gold, and green, the first time someone other than her mother had told her she was beautiful, the first time she'd felt that someone meant it.

It had been a blissful day.

Persephone's memories were interrupted by her phone ringing. It was Jaison.

She answered, her heart racing in her chest.

"Is everything okay?" She didn't even say hello.

"Yes, Persephone. I wanted to let you know that Lexa just came out of surgery."

"What? Why didn't you tell me earlier?"

"Because everything's fine."

How could everything be fine when Lexa had to go into surgery? Persephone couldn't help thinking Jaison had done this on purpose because of her inability to convince Hades to help.

"What if everything *hadn't* been fine?"

"This is why I didn't tell you earlier." His frustration was evident in his tone. "You freak out and it makes everything worse."

Okay, those words hurt.

"She had some internal bleeding. They caught it in time, and now she's stable and back in the ICU."

"I freak out? Excuse me for being concerned for my best friend, Jaison."

"Yeah, well, she's my girlfriend."

The line went dead, and Persephone pulled her phone away from her ear to find that Jaison had hung up on her.

What the actual fuck is happening?

Suddenly, she couldn't breathe, and her heart felt like it was beating in her head, irregular and quick. She looked around, vision blurred, and the only thing she could think was that she was dying.

She rushed from the store.

She heard her name being called as she left.

"Lady Persephone!"

She ran down the sidewalk and stopped in an alley-way. She pressed herself against the brick and leaned over, taking deep breaths.

"Lady Persephone? Are you okay?"

207

Leuce had followed her as she'd fled. It took Persephone a moment, but she finally straightened, her chest rising and falling. "Is it okay if we don't shop?"

Leuce's eyes were large—strangely innocent—and she nodded. "Of course. Whatever you want."

"Coffee," Persephone said.

"Sure."

They went to the Coffee House. It was the one place Persephone felt she could still go and not be bothered. She ordered two vanilla lattes—one for her and one for Leuce, who had never had coffee before.

They sat across from each other. Persephone kept her hands cupped around her drink, watching as the foam leaf atop melted into nothing.

"How do they make this picture?" Leuce asked, inspecting the foam like a rare specimen.

"Very carefully," Persephone responded.

The nymph took a tentative sip.

"Hmm," she hummed and took a bigger gulp. Persephone recalled the first time she'd had coffee. She hadn't actually liked it all that much, but Lexa had claimed that was because she'd had black coffee.

She'd been right—add a little cream, and it was her favorite drink.

"Just wait until you try hot chocolate," Persephone commented.

Leuce's eyes went wide.

Silence stretched between them. Persephone kept her gaze on her drink. She wasn't sure what to say to Leuce, and her body felt off, her earlier panic making her insides feel shaky.

"Do you want to talk about earlier?" Leuce asked.

Persephone met the woman's gaze and shook her head. "I'd rather not."

The nymph nodded.

"I'm sorry your friend is sick."

"She's not *sick*." Persephone didn't mean to snap, but the words just spilled out of her mouth. Plus, she was still a little freaked out about earlier. "She's hurt. She was hurt."

"I'm sorry." Leuce's voice was a whisper.

Persephone's shoulders fell. "Thank you. I'm sorry. It's...hard."

Leuce nodded. "I know."

Persephone met her gaze, and the nymph explained.

"I woke up a few days ago, and everything I knew had changed. Most of my friends are dead." The nymph paused. "I was angry at first. I think I still am."

Persephone wasn't sure what to say, but she was sincere. Now that she had distance from the situation, now that her anger toward Hades had lessened, she could think from Leuce's point of view.

"I'm sorry, Leuce."

She shrugged. "At least I am free."

It was strange to sit across from this woman and realize how similar they really were.

"Were you...*conscious* while you were imprisoned?"

"No," she said. "I think that might have been worse. Perhaps it was a mercy."

Persephone bit her lip. They were talking about Hades but indirectly.

"I don't...*blame* him for his anger," Leuce said. "I antagonized him. It was not a good relationship. It wasn't what you have."

"How do you know what I have?" Persephone asked.

"You have love," Leuce answered. "He loves you."

Persephone looked away. She didn't really want to talk about Hades with his ex-lover. Leuce seemed to sense this and changed the subject.

"Your friend, is she recovering well?"

Persephone wasn't sure how to answer that—she was really just staying the same. She shook her head. "I just wish I could heal her."

Leuce was quiet for a moment and then she answered, "I think I can help."

Persephone met the nymph's gaze, and the nymph leaned forward to whisper. "Have you heard of the Magi?"

She had. They were mortal practitioners of dark magic. She didn't know much about them, aside from the fact that Hecate often had to clean up after their spells.

Leuce offered a small smile. "I can tell you have. What have you heard?"

"Nothing good," Persephone answered.

"They aren't," Leuce said. "That is something that hasn't changed since ancient times, but some—the ones who are good at their jobs—can craft some powerful spells."

"What kind?"

"Any kind—love spells, death spells, *healing* spells."

"That is illegal magic."

It was illegal because it went against the gods. Love spells were Aphrodite's territory; death, Hades; and healing, Apollo's.

"Illegal, yes, but many would prefer owing a mortal than a god. I'm not saying you have to accept a contract with a Magi, but...I can get you into the same club as them. If you draw their attention, you get an audience with them."

"And how do they know I want an audience?"

"Because no one goes there unless they want something. Here," Leuce said, pulling a card from her pocket and handing it to her. It was black. A name was embossed on the surface.

Persephone read it aloud.

"Iniquity?"

"The club is true to its name. It's a den of wickedness and sin. It isn't a place for you."

Persephone offered a small, humorless smile.

"You don't know me very well if you believe that."

"Maybe not, but I do know Hades would turn me back into a tree if he knew I was telling you about it, but…it might be the only way to save your friend unless you want to make a deal with Apollo."

That was a huge no.

"How soon can you get me in?"

"Tomorrow, if you like."

Persephone tapped the card against her palm.

"Hades will be angry if he finds out."

Leuce smirked. "He always finds out."

"I will protect you," Persephone answered.

"I'm not worried about me," Leuce said. "Who will protect you?"

"From Hades?" Persephone was surprised by the question but knew the answer. There was no protecting herself from her lover. The air between them was raw. Even if she had wanted to, there was nothing she could do against the God of the Dead.

"I no longer have protection against Hades."

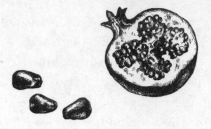

CHAPTER XIV
Iniquity

Persephone needed to be at Iniquity at midnight.

Earlier in the day, she'd told Hades she was going to stay at her apartment to be with Sybil. Instead, she spent the evening getting ready.

Her dress was revealing to say the least, and she wondered what Hades would say if he saw it. It featured a crisscross mesh top with a high neckline, long sleeves, and a short, black skirt. She paired it with a black bralette and strappy heels.

"You look stunning," Sybil said. She stood in Persephone's doorway in her pajamas—a blue shirt and gray shorts.

"Thanks."

"You don't look excited to be going out."

"It isn't for fun."

Sybil nodded. "Do you have to go?"

"I think so." Persephone met Sybil's gaze. "Is there anything I should know?"

She wasn't completely sure how Sybil's powers worked, but she liked to think if she was walking into anything dangerous, Sybil would let her know. The oracle shook her head.

Instead, she pushed away from the doorframe and said, "I'll call you a taxi."

Sybil disappeared.

Persephone looked at her reflection again. She almost didn't recognize the person staring back. She was different—changed.

It's darkness, she thought.

But it wasn't Hades who had coaxed it to the surface. It was Lexa's pain that had unleashed it.

Sybil returned. "Taxi's here."

"Thanks," Persephone said. She took a deep breath, feeling as though she couldn't quite breathe deeply enough. She collected her clutch and phone, and when she turned to leave, she found Sybil still standing in the doorway, watching her.

"Hades doesn't know where you're going, does he?"

Persephone opened her mouth and then closed it. There was no need to answer; Sybil already knew. So instead she said, "It isn't like he can't find me."

The oracle nodded. "Just…be careful, Persephone. I know you want to save Lexa, but what will you destroy to get there?"

Those words shivered down Persephone's spine. She didn't like what they implied. All Persephone wanted was for everything to go back to the way it was before Lexa's accident.

"I thought you said there was nothing I needed to know."

The oracle gave a wry smile. "You don't make promises, and oracles speak in riddles."

Fair.

Persephone had learned a lot about oracles from Sybil. They might *hear* prophecies, but how they were interpreted was up to the one who received them.

Persephone chose to interpret this as *there's no other way,* and so she left for Iniquity.

She tamped down the anxiety that flared in her stomach when she told the driver her destination. He glanced at her in the rearview mirror. The name clearly made him uncomfortable, but he didn't say anything, just nodded and took off into the night.

Persephone settled into the back seat and checked her phone.

It was a habit because she used to talk to Lexa all the time, but there were no new messages—none from Lexa, no updates from Jaison or Lexa's mother, nothing.

She spent the ride reading through previous text messages from Lexa, and by the time the cab stopped, her eyes were watery and her throat thick with tears. The emotion was motivating. It made it easier to swallow her guilt and look out the window.

The car had stopped in front of a plain, brick build-ing. The name was nowhere to be found on the exterior.

She hesitated before exiting.

"Is this…the right place?" she asked.

"You said Iniquity, right?" the driver asked, pointing to the building. "That's it."

She left the cab and stood outside alone, unnerved by the quiet. She had expected a crowd similar to Nevernight, even though Leuce had made it clear

214

Iniquity was different. It was invitation-only—exclusive to the underbelly of society. She shivered and started down the alleyway. The taxi driver had dropped her off at the front of the building, but Leuce had been clear in her instructions: the entrance was in the back, down the stairs, knock once.

Persephone continued down the dimly lit alleyway and found the door. She did as she was instructed, and a slot in the door opened. She jumped but couldn't see anything through the opening. It took her a moment to remember her password.

"Parabasis," she said.

The word shivered through her whole body, its meaning shaking her foundation.

To intentionally cross a line.

She knew that was what she was doing, but she had to try.

Lexa needed her—she needed Lexa.

Whoever was on the other side closed the slot and opened the door. Hesitantly, she entered the club. Like at Nevernight, she stepped into complete darkness. Whoever occupied the space with her was not visible, but she felt them.

They said nothing, just moved past her. After a brief moment, a set of curtains opened ahead of her, and she was let into an unfamiliar world colored in red, full of gems and feathers and burning lights. The floor of the club was packed with people. A stage towered over the crowd, framed with crimson curtains and blazing bulbs. Women danced there, dressed in shimmering bras, fishnet stockings, and enormous headpieces. They were glamorous, synchronized, and erotic, swaying to sensual music.

Persephone stood frozen, entranced.

The air was hot, heavy, and scented with vanilla. She inhaled it, and it filled her veins like her magic, shivering through her body, heating her skin. She rolled her neck and shoulders, loosening tense muscles, relaxing into the music. The part of her mind that told her to be on edge was fading.

A hand slipped into hers, and she twisted to find Leuce standing behind her. She didn't speak, just pulled Persephone along the back wall into a darkened hallway.

"This place—" Persephone breathed.

"Is meant to ensnare, Persephone." Leuce placed her hands on either side of the goddess's face. "Keep your wits about you and focus on your task. The air here is toxic. It will draw you in, a current you can't escape."

"That would have been great information to have before I got here," Persephone said, a little irritated.

The nymph smiled. "There's nothing I could have done to prepare you. You are either strong-willed or not. It's how they will choose you."

Persephone focused on the nymph. Her ice-blue eyes were intense. It was then she noted how the girl was dressed. Her white hair was curled and styled. She wore bright red lipstick, and her outfit was a short silver tassel dress that shimmered like all the stars in the sky. She looked like one of the dancers on stage.

"You work here?"

Again, it was information she would have liked to have before arriving, but Leuce didn't seem to think it was important.

"Focus on your task, Persephone. You wanted this, remember?"

That almost sounded like a threat.

She glared at the woman, eyes flashing. She suddenly wished to remind Leuce of who she really was.

"Then tell me what to do. How do I ensure they see me?"

"You dance," Leuce answered. "If they're interested, they'll come to you."

Persephone glanced over her shoulder where hundreds of people were crammed together on the floor.

"Are you telling me all these people are here for the same thing?"

"Not the same thing," Leuce said. "But they're here because they want something."

"Leuce, what else goes on here other than illegal magic?"

"That's not a conversation you want to have, Persephone. Trust me."

She was gone then, and Persephone was swallowed by the crowd. For a few seconds, it was like fighting a current, graceless and panicked, but like earlier, she found there was something bewitching about the music. It seemed to dance along her skin, seep through her pores, until she moved with the beat, rocking her hips and raising her arms over her head. Sweat beaded on her forehead, and images of sensual nights with Hades reeled through her mind—his soft mouth on hers, his silken tongue lapping at sensitive skin, his body glistening and hot, his cock filling, stretching, demanding. Her breath came short, and a moan escaped from her mouth.

She felt rabid, starved, desperate.

It got worse.

Her memories were suddenly infiltrated by another

face. It wasn't her body beneath Hades's—it was Leuce's, her back arched, her head thrown back, her mouth open as she screamed her lover's name.

It was enough to break the spell the music had cast upon Persephone. Suddenly, she was aware of her surroundings again—the bodies crowded her, their sweat-soaked skin brushing hers.

Hands gripped her hips, and a body moved behind her. She turned to face a man dressed in dark clothing, and in the red light, his eyes were black. At first, she wondered if he was here to summon her, but his hand remained fastened on her hips. She pushed him back, intending to break contact with him, when another set of hands clasped her shoulders.

Persephone wrenched from his grip. Her heart raced, her magic igniting in her blood, but as she turned to look at the other person who had touched her, both men disappeared into the crowd.

Unnerved, she pushed through the mass of people until she reached the outer edge of the dance floor. She sought darkness, wishing to become shadow, and she found it as she rested against a wall at the mouth of a hallway.

Her body still shook from the memories she'd recalled on the dance floor. She was both aroused and pissed. What sort of horrible magic encouraged such salacious thoughts? And why had they morphed into something that made her want to vomit? She didn't want to think of Leuce and Hades together. She didn't want to dwell on the fact that she and the nymph both knew Hades's body so well.

She liked to think she knew a different Hades and that the way he coaxed her to orgasm was different from how he'd treated others.

She felt ridiculous as these thoughts rolled through her head. Perhaps whatever magic had overcome her on the dance floor was still clinging to her aura.

As she hid there in the darkness, the crowd pulsing on the dance floor in front of her, something was suddenly thrust into her closed fist. The feeling was strange and sudden—*magic*, she realized as she opened her hand and found a piece of paper. Unfolding it, there was a number written in ink. 777. Below the number was an arrow, as if directing her to walk down the hallway.

She looked around and saw nothing but felt as if the whole room were watching her, even as she lurked in the darkness. Peeling away from the wall, she followed the arrow down the dark hall and happened upon an elevator, only visible because the numbers and doors were alight in red.

She pressed the button, and the elevator opened soundlessly.

Inside, she noted the floors only went up to eight. She assumed that she needed the seventh floor and that the number on the paper was a room.

After the roar on the dance floor, the silence in the elevator pushed against her ears. It unsettled her and left her to focus on what was ahead—the unknown. What if Leuce was wrong about the Magi? What if they wanted something she couldn't give? What if they couldn't help her?

When the elevator doors opened, she was let out into a hallway that led straight to a black door. She approached hesitantly, fear warring with the guilt in her mind. Finally, she knocked, and a voice on the other side directed her to come inside.

The handle was cold and made her skin prick as she entered. The room was dim and had black marble floors and dark walls. The only source of light came from the center of the room. It illuminated a raised, round platform and a large, plush chair upon which a familiar man was seated.

He was Kal Stavros.

He looked exactly like his pictures in the tabloids. He had a perfect, square face, a swath of thick, black hair, and blue eyes.

She hated his face.

Persephone narrowed her eyes, fingers tightening into fists. The surge of anger she felt at seeing this man was acute. It drove her magic wild.

"Persephone," Kal purred.

Was it possible to reach into his mouth and yank her name from it? Persephone thought.

"I hope Alec and Cy didn't frighten you, but I had to be sure it was you."

So those men from the dance floor worked for him.

"I can see why Hades is taken with you," he said, his eyes trailing her body, making her feel sick to her stomach. "Beauty and spirit, well-spoken and opinionated. Qualities I admire."

"Don't make me vomit," she said. "Just tell me what you want."

He chuckled. It was villainous—a sound contrary to his beauty.

"I'm so glad you asked," he said. "But you first— what brings you to Iniquity, the heart of sin?"

She hesitated. What was she still doing in this room?

She turned to leave, but instead of finding the door she had entered, she faced a wall of mirrors.

"Going somewhere?"

She twisted toward him.

"Are you holding me prisoner?"

"These are the rules of Iniquity. Once you enter the chamber of a dealer, you don't leave until a bargain is struck."

That wasn't what Leuce had said.

"What if I don't want to bargain with you?"

"You don't know what I'm offering."

"If it isn't a way out of this room, I don't want it."

"Even if it means saving your friend?"

Silence followed his question, and Persephone swallowed. "What do you know about that?"

Kal smiled, and it made the words that came out of his mouth next more callous. "I know she will die unless you can find a way to heal her."

"She isn't *dying*," Persephone said through her teeth. It wasn't true—it couldn't be. Neither Hades nor Sybil had said so...and wouldn't they say so?

"That is not what I see."

Persephone shifted slightly on her feet. She was uncomfortable in this dark room, closed up with a man who had already bargained with her—an exclusive in exchange for her job.

"Why should I trust you?"

"Because deep down, you know I'm right. If you thought Lexa was going to live, would you have come?"

She hated him.

"What do you want?"

He showed his teeth when he smiled this time.

"I have a deal for you. I'll give you the spell you need to heal your friend if you give me everything."

"Everything?"

"I want every detail of your relationship with Hades. I want to know how you met him, when he first kissed you, and all the scandalous details from the first time he fucked you."

"You're sick."

"I'm a businessman, Persephone. Sex sells." He sat back in the chair. "Sex with gods sells better, and you, my sweet—you're a *gold mine.*"

"I'm not the only one who's slept with Hades." She hated that she said the words at all, but it was true.

"But you're the first he's committed to, and that's worth more than the words of a fuck buddy. He's invested in you, which means he'll do anything to protect you and the details of your private life."

Persephone suddenly understood. "You want to blackmail Hades?"

"Well, he is the Rich One."

"But *you're* rich," Persephone argued.

"Not like him," Kal said. "But that's what you're going to help me with, and in exchange, you get to save your friend from certain death."

At that, Persephone froze. Up until this point, she would have given anything to have Lexa back, but now that she was presented with this opportunity, she wondered—could she really give up the details of her relationship with Hades in exchange for her best friend's life?

Guilt and shame slammed into her, as potent as the smell of Hades's magic in this room. Her gaze shifted to something black glimmering at the man's feet—snakes. They wound their way around his feet and his wrists. Kal only noticed when the serpent's scaly body curled over his neck. He screamed but froze when the creatures tightened their hold, hissing near his ear.

Hades materialized out of the darkness, surprising Persephone. She hadn't felt him at all.

His voice sounded calm and collected, but she felt his rage.

"Are you threatening me, Kal?" he asked.

"No...never!" The pitch of Kal's voice changed, rising with his fear.

Persephone turned to look at Hades. He was angry—it was present in his eyes and the press of his lips against hers as he bent to kiss her. His tongue demanded entrance, twining with her own. One of his hands cupped her neck and chin, the other knotting into her hair, tightening around the strands. He forced her mouth open wider, lapping at the back of her throat. When he pulled away, it was with her bottom lip between his teeth.

"Are you well?" His voice was rough.

She nodded, dazed.

Hades turned his attention to Kal and stalked toward him. The mortal began defending himself, still frozen beneath the white light. His hands dug into the arms of the chair, his body rigid as the snakes hissed and slithered over his body.

"I-I was following your rules! *She* summoned *me*!"

"My rules? Are you insinuating I would approve of a contract between you and my lover?"

"That would be making an exception," Kal replied. "There are no exceptions in Iniquity."

"Let me be clear," Hades said, and black spikes sprouted from his fingertips. He grasped Kal's face. The man cried out as blood bubbled beneath the spears digging into his skin. "Anyone who belongs to me is an exception to the rules of this club."

Hades lifted Kal out of the chair and tossed him to the ground. He landed with a loud thud, and the snakes went with him. They lashed out, their fangs sinking deep into his skin. Kal screamed, and Persephone watched, unflinching, as the man who had threatened her was tortured by her lover.

"You bastard!" he groaned, lying in a fetal position. His hands shook as he attempted to cover his wounds.

"Careful, mortal." Hades moved like smoke and came to stand beside Kal.

"I followed the rules," the man groaned. "I followed *your* rules."

Persephone looked at Hades's face—it was shadowed, his cheekbones, eyes, and forehead alight.

"I know the rules well, mortal. You don't fuck with me or my lover, understand?"

Kal rolled onto his hands and knees. He struggled to lift his head, but when he did, he met Persephone's gaze.

"Help me," he shouted.

"Do not speak to her, mortal."

Hades placed his boot against the man's side and pushed him to the ground. He landed on one of the snakes, which retaliated by biting into his flesh again. Kal screamed.

Persephone didn't even flinch.

What was wrong with her? She should stop this. Except that a part of her believed Kal actually deserved it.

Hades turned to Persephone. She met his gaze, unable to discern his thoughts from his expression.

"Shall I continue to punish him?" Hades asked.

Persephone stared at Hades, and her eyes dropped to Kal. She strolled toward him and knelt. His bloodied face was now streaked with tears.

"Will his face scar?" she asked Hades.

"It will if you wish it."

"I wish it."

Kal whined.

"Shh," Persephone crooned. "It could be worse. I am tempted to send you to Tartarus."

He quieted at her statement.

Then she continued, "Tomorrow, I want you to call Demetri and tell him you made a mistake. You don't want the exclusive, and you will never, ever tell me what to write again. Do we have an agreement?"

Shaking, he nodded his head.

Persephone smiled. "Good." She straightened and turned to Hades. "He can live," she said.

The god held her gaze for a long moment and then looked at Kal.

"Leave."

In the next second, the man and the snakes were gone, and Persephone was left alone with Hades. Despite their distance, anger built between them like a solid, stone wall.

Before he could say anything, she spoke.

"You ruined everything!"

He looked startled and then quickly took up the defense, moving toward her.

"*I* ruined everything? I saved you from making a huge mistake. What were you thinking coming here?"

"I was trying to save my friend, and Kal was offering a way to do that, unlike you."

"You would give up *our* private life—something you cherish most—in exchange for something that will only condemn your friend?"

"Condemn her? It will save her life! You bastard. You told me to have hope! You said she could survive."

They were nose to nose now. "You don't trust me?"

"No! No, I don't trust you. Not when it comes to Lexa. And what about this place, Hades? This is your club, isn't it? What the fuck?"

Hades reached for her, clasping her shoulders; he drew her flush against him.

"You were never to come here. This place isn't for you."

Persephone flinched.

"Leuce works here," she snapped.

"Because it's *Leuce*," Hades said, as if that explained everything. "You told me to give her job back, so I sent her here. You…you're…different."

She pushed away from him. "Different?"

"I thought we'd established this," Hades said through his teeth. "You mean more to me than anyone—*anything.*"

"What does that have to do with keeping this place from me?"

Hades was silent.

"Everything here is illegal, isn't it? The Magi are here. What else?"

Hades tried to remain silent again.

"What else, Hades?" she demanded.

"Everything you've ever feared," he answered, and she shivered. "Assassins, drug lords…"

Persephone felt the color drain from her face.

"Why?"

"I created a world where I could watch them."

"Watch them do what? Break the law? Hurt people?"

"Yes," he answered, his voice gritty.

"Yes? That's it? That's all you have to say?"

"For now," he said. His voice tightened, and his chest rose and fell with his anger, but instead of leaving, he moved toward her. She held her ground, unafraid, lifting her chin and glaring at him.

"Who brought you here?" he asked.

"A taxi."

"You think I won't find out?"

"I have free will. I *chose* to come here of my own accord."

"A choice that cannot go unpunished," he said and reached for her.

Instinctually, Persephone pushed his hands away.

His eyes gleamed. "Are you telling me no?"

She knew if she said no, he would stop, but she couldn't deny she wanted to see his punishment through. It would mean intense pleasure and it would be angry and rough and primal, and she needed release.

She shook her head once, and then Hades spun her around to face the mirrored wall. She used it for support as he bent her forward and watched him in the reflection. He nudged her legs apart and lifted her skirt, eyes hungry.

His hand brushed across her skin, and then he swatted her ass. She yelped, more from surprise than pain, and Hades glanced up, meeting her gaze in the mirror before drawing her underwear to her ankles and helping her step out of them. Her core tightened in anticipation as he shoved them in his pocket.

She gasped when his hand dipped between her thighs; her back arched as his fingers teased. She was molten for him—she didn't even need the foreplay.

Hades's inhale was a hiss. "So fucking wet. How long have you been like this?"

A moan stuck in her throat as she answered.

"Since I got here," she said. "I wanted you on the dance floor. I willed you to manifest from the dark, but you weren't there."

"I'm here now," he said and bent to kiss her shoulder, down her back, and then her bottom. All the while, his finger curled, going deeper while his other hand worked her clit in soft, aching circles. She could barely breathe, focusing on the feel of him inside her, mindless with need.

"Hades," she begged. "*Please*."

He withdrew, and Persephone gave a frustrated cry. She started to twist toward him. She felt rabid. She needed release, and if he would not offer it, she would chase it herself.

But Hades's hands clamped down on her hips.

"Stay," he commanded, and she glared at him in the mirror.

He offered a devilish smirk. "It wouldn't be punishment if I gave you what you wanted when you demand it."

She stuck her chin out and said, "Don't pretend you don't want me."

"Oh, I'm not pretending," he said as he unzipped his trousers, took out his cock, and entered her from behind. Persephone's breath caught in her throat. Was it possible Hades was somehow thicker? She took him in one, quick thrust, a guttural sound escaping her throat as he pumped into her.

At first, it was like Hades wasn't sure what to touch—his hands clasped her breasts, her stomach, her hips. Then he wrapped a fistful of her long hair around his hand like a bandage and pulled her head back so he could kiss her mouth. When he released her, his thrusts became languid, and she felt him in the bottom of her stomach.

"This is for us," he said. "You will share this with no one else."

All Persephone could manage was a breathy whine. She felt the intensity of his words like she felt the rawness of his sex inside her. His arm cut into her stomach as he held her in place, and her nails dug into his skin.

"Some things are sacred to me." Hades's breath grew ragged, but he kept speaking, his words interlaced with Persephone's moans. "This is sacred to me. You are sacred to me. Do you understand?"

Persephone nodded, sweat beading on her forehead, and her brows drew together in a hard line. She was barely holding on to her sanity.

"Say it," he ordered. "Say you understand."

"Yes," she sobbed. "Yes, gods-dammit. I understand! Make me come, Hades!"

The god spun her around to face him and kissed her, pressing her into the mirror, savoring her mouth before lifting her and entering her again.

Persephone groaned, fingers twining into his hair, and when he pulled away, his eyes glittered.

"I have never loved anyone as I love you." He spoke like he was confessing. "I can't put it into words—there are none that come close to expressing how I feel."

Persephone tightened her hold on him, bending toward his lips.

"Then don't use words," she said.

Their lips collided, and they slid to the floor. Persephone's knees were bent, pressing into the hard marble floor as she straddled Hades, but she didn't even notice, too focused on the pleasure building inside her. She interlaced her fingers with Hades's and guided his arms over his head, rocking against him.

"Fuck," Hades cursed, breaking her hold. He gripped her hips and helped her move faster, harder. Their eyes held until the pleasure became too much. Persephone's head lulled back as she came, and Hades followed soon after.

Persephone collapsed onto his chest, breathless and sated, comforted by the feel of Hades's arms around her. They didn't speak for a long time—not until their breathing had evened and their hearts had stopped racing.

Hades broke the silence.

"Marry me."

Persephone sat back. Hades was still hard inside her, and the movement made his eyes glitter like coals.

"What?"

There was no way she'd heard him correctly.

"Marry me, Persephone. Be my queen. Say you'll stand by my side...forever."

He was serious, and she was...confused. Not about her love for Hades—but so many other things.

"Hades...I..." She couldn't figure out what to say. "You were just angry with me."

He shrugged. "And now I am not."

"And you want to marry me?"

"Yes."

She stood, stumbling back as her legs struggled to hold her up. Hades held out his hands to help steady her, but she refused them.

"I can't marry you, Hades," she answered, her eyes welling with tears. "I…I don't know you."

Hades's brows knitted together. "You know me."

"No, I don't," she argued, indicating her surroundings. "You kept this place from me."

Hades dipped his chin, eyes narrowed. "Persephone, I have lived forever. There will always be things you learn about me, and you should know you won't like some of them."

"This isn't one of those things, Hades. This place is real, and it exists in the present. You hired Leuce to work here. I deserved to know just as I deserved to know about Leuce!"

When he said nothing, she asked, "Why didn't you tell me?"

"Because I was afraid," he snapped and fell silent. His words were angry, and she wondered if he was more frustrated at having to say something like that out loud or at having those feelings at all.

"Why?"

"Obviously because of your moral compass." He got to his feet and took a few steps away. She couldn't really explain how those words felt, but she wanted to argue that her moral compass wasn't very high, seeing as how she had turned Minthe into a mint plant and watched Hades torture a mortal.

He sighed. "I wanted time to think about how to

show you my sins. To explain their roots. Instead, it seems, everyone wishes to do it for me."

Persephone blinked, and her frustration was suddenly gone. Instead, she felt…sad. She hadn't expected Hades to feel insecure about this, much less be frustrated when others took away his chance to tell her, and she wasn't sure that was what Leuce intended either.

Her expression softened, and she took a step toward him.

"I'm sorry, Hades."

His brows knitted together. "What are you apologizing for?"

"I guess…everything," she said. "For coming here… for telling you no."

"It's okay. It's a lot to ask of you right now," he said. "With Lexa and your work. And I have put a lot on you tonight, shown you a side of me you haven't seen before."

"You aren't…upset?"

Hades considered this for a moment. "Do I wish you'd said yes? Of course."

Her shoulders fell. "I'm just…not ready."

"I know." He kissed her forehead, and as his lips touched her skin, she began to cry. Hades brushed her tears away. "Tell me."

"I ruined everything." She buried her face in his chest.

"Shh," he soothed. "You ruined nothing, my darling. You were honest with yourself and with me. That is all I ask."

"How could you want to marry me now? After I have told you no?"

"I will always want to marry you because I will always want you as my wife and queen."

She was comforted by the promise in his voice and hoped that when he asked again, she would be ready.

"Will you show me more of this place?" she asked, rubbing at her face to erase the tears.

"More of Iniquity?"

"Yes."

He groaned. "Do I have a choice?"

"If I am ever to be your queen? No."

CHAPTER XV
A Network of Secrets

As it turned out, there was more to Iniquity than her experience as a customer on the dance floor. It doubled as a hangout for New Athens crime families, secret societies, gangs, and freelance criminals. Their lair was in the basement of the building, accessible only with an ancient coin called an obol.

Persephone glanced at Hades. "I see you have repurposed the idea of paying to enter the Underworld."

He chuckled quietly but said nothing as he guided her down a long, dark hallway and into a spacious room, lit only by light that filtered in through a wall of windows. Persephone approached and found that the suite overlooked a casual sitting area. There was a bar and several smaller tables and chairs. People sat around, playing cards and chatting, drinking and smoking, filling crystal trays to the brim with ashes.

Persephone touched the glass and asked, "Can they see us?"

"No," Hades said.

"So you spy on them from up here?" she asked, glancing at the god who hung back, sticking to the shadow.

"You can call it spying if you like," he said.

She studied the people below and found a familiar face.

"That's Madelia Rella," Persephone said, surprised to see the madam and owner of the pleasure district—literally a whole neighborhood of brothels. She was a beautiful, middle-aged mortal. Her hair was dark, and she wore sequins and feathers. A jade cigarette holder was poised between her pointer and middle finger. Persephone had never seen anyone look so glamorous as they smoked.

Madelia was often in the news, advocating on behalf of sex workers, arguing for safer conditions and harsher punishments for offenses made against them.

"She is in debt to me," he said.

"How?"

"I loaned her the money to start her first brothel."

Persephone wasn't sure how to feel about that. "Why?"

"It was a business opportunity," he said, matter-of-fact. "In exchange for the money, I have a stake in her company, and I can ensure the safety of her escorts."

Persephone hadn't expected Hades to say that last part, but it didn't really surprise her. Hades was protective of women.

"Who else is down there?" she asked.

She felt the God of the Underworld beside her, and she glanced at him as he scanned the crowd below. He indicated a small, round table in a darkened corner where two men were playing cards.

"That is Leonidas Nasso and Damianos Vitalis. They are billionaires and the bosses of rival crime families."

"Nasso?" Persephone asked. "You mean…the owner of the Nasso Pizzeria chain?"

"The very one," Hades confirmed. "The Vitalises are also restaurant owners, but they make their real living from fishing."

Persephone also recognized that name from the Vitalis Fish Market. They were one of the oldest and most important fish wholesalers in the country.

"If they are rivals, why are they playing cards?"

"This is neutral territory. It is illegal to cause harm to another person on this property."

"I suppose you are the exception to that rule?" she asked, lifting a brow. He *had* tortured Kal.

"I am always the exception, Persephone."

"These people," Persephone said. "They are the elite of New Athens."

Hades offered a single nod. "They are the rich and the powerful, but they are rich and powerful because of me."

Persephone let that sink in, feeling a little unnerved by her reaction. She should feel shocked by this, but instead she felt curious.

Hades pointed out a few others: Alexis Nicolo, a professional gambler, Helene Hallas, an art forger, and Barak Petra, an assassin.

"Assassin? You mean he gets paid to *kill* people?"

Hades did not honor her question with a response, which was fair enough. She knew the answer, and somehow, confirmation would just make it worse.

She shook her head. "I don't understand. How can you be concerned with saving souls from a terrible existence in the afterlife when you offer these…*criminals* a place to assemble?"

"They are not all criminals," he said. "I am not under some delusion, Persephone. I know I cannot save every soul, but at least Iniquity ensures that those who operate in the underbelly of society follow a code of conduct."

"How is murder part of a code of conduct?"

"Murder isn't part of the code of conduct," he said. "Unless the code is broken."

She turned to face Hades.

"We cannot all be good, but if we must be bad, it should serve a purpose."

She narrowed her eyes, unsure of how to feel about all this. Hades was literally a mafia boss.

"I don't expect you to understand. There are many reasons for what I do. Iniquity is no different. I have a network of the most dangerous men and women attached to strings. I could take them all down with one pull. And they all know it, so they do what they can to please me."

She shivered. It was strange to realize that Hades wasn't just powerful because of the control he had over his magic. He was powerful because of the deals he'd made, and this proved it.

"You mean everyone but Kal Stavros?"

Hades shrugged. "I told you it was just a matter of time before someone tried to blackmail you."

"You never said anything about blackmail," Persephone countered. "What does Kal have against you?"

"Nothing," Hades said. "He merely wishes to have control over me, as all mortals wish."

It wouldn't be the first time a mortal had tried to gain some form of control over Hades. Every time they entered Nevernight to strike a bargain, it was an attempt to command the God of the Dead.

"Are you afraid of me?" he asked after a moment of silence.

The question surprised her. She knew it was born out of fear, and yet when she looked at him, his expression revealed nothing of his thoughts.

"No," she answered quickly. "But it is a lot to take in."

And an obvious example of why she couldn't marry him.

Not yet anyway.

How could he think of asking her to be his wife—his queen—when she had no idea about any of this? Was this not an empire she would also inherit?

Hades looked away, his throat constricting as he swallowed whatever unease had crept into his consciousness. "I will tell you everything."

She had no doubt. She would make sure of that. She had so many questions. She wanted to know every person who entered this club, what businesses they owned, and just how much of the world Hades controlled.

Part of her wanted to ask him what he thought she'd do when she found out about Iniquity, but it was obvious he thought she'd leave.

"I think I've heard enough tonight," she answered. "I'd rather go home."

"Would you like Antoni to take you?"

She smiled a little, realizing that he thought she meant she wanted to return to her apartment.

"You might as well take me," she said. "We are going to the same place, after all."

His lips curled, and he put an arm around her waist, drawing her close before teleporting to the Underworld.

Persephone couldn't sleep.

She lay still, cradled against Hades's warmth, and agonized. Not over what she had learned about the God of the Dead but over what Kal had said about Lexa.

If you thought Lexa was going to live, would you have come?

Kal was right, of course. Persephone couldn't deny that she had sought a cure for Lexa's injuries at Iniquity, and she'd done so out of the fear that her friend wouldn't recover. The fear that, even if she did, she might not be the same.

She closed her eyes against the pain and left Hades's chamber.

The halls of the palace were quiet and lit by the light of the night sky. Hades hadn't succeeded in capturing the brightness of the sun, but he'd managed the moon well.

Persephone cut through the dining hall and made her way into the kitchen. She'd never been in this part of the palace before. Hades always had food brought to them at the dining table or the library, the office or the bedroom.

Turning on the light, she found a modern and spotless kitchen. The cabinets were white, the countertops black marble, and the appliances stainless steel. She shuffled over the cold floor and began to search the cupboards for supplies, finding pans, mixing bowls, and utensils.

That was the easy part.

The hardest part was finding the ingredients to bake something.

Anything.

She ended up gathering enough ingredients to make a simple vanilla cake and icing. It took her a few minutes to figure out how the oven worked. The one she used in her apartment was much older and had knobs, not buttons.

Once the oven was preheating, she set to work, focusing on her task. There was something relaxing about baking. Maybe she liked it so much because it felt like alchemy, measuring each ingredient to perfection, creating something that would bewitch the senses.

Not to mention that the act always took her mind off things, but as soon as she popped her cake into the oven, an overwhelming sense of dread stole her breath. Frantic to stop it, she started to clean. Even though Hades's kitchen had a dishwasher, she scrubbed every item by hand, rinsed, dried, and replaced them in the cupboards. After that, she focused on cleaning the stainless steel she'd smeared with her fingerprints.

By the time she was finished, the only indication anyone had used the kitchen was the smell of her cake baking.

The timer on the oven still showed she had fifteen more minutes. Fifteen minutes to be alone with her tormenting thoughts.

She turned on her music, hoping it would provide the distraction she needed. She clicked through the first few songs, their timbre dark and cold. Those songs reminded her of Lexa, the lyrics tangling with her thoughts and dredging up memories she didn't want to recall. The longer she clicked through each song, the more she realized that it didn't matter how the music sounded, it all reminded her of Lexa.

She turned it off, suddenly feeling exhausted. Her eyes were gritty, and her limbs were heavy. She sank to the floor, her body illuminated by the oven light, and drew her knees to her chest.

"Couldn't sleep?"

The sound of Hades's voice made her jump. She swung around to find him leaning in the doorway, thick arms crossed over his bare chest. A black cloth hung low on his hips, and his hair pooled in dark layers around his face. He looked sleepy and beautiful.

"No," she said. "I hope I didn't wake you."

"You didn't wake me," he said. "Your absence did."

"I'm sorry."

He smiled a little. "Don't be—especially if it means you are baking."

Hades crossed the kitchen toward her. She thought he might pick her up and carry her off to bed with the cake still in the oven, but he surprised her and sat beside her on the floor.

She found herself looking at him—at the way his muscles rose to the surface of his skin, at the shadow of stubble gracing his jaw, the full curve of his lips. He was impossibly handsome, unimaginably powerful, and he belonged to her.

"You know I can help you sleep," he said.

She knew that because he had done it before.

"The cake isn't finished," she whispered her reply. It wasn't because she wished to be quiet; it was that her voice wouldn't go any higher as her exhaustion took over.

"I would never let it burn," Hades replied.

After a moment, he shifted, and Persephone rested her head against his chest. Hades's skin was warm, his scent as intoxicating as the vanilla in the air, and despite how much she wanted to see this all through to the end, she fell asleep in his arms on the floor of the kitchen.

CHAPTER XVI
Breaking Point

Persephone called Eliska to check on Lexa as she headed to work the next morning. In truth, she'd been avoiding Jaison since his hateful words after Lexa's surgery and his comments about Hades. It was hard enough to reconcile that Hades couldn't help, worse when Jaison questioned their love.

Lexa's mother sounded exhausted on the phone as she communicated that there were no changes in her vitals. The whole thing felt like a nightmare, except that the longer it went on, the more Persephone considered that she might have to live without Lexa.

After last night, that somehow seemed like more of a possibility.

"Good morning, Persephone!" Helen said as Persephone stepped off the elevator. Her cheery expression faded quickly. "Is everything alright?"

Her question made Persephone feel strangely violent.

"No," she snapped. Her stomach immediately filled

with guilt as she headed to her desk. She would have to apologize to Helen later, but right now, she needed to calm down.

She barely got settled before Demetri stepped out of his office.

"Persephone, have a moment?"

Her anger rushed to the surface again, unbidden and senseless. She should say no, ask if she could have more time to get settled, but she found herself following her boss into his office.

"I have good news," Demetri said, taking a seat behind his desk.

Persephone knew what he was going to tell her, but she waited, staring at him with more indifference than she had ever felt in her life. It was the first time since he'd given her the ultimatum that she realized how much this had affected her.

"Kal has decided against forcing the exclusive."

When she didn't react, Demetri frowned. "What's wrong? I thought you'd be happy."

"You thought wrong," she said. "The damage is already done."

"Persephone."

She hated the way her boss said her name, like he thought she was being unreasonable.

"Don't do this," Demetri begged.

"Don't do what? Call you out on your bullshit?"

"If it was bullshit, you would have quit when I had to give you the ultimatum. As much as you want to pretend you don't need this job, I know you do. It's the only way you can distinguish yourself from Hades."

She flinched. Those words stung.

Demetri sighed, his frustration palpable.

"I'm sorry. I shouldn't have said that."

"Why not?" She laughed bitterly. "It's the truth."

"Just because it is the truth right now doesn't mean it will be the truth forever. If anyone can make a name for themselves in this business, it's you, Persephone."

"Flattery will get you nowhere, Demetri."

He laughed humorlessly. "Will I ever earn your forgiveness?"

"Forgiveness, yes. Trust, no."

"I suppose I deserve that." Demetri's eyes fell to his hands as he twined his fingers together nervously. "You know I did it because I had no choice."

"I'm sure you had a choice like I had a choice."

He nodded his head, but his eyes were distant, as if he were recalling something that happened long ago. After a moment, he began to speak. "Kal is no Hades, but he is powerful. I…" He paused to clear his throat. "I sought his help."

A realization settled upon her—Demetri knew Kal was a Magi.

"In what way?"

"A love potion."

Persephone frowned. "I…don't understand."

Demetri raised his brows and then met Persephone's gaze. "In college, I met a man named Luca. He became my best friend, and I was so in love with him. One night, I decided to tell him how I felt. My feelings weren't recip-rocated…but…I couldn't imagine a life without him."

"So you gave him a love potion?"

She was appalled that Demetri would resort to such measures. A love potion was serious business. There was a reason their creation and distribution were illegal. It took away an individual's *choice*.

"It wasn't my proudest moment," Demetri admitted. "If I had to do it all over again, I would have let him go."

"You have to undo it," Persephone said. Demetri's eyes went wide. Clearly, he wasn't expecting her to say that.

"Undo it?"

"Or tell him what you did," Persephone urged. "Demetri...*you were wrong*."

"I didn't tell you this so you would tell me how I should fix it," he said, his face growing red. "I'm telling you this so you understand why I pushed you."

"I realize that, but Demetri...if you really loved—"

"Don't," Demetri snapped, and Persephone clamped her mouth shut. He took a deep breath. "This conversation is over."

"Demetri—"

"If I hear a whisper of what I have told you anywhere, Persephone, I will fire you. That's a promise."

Persephone pinched her lips together and stood, feeling dazed. She paused before leaving the office.

"You're no better than Apollo."

Demetri laughed, and it was cold and humorless. "I think that's the first time anyone's ever compared me to a god."

"It's not a compliment," Persephone replied. She knew it wasn't necessary to point it out. Demetri was well aware of the gravity of her comparison. Apollo and Demetri had essentially made the same decisions when it came to the people they supposedly loved, and the results were devastating for the mortals who remained.

She left Demetri's office and gathered her things.

"Oh…uh, Persephone?" Helen called as she walked past the desk to the elevator.

She didn't stop.

"Persephone?"

Helen came up beside her.

"What, Helen?" Persephone snapped.

"Are you—"

"Please don't ask me if I'm okay."

Helen's lips thinned, and she hesitated, stumbling over her words. "Um, this came for you."

She handed Persephone a white envelope.

"Who—?"

Persephone started to ask when Helen turned on her heels and returned to her desk.

Persephone sighed. She didn't blame the girl for practically running from her. Now she had two reasons to apologize to her, but she'd have to do that later, because she really wanted to leave.

She stepped inside the elevator and opened the envelope. Inside was a handwritten letter.

Dearest Persephone,

I see you did not like the rose. Perhaps you will find future gifts more acceptable.

—Your admirer

It was the first time she'd thought about the rose since it had arrived on her desk a few days ago. It was still there, wilted and forgotten after Lexa's accident. While she had assumed Hades had given it to her, she now realized it wasn't from him. She was going to have to tell Helen to stop accepting unmarked gifts and envelopes.

Suddenly uneasy, Persephone crushed the letter between her hands and threw it away as she stepped out of the elevator.

She called a taxi and headed to the hospital to visit Lexa.

She would never get used to this place. Just approaching made her anxious—a feeling that grew once she reached the second floor, making her way down the hall to Lexa's room. Suddenly, she halted, spotting Eliska and Adam speaking to the doctor.

"At this point, it is something to consider," the doctor was saying.

Lexa's parents looked distraught.

Persephone ducked behind a computer stand, listening.

"How long does she have? Once the ventilator is removed?" she heard Adam ask.

"That's really up to her. She could pass within seconds or days."

Persephone felt sick to her stomach.

"Of course, it is your decision," the doctor said. "I'll give you some time to think on it. If you have any questions, please let me know."

Persephone turned and ran down the hallway to the bathroom. She barely made it to the toilet before vomiting, and when nothing else came out, she heaved.

It took her far longer to compose herself than she imagined, and by the time she made it to Lexa's room, Eliska was alone. She looked up when Persephone entered and smiled.

"Hi, Persephone," she said.

"Hi, Mrs. Sideris. I hope I'm not bothering you. I should have told you I was coming."

"It's fine, dear." Eliska stretched. "If you're going to be here for a bit, I think I'll take a walk…"

Persephone managed a nod and a small smile. When Eliska left, she sat on Lexa's bed and carefully took her hand in her own. Lexa's skin was bruised from the IV and discolored from the tape they used to secure all the tubes going into her body.

Guilt settled heavily on Persephone's shoulders. She had failed to find a cure for Lexa's injuries. The ventilator breathed for her, kept her body going, and Lexa's parents wanted to take her off.

It was Persephone's worst fear realized.

What would be so terrible about seeing her enter the Underworld?

It was a question that should have a simple answer, but it was more complicated than that, and on the heels of Hades's proposal, the truth of her agonizing thoughts was exposed. What if she and Hades *weren't* meant to be together forever? What if she lost access to the Underworld and the souls? That would mean she would lose contact with Lexa too.

She recognized that even when she and Hades had broken up, the God of the Dead had allowed her to retain his favor. She could have gone to the Underworld at any point and visited the souls, but she hadn't. The thought of going had been too painful and filled her with worry. That wouldn't change if they split again.

"I don't know if you can hear me," Persephone said. "But I have so much to tell you."

As she held Lexa's hand, she launched into a summary of everything that had happened to her.

She talked about Kal's ultimatum.

"I should have told you the moment it happened." She paused and laughed a little. "I'm sure you would have told me to quit—go off and start my own newspaper or something."

She told her about Hades's deal with Apollo and how she foiled his plan to meet without her. She talked about Iniquity and all the things she'd learned about Hades.

Her eyes watered as she spoke. "And then he asked me to marry him, and I said no. I can hear you asking me what I was I thinking, and the truth is, I don't know." She paused and shook her head. "I just know that no matter how much I love him, I can't marry him right now."

The only answer was the sound of Lexa's ventilator.

She had never felt more alone.

"Lexa." Persephone's mouth quivered, and giant tears blurred her vision. She pressed a kiss to her best friend's hand, whispering, "*I need you.*"

Suddenly, the smell of wildflowers permeated the air, bitter citrus and mint. Persephone went rigid and collected herself as quickly as she could.

"Mother."

She cringed when she spoke. It was obvious she'd been crying. She didn't turn to look at Demeter. "What are you doing?"

"I heard about Lexa," Demeter said. "I came to see if you were okay."

Her friend had been in the hospital for days. If Demeter were really concerned, she would have showed up sooner.

"I'm fine."

She felt her mother move closer.

"Hades would not help her?"

Again, Persephone tensed. She hated this question; hated it because so many people assumed Hades *would* help, hated it because she'd let herself believe she might become an exception to his rule, hated it because he was the reason she had to say no.

"He said it was not possible," she whispered.

She released Lexa's hand and turned to look at her mother. The goddess had appeared in her mortal form and wore a tailored yellow dress. Her golden hair was sculpted into a tight ponytail that curled at the end.

"Why are you really here?" Persephone asked.

"Is it so hard to believe I am concerned for you?"

"Yes."

"I have only ever had your best interest in mind, even if you refuse to see it."

Persephone rolled her eyes. "We are not having this conversation, Mother. I made my choice."

"How will you live your life beside the god who let your best friend die?"

Persephone flinched. She thought about the threads he hid on his skin and the lives he had exchanged to get them. She would be lying if she didn't admit that she had wondered why he wouldn't choose to trade Lexa's soul for another.

Persephone narrowed her eyes, suddenly suspicious. "If I find out you had anything to do with this—"

"You'll what?" Demeter goaded. "Go on."

"I will never forgive you."

Demeter smiled coldly. "Daughter, for that threat to work, I would need to want forgiveness."

250

Persephone ignored the pain of Demeter's words.

"I did not hurt Lexa. Given the circumstances, I think you should consider—can a daughter of spring truly be death's bride? Can you stand beside the god who let your friend die?"

The truth was Persephone did not know, and that made her feel guilty and angry. She clenched her fists.

"Shut up," she gritted out.

"You should channel your anger against the Fates," Demeter said. "They're the ones who have taken your friend."

Persephone offered a sarcastic laugh. "Like you did? How did that turn out for you?"

Demeter narrowed her eyes. "That remains to be seen."

Persephone turned from her mother and looked at Lexa again. Seeing her like this was the hardest thing she'd ever experienced, and it was getting worse every time she stepped through the hospital door.

"Hades isn't the only god who could help you. Apollo is the God of Healing."

Persephone's body seized.

"Of course, you may have ruined any chance you might have had at securing his aid after that atrocious article you released."

"If you came to defend him, I won't hear it. Apollo hurt my friend and so many others."

"You think any god is innocent?" Demeter paused to laugh, and the sound was chilling. "Daughter, even you cannot escape our corruption. It is what comes with power."

"What? Being a bad person?"

"No, it is the freedom to do whatever you want. You

251

cannot tell me if, given the opportunity, you would defy the Fates in favor of saving your friend."

"Those decisions have consequences, Mother."

"Since when? Tell me the impact your articles have had on the gods, Persephone. You wrote about Hades, and he ended up with a lover. You wrote about Apollo, and he is still beloved." She paused to laugh. "Consequences for gods? No, Daughter, there are none."

"You're wrong. Gods always require a favor—favors mean consequences."

"Lucky you are a god. Fight fire with fire, Persephone, and quit sniveling over this mortal."

Her mother was gone, but the smell of her magic remained, and it made Persephone feel sick.

Or maybe she felt sick at the thought of going to Apollo for help.

She couldn't do it. How could she ask the god she'd criticized and proclaimed to hate for help? It would be betraying Hades and Sybil; it would be betraying herself.

When Eliska returned, Persephone prepared to leave, pressing a kiss to Lexa's forehead. When she turned back to Lexa's mother, she blurted, "Don't take her off the vent yet."

Eliska's eyes watered, already rimmed with red. Persephone was certain her walk was more of an excuse to go off and cry.

"Persephone," Eliska said, her mouth quivering. "We can't...keep letting her suffer."

She isn't even in there, Persephone wanted to say. *She is in limbo.*

"I know this is hard. Adam and I haven't decided on a course of action yet, but as soon as we do, I'll let you know."

Persephone left the ICU in a daze. She felt like she had the day she found out Lexa was in the accident. She was a ghost, frozen in time, watching the world continue. Ungrounded, she made her way to the elevator. She was so lost in her own thoughts, she almost didn't notice Thanatos leaning against a wall in the waiting room. Beneath the fluorescent lights, his blond hair looked colorless, and his black wings were very much out of place amid the sterile walls and stiff chairs.

Persephone knew he hadn't expected to see her there because when he caught her gaze, his striking blue eyes widened in surprise.

She tried to control the beating of her heart. *There are any number of reasons he might be at the hospital. Lexa's not the only one in the ICU,* she told herself. *He might be here for someone else.*

She approached him and managed a smile.

"Thanatos, what are you doing here?"

"Lady Persephone," he said and bowed. "I am… working."

Persephone tried not to cringe. Thanatos couldn't help that he was the God of Death, but somehow, it was different talking to him in the Underworld. There, she hadn't really thought too long on his purpose. Here, in the Upperworld, with her friend on life support, it was crystal clear. He severed the connection between the souls and their bodies. He left families devastated. He would leave *her* devastated.

"You mean you are reaping?"

"Not just yet," he said. His half smile was charming, and it made her want to vomit. "You look—"

253

"Tired?" she offered. It wouldn't be the first she'd heard it today.

"I was going to say well."

She could feel Thanatos's magic on the edges of her skin, coaxing her to calmness. Normally, she would take that as a sign of his caring nature, but not today. Today it felt like a distraction.

"I don't want your magic, Thanatos." Her words were harsh. She was frustrated, she was scared, and his presence was making her uncomfortable.

She didn't think the god could look any paler, but even more color drained from his face. It took her a moment to realize that the sparkle in his eyes was gone. She had hurt his feelings. She pushed past the guilt and asked, "What are you really doing here, Thanatos?"

"I told you—"

"You're working. I want to know who you're here to take." Her voice shook as she asked the question.

The god pressed his lips together, a mark of defiance, and answered, "I can't tell you that."

There was silence, and then Persephone said the words she knew Thanatos would be compelled to obey because Hades had ordered it. "I command you."

Thanatos's eyes glistened, as if this whole thing caused him physical pain. His brows drew together over desperate eyes, and he whispered her name, voice cracking as he spoke.

"*Persephone.*"

"I won't let you take her."

"If there were another way—"

"There *is* another way, and it involves you leaving." She pushed him a little. "Get out."

She spoke quietly at first, not wanting to draw attention, but when he didn't move, she said it again—firm this time, the words slipping through her teeth.

"I said get out!"

She pushed him harder, and he held up his hands, backing away.

"This isn't something you can prevent, Persephone. My work is tied to the Fates. Once they cut her thread...I have to collect."

She hated those words, and they set her off in a way she'd never imagined.

"Get out!" she yelled. "Get out! Get out! Get out!"

Thanatos vanished, and Persephone was suddenly surrounded by nurses and a security guard. They were questioning and directing, and the words filled her head to bursting.

"Ma'am, is everything alright?"

"Maybe you should have a seat."

"I'll get some water."

Pain formed at the front of her head. Despite the nurse trying to direct her to a chair, she broke free.

"I need to check on Lexa," she said, but when she tried to return to the ICU area, the security guard blocked her.

"You need to listen to the nurses," he said.

"But my friend—"

"I'll get an update on your friend," he said.

Persephone wanted to protest. *There was no time.* What if Thanatos had teleported to her room and taken her to the Underworld? Suddenly, the doors opened from the inside, and Persephone leapt at the chance. Pushing past the guard, she took off at a run for Lexa's room and promptly vanished.

Being teleported to another realm without warning felt like being in a vacuum. Suddenly, it was harder to breathe, her body felt void of moisture, and her ears popped painfully. The symptoms lasted a few seconds before she was overpowered by the scent of Hades's magic, burning her nose like frost.

As her eyes adjusted to the darkness, she realized she'd been deposited in Hades's throne room. It was always dark despite the hazy light that filtered in through slanted windows overhead. Hades sat upon his throne—a glassy piece of obsidian that was both artistic and monstrous. She could see nothing of the god but a slash of his beautiful face, illuminated by red light.

She could guess why Hades had brought her here—to prevent her from interfering with Thanatos's work, to lecture her once again about how they could not interfere in Lexa's life—but she didn't want to hear it.

She tried to gather her magic and teleport, knowing it was in vain—Hades was far more liberal in revoking any rights she had to leave the Underworld while he was angry.

And he was angry.

She could feel his frustration. It built between them, making the air tangible.

"You cannot just *remove* me from the Upperworld when you please!" she shouted at him.

"You are lucky I removed you and not the Furies."

The tone of his voice deepened and put her on edge. Still, she wanted to fight.

"Send me back, Hades!"

"No."

A searing pain erupted from Persephone's shoulder, her side, and her calves as thorns sprouted from her skin. It brought her to her knees before Hades. The god rose from his throne, illuminated completely by the red light. He looked horrified and deadly and moved toward her with predatory grace.

"Stop!" she commanded as he approached. "Don't come any closer!"

She didn't want him to see how bad her wounds really were.

Hades didn't obey.

He knelt beside her.

"Fuck, Persephone. How long has your magic been manifesting like this?"

Persephone didn't answer. Instead, she asked, "Don't you ever listen?"

He gave a humorless laugh. "I could ask the same of you."

She ignored his comment, focusing on breathing through the pain of her injuries. Her magic had manifested like this on several occasions, but this was probably the worst case. Hades placed his hands on her shoulder, then her side, then her calves, healing the wounds. When he was finished, he sat back on his heels, blood covering his hands.

"How long have you kept this from me?"

"I've been a little distracted in case you haven't noticed," she said. "What do you want, Hades?"

Hades's eyes flashed, and his concern for her quickly dissolved into anger.

"Your behavior toward Thanatos was atrocious. You will apologize."

"Why should I?" she snapped. "He was going to take Lexa! Worse, he tried to hide it from me."

"He was doing his job, Persephone."

"Killing my friend isn't a job! It's *murder*!"

"You know it isn't murder!" His voice was harsh. "Keeping her alive for your own benefit isn't a kindness. She is in pain, and *you* are prolonging it."

She flinched but recovered. "No, *you* are prolonging it. You could heal her, but you have chosen not to help me."

"You want me to bargain with the Fates so that she might survive? So you can have the death of another on your conscience? Murder doesn't suit you, goddess."

She slapped him—or tried to, but Hades caught her wrist and pulled her against him, kissing her until she was subdued in his arms, until all she could do was cry.

"I don't know how to lose someone, Hades." She sobbed into his chest.

He took her face between his hands, attempting to brush her tears away.

"I know," he answered. "But running from it won't help, Persephone. You are just delaying the inevitable."

"Hades, please. What if it were me?"

He released her so quickly, she almost lost her composure.

"I refuse to entertain such a thought."

"You cannot tell me you wouldn't break every Divine law in existence for me."

Persephone had noted the depth of Hades's eyes before—as if there were thousands of lifetimes reflected within them—but it was nothing like what she saw now. There was a flash of malice—a moment when she swore she could see every violent thing he'd ever done. She didn't doubt what he would go through to save her.

"Make no mistake, my lady, I would burn this world for you, but that is a burden I am willing to carry. Can you say the same?"

Something changed within Hades after her question, and just as suddenly as he seemed to open all his wounds, they closed. His eyes dulled and his expression became passive.

"I will give you one more day to say goodbye to Lexa," he said. "That is the only compromise I can offer. You should be thankful I'm offering that."

The god vanished.

Alone in the throne room, Persephone expected to feel overwhelmed by the reality that within the next twenty-four hours, Lexa would be dead.

Instead, she felt a strange sense of determination.

Consequences for gods? she thought. *There are none.*

She rose to her feet and teleported to her apartment. Sybil reclined on the couch, her eyes going wide when Persephone appeared, bloodied and bruised from her magic.

The oracle sat up.

"Persephone, are you—"

"I'm fine," she said quickly. "I need your help. Where does Apollo hang out most nights?"

CHAPTER XVII
The Pleasure District

Persephone navigated the narrow cobble streets of the pleasure district, passing white-washed shops and brothels with names like Hetaera, Pornai, and Kapsoura. The passages were filled to bursting with people. There were those who had come to enjoy the pleasures of the district, obvious because of the masks they wore to hide their identities. Then there were those who were here to give the pleasure—women in lace and topless men. They danced through the crowds, teasing potential customers with feather boas and chocolate. Their skin glistened from oils that smelled like jasmine and vanilla. Lights crisscrossed overhead, giving the entire place a strange, red glow.

Turned out this was where Apollo spent most evenings.

"He'll be at Erotas," Sybil had said. "He owns a suite there on the third floor."

The Goddess of Spring reached up to check the

mask Sybil had let her borrow, paranoid that somehow it would come loose and expose her identity. It was heavy and solid black. She only needed to wear it until she made it to Erotas. Once inside, every visitor was promised anonymity.

She recognized she had a choice, but it was one she wasn't willing to make. Her mother had been right. Why not ask Apollo to heal her friend? It was a bargain she was willing to make, and so she headed in the direction of Erotas.

She could see it from a distance—a giant, mirrored phallus at the very edge of the pleasure district. Being one of the most expensive and higher-end brothels, it had the best view of the ocean. When she was within view of the door, she shed her coat and mask. Beneath, she wore a simple black dress and strappy black heels—it was the attire worn by the women who served within Erotas, and if Persephone was lucky, she'd blend in enough to find Apollo.

She was surprised to find that the interior of the brothel was more traditionally decorated. The entryway was round and lit by a large crystal chandelier. The walls were red, decorated with ornate mirrors and sconces, and there was no one in sight as she crossed the marble floor toward an elaborate princess staircase that led to the second floor.

Easy enough, Persephone thought as her hand touched the wrought-iron rail.

"Where are you going?"

She froze and turned to find an older woman dressed in crimson. She was beautiful, slender, and had white hair. She assumed this woman was the madam—or manager—of the brothel.

"I have a client," Persephone said. "Waiting. Upstairs."

"You're lying," the woman said.

Persephone paled.

"None of the girls have gone up yet," the woman continued. "Come!"

Persephone hesitated but descended the stairs. The woman studied Persephone as she approached, trying to place her.

"What's your name?" she asked, eyes narrow.

"K-kora," Persephone managed.

"You are new," the woman said, and then she touched Persephone's face, as if inspecting her for imperfections. "Yes, you will fetch a high price."

"A high price?" Persephone's brows pinched together.

"I'm assuming that's why you were leaving. Nervous for the auction?"

Auction?

Persephone nodded.

"Do not worry, my sweet. Come."

The madam placed her arm through Persephone's and led her into a parlor beneath the staircase.

Inside, there were women and men of all ages and sizes dressed in black. Persephone wondered why it was the chosen color, as they all looked like they were at a funeral.

As the madam and Persephone entered, a man wearing a red cloth around his waist and a mask of the same color approached with a silver tray. The madam took a glass of champagne and passed it to Persephone.

"Drink," she said. "It will calm your nerves."

Persephone sipped the drink—it was sweet and light.

"Mingle, chat. The bidding will begin soon."

The madam left, and once Persephone was alone,

she was approached by a woman with dark curls and long lashes. Her lips were a bright red and her skin a rich shade of brown.

"I've never seen you before," she said. "I'm Ismena."

"Kora," Persephone said. "Um…can you tell me what's going on?"

Ismena laughed a little, almost like she thought Persephone was joking. "Did they just pull you off the street because you were pretty?"

Persephone's eyes widened.

"Does that happen?"

"Never mind," Ismena said. "It's an auction. You're given a number and let into a room sort of like an auditorium where you wait until your number is called. After that, you're led onto a stage and you just…stand there until they tell you to leave."

"And after that?"

"You're led to the room of your bidder."

Persephone's stomach soured.

"How'd you get into this line of work anyway?" Ismena asked. "You don't look prepared at all."

Persephone sort of laughed and offered the only thing she could. "Sometimes there aren't any choices. What about you?"

The woman shrugged. "It's good money, and most of the time, these men aren't even after sex. They just want conversation."

Well, that was good, because that was all Persephone had come for—conversation and a bargain.

The woman in crimson returned and clapped her hands, drawing everyone's attention.

"It's time, ladies and gentlemen."

Persephone followed Ismena's lead. They filed into an adjacent room where a series of chairs were arranged. As they entered, they were given numbers and took their seats. One by one, the madam summoned men and women, and as they disappeared into the darkness, Persephone's heart raced. She wondered what Hades would do if he found out she was about to auction herself off to the highest bidder in a brothel.

Then another thought occurred to her—what if she couldn't find Apollo?

She waited forever—until everyone in the room was gone except for her.

The madam entered.

"Your turn, Kora."

Persephone rose and followed the woman into the shadows. She was directed onto a round stage. She could see nothing beyond it, but she knew people were scattered in the dark beyond because she could sense them. A torrent of emotions hit her—intense loneliness and longing. Beneath that, there was a tinge of amusement. She looked up into the darkness and offered a soft half smile.

"I'm here for you, Apollo."

The madam appeared from the shadow, as quick as lightning, and snatched her by the wrist.

"How dare you! This auction is supposed to be anonymous."

A voice crackled through an intercom.

"Don't leave a bruise, Madam Selene, or you will face the wrath of Hades."

So much for anonymity.

The woman inhaled sharply and released her, eyes wide.

"You are Persephone?"

Apollo's voice crackled over the intercom again.

"Escort her to my suite."

Persephone turned to the madam expectantly. It took her a moment to move. The woman seemed frozen, staring at Persephone as if she were one of the dead herself. After a moment, she cleared her throat and bowed her head.

"This way, my lady."

The madam led Persephone out of the room and into a mirrored elevator. When the doors closed, Madam Selene stared at Persephone through the reflection.

"Why did you let me treat you like one of my girls?"

Persephone shrugged. "I was curious. Don't worry; if everyone in attendance tonight keeps my secret, I'll ensure Hades never finds out that you laid a hand on me. Understood?"

"Of course."

Madam Selene pulled out a key and inserted it into the panel, pressing the button for the third floor. They were silent until the madam asked, "Are you here to bargain with him?"

Persephone's heart raced. "Why would I bargain with Apollo?"

"Because you're desperate."

Persephone stared at the woman.

"I see desperation every day, my love. If you're seeking an end to it, trust me, Apollo's not the answer."

Persephone clenched her jaw. "Remember my promise earlier, Madam? You'd do well to stay quiet."

The woman smirked, and Persephone thought it hinted at her wickedness. "Apologies, my lady."

The elevator came to a halt, and Persephone stepped into a well-furnished and luxurious living room. The place was covered in rich fabrics, textured rugs, and fine artwork.

Persephone felt on edge as she moved into the space, thinking that the God of Music might appear out of thin air just to scare her, but as she rounded the sitting area, she found Apollo in an adjacent room. He was naked, relaxing in a giant bath. When he saw her, the god stretched out, resting his feet and draping his arms over the edge of the bath.

"Ah, Lady Persephone," he said. "A true pleasure."

"Apollo," she acknowledged.

"Come, join me!"

"Did you not just warn Madam Selene of Hades's wrath? He will cut off your balls and feed them to you if you touch me."

Apollo chuckled, as if he thoroughly enjoyed the visual Persephone had just given him.

"Would you deny me what I am due? I bought and paid for you, after all."

"Then that is your loss," she replied.

Apollo chuckled, narrowing those inky violet eyes.

Suddenly, the elevator doors opened again, and three nymphs entered the room. They were dressed in shimmery slips. One carried a bowl, the other a tray of various bottles, and the last a stack of towels.

"Put the oils in the bath. I have waited long enough," Apollo snapped as they approached.

The nymph with the tray didn't seem at all anxious at the god's rudeness. Her movements were unhurried and precise. She set the tray down, chose a bottle, and measured the oil with the cap. When that nymph was finished, the other scattered rose petals into Apollo's bath, and the last rolled up a towel and placed it beneath his head. Once the nymphs were finished, they left the room soundlessly.

"Did Sybil tell you where to find me?"

Persephone glared. "So you do remember her name."

He had refused to say it before.

The god rolled his eyes. "I remember the names of all my oracles, all my lovers, all my enemies."

"Are they not all the same?" Persephone challenged.

The god frowned, his face growing stony. "You should be more careful with your words, especially when you are here to ask for help."

"How do you know I am here to ask for help?"

"Am I wrong?"

She was silent, and the god laughed.

"So tell me, Lady Persephone, what do you want that your lover will not offer freely?"

Life.

All of a sudden, Persephone felt a rush of heat through her body. She hated that she was here, hated that she had come to Apollo for help. Hated that he knew she was here because Hades could not give her what she wanted.

"I need you to heal my friend," Persephone said. The words felt like thorns on her tongue. She knew she should not say them or ask Apollo to defy Fate…but here she was.

Apollo stared at her for a long moment, and then he threw his head back, laughing. Persephone despised the sound of it. The tone was off, full of false amusement. Except that when the god looked at her again, his eyes sparkled.

"And why would I help the journalist who slandered my name?"

Persephone's hands shook, and she clenched her fists to keep him from noticing. After a beat of silence, she spoke.

"Because. I am willing to bargain."

That got Apollo's attention. He sat up in the bath and stood, completely naked.

"You're willing to bargain with me?" he asked.

Persephone turned her head away, swallowing hard. If she were being honest, seeing Apollo naked was no different than seeing the statues in the Garden of the Gods at New Athens University, but there was something different about seeing flesh rather than stone.

"Yes, Apollo. That's what I said."

Water sloshed, and she knew without looking that he had gotten out of the bath.

"This...*friend*. She must be very important to you."

"She is everything."

"Apparently," Apollo said, amusement in his tone. "Especially if you are so willing to defy Hades and bargain with me."

Persephone's eyes snapped to Apollo. He had done nothing to cover himself.

"Will you help me or not? I did not come here for polite conversation."

"You call this polite?" the god scoffed.

Persephone's fists clenched tight, and Apollo narrowed his eyes. She wondered if he could sense her losing control of her glamour.

"Beg," he said. "On your knees."

Persephone was disgusted. "Never."

"Then I won't help you."

He started to turn when she called out, "Wait!"

Apollo paused, lifted a brow, and waited.

Persephone worked to keep her anger under control as she made her way to the floor, and when she spoke, her voice shook.

"*Please.*"

"No."

Apollo started to walk away just as vines erupted from the floor with no warning, trapping him.

"Well, well, well, you are full of surprises," the god said.

"*I said please.*" Her voice was venom. She would torture him, and she would take immense pleasure from the act.

"You are a goddess. A goddess masquerading as a mortal!" Apollo ignored her plea, his eyes glittering with excitement. "No one knows, do they?"

That wasn't exactly true, but instead of answering, the vines with which she held Apollo grew thorns. Sharp splinters exploded near his face and cock, silencing him.

"I believe we were having a conversation," she said, "that involved you saving my friend."

Apollo focused his gaze upon her, then attempted to snap the vines holding him. After a few tries, he gave up, panting. "What are these *made* of?"

Persephone blinked—she didn't know. But she was surprised that Apollo hadn't been able to break her magic. Maybe her anger and hatred for the god had something to do with their strength.

He met her gaze, eyes inquisitive. "You are a powerful little creature."

"I am not a creature."

"Yes, you are. You are a *leech,* sucking the fun out of my evening."

"You're the one who made this difficult."

"I hardly thought you were capable of…" He looked down at himself, narrowly missing having his face impaled by the massive thorn.

"Defeating you?" Persephone supplied.

"Restraining me," he corrected, and that mischievous glint entered his eyes again. "Am I correct in guessing this is one of Hades's favorite parts?"

"I'm not here to talk about Hades."

"Of course. Because if you were, we'd have to address the elephant in the room. He doesn't know you are here, does he?"

"Why does everyone keep asking that?" she complained. "I don't have to ask for permission to be here."

Apollo's lips curled. "Perhaps not, but I am certain he will feel utterly betrayed when he discovers you came to me for aid. After all, he offered up a favor of his own to save you from me last time."

Persephone ignored the guilt. "That was Hades's choice. I have also made a choice. I propose a bargain, Apollo. You heal my friend and I'll—I'll—"

Well, she wasn't exactly sure what she would do.

"You'll do whatever I want."

She hated how interested Apollo appeared at the prospect of an open request.

"Not whatever you want," Persephone said. "I won't do anything that will hurt Hades."

"Oh, but you already are, little goddess." He paused.

"Fine. I'll bargain with you, but only because this will entertain me."

She waited. She wanted the terms of their agreement.

"I can't think with this thorn in my face."

She considered telling him to deal with it but decided she should be a little accommodating. She was at his mercy when it came to this bargain.

She dismissed her magic and Apollo stretched, still naked.

"Is it too much to ask for you to get dressed?" she asked.

"Yes. Now, what do I want from you?" He considered the question as he walked to the corner of the room and retrieved a floral robe. His back was to her as he slipped it on. He did nothing to secure it, however, and it hung open, exposing his nakedness. She rolled her eyes. "I want you to hang out with me."

"What?" Persephone thought he was joking, but the look on Apollo's face said otherwise.

"You'll be my...*friend*. We'll party together, we'll attend events together, and you'll come to my penthouse."

"You want me to hang out with you?" Something didn't seem right about this. "For how long?"

"How much is your friend's life worth?"

Persephone wasn't going to answer that.

"What if we hate each other?" Because she was sure she would only hate him more by the end of this.

Apollo shrugged. "You'd be surprised by what I can handle."

She had never wanted to roll her eyes so much at one person.

"What does *hanging out* with you entail?" she asked.

"Someone's taught you well," he said.

271

"I won't sleep with you. I won't hurt people for you. I won't use my powers for you either."

"Anything else?"

"If your healing fails to work, the deal is off."

Apollo seemed to think that was particularly funny. "If my healing fails to work? Little goddess, do you know how many healers I have fathered?"

"I don't want to know anything about that part of your life, Apollo."

"Is that the end of your requests?"

"Six months," Persephone said. "I'll only do this for six months."

The god was silent as he considered her proposal. Finally, he said, "Deal."

"Deal?"

She couldn't help it; she had to ask. She hadn't expected him to be so accepting of the timeline.

Apollo chuckled. "Is it so unbelievable that I would help?"

"You aren't helping out of the goodness of your heart," Persephone countered. "You're helping because it benefits you in some weird way."

Apollo sulked. "Don't insult me—I can rescind my offer."

"No!" she said quickly, and her face grew hot. Not from embarrassment but anger. "I'm sorry."

The god stared at her. "You really care for your friend. But I must ask—what's so bad about her death? You are Hades's lover. It isn't like you can't see her in the Underworld."

Persephone hesitated to speak, and Apollo started to laugh.

"Uncertain about your relationship with the Rich One, huh?"

"I just," she stammered, uncertain of how to acknowledge what Apollo was saying. She thought of her mother's words—*you should consider, given the circumstances, can a daughter of spring truly be death's bride?* It was a question she couldn't answer. Could she exist beside Hades, the god who would let her best friend die? Could she rule a world that was responsible for the unbearable pain she felt? "There is no way I can be the goddess he wants."

Apollo snorted.

Persephone glared. "What?"

The god raised his brows. "It just sounds like you think he wants something other than you, which is not what I witnessed when I came to punish you in the Underworld."

She crossed her arms over her chest. "What would you know about it, Apollo?"

She didn't like how serious he suddenly looked. "More than you could ever imagine, little goddess."

She felt the truth of those words. She wanted to ask more questions—what exactly he witnessed when he came to the Underworld—but she didn't want Apollo to know she was curious.

"Just…heal my friend, Apollo."

"As you wish, goddess." He held out his hand. "Where are we going?"

"Asclepius," she said. "Second floor, ICU."

"Oh yes—my son's namesake. Did you know Hades complained of his skill so much my father killed him?"

"His skill?"

"He could bring the dead back to life," Apollo said. "I imagine Hades put him in Tartarus for that."

Apollo took her hand, and the pull of his magic made her stomach turn. He smelled like wood and eucalyptus.

They found themselves in Lexa's dark room. Her parents were asleep in the corner. The room smelled stale, and the air was sticky and hot. Persephone glanced at Apollo, surprised to see his face was drawn and grim.

"I can see why you were desperate to bargain," he said. "She's nearly gone."

The comment was an affirmation that Persephone had made the right decision, and as if Apollo heard that thought, he met her gaze.

"Are you sure you want this?"

"Yes." Her voice was a whisper in the dark, and in the next second, the God of Music was holding a bow and arrow. The weapon was ethereal—glowing and shimmering in the shadow of the room. It was bizarre to witness a god dressed in a floral robe, holding such a majestic weapon.

Apollo nocked the arrow, the veins in his arm popping as he pulled it back on the string, releasing soundlessly. The arrow hit the center of Lexa's chest and vanished into a shower of shimmering magic.

Silence followed.

And nothing happened.

"It's not working," Persephone said, already feeling a sense of terror at the thought.

"It will," Apollo said. "Tomorrow they'll take her off the ventilator, and she'll wake up and breathe on her own. She'll be a living, breathing miracle. Exactly what you wanted."

For some reason, those words left a horrible taste in Persephone's mouth. She looked back at Lexa, who was as still as a corpse.

"I'll be in contact," he said. "Your duties begin soon."

Then he vanished.

And in the noisy ICU, Persephone wondered what she had done.

CHAPTER XVIII
The Furies

Persephone arrived at the hospital with Sybil the next morning. She was too anxious to stay away. It wasn't that she didn't trust Apollo's healing powers, but she couldn't shake the feeling that something was about to go horribly wrong. She could feel it—a tangible darkness gathering behind her, gaining speed and depth and weight.

Would Lexa be healed enough by the time they took her off the ventilator? Would Hades intervene? What would happen once he discovered she'd bargained with Apollo? Would he see her decision as betrayal?

The guilt made her nauseous and light-headed, and as she headed into the elevator with Sybil, she worried she'd have another panic attack. She wondered if the oracle sensed her turmoil, especially when she glanced in her direction.

Instead, Sybil asked, "Did you do it?"

Persephone didn't look at the oracle. She kept her gaze on the red number as it changed from floor to floor.

"Yes."

"What did you offer in exchange?"

She'd hoped to keep her bargain secret for as long as possible. She didn't want to know what her friend actually thought of her choice.

"Time."

Persephone had yet to really understand what she'd agreed to when it came to Apollo's demand for her attention, but the worry was already sinking into her bones. In the hours after she'd left the hospital, she'd gone over the terms of their agreement. She was certain she'd missed something, and it was just a matter of time before Apollo asked her to do something she couldn't refuse.

If Lexa is alive, it will be worth it, she thought.

She hoped.

When they arrived on the second floor, Jaison was already there, sitting in the same wooden chair he'd occupied since Lexa's accident with his eyes closed. He stirred as they approached and looked at them.

"Hey," Persephone said as gently as she could. "How are you?"

Jaison shrugged. The whites of his eyes were yellow, his skin pallid.

"How long until we hear something?" Sybil asked.

"They plan to take her off life support at nine." His voice was hollow.

Persephone and Sybil exchanged a glance. Jaison leaned forward and rubbed his face vigorously before standing.

"I'm going to get some coffee."

He walked off, and Persephone watched him until he disappeared. No wonder mortals begged Hades to return their loved ones. The threat of death took more than one life. The thought brought tears to her eyes.

How was she supposed to rule a kingdom that caused so much pain? That brought suffering to the living?

"He doesn't know, does he?" Sybil asked.

Persephone shook her head. He still thought he was losing Lexa today.

"No one needs to know," she said. "Let them think it was a miracle."

The two took a seat and waited. Jaison eventually came back with a steaming cup of coffee and sat beside her. They didn't speak, which was fine with her. She was lost in thought, unable to focus on any one thing. The longer the silence stretched, the more her anxiety grew.

At some point, Lexa's family began to arrive. Soon, they were led to a larger room where Lexa had been moved. Lexa's parents were nearest to her, then Jaison, several aunts and uncles and friends from her hometown of Ionia. Each person in the room approached her and said their goodbyes, touching her, holding her hand, or kissing her face.

When it was Persephone's turn, she scooped up Lexa's hand and pressed a kiss to her cold skin.

"Please, please wake up," she prayed to no one but Apollo's magic, and to Persephone's surprise, Lexa squeezed her hand. She looked up and met Jaison's gaze, but she could tell by his expression that he hadn't seen what happened.

"She squeezed my hand." Persephone's voice was high-pitched, unfamiliar to her ears, but she was experiencing a rush of adrenaline.

"What?" Jaison looked down at Lexa and clasped her other hand. "Lexa, Lexa, babe. If you can hear me, squeeze my hand!"

There was a flurry of activity after that. Everyone but Lexa's parents were ushered out of the room, and the doctors were called in to check her vitals. Sometime later, Lexa's father came to the waiting room to let everyone know that her body had healed enough in the last twelve hours to support life-sustaining activity.

"It's a miracle," he said, eyes watery. "A miracle."

Persephone's eyes watered too, and her body trembled. Her sacrifice had been worth it! Lexa was back.

"You did it," Sybil whispered, and the two hugged. It was then Persephone noticed Jaison standing apart from them. She approached, hesitant.

"Are you okay?" she asked.

"Yeah," Jaison said. He sniffed, wiping his eyes. After a moment, he embraced her, his breath releasing in a harsh gasp. "Thank you, Persephone."

His expression of gratitude seemed misplaced given what Persephone had done, so instead of speaking, she remained quiet, hugging him tighter.

They lingered in the waiting room for a little while, talking and laughing. Everything felt strange but hopeful, like the sun was still managing to shine through thick, black clouds. At some point, Persephone decided it was time to sneak away. She needed a shower and a few hours of sleep. She said goodbye to Jaison, Sybil, and Lexa's family and left.

She made it outside before the hair on the back of her neck stood up and a terrifying hiss drew her attention skyward where three women hovered, black, leathery wings spread wide. Their limbs were pale white, and black snakes twined around their bodies. Their hair was inky and seemed to float around them as if they were underwater. Each wore a crown of thick spires, resembling black blades.

They were Furies—goddesses of vengeance—and they only popped up when someone broke Divine law.

"Persephone, daughter of Demeter."

They spoke in unison, their voices echoing in her mind like the hiss of a snake.

"*Fuck.*"

"You have broken a sacred law of the Underworld and therefore must be punished."

A shiver of fear shook her spine. She had not considered that her decision to help Lexa would be punishable by the three goddesses.

Suddenly, serpents slithered around her feet. Persephone jumped.

"Oh no! Fuck, fuck, fuck!"

She tried to jump from the middle of the pool of snakes, but they were quick to surround her, slithering up her legs, torso, and shoulders. Their scales were slippery and rough and tightened around her like rope. A faint whisper reached her ears—*punish, punish, punish.* Then one of the serpents sank its fangs into her shoulder.

Persephone screamed. The pain was sharp, and the venom burned. Suddenly, she was frozen—her scream dried up in her throat and her legs wouldn't work. She tried to move but fell, striking the cement hard. Her body felt like it was being torn apart, and all of a sudden, everything was dark, and she was falling.

She appeared on the floor of Nevernight.

She was surprised when Apollo landed on his face beside her. The god groaned, rolling onto his back. Persephone regained movement in her limbs and started to get to her feet when she saw Hades standing over her like a dark cloud. There was an acute fury in his eyes, and she felt like he was skinning her alive with that stare. She had never experienced fear standing opposite him, even after she had published her story on Apollo, but right now, it settled heavy and cold in her stomach.

Was this what it was like to come before Hades, King of the Underworld—judge and punisher?

"Fucking Furies," Apollo said as he got to his feet, brushing himself off. Persephone glanced at the god, who now spotted Hades. "You know you could upgrade to something a little more modern to enforce natural order, Hades. I'd rather be carried off by a well-muscled man than a trio of albino goddesses and a serpent."

"I thought we had a deal, Apollo," Hades gritted out.

Persephone marveled at how her lover could appear so calm and yet infuse his voice with a quiet fury. She felt it in the air, and it settled on her skin, drawing goose bumps to the surface.

"You mean the deal where I stay away from your goddess in exchange for a favor?"

Hades said nothing. Apollo knew the deal.

"I'd have been more than obliging, except your little lover showed up at Erotas demanding my help. While I was in the middle of a bath, I should add."

"No, you shouldn't," Persephone hissed.

"She can be very persuasive when she's angry," Apollo continued, ignoring her. "The magic helped."

Apollo didn't even need to say the last part; Hades knew what it meant when she got angry—loss of control.

"You never said she was a goddess. No wonder you snatched her up quickly."

Why does everyone say that? she wondered.

"I could hardly deny her request when she had razor-sharp thorns pointed at my nether regions."

Persephone wanted to vomit, but she glanced at Hades and noted that despite the anger clouding his face, he seemed a little proud.

"So we struck a deal. A *bargain,* as you like to call it." Hades's eyes darkened.

"She asked me to heal her little friend, and in exchange, she provides me with…companionship."

"Don't make it sound gross, Apollo," Persephone snapped.

"Gross?"

"Everything that comes out of your mouth sounds like a sexual innuendo."

"Does not!"

"Does too."

"Enough!" Hades's voice cracked like a whip, and when Persephone looked at him, she saw fire in his eyes. Though he addressed Apollo, his gaze didn't leave her, and she felt it tear away all her layers, exposing the raw and real fear she felt beneath. "If you are no longer in need of my goddess, I would like a word with her. Alone."

"She's all yours," Apollo said, who had the good sense to evaporate and say nothing else.

Persephone stood still, staring at Hades. The silence on the floor of Nevernight was tangible. It set heavy on her shoulders and pressed against her ears, and when his voice erupted, burning away the quiet, it promised pain. She could already feel her heart breaking.

"What have you done?"

"I saved Lexa."

"Is that what you think?" He seethed. She could see

tendrils of his glamour coming off him like smoke. She'd never seen him lose control of his magic.

"She was going to die—"

"She was *choosing* to die!" Hades snarled, advancing upon her. His glamour fell away, and he stood before her, stripped of his mortal form. He seemed to fill the room, an inferno, spreading his heat, his anger billowing, eyes inflamed. "And instead of honoring her wish, you intervened. All because you are afraid of pain."

"*I am afraid of pain,*" she snapped. "Will you mock me for that as you mock all mortals?"

"There is no comparison. At least mortals are brave enough to face it."

She flinched, and her anger ignited, a searing pain erupting from all over as thorns sprouted from her skin.

"*Persephone.*"

He reached for her, but she stepped away. The movement was painful, and she inhaled between her teeth.

"If you cared, you would have been there!"

"I was there!"

"You never once came with me to the hospital when I had to watch my best friend lie unresponsive. You never once stood by me while I held her hand. You could have told me when Thanatos would start showing up. You could have let me know she was...*choosing* to die. But you didn't. You hid all that, like it was some fucking secret. *You weren't there.*"

For the first time since she was dumped in front of him by the Furies, he looked shocked and sounded a little lost when he said, "I didn't know you wanted me there."

"Why wouldn't I?" she asked, and there was a twist in her voice, a note of her sadness she couldn't hide.

"I'm not the most welcomed sight at a hospital, Persephone."

"That's your excuse?"

"And what's yours?" he asked. "You never told me—"

"I shouldn't have to *tell you* to be there for me when my friend is dying. Instead, you act like it's as…normal as breathing."

"Because death has forever been my existence," he snapped, growing more and more frustrated.

"That's *your* problem. You've been the God of the Underworld so long, you've forgotten what it is really like to be on the brink of losing someone. Instead you spend all your time judging mortals for their fear of your realm, for their fear of death, for their fear of losing who they love!"

She was a little shocked by the words coming out of her mouth. To be truthful, she hadn't realized how angry she'd been until this very moment.

"So you were angry with me," he said. "And once again, instead of coming to me, you decided to punish me by seeking Apollo's help." He spat the god's name, his hatred evident.

"I wasn't *trying* to punish you. When I decided to go to Apollo, I no longer felt like you were an option."

Hades's eyes narrowed. "After everything I did to protect you from him—"

"I didn't ask that of you," she snapped.

"No, I suppose you didn't. You have never welcomed my aid, especially when it wasn't what you wanted to hear." He sounded so bitter, she flinched.

"That's not fair."

"Isn't it? I have offered an aegis, and you insisted you

284

do not need a guard, yet you are regularly accosted on your way to work. You barely accept rides from Antoni, and you only do now because you don't want to hurt his feelings. Then, when I offer *comfort,* when I *try* to understand your hurt over Lexa's pain, it isn't enough."

"*Your comfort?*" she exploded. "What comfort? When I came to you, begging you to save Lexa, you offered to let me grieve. What was I supposed to do? Stand back and watch her die when I knew I could prevent it?"

"*Yes,*" Hades hissed. "That's exactly what you were supposed to do. You are not above the law of my realm, Persephone!"

Clearly not. The Furies had come after her.

"I don't see why her death matters. You come to the Underworld every day. You would have seen Lexa again!"

"Because it's not the same," she snapped.

"What is that supposed to mean?"

She glared at him, arms crossed tight over her chest. How was she supposed to explain this? Lexa was her first friend, her closest friend, and just when she thought she had her life in order, she met Hades, who threw it all out of orbit. Lexa was the only anchor to her old life, and now Hades wanted to take her too?

Which led to the real problem, and it hurt to say, because she was admitting her greatest fear.

"What happens if you and I." She paused, unable to say the words. "If the Fates decide to unravel our future? I don't want to be so lost in you, so anchored in the Underworld, that I don't know how to exist after."

Hades's eyes narrowed, but when he spoke, his voice was desolate. "I'm beginning to think that maybe you don't want to be in this relationship."

Those words made her chest feel as if it were caving in. "That's not what I'm saying."

"Then what are you saying?"

She shrugged, and for the first time, she felt tears building behind her eyes. "I don't know. Just that…right when I was really starting to figure out who I was, you came along and fucked it all up. I don't know who I'm supposed to be. I don't know—"

"What you want," he said.

"That's not true," she argued. "I want you. I love—"

"Don't say you love me," he interrupted her again. "I can't…hear that right now."

The silence that followed made her feel even more hopeless. Her face felt wet, and she touched her cheek, wiping away the tears.

"I thought you loved me," she whispered.

"I do," he said, staring at the floor. "But I think I may have misunderstood."

"Misunderstood what?"

"The Fates," he said bitterly. "I have waited for you so long, I ignored the fact that they rarely weave happy endings."

"You cannot mean that," she said.

"I mean it. You'll find out why soon enough."

Hades restored his glamour and straightened his tie, his eyes devoid of emotion. How could he recover so quickly when she felt like her insides were destroyed? Then, as if he hadn't already torn a hole through her heart, his parting words reached her—ice cold and haunting.

"You should know that your actions have condemned Lexa to a fate worse than death."

CHAPTER XIX
Goddess of Spring

Alone, Persephone collapsed in tears. As she hit the floor, the thorns bursting from her skin were jarred, and she cried out in pain.

"Oh, my love." Persephone felt Hecate's hand on her back. She didn't look at the goddess, sobbing into her blood-covered hands.

"I messed up, Hecate."

"Shh," the goddess soothed. "Come, on your feet."

Hecate lifted Persephone, careful to avoid touching the thorns sprouting from her body, and teleported to her cabin. Hecate sat Persephone down, placed her hands over the thorns that had broken her skin, and began to chant. Warmth emanated from her palms. Persephone watched as the barbs began to grow smaller until nothing of the malady was visible. When the wounds were healed, Hecate cleaned the blood away and sat down opposite Persephone.

"What happened?"

Persephone burst into tears again, guilt and agony

warring in her mind. She told Hecate everything—the conversation she'd overheard about taking Lexa off life support, her mother's visit, and her trek to the pleasure district.

"When it came down to losing her…I couldn't." She choked on a sob. Hecate reached out and covered Persephone's hand with hers. "And my mother just made it all worse. There may not be consequences for gods, but there are consequences for me."

"There are always consequences. The difference between you and other gods is that you care about them."

Persephone was silent for a moment and then repeated what Hades had told her. "I have condemned Lexa to a fate worse than death." She paused. "I just wanted her with me."

"Why do you hold on to the mortal realm?"

Persephone looked at Hecate. "Because it is where I belong."

"Is it?" Hecate asked. "What about the Underworld?"

When Persephone didn't respond, Hecate shook her head.

"My dear, you are trying to be someone you're not."

"What do you mean? All I have been trying to do is be myself."

And that had been more difficult than she could ever imagine.

"Are you?" Hecate asked. "Because the person who sits before me now does not match the one I see beneath."

"And who do you see beneath?" Persephone asked, her voice verging on sarcasm.

"The Goddess of Spring," Hecate answered. "Future Queen of the Underworld, wife of Hades."

Those words made Persephone shiver.

"You are holding on to a life that no longer serves you. A job that punishes you for your relationships, a friendship that could have blossomed in the Underworld, a mother who has taught you to be a prisoner."

Persephone bristled at those words.

"And if you need any more evidence that you are denying yourself, look no further than the way your magic is manifesting. If you do not learn to love yourself, your powers will tear you apart."

Persephone's brows knitted together. "What are you saying, Hecate? That I should abandon my life in the Upperworld?"

Hecate shook her head. "You think in extremes," she said. "You are either a goddess or a mortal. You either live in the Underworld or the Upperworld. Do you not want it all, Persephone?"

"Yes," she said, frustrated. "Of course I want it all, but everyone keeps telling me I *can't*!"

A slow smile crept across Hecate's face. "Create the life you want, Persephone, and stop listening to everyone else."

Persephone blinked, absorbing Hecate's words.

Create the life you want.

Up until this point, she thought she knew what kind of life she wanted, but what she was realizing now was that things had changed since meeting Hades. Despite her struggle to accept herself and understand her power, he had shifted something inside her. With him came new desires, new hopes, new dreams, and there was no way to attain those without letting go of old ones.

She swallowed hard, her eyes watering.

"I messed up, Hecate," she said again.

"As we all do," the goddess replied, standing. "And as we all will. Now let's channel some of that pain and clean up the mess you made in the grove. Consider it practice."

Persephone didn't argue, finding that she was strangely motivated.

The two left Hecate's cottage for the grove. Persephone knew when they were close because she could smell rotten fruit—a terrible mix of sugar and decay.

"The goal is to collect all the dead pieces and make them into ripe pomegranates," Hecate said.

"How do I do that?"

"The same way you destroyed them—except you want to control how much power you use."

Persephone wasn't sure she could, but she remembered the time she'd spent with Hades and how he taught her to focus her power. That memory made her chest ache in a way she never thought possible.

Magic is balance—a little control, a little passion. It is the way of the world.

"Imagine the pomegranate whole, a delicious crimson color."

Hecate's voice faded away as Persephone focused on her task.

Close your eyes, she heard Hades whisper in her ear, and she obeyed as her breath caught in her throat. She could have sworn she felt the scrape of his cheek against hers.

He continued to whisper.

Tell me what you feel.

Warmth, she thought.

Focus on it.

As before, it started low in her stomach, and she fed it, tortured by thoughts of Hades.

Where are you warm?

"Everywhere," she whispered and imagined all that warmth in her hands, the energy growing so bright she could barely look at it, like a sun in the palm of her hands, or a dying star.

Open your eyes, Persephone. She swore his breath caressed her skin.

She did, and the shimmering image of a pomegranate sat between her hands. She took a deep, deliberate breath, guiding her hands to the earth, and as she did, pieces of rotting flesh rose from the ground and gathered. Before long, the grove smelled of fresh, ripe fruit, and several whole, red pomegranates lay at her feet.

When she looked at Hecate, the goddess was clearly surprised.

"Very good, my love," she said.

Persephone would have smiled, but she found that her success at reconstructing the pomegranates was overshadowed by an acute sadness. It made the world feel heavy and her body feel sluggish. She blinked rapidly, hoping to keep her tears at bay.

She wasn't sure if Hecate could sense her turmoil, but the goddess was quick to distract her.

"Come. I will teach you to make poisons as promised."

The two returned to her cottage, and Persephone sat beside Hecate, who had picked and bound several varieties of plants.

"What is all this?"

"The usual. Hemlock, daphne, deadly nightshade, death cap, angel's trumpet, curare."

The goddess explained which parts of each plant were deadly and how much it would take of each to kill a target. She also seemed to delight in explaining *how* the plant would kill.

"What would poison do to a god?" Persephone asked.

A ghost of a smile touched the goddess's lips.

"Thinking of poisoning Apollo?"

Persephone could feel her cheeks redden. "N-no!"

Hecate laughed quietly. "Do not feel guilty for contemplating murder, my dear. Most gods have done far worse."

Persephone knew that was true.

"Poison would likely have little impact on Apollo, except to make him very sick, which would be just as fun. Talk about no consequences."

Persephone laughed and filed that bit of information away for later.

They spent a while crushing leaves and oils into powerful concoctions until Persephone's hands hurt from using the mortar and pestle and her eyes stung from the potency of the plants. At one point, she started to rub her eyes, but Hecate's hand clamped down on her wrist.

Persephone yelped, mostly from surprise. She didn't know Hecate could move that fast.

"Don't."

Hecate led Persephone to a basin. Persephone washed her hands and waited for Hecate to finish up before they made their way to Asphodel.

"I have finalized your gown for the summer solstice," Hecate said. Persephone's stomach felt unsettled. She knew what the goddess was trying to do. She'd already commissioned a new crown for Persephone to wear for the occasion. She was trying to turn her into some sort of queen, and on the heels of her fight with Hades, that made her anxious.

When Persephone and Hecate arrived, the souls swarmed. She wasn't sure why, but today their excitement, kindness, and clear devotion brought tears to her eyes. Maybe it had something to do with her conversation with Hecate. She'd always known the people of the Underworld considered her a goddess. More than that, they'd immediately accepted her as part of their world and hinted at her potential to become Queen of the Underworld, and all she'd ever done was resist.

She was afraid.

Afraid she would somehow disappoint them like she had disappointed her mother, like she had disappointed Hades.

She took a deep breath, forcing down the emotion thick within her throat, and pretended like everything was fine. She helped finalize decisions for the solstice celebration, tasted samplings of various meals, approved decor, and played with the children before returning to the Upperworld.

When she arrived home, she broke down.

Sybil didn't ask any questions. More than likely, she had already guessed what had happened. The oracle just held her as she cried herself to sleep.

Before work on Monday, Persephone stopped by the hospital only to find that Lexa was asleep.

"She woke up briefly," Eliska said. "But she was very confused. The doctor gave her a sedative."

"Confused?"

Persephone's anxiety spiked, making her stomach feel sick.

"They think it's temporary psychosis," Eliska explained. "It isn't unusual for patients who have been in the ICU."

Psychosis. Temporary.

Persephone's relief was immediate. It was probably too much to expect that Lexa would bounce back. Still, Persephone had let her hopes rise. She'd thought that Divine magic would work differently from traditional medicine. That when Apollo talked about miracles, it would mean skipping the recovery too.

"Persephone, are you alright?" Eliska asked.

The goddess met the mortal's gaze and nodded. "Yes, I'm fine. Will you...text me when Lexa wakes up?"

"Of course, dear." Eliska paused, studying her. Whatever she was seeing in Persephone's expression had her suspicious because she asked again, "Are you sure you're okay?"

No, Persephone thought. *My whole world is falling apart*. She nodded. "Yeah, just...tired." She felt silly saying that. Eliska was tired too.

"I understand. I promise to text you as soon as Lexa wakes." She reached for Persephone, hugging her close. "I'm so thankful Lexa has a friend like you."

Persephone swallowed hard, and her eyes watered. Again, Hades's words erupted in her mind.

You should know that your actions have condemned Lexa to a fate worse than death.

They'd attached themselves to her, like a leech, hungry for blood. They made her head and heart ache. They made her want to scream.

I am not a good friend. I am not a good lover. I am not a good goddess.

Work was awkward.

Persephone didn't feel comfortable around Demetri since learning about the bargain he'd made with Kal Stavros. She realized that she had all but done the same, but somehow his situation just seemed different.

Or rather she kept telling herself it was different.

To make matters worse, he had resorted to assigning her menial tasks like making copies, verifying another coworker's work, and researching a privacy law for him. He'd sent her the to-do list in an email with an end of day deadline, which meant she couldn't work on any of the stories she had in her queue.

She rapped on Demetri's open door.

"Have a moment?" she asked when he looked up from his tablet.

"Not really," he said. "Another time?"

"It's about the to-do list."

Demetri took off his glasses and stared at her. "It's three things, Persephone. How hard can it be?"

His comment flustered her. "It isn't," she snapped. "But I have other stories—"

"Not today," he cut her off. "Today, you have three things to accomplish by five."

Persephone set her teeth so hard, she thought her jaw might break.

"Close the door as you leave."

She slammed it. Probably not the best move, but it was better than filling the guy with holes from the thorns she wanted to throw at him. She took a few breaths, deciding it would be best if she just got through the tasks Demetri had assigned.

When she was finished, she could comb through the information she'd received over the last few weeks, trying to decide on her next story.

She had several options available to her and a million lines of inquiry, but the information she gravitated toward always included her mother. The Goddess of Harvest should be renamed the Goddess of Divine Punishment, because she was definitely fond of torture, and her methods were vicious, often forcing mortals into starvation or cursing them with an unquenchable hunger. Now and then, when she was really pissed off, she would create famine, killing off whole populations.

My mother is the worst, Persephone thought.

By the time lunch rolled around, Persephone was entertaining herself with thoughts of writing about Demeter. She could see the headline in black, bold letters:

Nurturing Goddess of Harvest Deprives Whole Populations of Food

Then she cringed, imagining the fallout.

It was likely Demeter would take revenge in the only way Persephone could imagine—revealing that she was actually Demeter's daughter.

With that thought, Persephone left the Acropolis and met Sybil at Mithaecus Café for lunch.

Her mind was chaotic, going in several directions—dwelling on Lexa's healing and Hades's anger, making it hard for her to focus on anything the oracle was saying, which made her feel guilty because Sybil had news.

"I got a job offer today," she was saying, which got Persephone's attention. "From the Cypress Foundation."

Persephone lit up. "Oh, Sybil! I'm so happy for you."

"I should be thanking you," Sybil said. "I'm sure you're why they picked me."

Persephone shook her head. "Hades knows talent when he sees it."

The oracle didn't look so certain.

Persephone couldn't explain why, but her excitement for Sybil dwindled quickly, as a heavy feeling settled on her chest. It was a combination of emotions—guilt, hopelessness, and a ton of unspoken feelings.

"I have to hang out with Apollo," she said abruptly.

Sybil stared at Persephone.

"That was the bargain," Persephone explained. "I just…want you to know."

"I'm glad you told me," Sybil replied, and Persephone couldn't help thinking she was too nice, too understanding.

"Do you remember at the gala, when you told me my colors and Hades's colors were all…?"

Her voice faltered, the question poised on her tongue. Sybil's eyes were searching, and she pressed her lips together. Persephone wasn't sure if it was because she was trying to keep from saying something she would regret or if she was trying not to smile. Either way, Persephone had to ask.

"Are they still…tangled up?"

"They are," Sybil said quietly. "I wish you could see it. It is beautiful, sensual, and chaotic."

Persephone offered a humorless laugh. "Chaotic is right."

Sybil smiled. "Well, I did say it was a tangle."

Persephone gave her a questioning look.

"It is what happens when two powerful people meet."

"Discord?" Persephone asked.

"And passion and bliss." Sybil was smiling completely now.

Persephone looked away. She and Hades definitely had all those things, but were they possible to reclaim? After all she had done?

Sybil placed a hand on Persephone's.

"You were always meant for greatness, Persephone, but getting there will be war." Persephone shivered.

"Not literal war, right?"

Sybil didn't say.

They left, walking in opposite directions, Persephone to work and Sybil to the hospital to visit Lexa. Persephone hadn't heard from Eliska, so she assumed Lexa had yet to wake up. The thought made her anxious. Did that mean Apollo's magic hadn't worked? She pushed those thoughts aside. Apollo was an ancient god, his magic well-practiced.

Lexa is still healing. She is tired, Persephone told herself. *She needs her rest.*

She took a shortcut back to the Acropolis. She was getting used to avoiding the attention of journalists and rabid fans of the Divine, and that meant avoiding the main roads in favor of narrow alleyways. While they weren't as pleasant as the well-landscaped sidewalks of New Athens, she'd learned it was the easiest way to get where she needed in the least amount of time. There were fewer people, and those she did encounter didn't seem to care that she was there. Which was probably why she noticed a snowy cat with large, green eyes following her.

She knew by its mannerisms—strangely human and attentive—that the creature was a shape-shifter. Shape-shifters didn't use glamour to mask appearances. Their biology allowed them to change forms, which meant Persephone couldn't see what they were beneath their animal form.

Persephone continued walking for a while, pretending that she hadn't noticed the cat wandering the alleys with her. When she was sufficiently out of sight of any onlookers, she stopped. The cat seemed surprised and halted too.

Then, as if remembering it was supposed to be a cat, the creature began to lick its paw.

Gross, Persephone thought. *This stone is not clean.*

"Shift," she ordered.

If it was sent, as she suspected, by Hades, the shifter would have no choice but to expose itself. Despite this, the cat attempted to run away. Clearly, it hadn't expected Persephone to confront it.

Mid-run, its body straightened and grew, transforming into a slender woman who was now standing still. She was tall and dressed in gold armor. Her dark hair was braided and fell over her shoulder to her waist. Persephone noted several weapons attached to her body—a long sword at her hip, a set of knives crossed on her back, a dagger around her bare thigh.

She was an aegis and an Amazon—a daughter of Ares bred for brutality and war. She knelt on one knee, pressing a hand to her chest as she did, and said, "My lady."

"Don't." Persephone's voice was sharp, and the warrior met her gaze, standing. "Hades sent you?"

"It is an honor to serve you, my lady."

"I didn't ask for this," Persephone said.

"Lord Hades worries for you. I will keep you safe."

She really hated the way those words made hope bloom in her chest.

"I don't need you to keep me safe. I can take care of myself. I've lived in the mortal world for years, and trust me, if an Amazon comes to my rescue, it'll only make things harder for me."

The woman raised her head, defiant. "I will do as Lord Hades commands."

"Then I will speak with Lord Hades," Persephone replied, twisting on her heels.

"*Please.*"

Persephone was stopped by the shakiness in the Amazon's voice. She faced the woman.

"I shouldn't expect you to care, but I need this. I need this charge. I need this honor."

"Why?" Persephone was genuinely curious, but she didn't like the change it inspired in the Amazon. The woman looked at her feet, and her shoulders fell. Whatever her reasoning, it was a burden.

Then she said, "I do not wish to expose my shame."

A strained silence followed, and after a moment, Persephone asked, "What's your name?"

The woman looked bewildered.

"You may call me Aegis, my lady."

"I prefer to call you by your name," Persephone answered. "Just as I prefer you call me Persephone."

"Lord Hades—"

"I really wish Lord Hades's staff would stop telling me what he dislikes or likes. Clearly, he hasn't made that consideration for me."

She regretted the outburst.

But the woman smiled. "It's okay." She paused. "I'm Zofie."

"Zofie," Persephone said her name. "If it is that important to you, I will not dismiss you."

But she would have words with Hades…when she decided to talk to him again.

"Thank you…Persephone."

"I'm running late," she said and began to back away, and then she pointed at what the woman was wearing. "We'll talk about the armor later."

Zofie advanced. "Lord Hades said not to let you out of my sight."

Persephone rolled her eyes. "I can't bring you into my office, Zofie…not dressed like this *or* as a cat."

"I'm content to wait for you outside," Zofie offered.

Persephone sighed. "Fine. We'll talk about that later too."

Persephone left the alleyway, and her new aegis followed. She had a lot of questions for the woman—namely, where was she from and why was it so important for her to keep this position? Persephone couldn't refuse when she'd seen the look in Zofie's eyes, because she had recognized it in herself. It was hopelessness.

She wondered if the God of the Dead had chosen her aegis strategically, knowing Persephone wouldn't be able to deprive Zofie of her dream.

CHAPTER XX
Competition

Persephone decided to deal with Zofie's armor quickly.

Upon leaving work, the Amazon trotted alongside her toward Hades's Lexus and hopped inside.

"To the Pearl, Antoni."

She wondered if Aphrodite would be in the boutique. Since Zofie was Hades's employee and she had been appointed to guard Persephone in the Upperworld, surely he wouldn't mind if she charged clothing, shoes, and accessories to his account.

And if he did, well, it was his fault for undermining her.

Antoni glanced in the rearview mirror.

"I see you met Zofie," he said.

"Don't tell me you knew about this, Antoni."

The cyclops ducked his head a little as if to hide from her frustration. "I think it was inevitable, my lady."

Persephone didn't respond. She looked out the window as they passed marble-white buildings, stoic churches, and colorful apartments until they came to Aphrodite's shop. Persephone picked up Zofie, who protested with a loud whine.

"Shh!" she commanded. "No one lets their cat walk into a shop of their own free will."

She stepped out of the limo and into the shop.

"I didn't know you liked pussies," Aphrodite said, materializing as soon as Persephone set the cat on the floor. The goddess was a little more covered than usual, wearing a silk champagne dress embossed with flowers. It had thin straps, came to her midcalf, and looked more like a nightgown than something to wear in public, but Persephone was discovering that was Aphrodite's modus operandi.

"Shift," Persephone ordered, and Zofie became human again.

Aphrodite's eyes narrowed upon the Amazon. "A daughter of Ares," she said. "I'm not surprised."

Persephone's brows drew together. "What do you mean?"

"Hades would only ever assign the best to protect you."

Zofie bowed her head. "It is an honor for you to say, Lady Aphrodite."

The Goddess of Love offered a half smile, but it was not kind.

"Of course. Everyone knows Amazons are brutal, aggressive, and full of bloodlust. You're all just like your father."

Zofie stiffened beside her, and Persephone wondered why the goddess felt the need to be so cruel.

"Aphrodite, I'm hoping to purchase a new wardrobe

for my aegis," Persephone said quickly. "I need her to blend in if she's going to...*protect* me."

It was hard for Persephone to say the word. She didn't want to need protection. She wanted to protect herself, but at this point, after what had happened a few days ago, it was likely she'd just rip herself apart.

"What's the matter? Wartime chic too flashy for you?"

Persephone gave Aphrodite a dull look as she began pulling clothing off racks and handing it to the attendants.

"What colors do you like, Zofie?" Persephone asked.

"I don't know," Zofie said. "I've never thought about it."

Persephone paused and looked at her. "Never thought about it?"

"We are warriors, Lady Persephone."

"That doesn't mean you can't enjoy fashion," Persephone remarked and then laughed to herself. She sounded like Lexa.

When the attendant's arms were piled high with clothes, Persephone ushered Zofie into one of the changing rooms and took a seat. Aphrodite lounged nearby.

"How's the love life?" Aphrodite asked.

"Why do you always ask that?" The question frustrated Persephone for obvious reasons. She hadn't seen Hades since their fight, and she'd agonized over the status of their relationship since.

"I've never asked it of you before. I can usually smell it."

Persephone rolled her eyes, still repulsed by Aphrodite's unusual skills.

"Then I guess you have your answer."

Persephone didn't look at Aphrodite. She stared at the curtain that Zofie had disappeared behind.

"You might not be having sex, but you still love him," Aphrodite said.

"Of course I love Hades."

No one needed magic to see that.

"Have you told him?"

"I tried," Persephone said.

Don't say you love me.

Aphrodite was quiet for a long moment and then said, "I have never told anyone I loved them and meant it."

"What about Hephaestus?"

"I have never told him that I loved him."

There was an uncomfortable pause, and then Persephone asked, "Is that because you really do love him?"

Aphrodite didn't answer, and Zofie picked that moment to leave the changing room in a tailored blue dress that made her look remarkably tan and accentuated her athleticism.

"Oh, Zofie! You look beautiful."

The Amazon flushed crimson and stood in front of the mirror, smoothing her hands over the fabric. "It's not very conducive to fighting," she commented, attempting to kick out her feet and squat.

"Oh, darling. If you cannot fight in heels and a tailored dress in this age, how can you call yourself a warrior?" the Goddess of Love asked.

Persephone couldn't tell if Aphrodite was being serious or not. It was easy for an immortal to say something like that. Gods were virtually invincible.

"Let's hope you won't have a reason to fight anyone while you're guarding me," Persephone said.

Zofie disappeared behind the curtain again. She tried on several outfits, preferring pantsuits over skirts and dresses. Persephone did manage to convince the Amazon to buy one dress, a floor-length gown in the same color blue as the first one she'd tried on, arguing that if the warrior was going to be her aegis, she would have to attend formal events.

When they were finished shopping, Persephone and Zofie stood outside Aphrodite's shop.

"Do you have a home?" Persephone asked.

"My home is in Terme," Zofie answered.

That was north and several hundred miles away. "Do you have a place to stay here in New Athens?"

Zofie frowned and seemed confused. "I must go where you go, Persephone."

A thought occurred to her.

"Where would you have stayed had I not discovered you?"

"Outside," Zofie said.

"Zofie!"

"It is fine, my lady. I am resilient."

"Resilient I have no doubt. I won't have you sleeping outside—as a cat or otherwise. You can sleep on the couch for now."

They would work out sleeping arrangements again once Lexa returned home. Sybil had taken Lexa's bed for the time being, and it wasn't likely Persephone would be sleeping in the Underworld for the next few weeks.

"I cannot sleep," Zofie said.

"What do you mean?"

"I do not need sleep. Who will watch over you if I am not awake?"

"Zofie, I've survived this long without being abducted. I'm sure I'll be fine."

But as the words left her mouth, she felt foreign magic grip her and the familiar pull of being sucked into a void.

Someone was forcing her to teleport.

"Zofie—"

The Amazon's eyes widened, and the last thing Persephone saw before she vanished was the determined look on Zofie's face as she reached for her.

A second later, Persephone was thrust into the middle of a screaming crowd. The air was hazy and sticky. It smelled like tobacco and body odor.

"There she is!" Apollo wrapped an arm around her neck and hauled her against him. He was sweaty and dressed casually, in a polo shirt and jeans.

"What the actual fuck, Apollo?" Persephone demanded, pushing away savagely, but the god held her tight, pulling her along through the crowd toward a small stage at the front of the room. As he did, he turned his head toward hers, whispering against her ear.

"We had a bargain, Goddess."

She hated the feel of his breath on her skin. She should have expected Apollo to abduct her at any given moment. It was a part of the deal she'd forgotten to clarify, and now she regretted it.

She was thrust beneath bright lights. They blinded her and made the whole place appear darker, so it was hard to tell just how many people were in the crowd in front of her.

Apollo grabbed the mic and cried into it.

"Persephone Rosi, everyone! You may know her as Hades's lover, but tonight, she's our jury, judge, and executioner!"

The crowd erupted into boos and cheers.

Apollo returned the mic to its cradle and reached for Persephone's arm. She recoiled, but the god placed his hand on her back, guiding her to a chair to the side of the stage.

"Stop touching me, Apollo," she said through her teeth.

"Stop acting like you don't like me," the god replied.

"I don't. Liking you wasn't part of the deal," she snapped.

Apollo's eyes flashed. "I'm not opposed to ending the bargain, Persephone, if you can live with the death of your friend."

She glared and sat. Apollo smiled.

"Good girl. Now, you are going to sit here with a smile on that pretty face and judge this competition for me, got it?"

Apollo patted her face. She wanted to kick him in the balls but refrained, gripping the edges of her chair. As he turned back to the crowd, they began to chant his name. The god encouraged this by pumping his arms in the air.

"Ladies and gentlemen of the Lyre, we have a challenger in our midst."

The crowd booed, but Persephone felt relieved that she finally knew where she was. The Lyre was a venue in New Athens where musicians of all kinds performed. It was located in the arts district at the edge of the city.

"A satyr who claims he is a better musician than me!"

More boos from the crowd.

"You know what I say to that? Prove it."

He drew away from the mic, his face awash in the light from the stage.

"Bring forth the competitor!"

There was a disruption, and Persephone watched as the crowd split. Two burly men dragged a satyr between them. He was young and blond, his hair a nest of curls atop his head. His jaw was set, and his chest rose and fell quickly, giving away his fear, but his eyes were narrowed, black, and set upon Apollo with a hatred that Persephone could feel.

"Satyr! Your hubris will be punished."

The crowd cheered, and Apollo motioned for the men to bring the young man forward. They shoved him onto the stage, and he stumbled, falling to his knees. Persephone watched as Apollo summoned an instrument from thin air. It looked like a type of flute, and when the satyr saw it, his eyes widened. Clearly, it was important to him.

Apollo tossed it to him, and he caught it against his chest.

"Play it," the god ordered. "Show us your talents, Marsyas."

For a moment, the boy seemed even more frightened at hearing his name leave the god's mouth, and then she watched as he rose to his feet, his expression determined.

Marsyas put the flute to his lips and began to perform. At first, Persephone could barely hear the music he created because the crowd was so unruly. She couldn't help thinking that they seemed to be under some sort of spell, but slowly, they fell silent. Persephone watched Apollo, noting the way he clenched his fists and the tension in his shoulders. Clearly, he hadn't expected the satyr to be good.

His music was beautiful—it was sweet, and it swelled,

filling the whole room, seeping into pores and twining with blood. Somehow, it knew exactly how to target each dark emotion, each painful memory, and by the end, Persephone found herself crying.

The crowd was quiet, and Persephone couldn't tell if they were stunned into silence or if Apollo was preventing them from reacting with his magic, so she started to clap, and slowly, the rest joined in, whistling, cheering, and chanting the satyr's name. Apollo's face reddened, and he gazed menacingly at Persephone and the young man before summoning his own instrument, a lyre.

As he strummed, a pretty tune emerged, and each note seemed to carry longer than the last. It was a strange and ethereal sound, one that didn't calm but commanded attention. Persephone felt as if she were on the edge of her seat, and she couldn't figure out why. Was she fearful of Apollo? Or was she waiting for the music to transform into something more?

When he ended, the crowd erupted into applause.

Persephone felt like an invisible hand had clasped her heart and just released it. She sagged into her chair, taking deep breaths.

Apollo bowed to the crowd and then turned to Persephone.

"And now let us welcome our beautiful judge!" He smiled, but his gaze was threatening.

He gestured for Persephone to join him in the spotlight. She did, cringing when his arm snaked around her waist.

"Persephone, beautiful *goddess* that you are, tell us who is the winner of tonight's competition? Marsyas." He paused to let the crowd boo, the earlier hypnosis they'd experienced while listening to his music gone. "Or me, the *God* of Music."

The crowd cheered, and Apollo shoved the mic in her face. She could feel her heart beating hard in her chest, and sweat beaded on her forehead. She hated these lights; they were too bright and too hot.

She looked at Apollo and then at Marsyas, who seemed just as frightened by what she might say.

She spoke, her lips brushing the hard metal of the mic. "Marsyas."

That was when all hell broke loose.

The crowd cried in protest and some rushed the stage. At the same time, the burly men who had dragged the satyr to the stage returned and grabbed him again, forcing him to his knees.

"No, no, please!" It was the first time the young man had spoken. He pleaded with her, his dark eyes desperate. "Take it back! Lord Apollo, I was wrong to speak against your talent. You are superior!"

But his pleas fell on deaf ears, because Apollo only had eyes for Persephone.

"You dare defy me?" he said through his teeth. His jaw was clenched so hard, the veins in his neck popped.

"There is no fine print, Apollo. Marsyas was better than you."

It didn't help that she had never actually liked Apollo's music.

The god's fury soon turned to amusement, and a wicked smile cut across his beautiful face. The sudden change in his demeanor turned her blood to ice.

"Jury, judge, and executioner, Persephone."

He turned toward the crowd.

"You have heard Persephone's verdict," he cried into the mic. "Marsyas, the *winner*."

The crowd was still angry. They shouted obscenities and threw things at the stage. Persephone ducked behind Apollo.

"Careful," he warned. "She is protected by Hades."

She found it odd that he would say that, thinking he might prefer that she face the abuse, but at his reminder, the crowd calmed.

"Though Marsyas is the winner, he is still guilty of hubris. How shall we punish him?"

"Hang him!" someone yelled.

"Gut him!" another said.

"Flay him!" several cried. The cheers were the loudest then.

"So be it!" Apollo returned the mic to its cradle and twisted toward Marsyas, who was struggling in the arms of the men who held him.

"Apollo, you cannot be serious!" Persephone reached for him, and the god shoved her aside.

"Hubris is the downfall of humanity and should be punished," he said. "I will be the punisher."

"He is a child!" she argued. "If he is guilty of hubris, you are too. Is your pride too wounded to let him live?"

Apollo clenched his fists. "His death is on your hands, Persephone."

The goddess jumped in front of him, blocking Marsyas from view.

"You will not touch him. You will not hurt him!" She was desperate, and she feared she might lose control. She could feel her magic pulsing, making her flesh tingle and her hair rise.

Apollo laughed. "And how will you stop me?"

Apollo's magic surrounded her, suffocating her with the smell of laurel. She glared at him.

"Now." He turned back to Marsyas. "Let the skinning begin."

Persephone felt nauseous.

This can't be happening.

Apollo summoned a blade from thin air; its edges gleamed beneath the burning lights.

Persephone struggled to free herself, but the more she resisted, the heavier Apollo's magic felt.

She watched, wide-eyed and terrified as Apollo knelt before the satyr and pressed the blade to his cheek.

When she saw blood drip down his face, she lost control.

"Stop!" she screamed at the top of her lungs. Her magic fled from her body. It was an unusual feeling, like it was coming out of all her pores and her mouth and her eyes. It burned as if it were tearing skin and blinded as if it were pure light.

When the feeling faded, she was shocked to find everyone frozen: Apollo, his men, the crowd, everyone except Marsyas.

The satyr stared at Persephone, face pale and stained with crimson from the wound Apollo had made.

"Y-you're a goddess."

Persephone rushed to him and tried to pry the man's fingers from the satyr's arm, but they were wrapped too tightly. Frantic, she looked for another option. She didn't know how long her magic would hold. She wasn't even sure how she'd managed to freeze the whole room.

Then her eyes fell to the knife Apollo held inches

from Marsyas's face. She reached for it, and the slick handle slipped from his grasp. She took a few deep breaths before cutting into the man's fingers so that Marsyas could free himself.

"Run," she said.

"He will find me!" he argued, rubbing his arm.

"I promise you he won't come after you again," she said. "Go!"

The satyr obeyed.

She waited until he was out of sight to turn to Apollo and kick him hard in the balls.

The release of aggression was enough, and the whole room came to life again.

"Motherfucker!" the man behind her roared, clutching his hand to his chest while Apollo collapsed to the ground, groveling.

Persephone loomed over him.

"Don't you *ever* put me in that situation again." Persephone's voice shook with anger. Apollo breathed heavily, glaring up at her. "We might have an agreement, but I will not be used. Fuck you."

She left the building with a smile on her face.

CHAPTER XXI
A Touch of Betrayal

When Persephone returned home, she found Sybil, Zofie, and Antoni in her living room.

"Oh, thank the gods!" Sybil said, rushing to embrace her. "Are you okay?"

"I'm fine," Persephone said. Truthfully, she hadn't felt this good in a while.

"Where were you?" Zofie demanded.

"The Lyre. Apollo decided today was the day he would take advantage of our bargain," Persephone said.

Zofie's eyes widened. "You have a bargain with Apollo?"

Persephone didn't respond and moved into the living room to sit on the couch, suddenly exhausted. The three followed her. "Did you tell Hades I was abducted?"

Antoni rubbed the back of his neck and turned a little pink. He didn't need to answer; she knew the cyclops had.

Persephone sighed. "Someone should let him know I'm okay so he doesn't destroy the world."

Antoni and Zofie exchanged a look.

"I'll do it," Antoni said. "I'm glad you're okay, Persephone."

She smiled at the cyclops. Once he was gone, Sybil sat beside Persephone.

"What did Apollo make you do?"

Persephone told Sybil and Zofie what had happened, leaving out how she managed to freeze everyone in the whole room and that she'd cut someone's fingers off. She decided she did want them to know she had kicked Apollo in the balls, though. Sybil laughed. Zofie tried to hide her amusement, probably because she feared retaliation.

"I don't think he'll force me to judge another competition any time soon," Persephone said. "Or abduct me from the street."

There was silence for a long moment.

"Any updates on Lexa?" Persephone asked Sybil.

The oracle shook her head. "She was still asleep when I visited."

More silence. A strange kind of exhaustion seemed to settle upon them all at once, and Persephone sighed.

"I'm going to bed. See you guys tomorrow."

They said good night, and Persephone made her way to her room. She paused as she opened the door, overwhelmed by Hades's scent. Her heart beat faster in her chest and her skin was hot. She felt silly, both excited and anxious at the possibility of seeing and speaking to him.

She closed the door and said, "How long have you been here?"

"Not long." His voice came from the darkness. There was a rough undercurrent to his tone. She knew he was trying to keep a cap on his emotions. She could

316

feel them raging around her: anger and fear and lust and longing.

She would take them all if it meant being close to him.

"You know what happened?" she asked.

"I overheard, yes."

"Are you angry?" She whispered the words and found that she feared his response.

"Yes," he said. "But not with you."

He had kept his distance until that point, and then she felt him, his energy reaching for hers. His hands found her arms, her shoulders, and then her face. She inhaled sharply at his touch.

"I couldn't sense you," he said. "I couldn't find you."

Persephone placed her hands over his. "I'm here, Hades. I'm fine."

She thought he might kiss her, but instead he let go and turned on her light. It burned her eyes.

"You will never know how difficult this is for me."

"I imagine as difficult as it's been for me to deal with Minthe and Leuce." Hades's eyes darkened. "Except that Apollo has never been my lover."

He scowled. She was provoking him, but she needed to see his emotion, to see that he cared.

"You have not been to the Underworld."

Persephone folded her arms over her chest.

"I've been busy," she said—*and angry and afraid.*

"The souls miss you, Persephone," Hades said at last. She looked at him, unsure where he was going with this. Did he miss her? "Do not punish them because you are angry with me."

"Don't lecture me, Hades. You have no idea what I've been dealing with."

"Of course not. That would mean you'd have to talk to me."

She glared. "You mean like you talk to me? I'm not the only one with communication problems, Hades."

"I didn't come here to argue with you," he said. "Or *lecture* you. I came to see if you were okay."

"Why come at all? Antoni would have told you."

"I had to," he said and looked away, setting his jaw. "I had to see you myself."

She could feel what he didn't say. The emotions that swelled between them were heavy with desperation and fear, but why wasn't he *saying* that?

"Hades, I—" She took a step toward him. She wasn't sure what she was going to say. Maybe, *I'm sorry?* Those words didn't quite seem like enough, though, and she didn't have a chance to figure it out before Hades spoke.

"I should go. I'm late for a meeting."

He vanished, and Persephone exhaled, leaning against her door for support. Her body suddenly felt heavy, and torturous thoughts rolled through her head.

He couldn't get away from you fast enough, she thought.

Sadness curled into her chest, aching and hot. She made her way into the shower and stood under the hot spray until it was ice cold. After, she climbed into bed.

She missed Hades.

His comfort.

His conversation.

His touch.

His teasing.

His passion.

She missed everything about him.

She groaned and rolled onto her side.

Funny, she could hear Lexa's voice in her head. *Why didn't you just ask him to stay?*

He didn't give me the chance. He was busy anyway.

Did you even try to stop him?

No.

They'd already been arguing. What would they have done if he'd stayed?

Had really hot makeup sex, Lexa commented in her head.

She managed to smile despite the tears that pricked her eyes. For a moment, her thoughts spiraled. How had she gotten here? She'd severed her relationship with her mother and ended a bargain with Hades just to jump into another with Apollo. Her best friend was in the hospital, her future still uncertain, and Persephone hadn't really liked her job since Demetri's ultimatum.

What the fuck are you doing, Persephone? she whispered aloud.

Your best, she heard Lexa reply before she fell into a deep sleep.

———

With no update on Lexa from Eliska, Persephone headed straight to work. Antoni came to a stop in front of the Acropolis, glancing in the rearview mirror.

"Would you like me to escort you?"

She was looking out the window when he spoke, and his voice filled her with dread. Not because he was asking to escort her but because she had to get out of the car.

She'd been trying her hardest to embrace the screaming crowd, but today, she didn't feel like faking it.

She was sad.

She looked at the cyclops. "No, but thank you, Antoni."

Besides, Zofie was out there somewhere, watching. If things got out of hand, the aegis would intervene.

Persephone left the Lexus, entering the throng of screaming fans and reporters.

"Persephone! Persephone!"

She kept her head down, walking with determined steps toward the Acropolis.

"Persephone! Have you seen the *Divine*?"

"Do you know the woman Hades was seen with last night?"

Her steps faltered, and she paused, searching the crowd for the person who'd asked the question, when her eyes settled on a paper one of the mortals held. On the front page of the *Delphi Divine* was a photo of Hades and Leuce hand in hand. The title screamed back at her:

Hades Steps Out with Mysterious Woman

She walked up to the mortal and snatched the paper from his hands. Everything around her suddenly felt distant, the sound drowned out by a rushing in her ears.

I'm late for a meeting. She heard Hades's voice in her head.

Late for a liaison, she thought bitterly.

Gods, I'm so stupid.

Had he been so angry with her he'd sought Leuce's comfort? And so publicly too. He must want to torture her. Months ago, he'd never allowed himself to be photographed, but suddenly, he was appearing on the front page of the *Divine*.

But she didn't just feel betrayed by Hades.

She felt betrayed by Leuce. After everything she'd done to help the nymph, this was how Leuce repaid her?

Persephone headed inside, the paper clutched in her fist. Helen looked up when she got off the elevator, and for the first time since she'd started at *New Athens News*, she didn't ask Persephone if she was okay.

The goddess stowed her stuff, including the paper. She wasn't sure why she wanted to keep it, maybe so she could shove it in Hades's face when she saw him again. Maybe because she liked torture. She turned on her computer and made coffee, her mind whirling with so many emotions she couldn't concentrate, and she felt like she was having hot flashes. One moment, she was angry; the next, she could barely keep her tears at bay.

At some point, she moved on to trying to rationalize the situation.

Maybe it was all a misunderstanding.

She knew the media could deceive. One photo only told part of the story.

She pulled out the paper again and studied the picture. Hades and Leuce looked determined, their expressions serious.

Because they knew they'd been caught, she thought.

What explanation would Hades give? Did she even want to hear it?

Her stomach was in knots, and the back of her throat felt swollen. She was going to vomit.

As she stood, there was a commotion up front, and Persephone looked in time to see Hades striding toward her. He appeared angry, purposeful, and he only had eyes for her.

"You need to leave," she said immediately. He was causing a scene. Everyone on the workroom floor had stopped what they were doing to watch them.

"We need to talk," he said.

His scent hit her hard, his presence harder. He was an executive of death, well dressed, handsome, and brooding.

"No."

"So you believe it then? The article?"

"I thought you had a meeting," she said.

"I did," he said.

"And you conveniently left out the fact that it was with Leuce?"

"It wasn't with Leuce, Persephone."

"I don't want to hear this right now. You need to leave," she said and stepped out from behind her desk. She started toward the elevator—she would escort him.

"When are we going to talk about this?" he asked.

"What is there to talk about? I have asked you to be honest with me about when you are with Leuce. You weren't."

She pressed the button to summon the elevator.

"I came to you immediately after I saw Leuce home," he said. "But I didn't feel good about waking you. When I saw you yesterday, you looked exhausted."

She twisted toward him, her eyes glistening. "I *am* exhausted, Hades. I'm *tired* of you and *sick* of your excuses." She pointed to the elevator doors as they opened. "Leave."

Hades glared at her, and without warning, he snatched her about the waist and shoved her into the elevator. His magic flared, and she knew he was keeping anyone from entering or using the lift.

"Let me go, Hades!" She wiggled against him, and he pressed her harder into the wall. "You're embarrassing me. Why did you have to do this now?"

"Because I knew you'd jump to conclusions."

She glared up at him, but his expression was just as fierce.

"I'm not fucking Leuce."

"There are other ways to cheat, Hades!" She pushed against his chest, but the god didn't move. He was solid rock, an immovable, frustrating mountain.

"I'm not doing any of them!"

She stared at his chest and tried not to cry.

"Persephone." Hades said her name, and she closed her eyes against the desperation in his voice. "Persephone, please."

"Let me go, Hades."

He was quiet for a long moment.

"If you won't listen now, will you let me explain later?"

"I don't know," she whispered.

"Please, Persephone. Give me the chance to explain."

"I'll let you know," she whispered, her voice thick with emotion.

"Persephone." He reached to brush her cheek, and she retreated from his touch, still not looking at him, which meant she didn't see the expression on his face before he vanished.

When he was gone, the elevator doors opened, and Persephone found the whole newsroom gathered in front of the doors.

"What the fuck are you all staring at?" she snapped.

"Persephone." Demetri was at the front of the group and jerked his thumb toward his office. "A moment."

Grudgingly, she obeyed his direction and followed him. Once the door was closed, her boss took a seat beside her instead of behind his desk.

"You don't have to tell me what's really going on," he said. "But you cannot act this way at work."

"What way?"

"The elevator, the profanity," he said.

"The elevator wasn't my fault—"

She didn't even want to imagine what people thought about the elevator. It was the dining room all over again.

Demetri held up his hand. "Look, I saw the *Divine* this morning. I know you're going through some stuff. Why don't you take the rest of the day off?"

"No, I'm fine. I need the distraction," she said.

"No, Persephone. You need to deal with your problems. Seriously. Leave."

Persephone obeyed, feeling dazed as she left Demetri's office, gathered her things, and headed to the first floor. She halted, seeing the crowd waiting outside. She couldn't face them or rehash what was in the paper today, so she entered the elevator again and chose to go to the basement.

She found Pirithous in the maintenance office. He sat at his desk, distracted by something in front of him.

"Hey," Persephone said.

Pirithous did a double take. Clearly, he hadn't expected to see her in the doorway of his office. He rushed to cover what he was working on, and Persephone rose on her tiptoes, curious.

"What are you up to?" she asked.

"Oh, nothing," he said and stood awkwardly. "Can I help you?"

He seemed nervous, rubbing his hands on his uniform, so she smiled.

"I need help," she said. "Can you get me out of here?"

"S-sure," he said. "You want the getaway vehicle again?"

"It's not my preferred method of escape, but if it's the only choice…"

He smiled, more at ease now. She wondered what had him on edge.

"I might have something better."

Pirithous grabbed his keys, shut off the light, and locked up before leading her to an unmarked door at the end of a hallway.

It was the entrance to an underground tunnel.

She glared at him.

"You made me get into a trash can when you knew this existed?"

Pirithous laughed. "I didn't have a key then."

"Oh," she said. "Well, in that case…"

"Come on." He gestured for her to enter, and Pirithous closed the door behind them. The tunnel was cement, cold, and lit by track lighting that made everything look pale green.

"Where does this lead?"

"Olive & Owl Gastropub in Monastiraki Square."

Pedestrian tunnels were common in New Athens, but Persephone had never been in one.

"Is there a reason it isn't open to the public?"

"Probably because the executives of the Acropolis don't want to share."

Huh. That makes sense.

"You're leaving work early today," Pirithous observed.

"I just need a mental health day," Persephone said. She didn't want to explain what was in the paper or that Hades had come to her work and caused a scene.

Luckily, Pirithous didn't press. He just nodded and said, "I understand that."

They walked in silence for a little while, and then Persephone asked, "What were you working on earlier?"

"A list," he answered. "Just some…supplies I need."

She thought about asking him what kind of supplies, but he didn't seem interested in talking about it. In truth, he seemed just as distracted as she felt.

Finally, they came to the end of the tunnel, and Pirithous unlocked the door.

"Thank you, Pirithous. I owe you."

He shook his head. "Haven't you learned anything about owing people?"

Those words hit her hard, and his question gave her pause, but the mortal was quick to change the subject.

"Be careful, Seph."

He closed the door, and she heard the lock click into place on the other side.

Persephone made her way through the Olive & Owl Gastropub, exiting into Monastiraki Square, a stone-covered courtyard with several pubs, coffee-houses, and a large church. The clouds had thick-ened in her time underground, and a light mist hung in the air, coating everything in a slick layer of rain. She shoved her hands in the pockets of her dress and headed to her apartment.

On the way, Persephone received a text message from Eliska that Lexa was awake. She changed directions and headed for the hospital instead.

She wasn't sure what she expected when she had imagined her reunion with Lexa, but when she laid eyes on her best friend, she knew she had let her hopes get too high.

Lexa looked exhausted. She was pale, and there were dark circles under her eyes. Her lips were chapped, and her dark hair was knotted, parts of it stuck to her face.

Then there were her eyes.

Unlike her body, they had not regained life, and when she met Persephone's gaze, there was no spark of recognition. Still, Persephone managed to smile, despite feeling something dark gather in the back of her mind.

Something is wrong.

"Hey, Lex," Persephone said quietly, approaching the bed. Lexa's brows drew together, and when she spoke, her voice was low and rasped.

"Why am I here?"

Persephone hesitated and glanced at Eliska for clarity.

"She's been saying that since she woke up," she explained. "The doctor says it's part of the psychosis."

"Why am I here?" Lexa repeated.

Eliska went to her and sat on the edge of her bed, taking her hand.

"You were in an accident, baby," she answered. "You were hurt really bad."

Lexa looked at her mom, but it was like she didn't recognize her either.

"No, *why am I here?*" Lexa's questioning was more aggressive, and her eyes became unfocused. "I'm not supposed to be here!"

Persephone could feel the color drain from her face. She knew what Lexa was saying. She wasn't asking why she was in the hospital; she was asking why she was in the Upperworld.

Eliska looked at Persephone and saw the desperation in her eyes. It was one thing to have Lexa back, another to handle the aftermath and impact of her trauma.

"I'll get the nurse," Eliska said. "That will give you some time alone with her."

"I'm not supposed to be here," Lexa repeated as her mother left the room.

Persephone sat on the end of her bed.

"Lexa," the goddess called her name.

It took her a moment, but Lexa finally lifted her head and met Persephone's gaze.

"You don't remember."

Lexa's eyes glistened with tears. "I was happy," she said.

"Yes, you were happy," Persephone said, hope ballooning in her chest. Maybe Lexa was remembering. "The happiest person I knew, and you were in love."

That gave Lexa pause and her brows knitted together. "No." She shook her head. "I was happy in the Underworld."

Persephone was stunned. That was the last thing she expected her to say.

"Why am I here?" Lexa asked again and again. "Why am I here? Why am I here? Why am I here?"

Her voice grew louder, and she started to rock, shaking the bed.

"Lexa, calm down."

"Why am I here?" she screamed.

Persephone stood. "Lexa—"

The door to her room burst open, and Eliska and two nurses hurried to subdue her. Lexa was screaming now—it was a sound Persephone had never heard her best friend make. She backed away from the scene until she reached the door, then fled.

Lexa's cries followed Persephone until she entered the elevator. She waited until the doors were closed to burst into tears.

"Are you happy with the results?"

Persephone whirled to face Apollo.

He was dressed in a gray suit and white button-up shirt, his dark hair a perfect mess of curls. He looked beautiful and cold all at the same time.

"You!" Persephone advanced on him. Apollo lifted a sharp brow and didn't move. She hated that he seemed so unafraid of her. "You said you'd heal her!"

"I did heal her. Obviously. She's awake."

"I don't know who that person is, but it isn't Lexa!"

Apollo shrugged, and his dismissal angered Persephone so much, vines began to sprout from her skin. She didn't even feel the pain.

Apollo looked disgusted. "Get a hold on your anger. You're making a mess."

"The deal is off, Apollo."

"I'm afraid it's not," he said, suddenly seeming far taller and imposing than before as he straightened and uncrossed his arms. "You asked me to heal her, and I did. What you failed to realize is that it wasn't just her body that was broken. Her soul was too, and that, I'm afraid, is your lover's wheelhouse, not mine."

It was like she was being told Lexa was going to die all over again.

She didn't know a lot about souls, didn't know what it meant to have a broken soul.

But she could guess.

It meant that she would never have the Lexa she knew before the accident.

It meant that nothing would be the same ever again.

It meant that she'd made a deal with Apollo for nothing.

She knew this was what Hades had meant.

Your actions have condemned Lexa to a fate worse than death.

It took a moment for Persephone to focus. "You really are the worst."

She turned on her heels and left the elevator as its doors opened. Apollo followed close behind.

"Just because you failed to recognize the flaws in your bargain doesn't make me a bad person."

"No, everything else you do makes you a bad person."

"You don't even know me," he argued.

"Your actions speak loud and clear, Apollo. I saw all I needed at the Lyre."

"There are two sides to every story, love nugget."

"Then by all means, tell me your side," she snapped.

"I don't need to explain myself to you."

"Then why do you keep talking?"

"Fine, I won't."

"Good."

There was silence as they crossed the main floor of the hospital and exited the building, then Apollo spoke again.

"You're trying to distract me from my purpose!"

"I thought you weren't talking," she complained and then asked, "What purpose?"

"I came to summon you," he said. "For a date."

"First, you don't summon someone for dates," she said. "Second, you and I aren't dating. You asked for a companion. That's it."

"Friends go on dates all the time," he argued.

"We're not friends."

"We are for six months. That's what you agreed to, honey lips."

Persephone glared. "Stop calling me names."

"I'm not calling you names."

"Love nugget? Honey lips?"

He grinned. "Pet names. I'm trying to find the right one."

"I don't want a pet name. I want to be called by *my* name."

Hermes had given her a nickname, and she'd come to think of it as endearing.

"Too bad. Part of the bargain, baby."

"No, it wasn't," she said.

"You missed it. It was in the fine print."

Persephone knew her eyes were glowing bright green.

"It's not an option, Apollo." She cut him off. "You will call me Persephone and nothing else. If I want to be addressed in another way, I'll tell you."

Apollo had a lot to learn about respecting people's wishes. She noted how his jaw ticked, and she wondered what he would do next.

"Fine," he said between his teeth. "But you will join me tonight. The Seven Muses. Be there at ten."

"Tonight really isn't a great night, Apollo."

She needed to go to the Underworld and hear Hades's explanation for why he was with Leuce, plus she needed to finalize preparations for the summer solstice celebration tomorrow night.

"I didn't ask you if the timing worked for you," the god replied. "I'm telling you to get ready. We have an event."

CHAPTER XXII
The Seven Muses

Persephone was in her closet, searching for something to wear. She groaned. "What am I supposed to wear to the Seven Muses?"

"Let me help," Hermes said. Taking Persephone's place in the closet, he assessed her wardrobe. "You know Apollo will be pissed when I show up with you," Hermes said.

Persephone had summoned him as soon as she got home. When she called his name, he'd appeared immediately and asked, "*Who do I need to kill, Sephy?*"

"*Your brother,*" she'd responded.

"*Ohh. Can I get a rain check?*"

She'd given him another option—accompanying her tonight.

"He never said I had to be alone."

Apollo was quick to point out where Persephone had failed when agreeing to their bargain, so she would do the same. She had no interest in being alone with the God of Music.

Hermes poked his head out of Persephone's closet.

"Does Hades know you're going out?"

"Why does everyone ask that?" Persephone complained. "He doesn't have to know every move I make."

Hermes raised his brows. "Triggered much? I'm only asking in case there's a possibility you run into him tonight."

"What does that have to do with what I wear?"

"It has everything to do with what you wear," Hermes said, disappearing into her closet again. After a moment, he reappeared. "I think you should wear this."

He held a dress that looked like a patchwork of strategically placed gold-leaf appliqués held together with air.

"Where did you get that?" she asked, because she knew she didn't own anything like it.

Hermes grinned. "Wouldn't you like to know?"

She narrowed her gaze. "Did you steal it?"

He'd probably teleported while he was in the closet.

"Just put it on," he said, laying it on the bed.

"I can't wear that, Hermes."

"Why not?"

"Because it will look like I'm wearing…nothing!"

"No, it won't. It will look like you're wearing strategically placed gold leaves."

She glared at him. "Did you miss the part where I have to go out with Apollo?"

"Did you miss the part when I asked about Hades?"

"You're just going to piss him off."

"You want Hades pissed off. Don't lie to me, Sephy. You're looking forward to hot makeup sex when you two reconcile." Hermes shoved the dress into Persephone's hands. "Now go."

She headed for the bathroom.

There was a part of her that wanted to make Hades jealous, especially after the whole Leuce situation.

She slipped into the dress. She was a little surprised by how perfectly it fit and stepped out of the bathroom to show Hermes, who whistled.

"That's the dress!"

"Let me get this straight. You want me to wear this in the event that I run into Hades tonight?"

Hermes shrugged. "There's always the possibility, but if you don't see him, you know there'll be pictures."

"I can't wear this," Persephone said. She started toward the bathroom again to change, but when she turned, Hermes was blocking the door.

"Look, you need to show Hades what he's missing."

"What if Apollo thinks I'm dressing up for him?"

Hermes snorted, and Persephone glared.

"Okay, okay. Look, Apollo's a lot of things, but he knows you belong to Hades. He might flirt with you, but he won't try anything. Despite what you think, he knows when he's in danger of losing his balls."

"If that were the case, he wouldn't have struck a bargain with me at all."

"Sephy, I have known Apollo for a long time. He's a lot of things—selfish and self-centered and rude—but he is also lonely."

"Well, maybe if he wasn't so selfish and self-centered and *rude,* he wouldn't be lonely."

"My point is, he wants a friend. And yeah, it's a little pathetic that he had to make bargains just to have friends, but in case you haven't noticed, Apollo doesn't know anything about genuine relationships. It's why he fucks up all his lovers."

334

"He doesn't even try to get better."

"Because he doesn't have to. He's a god."

"That isn't an excuse."

"And yet it is still an excuse."

"You aren't like him."

"No, but have you ever considered that I am in the minority? Most of the Divine are just like Apollo. He was just unlucky to catch your wrath."

"You make it sound like I did something wrong."

"Feeling guilty?"

"No. Of course not. Apollo needed to answer for his behavior."

"And how did that work out for you?"

It hadn't.

"I'm not saying what you did was right or wrong. What I am saying is it isn't the way to get Apollo to listen to you."

"Then what do you suggest?"

He shrugged. "Just…be his friend."

Persephone wanted to laugh. She didn't like Apollo. He had hurt people—Sybil, specifically. He had deceived her, healing Lexa while knowing her soul was still broken. How was she supposed to be friends with someone like that?

As if Hermes guessed her thoughts, he added, "People like Apollo are broken, Sephy."

"Apollo's not a person."

"And yet he, like all of us, suffers human flaws." Switching gears, Hermes clapped his hands together. "Now, what shall I wear?"

Hermes decided on all-white attire—a silky shirt, jeans, and shiny shoes. Just as they were about to leave, Zofie burst into the room.

"Where do you think you're going?" she demanded.

"How did you know we were going anywhere?" Persephone asked. She'd told Zofie she was going to bed when she'd gotten home.

"I was listening at the door," the Amazon said.

"Okay, we're going to have to make a rule about that," Persephone said.

"And we're going to be late." Hermes took Persephone's hand. "So if you don't mind…"

Zofie drew her blade. "Release her or feel my wrath!"

Hermes laughed. "Where did you get her?"

Persephone sighed. "Zofie, put that away."

"Wherever you go, I must go too, Lady Persephone." She glared at Hermes. "To protect you."

Hermes was still laughing. "She knows I'm a god, right?"

Persephone elbowed him. "Help Zofie find something to wear. She's coming with us."

———

When they appeared outside the Seven Muses, people screamed their names.

Persephone glared at Hermes as they were ushered inside by two centaurs.

"You just had to let the world know we were here, didn't you?"

He grinned. "How else is Hades supposed to know about the dress?"

She elbowed the god again.

"Ouch! You're violent tonight, Sephy. I'm only trying to help."

They barely made it inside the club when their way

was blocked by Apollo. The god glared at Hermes. "What are you doing here?"

"I was invited," the God of Trickery said.

Apollo's gaze moved to Zofie. "An Amazon?"

Zofie glared at him, and Persephone had a feeling the Amazon hadn't forgiven him for abducting Persephone.

"She's my aegis," Persephone said. "Her name is Zofie." He frowned, and Persephone smirked as she said, "You never said I couldn't bring a friend."

He rolled his eyes and sighed.

"Come. I have a booth."

Apollo twisted, and the three followed. Persephone noted that the God of Music had chosen black leather pants and a mesh shirt as his club attire. Beneath the mesh, the contours of his muscles were visible. He was chiseled and athletic. She found herself comparing him to Hades again. Hades, whose body seemed to be built to destroy, with broad shoulders and large muscles.

Apollo's table was more like a lounge. White couches faced each other, and sheer, white curtains provided a small amount of privacy. The air was clouded with smoke and laser lights—something they did not escape, even in their booth.

The God of Music collapsed dramatically on one of the couches, his arms draping over the back, one leg resting on a cushion.

Persephone, Hermes, and Zofie all sat beside each other. The goddess felt uncomfortable in her revealing dress and sat with her back straight, hands on her knees.

"So how long have you known each other?" Apollo raised a pale brow, looking between her and his brother. He sounded frustrated.

"Oh, we've been friends forever," said Hermes, then he downed a shot of whatever was on the table. "Yum, you should try this."

He tried giving Zofie one of the drinks, but the Amazon's glare caused him to reconsider.

"Never mind," he said and took another shot.

"He means six months," Persephone said. "Hermes and I have known each other for six months."

"Seven," the God of Trickery corrected. "I pulled her out of a river and got thrown across the Underworld for my trouble." He looked at Persephone. "That's when I knew Hades was in love with you, by the way."

Persephone looked away, and an awkward silence descended between them, or maybe Persephone was just feeling out of place because Hermes began to chuckle beside her.

"Remember when you served mortals, Apollo?" he asked.

Apollo did not look amused. "Well, who taught Pandora to be curious, Hermes?"

The God of Trickery glared. "Why does everyone always bring that up?"

"One could argue you are responsible for all the world's evil." A smile pulled at Apollo's lips. It was actually...charming.

"Who put evil in a box anyway?" Persephone asked. "That seems stupid."

The brothers exchanged a look. "Our father."

Persephone rolled her eyes.

Power wasn't a replacement for intelligence.

After a couple of shots, Hermes dragged Persephone and Zofie to the dance floor. The music had an electronic beat and vibrated through her. For a while, they all danced together. Even Zofie, who had been on edge, loosened up, letting herself get swept into the fold of bodies.

Persephone continued to move. She shook and shimmied, matching Hermes's movements until his attention was taken by a handsome man who sidled up behind him.

Persephone cheered him on but found herself face-to-face with Apollo. He wasn't dancing, just standing in the center of the crowd, staring at her.

"So you were afraid to be alone with me?" Apollo asked.

"I am not afraid to be alone with you. I just didn't *want* to be alone with you."

"Why?"

"Why?" she asked, dumbfounded by the question. "Do you not understand what you put me through? You almost killed a *kid*!"

"He spoke slander—"

"This isn't the ancient world, Apollo. People are going to disagree with you, and you're going to have to deal with it. For fuck's sake, I don't even like your music."

Persephone's eyes widened. Had she just said that out loud?

Apollo pressed his lips together tightly, and after a moment, he said, "Wanna shot?"

"Are you going to poison it?"

Again, he offered that crooked smile.

They left the dance floor and headed for the bar, ordering a round.

Apollo downed his shot, slamming his glass on the counter, and looked at Persephone.

"So how did your lover take the news of our bargain?"

Persephone stared at the empty glass. "Not well. I guess I can't blame him."

She'd promised Hades a lot and had let him down.

"I think he hates me," she said, so quietly she didn't think Apollo could hear.

"Hades doesn't hate you," Apollo almost scoffed. "He doesn't have it in him."

"You didn't see the way he looked at me."

"You mean all broken?" Apollo asked. "I think I get it, Persephone."

She blinked at him.

"He's just hurt and frustrated. We all have things that are important to us—things we value above others. Hades values trust. He values the process of earning trust. He feels like he failed."

Persephone frowned. "How do you know that?"

"The Olympians have had a long history. We know each other in ways that would make you cringe—inside and out."

Persephone shivered.

"Hades doesn't feel worthy without trust. He needs you to believe in him, to find strength in him."

Persephone frowned. She knew Hades had a difficult time feeling worthy of his people's worship, but she never thought he would have the same difficulty feeling worthy of her love.

What had happened to him over his many lifetimes?

"What happened to you?" Persephone asked Apollo. "No one does what you do without…some sort of trauma."

It took Apollo a long time to speak, but he finally

answered. "He was a Spartan prince. Hyacinth. He was beautiful. Admired and pursued by many gods, but he chose me." He swallowed. "He chose me."

Apollo paused and then began again.

"We hunted and climbed mountains. I taught him to use a bow and the lyre. One day, I was teaching him quoit." Quoit was one of the games played during the Panhellenic Games. It involved throwing a heavy metal disc. "Hyacinth liked to challenge me and wanted to compete. He knew I wouldn't deny him—or a chance to win. I threw first. I didn't think about the strength behind the toss. He went to catch the disc, but there was too much power behind my throw, and it bounced off the ground and hit him in the head."

Apollo's chest rose with a deep inhale. "I tried to save him. I'm the fucking God of Healing. I should have been able to heal him, but each time my magic worked to close his wound, it opened again. I held him until he died."

His voice trembled now.

"I hated Hades for a long time after that. I blamed him for what the Fates had taken from me. I blamed him for refusing to let me see Hyacinth. I...I did some unfor-givable things in the aftermath of Hyacinth's death. It's why Hades hates me, and honestly, I don't blame him."

"Apollo," Persephone whispered. Hesitantly, she placed a hand on his arm. "I'm so sorry for your loss."

He shrugged a shoulder. "It was a long time ago."

"That doesn't make it any less painful."

While this didn't excuse Apollo's actions, she under-stood him a little better. He'd been broken a long, long time ago, and since then, he'd been searching for ways to feel whole.

"Another round!" he called to the bartender, who was quick to comply. Apollo handed Persephone a shot.

"Cheers," he said.

Things were a blur after the last shot. Persephone's head swam, her words slurred, and everything was funny. She danced with Apollo until her feet hurt, until the lights stung her eyes, until sweat beaded off her skin. When the perspiration turned cold, she suddenly didn't feel well and stumbled off the floor, running into something hard.

"Oh, hi, Hermes."

He frowned. "Are you okay?"

She responded by vomiting on the floor.

Her next lucid moment was when she found herself lying on the couch in Apollo's booth, a blurry Hades casting a shadow over her.

He looked impassive, and that hurt more than she anticipated.

"Why did you call him?" she asked Hermes. "He hates me."

"Blame Zofie," Hermes said.

Hades knelt beside her. "Can you stand? I'd rather not carry you out of this place."

Another blow. She sat up. Hades tried to hand her water, but she pushed it away.

"If you don't want to be seen with me, why don't you teleport?"

"If I teleport, you might throw up. I've been told you've already done that once tonight."

He didn't sound pleased.

She got to her feet. It took a moment for the world to stop spinning, and she swayed into Hades, who was quick to embrace her.

The feel of him against her skin was like a sexual experience. It made her quake to her very core. It made her hot all over. It made her want to moan his name.

She was being ridiculous.

She pushed away from him.

"Let's go."

She led the way outside where Hades's black Lexus waited. Antoni offered his crooked smile when he saw her.

"My lady."

"Antoni," she said and breezed past him, climbing into the back of Hades's car on her hands and knees. Hades followed close behind. She knew because she could smell him—spice and ash and sin.

She'd never considered the smell of sin before, but now she knew it for what it was—sultry and sexual. It filled her lungs, ignited her blood.

They sat in silence on the way home, the air thick with warring emotions. Persephone was busy building a wall against whatever Hades was feeling—it was dark. She could feel it twisting toward her, like the tendrils of his magic.

She was so relieved when they arrived at Nevernight, she opened the door before Antoni was out of his seat. As she exited, she missed the curb and fell, her knee striking the concrete hard.

"My lady!" Antoni cried. He reached for her arm, but she pushed it away.

"I'm fine."

She rolled over and sat. Her knee was a mess, and pieces of dirt stuck to the blood. Hades stood beside Antoni, and they stared down at her.

"It's okay. I don't even feel it."

She tried to stand, but her head was pretty fuzzy, and she was aware she was slurring some of her words. She hated that she was in this state.

She blew out a long breath. "You know, I think I'll just sit here for a little while."

Hades said nothing, but this time, he scooped her up into his arms and carried her into Nevernight.

The club was empty, which told her it was later than she had originally thought. She expected him to teleport to the Underworld, but instead he carried her down the stairs, across the floor, and to the bar. When he sat her down, it was on the edge of the table. He turned and started to work.

"What are you doing?"

Hades handed her a glass of water. "Drink."

She did. This time, she was thirsty.

While she drank, Hades shed his jacket and filled another glass of water. He cleaned her wounded knee, washing away the dirt and blood. After, he covered it with his hand, and his warmth healed.

"Thank you," she whispered.

Hades stepped back, leaning against the counter opposite her. She had to admit, she didn't like the distance. It was like he still had a hold of her heart and was stretching it as he moved.

"Are you punishing me?" Hades asked.

"What?"

"This," he said, pointing to her. "The clothes, Apollo, the drinking?"

She frowned and looked down at her dress.

"You don't like my clothes?"

He glared at her, and for some reason, that made

her angry. She pushed off the counter and shimmied the dress up over her hips.

"What are you doing?" Hades asked. His eyes glinted, but she couldn't tell if he was amused or aroused.

"Taking off the dress."

"I can see that. Why?"

"Because you don't like it."

"I didn't say I didn't like it," he replied.

Still, he didn't stop her.

The dress was off. She stood naked in front of him.

Hades's eyes raked her frame.

Gods.

Her whole body tingled, like her skin was a collection of exposed nerves. Her fingers itched to touch, to pleasure—either herself or him, she really didn't care.

"Why weren't you wearing anything under that dress?"

"I couldn't," she said. "Didn't you see it?"

Hades's jaw ticked.

"I'm going to murder Apollo," he said, mostly under his breath.

"Why?"

"For fun." His voice was gruff, and Persephone giggled.

"You're jealous."

"Don't push me, Persephone."

"It wasn't like Apollo knew," she said, watching Hades drink straight from a whiskey bottle he'd retrieved from the wall. "Hermes was the one who suggested it."

The bottle shattered. One moment, it was whole in Hades's hands, and the next moment, glass and alcohol covered the floor at Hades's feet.

"Motherfucker."

345

Persephone wasn't sure if the curse was from what she'd said about Hermes or the whiskey he'd just wasted.

"Are you okay?" she asked quietly.

"Forgive me if I am a little on edge. I have been forced into celibacy."

Persephone rolled her eyes. "No one ever said you couldn't fuck me."

"Careful, Goddess," his voice rumbled, deep and terrifying. It was the voice he used when he punished. "You don't know what you're asking."

"I think I know what I'm asking for, Hades. It's not like we've never had sex."

He didn't move, but he tilted his head a little, and her body tightened, knowing whatever he was about to ask would make her body quiver.

"Are you wet for me?"

She was, he knew it, and his restraint was pissing her off. She tilted her head and challenged, "Why don't you come and find out?"

She waited, and Hades's chest rose and fell quickly, his knuckles turning white as he grasped the counter behind him. When he didn't move, she decided she'd just bring up Apollo—it was what he deserved.

"Why didn't you let Apollo see Hyacinth after his death?"

"You really know how to kill a boner, darling, I'll give you that."

The god turned back to the array of liquor and found another bottle. Persephone crossed her arms over her chest, the buzz from the alcohol wearing off. She suddenly no longer felt like being naked. She reached for Hades's jacket. As she slipped it on, it swallowed her.

"He said he blamed you for his death."

"He did." Hades response was short. "Much like you blamed me for Lexa's accident."

"I never said I blamed you," she argued.

"You blamed me because I couldn't help. Apollo did the same."

Persephone pressed her lips together and took a breath. "I'm not...trying to fight with you. I just want to know your side."

Hades considered this as he took a drink from the bottle. She couldn't tell what it was—but it wasn't whiskey.

Finally, he spoke. "Apollo didn't ask to see his lover. He asked to die."

Persephone's eyes widened. That wasn't what she'd expected Hades to say.

"Of course it was a request I could not—would not—grant."

"I don't understand. Apollo knows he cannot die. He is immortal. Even if you were to wound him..."

"He wished to be thrown into Tartarus. To be torn to pieces by the Titans. It is the only way to kill a god."

Persephone shivered.

"He was outraged, of course, and took his revenge in the only way he knows how—he slept with Leuce."

Things were falling into place.

"Why didn't you tell me?" Persephone demanded.

"I tend to want to forget that part of my life, Persephone."

"But I—I wouldn't have—"

"You already broke a promise you made. I doubt my story of betrayal would have prevented you from seeking Apollo's help."

She didn't know what to say to that—his words were harsh but warranted. She flinched and hugged herself a little tighter. She wasn't sure if Hades noticed her reaction or decided he was finished with this conversation, but he pushed away from the bar and said, "You are probably tired. I can take you to the Underworld or Antoni will see you home."

She studied him for a long moment and then asked, "What do you want?"

What she was really asking was: *Do you want me?*

"It is not my decision to make."

She looked away, swallowing a lump in her throat, but Hades's voice drew her back.

"But since you asked…I always want you with me. Even when I'm angry."

"Then I'll come with you."

He drew her close, his arm a hook around her waist. She braced herself against his biceps as their middles touched and their eyes held. She wanted to kiss him—it wouldn't take much. They were already so close, but she was hesitant—she had vomited earlier and still felt disgusting. On top of that, Hades didn't move closer, and the pain that pulled at his features kept her frozen and hardened her own heart.

She still had a whole night to go, sleeping beside him.

This was going to be rough.

CHAPTER XXIII
The Solstice Celebration

Persephone woke up alone.

She ignored the way her chest tightened as she rose to get ready. Once she was dressed, she found Hecate in the palace ballroom, instructing souls, nymphs, and daimons in their tasks as they prepared for the solstice celebration tonight.

When Persephone arrived, Hecate smiled, and several voices erupted all at once.

"My lady, you've arrived!"

There was so much excitement and energy in the room, Persephone couldn't stay sullen.

"I hope you haven't waited long," she said.

"I was just finishing assigning tasks," Hecate said.

"Great. What can I do?"

Persephone saw the hesitation on Hecate's face.

"Of course, you should supervise."

Persephone frowned. "I'd like to help," she said and looked at the people gathered in the room. "Surely some of you could use an extra set of hands?"

At first, she was met with silence, and then Yuri spoke up. "Of course, my lady. We'd be happy to have your assistance with the flower arrangements!"

Persephone grinned. "Thank you, Yuri. I would like that very much."

Not to mention she needed a distraction—anything to keep her mind off the last few weeks.

"Let's get to work!" Hecate called, and the crowd dispersed.

Persephone worked with a group in the ballroom, making floral arrangements, garlands, and floral crowns from flowers the souls had picked from the gardens of the Underworld.

"You are quieter than usual," Hecate said, coming to work beside Persephone. She trimmed leaves from stems while Persephone arranged them in a large urn.

"Am I?"

She'd been so engrossed in her work, she hadn't paid much attention to what was going on around her.

"Not just today," Hecate said. "You haven't been to the Underworld for days."

Persephone froze for a moment and then continued with her project. She didn't know what to say—was she supposed to apologize? Her eyes blurred with tears, and before she knew it, Hecate was leading her out of the ballroom, down the hall, and into Hades's library.

"What's wrong, my dear?" Hecate asked, guiding Persephone to sit and kneeling before her.

"I messed up terribly."

"I'm sure it is nothing that can't be fixed."

"I'm sure it cannot," Persephone said. "I have made so many mistakes, Hecate. I have destroyed my best friend's life, bargained with a terrible god, and sacrificed my relationship with Hades."

"That is a lot." Hecate's words made Persephone feel even more miserable. "But I think it is not true."

"Of course, it's true." She stared at Hecate, confused by the goddess.

"Did you strike Lexa with a car?" Hecate asked.

Persephone shook her head.

"You did not ruin your best friend's life," she said. "The mortal driving that car did."

"But she's not the same—"

"She's not the same. Even if she had recovered on her own without Apollo's magic, she wouldn't have been the same. You have bargained with a god, yes—terrible?" Hecate shrugged. "If anyone can help Apollo become more compassionate, it's you, Persephone."

She wasn't sure about that, but after learning about Apollo's past, she knew she wanted to do something for him. Maybe if she showed him kindness, he would learn kindness toward others.

"Compassion or not, it doesn't change how Hades thinks of me now. He does not trust me, nor does he think I trust him."

"Hades trusts you," Hecate said. "He gave you his heart."

"I am sure he regrets that decision."

"You cannot be sure of anything unless you ask, Persephone. It is more unfair to assume you know Hades's feelings."

Persephone considered this. She'd wanted to ask him a lot of things yesterday, but fear and embarrassment kept her from it.

"And I have a feeling our dark ruler hasn't been all that fair to you."

Persephone wasn't sure if fair was the right word.

"He has been honest about how angry he is with me."

"Which is probably why you want to avoid him. I would. No one likes Hades when he's angry."

Persephone laughed a little.

"My point is you both have a lot to learn from this. If you want this relationship to work, you must be honest. It doesn't matter if your words sting. They're important."

She had a lot of words.

"Do not worry, my dear." Hecate rose to her feet, bringing Persephone with her. "All will be well."

Before they left the library, Persephone paused. "Hecate, do you know how to find a soul in the Underworld?"

Hecate smiled. "No, but I know who does."

Persephone and Hecate returned to the ballroom and finished up their floral arrangements. After, they made their way to the kitchens where Milan, a daimon, and a staff of several souls who had been chefs in previous lives worked on the solstice feast. Milan insisted they try an assortment of jams, preserves, grapes, figs, pomegranates, blackberries, pears, and dates. There were cured meats and various cheeses, crackers and fresh herbs.

"My lady Persephone...do you happen to have the recipe for that sweet bread you made?" Milan asked.

It took her a moment to understand what Milan was talking about. "Oh, you mean the cake!"

"Whatever it was, it was delicious," Hecate said. "And almost started a war."

Persephone laughed. She'd baked the cake, left it to cool overnight, and completely forgotten about it.

"It's very easy, Milan. I'll teach you."

The daimon grinned, and Persephone spent the rest of the afternoon baking in the kitchen until Hecate pulled her away to get ready for the festivities.

They hung out in Hades's bedchamber. Hecate's nymphs, lampades, worked Persephone's hair into smooth curls, then braided pieces, sculpting part of it into a half-up style. Her makeup was darker than usual. A shimmering black shadow and thick liner made her eyes appear wider and more open; the color also brightened her irises. A burgundy lip completed the look.

As she watched herself transform in the mirror, she was reminded of the evenings she and Lexa had spent getting ready for events. Persephone hadn't grown up around mortals, so when she'd come to New Athens University, she'd had no experience with makeup or fashion. Lexa had shown her the ropes, and she'd been amazing at it.

Is amazing at it, Persephone corrected herself.

Lexa *was* alive.

Except that Persephone almost felt as though Lexa might as well be gone. The person sitting in that hospital room looked like her best friend but didn't act like her.

Persephone's eyes watered, and she took a breath, looking toward the ceiling. The lampades sensed her distress and patted her face and hair.

"I'm alright," she whispered. "Just thinking about something sad."

"Perhaps this will take your mind off it," Hecate said, entering Hades's chamber.

Persephone turned in her seat as the Goddess of Witchcraft approached with a long white box. Inside was a beautiful gown. It was black with gold accents. The sleeves were off the shoulder, long, but split, giving the illusion of a cape.

"Oh, Hecate. It's beautiful," Persephone said, twisting in front of the mirror after she'd put it on.

The dress wasn't the only surprise Hecate had for her. She stood behind Persephone and moved as if she were placing something on her head. As she did, a crown appeared between her hands. It was iron and jagged, and it gleamed with shining obsidian, black pearls, and diamonds. Upon Persephone's head, it resembled a dark halo, ignited against her bright hair.

"You look beautiful," Hecate said.

"Thank you," Persephone breathed.

She didn't recognize herself in the mirror, and she wasn't sure what was different—the crown, the dress, the makeup, or something else? A lot of things had happened in the last month, and she felt the weight of them on her shoulders, on her chest, settling at the bottom of her stomach.

"Has Hades arrived?"

"I am sure he will come later," Hecate said.

Persephone met her friend's gaze in the mirror. She wanted Hades. They didn't even need to talk; she just wanted his presence for comfort.

"Come. The souls have a surprise for you."

Hecate reached for Persephone's hand, and they left Hades's chamber. The lampades followed, zipping away to take their place outside.

The palace was decorated throughout. The bouquets of flowers Persephone and the others had arranged brought life to the shadow. Banquet tables were crowded with food and candlelight. The smells were mouthwatering. The French doors in the ballroom were open and led to the courtyard, where a fire blazed and the souls had erected a maypole.

As Persephone stepped outside, the souls and daimons and nymphs cheered.

Yuri ran forward, taking Persephone's hands.

"Persephone! Come. The children have a surprise for you!"

Yuri led her away from the stone courtyard to the springy grass where the lampades had gathered in a circle. Souls followed behind them.

Persephone was surprised when Yuri directed her to a throne that sat at the top of the circle. Unlike Hades's, it was a chair made of gold. The metal had been shaped into flowers, and the cushions were white.

"Yuri, I am not—"

"You might not be queen by title, but the souls call you their queen."

"That does not mean I should wear a crown or sit upon a throne in the Underworld."

"Do this for them, Persephone," Yuri pleaded. "It is part of the surprise."

"Okay," Persephone said, nodding. "For the souls."

She took a seat, and Yuri clapped her excitement.

After a moment, children from the Underworld appeared from the darkness, wandering into the circle of light, dressed in colorful clothing. They began their performance by stomping their feet and clapping their hands in unison. The effect was musical, increasing in tempo the longer they went. Soon, their voices joined the clapping and stomping, and they began to move about, creating different lines and shapes with their bodies. By the end of the performance, Persephone was clapping along and smiling so wide, her face hurt.

The children grinned, bowing to the applause.

Then a flute began to play, and the children started to sing, their voices rising and falling in a haunting melody. The song they sang was the tale of the Lethe, the river of forgetfulness, and told of a woman who drank from its waters and forgot the love of her life. When the song ended, a hard knot settled at the back of Persephone's throat. She stood as she clapped, and the children ran to her, hugging her legs.

"Thank you," she told them. "You were all so wonderful!"

After the children's performance, the real festival began, and the residents dispersed. Some danced and played instruments while others played games—races, disc tosses, and jumping competitions. A group headed inside the ballroom to eat, and the children gathered around the maypole.

"Persephone!" Leuce approached, throwing her arms around the goddess's neck, a glass of wine in hand.

"Leuce, I'm so glad you could make it."

The nymph drew back. "Thank you for inviting me. This is truly amazing. I've never seen the Underworld so vibrant. Drink," she said, handing Persephone the wine she held. "The wine tastes like strawberries and summer."

Leuce twirled away, disappearing into the crowd of souls.

"Well, don't you look like the Queen of the Underworld," Hermes said, appearing out of thin air.

"Hermes!" She threw her arms around him. "I'm so glad you're here!"

Persephone smiled at the God of Trickery. He was dressed like an ancient god—gold armor and a leather skirt. His sandals wrapped around his strong calves, a circlet of laurel leaves crowned his head, and his white-feathered wings draped his body like a lush cloak.

"Wouldn't miss it for the world, Sephy," he said and then winked, holding up a bottle of wine he'd swiped from the ballroom. "The wine helps. Where's your brooding lover? He wasn't too angry with you, I hope?"

At the mention of Hades, Persephone was reminded that the God of the Underworld still hadn't made an appearance. She frowned.

"I'm not sure where he is. He left before I woke."

"Uh-oh. Don't tell me, Sephy. No makeup sex?"

When had talking about sex become a regular conversation between her and Hermes?

"No."

"I'm sorry, Sephy," Hermes said and then poured more wine into her cup. "Drink up, gorgeous. You're going to need it."

But Persephone didn't feel like drinking, and soon, Hermes was distracted.

"Nemesis!" Hermes yelled when he glimpsed the Goddess of Divine Retribution and Revenge. "I have a bone to pick with you!"

Persephone tried not to laugh. Hearing Hermes use mortal idioms was hilarious. She started to turn when she noticed Apollo. He must have just arrived, as she was certain she would have sensed his menacing presence before now. He felt like static in the air.

He wore red robes, secured by embellished gold leaves. She'd never seen his horns before, but tonight, they were on full display. In total, he had four, a set of two, curling on each side of his face. They almost looked like a helm worn during battle.

She smiled at him and approached.

"Last time I checked, I was the one who was supposed to do the summoning," he said.

"I didn't summon you," Persephone said. "I invited you. You didn't have to come."

Apollo's jaw tensed.

"But I'm glad you did," she added, and the god's brows rose. "Come. I'd like you to meet someone."

She led Apollo outside where the maypole was raised and the dead danced. It took her a moment, but she finally found him standing with a crowd of souls: Hyacinth, the young man Apollo loved. He was well-muscled and beautiful, with a swath of golden hair. When he smiled, his teeth gleamed; when he laughed, it was like music. She knew when Apollo saw him, because he stiffened beside her.

"Go to him, Apollo," she said.

He hesitated and paled. "Does he remember…?"

"He still loves you," she said. "And he has forgiven you."

She was surprised when Apollo looked at her with a severe expression on his face.

"Why?" he demanded.

She blinked. "What?"

"Why would you do this for me?" he asked. "I have been so unkind to you."

"Everyone deserves kindness, Apollo."

Especially those who hurt others, she thought but didn't say.

"Go," she encouraged. "You don't have much time, and you must make the most of it."

Still he stared at her, as if he couldn't figure her out.

After a moment, he turned and took a deep breath, set his shoulders, and strolled toward Hyacinth. The young soul did a double take, and his expression melted into shock when he spotted the God of Music approaching. He put his drink down and threw his arms around Apollo's neck, drawing him close. When their lips met, Persephone felt a pang in her chest—a reminder of how much she missed Hades.

She shook her head and wandered from the courtyard into the gardens. She hoped to spend a few minutes alone but stumbled upon a shadowy figure, startling her.

"Thanatos," she breathed, her heart calming. "You startled me."

"I am sorry. That was not my intention."

She frowned. She hadn't seen the God of Death since she'd yelled at him in the hospital. She could feel a difference in the air between them. Once friendly, it was now tender.

"What are you doing out here?"

"Enjoying the revelry," he answered. He wasn't looking at her as he spoke, his eyes on the maypole ahead, illuminated by the nymphs' light.

"Why don't you join them?" she asked.

Thanatos's smile was sad. "I am not made for merriment, my lady."

She frowned. "Please call me Persephone, Thanatos."

He bowed his head. "Right. I'm sorry."

"No, *I'm sorry,*" she said. "There is no excuse for how I treated you. I can…scarcely believe it myself."

"It's okay, Persephone. I'm used to it."

She winced. "It pains me to know that. I wish it weren't so. You deserve better, especially from a friend."

Thanatos met her gaze, smiling. "Thank you, Persephone."

They stood together for a while, watching the residents of the Underworld celebrate.

At some point, Persephone reentered the palace. She roamed from room to room, looking for Hades. The more time that passed without his presence, the more frustrated she became. How could he not come to a celebration in his own realm? Not only was it important to his people, it was important to her. She'd helped plan it, and he knew it was happening tonight. *What was keeping him?*

The party neared its end with no sign of Hades. Unable to rest, she waited up for him.

And waited.

And waited.

It was close to five in the morning before he returned. His presence was familiar, and unlike previous times when he had inspired need within her, she felt cold.

When Hades entered the room, she turned to face him. His dark gaze assessed her from head to toe. She hadn't removed the crown Ian had made for her or the dress Hecate had crafted. Hades did not comment on her ensemble. Instead, he said, "I did not think you would be awake."

"Where were you?"

"I had a few things to take care of."

Persephone's fingers fisted. "Were these things more important than your realm?"

Hades's brows lowered. "You are angry that I was not at your party."

So he didn't forget.

"Yes, I am angry. You should have been there."

"The dead celebrate everything, Persephone. I won't miss the next one."

"If that is your view, I'd rather you not come at all."

Hades seemed surprised by her comment. "Then what do you want from me?"

"I don't fucking care how much they celebrate. What's important to them should be important to you. What's important to me should be important to you."

"Persephone—"

"Don't," she cut him off. "I understand you don't know what I don't tell you, but I expect you to be aware of what I am planning and show interest—not only for me but for your people. You never once asked about the solstice celebration, not even after I asked you for permission to host it in the courtyard."

"I'm sorry."

"You aren't," she snapped. "You are only saying that to appease me, and I *hate* it. Is this why you want a queen? So you don't have to attend these events?"

"No, I wanted *you*," he said, a hint of frustration in his voice. "And because of that, I wished to make you my queen. There are no ulterior motives."

But she hadn't missed that everything he'd just said was in the past.

She narrowed her eyes.

"Look, Hades. If you don't…want this anymore, I need to know."

Hades's head jerked, and he stared at her. "What?"

Obviously, she wasn't making sense. "If you don't want me—if you don't think you can forgive me, I don't think we should be in a relationship, the Fates be damned."

It was the first time Hades moved since he'd entered the room.

He took deliberate strides toward her and spoke as he moved.

"I never said I didn't want you. I thought I made that clear yesterday."

She rolled her eyes. "So you want to fuck me? That doesn't mean you want an actual relationship. It doesn't mean you will trust me again."

Hades stopped inches from her and narrowed his eyes. "Let me be perfectly clear. I do want to fuck you. More importantly, I love you—deeply, endlessly. If you walked away from me today, I would love you still. I will love you forever. That's what Fate is, Persephone. Fuck threads and colors…and fuck your uncertainty."

He bent closer to her as he spoke, his face inches from hers.

"I'm not uncertain," she said. "I'm afraid, you idiot!"

"Of what? What have I done?"

"This isn't about you! Gods, Hades. You'd think you of all people would understand."

She turned her head away, unable to look at him.

After a moment, Hades spoke again, urging, "Tell me."

Persephone's mouth quivered. "I've longed for love all my life," she said. "Longed for acceptance because my mother dangled it in front of me like something I had to earn. If I adhered to her expectations, she would grant it; if I didn't, she'd take it away. You want a queen,

362

a goddess, a lover. I can't be what you want. I can't...
adhere to these...*expectations* you have of me!"

There was something freeing about saying all that
out loud. She suddenly felt lighter, like she'd let go of a
boulder she'd been carrying on her back.

"Persephone—" Hades's fingers pressed beneath her
chin. She met his gaze. "What do you think of when
you think of a queen?"

Persephone's brows knitted together, and she shook
her head as she admitted, "I don't know. I know what I
would like to see in a queen."

"Then what would you like to see in a queen?"

"Someone who is kind...compassionate...*present*."

Hades's thumb brushed her lips. "And you do not
think you are all those things?"

She didn't answer, and Hades said, "I'm not asking
you to be a queen. I'm asking you to be yourself. I'm
asking you to marry me. The title comes with our
marriage. It changes nothing."

Persephone swallowed. "Are you asking me to marry
you again?"

"Will you?"

Her breath caught in her throat. She couldn't answer.
For the last few weeks, she and Hades hadn't exactly
been on speaking terms. They had too much to reconcile. Her eyes watered, and tears streaked her face. Hades
brushed them away.

"My darling, you do not have to answer now. We
have time—an eternity."

Their lips met—their kiss sinful and rough and
desperate. Persephone felt feverish and frenzied. The
adrenaline made her bold, and she reached into his

pants, working his cock with her hand. Hades groaned, his teeth skimming her bottom lip as he pulled away to explore her jaw and neck and breasts.

He looked stunned when she pushed him away. They stood apart for a moment, breathing hard, hot and wet and wild. Then Persephone planted a hand on his chest and directed him backward until the back of his knees hit the bed.

"Sit," she commanded, removing her crown and setting it aside.

Hades obeyed, and she held his gaze as she knelt before him. His eyes glittered like obsidian.

"You look like a fucking queen," he said.

A corner of her mouth lifted. "I am your queen."

She wrapped her hand around his length and stroked him from root to tip, her thumb moving lightly over the head of his cock.

"*Persephone.*"

He growled her name, and she took him into her mouth. Hades moaned, his fingers twining into her hair. She took him deep—to the back of her throat, and then into the side of her cheek. She paused to lick and suck, reveling in the taste of him.

"Yes," he hissed. She could feel him growing thicker, pulsing, and when he came, she drank from him like she had never tasted anything so sweet. Hades drew her to her feet—he kissed her, possessed and paralyzed her. He left her dress in a puddle on the floor and guided her to his bed, divesting himself of his own clothes before covering her body.

He was warm and solid, and he fit against her like he was made for every contour of her. As he loomed over her, she reached up and drew a piece of his silken hair around her finger.

"Why do you wish to be married?"

Hades's brow rose; clearly the question amused him. "Haven't you always dreamed of marriage?"

"No," she said, and she was being honest. She had never really considered marrying someone as a possibility before. Her mother made sure she never met anyone for the first eighteen years of her life, and once she was free, she was so focused on college and landing a job, she hadn't thought much about relationships. "You didn't answer my question. Why is marriage important to you?"

"I don't know," he answered truthfully. "It became important to me when I met you."

Persephone held his gaze and drew her legs apart, wrapping them around his waist. She could feel the head of his cock pressing against her entrance. Hades sank into her with a groan. She gasped, gripping his arms. There was something sweet about the beginning. Hades bent to kiss her, letting his forehead rest against hers, and breathed her breath. Then everything changed. Hades's thrusts became urgent, and his head fell into the crook of her neck, his teeth grazing and biting her skin.

"So fucking sweet," Hades hissed, looking into her eyes. "Take me deeper, darling."

She wasn't sure it was possible; she could already feel him in the bottom of her stomach. Hades's arms looped under her knees, and he lifted her slightly. Pleasure ripped through her, and she dragged her nails along his skin.

"Harder!" she commanded.

He drove into her, pumping his hips. She clenched

around him, her orgasm building inside, clawing its way to the surface.

"Come, darling."

With his permission, she climaxed, and as she came down from her high, Hades groaned, throwing his head back and shuddering.

In the aftermath, they lay together, kissing and touching and breathing.

"Gods, I missed you," Persephone said, resting against Hades, her head on his chest.

Hades chuckled, and they glanced at one another. After a beat of silence, Persephone spoke in a low voice. "You were going to tell me about Leuce."

"Hmm. Yes," he said, and after a moment, he pulled her on top of him. "I had a meeting with Ilias at my restaurant. I didn't know Leuce was there. She hurried after me as I was leaving and grabbed my hand. Old habit."

Persephone glared.

Hades pressed a finger to her pouting lips. "I jerked away and kept walking. She was asking for a new job."

"That's it?"

"Afraid so."

She collapsed on him. "I feel like an idiot."

Hades wrapped his arms around her.

"We all get jealous. I like when you're jealous… except when I think you might actually leave me."

She rose again, straddling him now.

"I was angry, yes, but…leaving you never occurred to me."

After a moment, Hades followed her into a sitting position.

"I love you. Even if the Fates unraveled our destiny, I would find a way back to you," Hades said.

Persephone twined her arms around Hades's neck.

"Do you think they can hear you?" she teased.

"If so, they should take that as a threat."

Persephone laughed, and they came together again. Later, as she dozed off, she couldn't help wondering about the Fates.

Would they really unravel her destiny with Hades?

———

Hades's absence drew Persephone from sleep.

She sat up, holding his sheets to her chest. The fire blazed, and it was still dark in the Underworld.

Something isn't right, she thought.

She got out of bed, slipped on her robe, and made her way into the garden. Hades had a habit of wandering into the night just to sit beneath the stars and wisteria. She walked the length of the garden, coming to the edge where it emptied into a field of flowers. From here, she could see the lights of Asphodel and the muted fire of Tartarus.

Perhaps he's gone there, she thought.

She wandered into the field. A warm breeze carried the smell of ash and made the grass rustle around her. It was almost loud enough to drown out the sound of Cerberus, Typhon, and Orthrus's footsteps, but Persephone heard their panting and turned in time to see the three Dobermans burst through the grass.

"Oh, my sweet boys." She patted each one on the head. "Have you seen your papa?"

The three whined. She assumed that was a yes.

"Will you take me to him?"

The three led Persephone through the field and into a tangled wood. She had never been here before and guessed this was a newer addition to the Underworld. Hades's realm was ever changing, and she suspected that was to make it harder for people to enter and escape.

The woods seemed to go on forever—deep and dark. Tree limbs interlaced, creating an archway overhead, and though they were bare, lampades rested there, lighting the path as if it were a starry sky.

The dogs kept their noses to the ground and surprised Persephone when they bolted from the path, into the forest beyond.

Would Hades really be so deep in these woods?

She followed, her way lit by the nymphs, until she lost sight and sound of Cerberus, Typhon, and Orthrus.

A breathy moan drew her attention. It came from behind her and grew in frequency.

Persephone moved toward the sound. Her heart hammered in her chest, and the air suddenly felt heavy and solid. It wasn't long before she saw them in a clearing— Hades and Leuce tangled together just as tightly as the branches overhead, the nymphs' light illuminating their lovemaking.

PART III

"The path to paradise begins in Hell."
—DANTE ALIGHIERI

CHAPTER XXIV
A Touch of Madness

For one horrifying second, Persephone couldn't move.

She was frozen, numb.

Her legs felt shaky, and her chest ached in a way she'd never thought possible. It was like her shock had become a monster, and it was clawing its way out from the inside.

Then an awful sound escaped her mouth.

The two froze and turned in her direction. Hades pulled away from Leuce, and the nymph collapsed to the ground, unprepared for his sudden movement.

"Persephone—"

She barely heard him say her name over the roar in her ears. Her power churned inside her, boiling her blood, rushing to the surface of her skin.

She saw nothing but red.

She would destroy him. She would destroy her. She would destroy this world.

Persephone screamed her rage, and everything around

her began to wilt. The trees rotted before her eyes, the leaves withered and fell, the grass yellowed and faded until all the earth around her was barren. She would strip Hades's world of life like he had stripped her of happiness.

Leuce fled, and Hades came toward Persephone. At his approach, she felt the devastating blow of his betrayal all over again.

"Persephone!"

"Don't say my name!"

Her voice sounded different, guttural.

Her power was hot in her hands, and she fed her anguish into it. The ground beneath her feet began to rumble.

"Persephone, listen to me!"

She had listened to him. She had listened and believed him.

I love you—deeply, endlessly.

She wasn't listening anymore.

He took a step toward her.

"Don't!"

As she spoke, the earth between them split, and a massive chasm opened between them.

Hades's eyes widened.

"Persephone, please!" He sounded desperate, but that was expected.

She was destroying his realm.

She screamed, her voice rang with fury and violence, and her magic was like fire against her skin. She didn't know what she was doing, but she felt guided to bring her hands together, and the power that gathered there was immediate. It blasted Hades, sending him flying backward into the desolate landscape.

He landed on his feet and dropped his glamour. He was a manifestation of death—dark and menacing.

This is how he looked upon the battlefield, she thought, and for a moment, Persephone's heart beat harder with the fear that he might overpower her.

Shadows peeled away from his form and raced toward her. He was trying to subdue her, and the thought sent a burst of raw anger through her. She screamed again, and her magic tore from her, freezing the shadows just as she'd frozen everyone at the Lyre.

A deafening silence followed, and she met his gaze before sending Hades's shadows racing back toward him with a burst of her own magic.

Hades lifted his arm, and the shadows disintegrated into ash.

"Stop!" he commanded. "Persephone, this is madness."

Madness? She would show him madness.

"You would burn the world for me?" she asked, recalling words he'd used when she'd spoken to him about Apollo, recalling how fervent he'd been when he'd told her never to use the god's name in their room again. *Their* room. Power gathered in her hands. "I will destroy it for you."

Hades's eyes widened just as a terrible cracking sound filled the air. Massive roots split the sky, barreling toward the earth. She was drawing the life from the Upperworld into the Underworld.

The roots hit the ground with a deafening explosion, shaking the earth and destroying mountains.

"Hecate!" Hades's voice was powerful and resonant as he summoned the Goddess of Magic. She appeared immediately, manifesting beside Hades. Together, their power fought Persephone's, and as more roots threatened to spear the Underworld, they were halted midair.

"What happened?" Hecate cried.

"I don't know. I felt her anguish and came as soon as possible."

Hades's answer incensed her.

Felt my anguish? He saw it! Why is he acting like he isn't the traitor here?

Persephone's rage continued. She fought hard against Hades and Hecate. Combined, their magic was like an impossible weight. The more she pushed against it, the more drained she felt, but she wasn't just exhausted physically.

Inside, her rage was turning to despair.

Inside, she was broken.

"My dear." It was like Hecate was right beside her, speaking into her ear, though she stood on the other side of the cavern. "Tell me."

Persephone's eyes blurred with tears, and she shook her head.

"Persephone, tell me what happened."

Tears slid down Persephone's face as the memory of what had unleashed her terror welled to the surface, unbidden. If Persephone could, she would have repressed it for the rest of her life, but at Hecate's words, she relived the terror of discovering Hades inside Leuce. Seeing the pleasure on the nymph's face made her want to vomit.

This time, instead of inspiring the anger that fueled her power, the memory exhausted her. She felt unstable on the inside, defeated, and sick. The power rushing through her body died, and she swayed. Hecate caught her in her arms just as she vomited.

Slowly, the goddess helped her to the ground, and Persephone rested in her arms. She brushed her hair from her face, soothing, "It wasn't real, my dear, my love, my sweet."

Persephone sobbed, turning her head into Hecate's chest. "I cannot unsee it. I cannot live with it."

"Shh. You will, my dear. Rest."

Then she was embraced by darkness.

———

Persephone woke in the queen's suite; her face felt swollen, and her head hurt. Plush blankets cradled her weak body, and bright light filtered in through the windows. It took her a moment to recall how she'd gotten here, but soon the memories returned, flooding her mind like a living nightmare. Tears formed in her eyes and slid down the side of her face.

"Do not cry, my sweet," Hecate said.

Persephone turned her head and found the goddess sitting beside the bed. Persephone rubbed her eyes, trying to make the tears disappear, but she just sobbed harder.

Hecate took Persephone's hand. "Breathe, my dear. What you saw wasn't real."

Persephone took several deep breaths and looked at her friend. "What are you saying?"

"You walked through the Forest of Despair, Persephone. What you saw was a manifestation of your greatest fear."

Persephone was quiet for a moment, trying to grasp what Hecate was saying, but the terror of those memories was embedded in her mind.

Hecate sighed. "And I see the enchantment hasn't worn off yet."

"Enchantment?"

"We think that's how you ended up in the forest," she said.

"You think someone enchanted me?" Persephone frowned. "Who?"

The goddess offered a small smile, but there was nothing humorous about it. "Hades is on the hunt."

Persephone shivered. She could just imagine what that meant, recalling how he'd looked in the forest after she'd drained it of life. Still, she couldn't help hoping he found whoever had done this, because what she had seen last night was torture.

Persephone sat up, leaning against the headboard, her head spinning. "Why would Hades have such a horrible place in the Underworld?"

"Well, it is an extension of Tartarus," Hecate said. "And you weren't meant to be there."

Persephone pushed the covers away and tried to stand up, but she felt so weak.

"I'd like to go outside," she said.

Hecate helped her stand, and they stepped outside. It was late afternoon, and Persephone was relieved when she strode onto the balcony and saw that the Underworld was lush and green.

Suddenly, she was frantic. "The souls! Did I—"

She'd used so much power; she'd shaken the ground and cracked the sky, giving no thought to the people she might have hurt.

"Everyone is fine, Persephone," Hecate assured her. "Hades has restored order."

Persephone closed her eyes and let out a long breath. *Thank the gods,* she thought.

They entered the garden and found a spot to sit beneath the purple wisteria.

"You demonstrated great power in the forest, Persephone," Hecate said. Persephone couldn't place the tone of the goddess's voice, but she sensed a mix of admiration and fear.

She looked at the goddess. "Are you...afraid?"

"I'm not afraid of you," Hecate said. "I'm afraid *for* you."

Persephone's brows drew together, and Hecate sighed, looking down at her hands. "It was a fear I had from the moment I met you, that you would be powerful...terribly so."

Persephone shook her head. "I...don't understand. I'm not..."

"You halted Hades's magic. You *used* his magic against him, Persephone. He is an ancient god, well-practiced. If the Olympians find out..."

"If they find out...?" she prompted when Hecate's voice faded away.

It was the other woman's turn to shake her head. "I suppose anything could happen. They might want you to become an Olympian, or..."

"Or?"

"They might perceive you as a threat."

Persephone couldn't help it. She laughed, but one look at Hecate told her just how serious the goddess was about this.

"That's ridiculous, Hecate. I can barely control my power, and apparently, I can't maintain my strength."

"You're learning control, and strength comes with practice," Hecate said. "Mark my words, Persephone. You will become one of the most powerful goddesses of our time."

Persephone didn't laugh.

They were quiet for a while after that, and soon, Hecate rose to depart.

"I must go. I promised Yuri we'd have tea. I didn't think you'd be up for it."

Persephone smiled. The goddess was right; she didn't feel up for much. She was exhausted and still unsettled by the events that had unfolded last night.

Hecate leaned forward and kissed Persephone's hair before departing.

Alone, Persephone's thoughts turned to Hades. She'd thought she'd manifested her greatest fear when she'd almost lost Lexa, never really considering that Hades's betrayal could be just as horrific. She still felt unfathomable pain when she thought of him and Leuce together, despite Hecate's explanation for what she'd seen in the Forest of Despair.

She sighed and rose to her feet, wandering through Hades's garden, halting when the god walked into view from the opposite direction. He was in his Divine form, his strong frame draped in robes, and his long hair was pulled up into a messy bun. His horns were like black slashes, rising into the sky. He looked exhausted and pale and beautiful.

She held her breath in his presence, feeling as if there were oceans between them.

"Are you well?" he asked.

The question always warmed her, but this time, it

ignited her. She felt so much for him in a single moment, she could hardly make sense of it all, love and desire and compassion.

"I will be," she answered.

Hades watched her for a moment, gaze searching.

"May I join you on your walk?" he asked.

"This is your realm," she answered.

Hades frowned but said nothing, and as she moved forward, he fell in step beside her. They didn't hold hands or walk arm in arm, but now and then, their fingers would brush, and the sensation was electric. Every inch of her skin felt like an exposed nerve. It was so strange. After everything they'd been through in the last few days, her body still responded to him as if none of that had happened.

She found herself wondering if Hades felt the same, then noticed his fists clench at his side.

She took that as confirmation.

They walked in silence until they came to the edge of the garden, where Persephone had found herself last night before venturing into the Forest of Despair. Finally, Hades turned toward her and spoke.

"Persephone. I...I don't know what you saw, but you must know—*you must know*—it wasn't real."

He sounded so broken, so desperate for her to understand.

"Shall I tell you what I saw?" She whispered the words, and while she didn't feel angry, she too wanted him to understand. "I saw you and Leuce together. You held her, moved inside her like you starved for her."

She shook as she spoke, and her nails dug into her palm.

"You took pleasure from her. Knowing she was your lover was one thing. Seeing it was…devastating."

She closed her eyes against the nightmare as tears streamed down her face.

"And I wanted to destroy everything you loved. I wanted you to watch me dismantle your world. I wanted to dismantle *you*."

"Persephone," Hades whispered her name, and then she felt his fingers beneath her chin. He tilted her head up, and her eyes fluttered open. "You must know that wasn't real."

"It felt real."

Hades's fingertips slid across her skin, collecting her tears.

"I would take this from you if I could."

"You can," she said, drawing close. "Kiss me."

Hades's lips pressed to hers. His tongue teased her lips before thrusting into her mouth and coiling with her own. His mouth was brutal and bruising, and he tasted smoky and sweet, and as he explored, her hands sought, running down the planes of his hard stomach and gripping his cock through his robes.

An unnatural groan escaped his mouth, and he pulled away; his gaze burned into hers.

"Help me forget what I saw in the forest," she said, breathing hard. "Kiss me. Love me. Ruin me."

They collided, tearing at each other's clothes until they stood naked beneath the pallid Underworld sky. Their lips crashed, tongues tasting, breath mingling. Hades's hand cupped the back of her head; the other moved down, over her belly and into the nest of curls between her thighs. She moaned as his fingers dipped into her hot flesh. For a moment, she was lost in the pleasure of him, in the ache at her core.

When Persephone could no longer stand, Hades knelt with her. She settled back, cradled by his robes, while he sat on his heels, staring at her unclothed body, eyes like the fires of Tartarus.

"Beautiful," he said. "If I could, I would keep us here in this moment forever, with you spread out before me."

"Why not fast forward," she asked, "to when you are inside me?"

Hades grinned. "Eager, darling?"

"Always."

He pressed a kiss to the inside of her knee and then trailed them down her thighs until his mouth closed over her cleft, his tongue playful, before parting her slit and spearing her. She bucked against him, and Hades pushed her knees down, spreading her wider. She could feel herself clenching around him, her arousal so heightened, it was almost painful.

She came, gasping his name, threading her fingers through his hair so she could pull him up her body to kiss him. His lips crashed against hers, trailed her neck and then her breasts, his tongue swirling around each tip, making them rock solid.

"There was no greater torture than feeling your anguish," he said. "I knew I was somehow responsible, and I could do nothing about it."

She pressed her fingers to his swollen lips. "You can do something about it."

She reached between them, where Hades's hard-as-steel cock pressed into her leg. She guided him to her center. They came together viciously. Hades's hips dug into hers as his cock split into her, and she reveled in the ache of him filling and stretching. Her head snapped back, pressing into the ground, and she arched against him, a guttural cry escaping her mouth.

Hades bent to kiss her lips, capturing the sound. She couldn't find a place for her hands. Her fingers clutched at his silk robes, at the grass, then his arms.

"Fuck!"

Maybe he'd cursed because she'd broken skin, she wasn't sure—but either way, he pinned her wrists above her head. His eyes were wild and unfocused, and his tempo increased as he chased his orgasm, slamming into her harder than ever.

Hades collapsed atop Persephone, his head resting in the crook of her shoulder. They were slick with sweat, and their breaths came in harsh gasps. After a moment, Hades lifted himself onto his elbows and brushed Persephone's hair from her face.

"Are you well?"

"Yes," she whispered.

"Did I…" He hesitated. "Did I hurt you?"

She smiled at the question because she had never felt better. "No."

She touched his face, tracing his brows, his nose, his kiss-swollen lips, and whispered, "I love you."

A faint smile touched Hades's lips. "I wasn't sure I would hear those words again."

Hades's admission hurt her heart.

Her eyes began to water. "I never stopped."

"Shh, my darling." Hades's gaze was tender. "I never lost faith."

But *she* had, and the thought nearly destroyed her.

Hades gathered her into his arms and brought her to his bed. There, he kissed her, drawing her from her darkness. He nudged her legs apart with his knee, and just as he prepared to consume her once again, there was a knock at the door.

Persephone froze, and to her surprise, Hades directed the person at the door to enter.

"Hades!"

The god rolled off her and sat up in bed, his naked chest exposed. Persephone sat up beside him, holding his sheets to her chest as Hermes entered their bedroom.

"Hey, Sephy," he said, giving her a sheepish smile.

"*Hermes,*" Hades called his attention.

"Oh yeah," he said. "I found the nymph, Leuce."

"Bring her," Hades ordered.

Persephone gave Hades a questioning look as Leuce appeared in the center of the room. It had been a while since Persephone had seen the nymph, and she looked exhausted and scared. Her eyes were wide, and her whole body shook. When her gaze fell upon Hades and Persephone, a horrible sob exploded from her throat.

"Please—"

"Silence," Hades commanded, and it was like Leuce lost her ability to emit sound. "You will tell Persephone the truth. Did you send her to the Forest of Despair?"

Tears spilled down Leuce's face as she nodded.

The wine, Persephone realized—*Drink! The wine tastes like strawberries and sunshine.* Persephone's instinct was to feel betrayed, but something seemed...off.

"Why?" she asked.

"To tear you both apart," Leuce answered.

There was no hint of venom in her voice, and

Persephone found that strange. If the nymph had truly wanted this, why was she so…remorseful? She shifted, moving closer to the end of the bed.

"Why?" Persephone asked.

Leuce's eyes widened, and she shook her head, refusing to speak.

"You will answer," Hades said.

Persephone didn't think it was possible for Leuce to cry harder, but she did, and this time, the nymph collapsed to her knees. "She will kill me."

"Who?"

"Your mother," Hades said.

The revelation shouldn't have shocked Persephone, but it did.

"Is this true?" she asked, turning to Leuce.

"I lied when I said I didn't remember who gave me life," she admitted. "But I was afraid. Demeter reminded me over and over that she would take it all away if I didn't obey. I'm so sorry, Persephone." Leuce hid her face. "You were so kind to me, and I betrayed you."

Persephone gathered the sheets around her and slid off the bed, ignoring the fact that she left Hades bared to the room. She approached and knelt before Leuce.

"I don't blame you for fearing my mother," Persephone said, and as she spoke, Leuce met her gaze. "I feared her for a long time too. I won't let her hurt you, Leuce."

The nymph collapsed into Persephone, and the goddess held her for a long moment, until she was able to collect herself.

"Hermes," Persephone said. "Will you take Leuce to my suite? I think she deserves some rest."

"Yes, *my lady.*" He gave an exaggerated bow and smirked.

Once they were gone, Persephone turned to Hades, who had a peculiar look on his face.

"What?"

He shook his head, a smile growing.

"I am just admiring you."

She was temporarily distracted by his comment and then said, "I suppose we should summon my mother to the Underworld."

Hades's brows rose. He clearly had not expected her to say that. "Shall we call upon her now?" he asked. "Perhaps we should make love so that she has no reason to suspect her plan worked."

"*Hades!*" Persephone chided but smiled too.

CHAPTER XXV
Collecting Pieces

Hours later, Hades, Persephone, and Leuce gathered in the throne room. Hades was in his Divine form, as was Persephone. They sat side by side, Hades on his obsidian throne and Persephone on gold and ivory. Leuce stood by Persephone, shaking.

"She will lash out," Leuce said. "I am sure of it."

"Oh, I expect it," Persephone replied and looked at the nymph. "She is my mother."

"Hermes has returned," Hades commented. He'd sent the god to retrieve the Goddess of Harvest—a task Hermes hadn't been eager to accept.

"*I think you just want her to disfigure my face,*" Hermes had said. "*She will bite my head off when I tell her you've commanded her appearance in the Underworld.*"

"*Then don't tell her Hades sent for her,*" Persephone had replied. "*Tell her I command it.*"

Hermes had grinned, just as Persephone was doing now.

She felt empowered in a way she had never felt before, and she couldn't really explain why. Maybe it had something to do with what Hades had said the night of the solstice celebration—that he loved her for who she was, and it was those qualities he wanted in his queen.

It meant that she could be herself without sacrifice, and the first step toward that would be dealing with her mother.

Hermes escorted Demeter into the room, and despite the severe mask she attempted to maintain, Persephone recognized the look of contempt on her mother's face when she saw Hades and Persephone sitting side by side like royals upon the dark precipice.

Her lips were pinched and her stare hard. She halted when she reached the center of the room.

"What is this about?" Demeter demanded, her voice tinged with fury.

"My friend tells me you have threatened her," Persephone said. If Demeter wasn't going to feign pleasantries, Persephone wouldn't either.

Demeter glared at the nymph and then looked at Persephone. "You would believe your lover's whore over me?"

"That is unkind," Persephone said tightly. "Apologize."

"I will do no such—"

"I said 'apologize,'" Persephone commanded, and Demeter was sent to her knees, the marble beneath her cracking with the force of her fall. Persephone didn't mean to use so much force, but the result had the desired effect.

Demeter's eyes widened in surprise. She hadn't expected to be taken to the ground by her own daughter. Her expression quickly turned into a glare, her anger filling the room. "So," she said, her voice shaking. "This is how it will be?"

Persephone said nothing. Demeter had chosen this path with her actions.

"You could end your humiliation," Persephone said. "Just...apologize."

Those words were like declaring war.

"Never." The word left Demeter's lips in a shuddering breath.

A shock wave of Demeter's power rushed through the throne room as the goddess attempted to rise. The surge in strength took Persephone off guard for a moment, her own magic rushing forward to quash it. She glanced at Hades. She could feel his power all around, lapping at the edge of her own, lying in wait.

Persephone stood and descended the few steps that separated her from her mother. As she approached, the floor beneath Demeter continued to crack and crumble. Finally, Demeter relented, her power waned, and she glared up at her daughter.

"I see you have learned a little control, Daughter."

Persephone might have smiled, but she found that when she looked at her mother, all she felt was resentment. It was like a curse, working through her body, coating everything in darkness.

"All you've ever had to do was say you were sorry," Persephone said fiercely. She realized they were no longer talking about Leuce. "We could have had each other."

"Not when you're with him," Demeter spat.

Persephone stared at her mother for a moment and then said, "I feel sorry for you. You would rather be alone than accept something you fear."

Demeter scowled at her daughter. "You're giving up everything for *him*."

"No, Mother, Hades is just one of many things I gained when I left your prison."

She released Demeter from her magic, but the goddess shook visibly and did not rise to her feet.

"Look upon me once more, Mother, because you will never see me again."

Persephone expected to see fury in her mother's eyes. Instead, they gleamed with pride, and an unsettling smile curled her lips.

"My flower...you are more like me than you realize."

Persephone closed her fingers into a fist, and Demeter vanished.

There was a beat of silence in the aftermath before Leuce hurried forward and embraced her.

"Thank you, Persephone."

When the nymph pulled away, Persephone smiled, maintaining her composure. On the inside, she was trembling. The look on her mother's face was one she knew well.

War was coming.

———

Persephone was anxious as she approached the hospital. It had been a few days since she had visited Lexa. Most of that was because Lexa was still struggling with delirium—or rather what the doctors were calling delirium. Persephone knew the truth of her psychosis. Her soul was struggling to understand what it was doing in the Upperworld.

Guilt made Persephone feel nauseous.

She'd been selfish. She knew that now—but the realization came too late.

Persephone headed to the fourth floor—the general ward where Lexa had been moved after being taken off the ventilator—and caught Eliska leaving Lexa's room.

"Oh, Persephone. I'm glad you're here. I was just going to get some coffee. Want anything?"

"No, thank you, Mrs. Sideris."

Eliska glanced back at the room. "She's having a good day," Eliska said. "Go ahead. I'll be right back."

Persephone entered the room. The television was on, and the curtains were drawn. Lexa sat up in bed, but she looked boneless. Her shoulders sagged, and her head lolled to the side. It was almost as if she were asleep, but her eyes were open and she seemed to be staring at the wall.

"Hey," Persephone said quietly. She took a seat near Lexa's bed. "How are you doing?"

Lexa stared.

And stared.

And stared.

"Lex?" Persephone brushed Lexa's hand, and she jerked, but the touch had gotten her attention. Except now that Lexa was looking at her, she felt…unsettled. The woman had the body and face of her best friend, but the eyes didn't belong.

These eyes were vacant, lackluster, lifeless.

She had the feeling that she'd just touched a stranger.

"Is this Tartarus?" Lexa asked. Her voice was hoarse, as if it had rusted from disuse.

Persephone's brows knitted together. "What?"

"Is this my punishment?"

Persephone didn't understand. How could she think her eternal sentence would be Tartarus?

"Lexa, this is the Upperworld. You—you came back."

She watched as Lexa closed her eyes, and when Lexa opened them again, Persephone felt like she was looking at her best friend for the first time since she'd awoken.

"You spend all your time in the Underworld and yet know nothing about death." Lexa was silent for a moment. "I felt...*peace.*"

She exhaled, as if the word brought pleasure, and continued.

"My body clings to the ease of death, searches for its simplicity. Instead, I am forced to exist in a distressed and complicated world. I cannot keep up. I don't want to keep up."

Lexa looked in Persephone's direction.

"Death wouldn't have changed anything for us, Seph," Lexa whispered. "Being back? That changes everything."

———

Lexa's parting words were heavy upon Persephone's mind as she returned home from the hospital. They made her afraid, and her mind turned to chaos as she attempted to divine the meaning behind them. What exactly did being back change for Lexa and her life?

Persephone had a feeling she knew the answer, though she was afraid to acknowledge it. The truth was, Lexa didn't want to be back, but Persephone had forced her to return. Now she had another question—how did souls who had experience such serenity live in a world without such promise?

Persephone had just poured herself a glass of wine when someone knocked. She was paranoid about answering the door when she was home alone, so she ignored it, thinking whoever was there would go away.

Except they didn't.

The knocking became excessive. Persephone

approached; her heart stuttered in her chest. She peeked out the window and screamed.

"Apollo!" she yelled. The god's face was pressed against the glass. She threw open the door. "Why are you knocking?"

"I am practicing respecting boundaries," Apollo said. "Is this not a mortal custom?"

She would have laughed, but he had scared her.

"I think I preferred you just appearing wherever you're not wanted."

To her surprise, he smirked. "Careful what you wish for, Seph."

She thought about correcting him but let the nickname slide. At least he hadn't called her honey lips.

"What are you doing here?"

"I came to bring you this," he said and pulled something from behind his back. It was a small, gold lyre.

Persephone took the instrument. "It's beautiful," she said and then met his violet eyes. "Why?"

"To say thank you."

She smiled. "I think that's the first time you ever thanked me."

"It's the first time you gave me a reason," he teased and then nodded to the instrument. "I can teach you to play it...if you want."

"I'd like that."

After a beat, he became serious again, his jaw tightened, and his eyes hardened.

"I'm really sorry about Lexa, Persephone. If it means anything to you, just know...I didn't actually know her soul was broken when I healed her."

Persephone looked at her feet. She hadn't known

either, hadn't known what it would mean for Lexa or her loved ones.

"Thanks," she said, looking at him again. "Wanna come in for some wine?"

"No," he said quickly and then laughed. "I would like to keep my balls, thank you."

Persephone wouldn't put it past Hades to manifest without warning. Still, even with the offer, Apollo lingered.

"There's something else."

Persephone waited.

"I'd like to let you out of the contract," the god said at last.

Persephone's eyes widened. "What?"

The god smiled ruefully. "I'm trying to change."

"I see that," she said and paused. "But I prefer to hold to my bargains, and if my calculations are correct, we still have five months and four days left."

She appreciated how Apollo was trying to be different, and she knew change took time. She wanted to spend these next few months watching him, guiding him. She trusted he could change with her, but with other people? She wasn't certain.

Apollo raised a brow and challenged, "Coffee tomorrow, two o'clock?"

"Is that a demand or a request?"

"Both?"

"Fine, but I get to pick the place."

Persephone swore she saw a moment of hesitation in Apollo's eyes—a gut reaction to disagree and demand control, but then his eyes softened.

"Fine. See you then."

And he was gone.

CHAPTER XXVI
A Touch of Serenity

Two weeks later, Lexa was released from the hospital. Their apartment felt smaller with six people inside, all fawning over Lexa. Eliska and Adam bought groceries and stocked their pantry to overflowing; Jaison had moved more of his things into Lexa's bedroom and took immediate responsibility for her medicines. Sybil, Persephone, and Zofie hung back, watching everything unfold, unsure of what to do.

Persephone wasn't sure what the worst part was—the fact that Lexa seemed to be completely detached from the situation or that her parents and Jaison were ignoring how different she was. She spent long stretches of time sleeping, and when she wasn't asleep, she stared at the wall. When asked direct questions, she just gaped at the person speaking until they repeated themselves, and sometimes, even then she didn't answer.

"She's not the same," Persephone had said one night after she'd asked Lexa to join them in the living room to watch *Titans After Dark*. It wasn't Persephone's favorite, but she remembered how her best friend would light up when discussing the gritty details of the primordial drama.

Lexa hadn't looked at Persephone when she'd answered with a quiet, "No."

When Persephone had spoken in the kitchen, she'd mostly been talking to herself. It was her own attempt to process grief. Lexa might not have died, but they'd lost her either way.

"She was hit by a freaking car," Jaison snapped. "She's not going to bounce back."

Persephone blinked, shocked by his anger.

"I know. I didn't mean—"

"Maybe if you weren't so wrapped up in your own problems, you'd see that."

He stomped back to Lexa's room without another word.

"He's just upset," Sybil said. "He knows she isn't the same."

"This mortal has distressed you," Zofie said. "Do you want me to kill him?"

"What? No, Zofie. You can't just kill people who upset you."

The aegis shrugged. "You can where I'm from."

"Remind me to hide all your weapons," Persephone said.

The tension remained throughout the next week. Persephone was glad to have an escape in the Underworld but made sure to check in with Lexa every day—it became a new routine, a new normal. Wake up, check on Lexa, work, check on Lexa, Underworld.

She went on like that for weeks until one morning

after returning from the Underworld, Persephone wandered into the kitchen and halted in her tracks.

Lexa was making coffee.

She stood in her pajamas, hair in a messy bun, and when she looked up at Persephone, she smiled. She looked…normal.

"Good morning," she chimed.

"G-good morning," Persephone said, a little suspicious.

"I thought you might like some coffee."

"Yes," Persephone said and gave a breathy laugh. "I love coffee."

Lexa laughed, filling a mug and pushing it toward her. "I know."

Persephone cupped the drink between her hands. For a moment, she couldn't move. She just stood there, staring awkwardly at Lexa.

She cleared her throat. "I'd…better get ready for work," she said, reluctant to leave, afraid that if she did, she'd realize this was all just a dream.

Lexa offered a small smile again. "Lucky," she said. "I would like to work again."

"You will soon."

Persephone made her way back to her room. As she did, she sipped the coffee Lexa had made and promptly spit it back into the cup. It was strong and bitter and thick.

Not like the coffee Lexa had made before the accident.

She's trying, Persephone thought. *That's all that matters.*

She'd drink a million cups of this coffee if it meant Lexa was healing.

Persephone got ready for work. She hated how her perception of her job had changed. She used to look forward to days spent at *New Athens News.* Now they filled her with dread, and it had nothing to do with the crowd that hung out to see her every day—it was her boss. Demetri had continuously given her busy work, keeping her from working on stories. She decided if he did it again today, she would challenge him.

"Hi, Persephone!" Helen said as she exited the elevator.

"Hello, Helen," Persephone said, smiling at the young woman. She was about the only thing Persephone enjoyed about her job anymore.

She crossed the workroom floor, and before she made it to her desk, Demetri popped out of his office, handing her a stack of papers.

"Obituaries," he said.

When Persephone didn't take them, he dropped them on her desk.

"You have to be kidding me, Demetri. I'm an *investigative* journalist."

"And today you are editing obituaries," he said.

He turned and went back into his office.

She followed. "You've given me menial tasks since Kal called off the exclusive." *Since I found out about your fucked-up love potion,* she wanted to say. "Was this the trade-off?"

"You wrote an article that resulted in negative publicity for this company and hurt your reputation. What do you expect?"

"It's called journalism, Demetri, and I expect that you'll stand up for me."

"Look, Persephone, no offense, but when it comes down to saving my own ass or saving yours, I'm choosing myself."

Persephone nodded. "You'll regret this, Demetri."

"Are you threatening me?"

"No," she said. "I'm offering you a peek into the future."

"Do us a favor, Persephone. Stop sending your god after your problems."

"You think Hades will be the one to dismantle you?" Persephone asked, taking deliberate steps toward the mortal.

Demetri tensed, unnerved by whatever he saw in her expression.

She shook her head and continued, "No. Your fate is mine to unravel."

With the prophecy spoken, Persephone turned on her heels and left Demetri's office.

———

Lexa was in the kitchen the next morning with another pot of coffee. The same thick, burnt sludge she had made the day before, but Persephone didn't care. She accepted the drink, sitting at the bar.

"Are you alright?" Lexa asked.

Persephone was so surprised by the question, she burned her lips trying to sip her coffee. "I'm sorry, what?"

"Are you alright?"

Persephone set down her mug. "I should be asking you that question," she said and sighed. "I guess I'm just not looking forward to work."

She explained what had happened the day before.

"When I started there, I was so...ecstatic. I was ready to find the truth, to give a platform to the voiceless. Instead, I'm made to run copies, edit obituaries, and make up predictions."

"I think it's time to start your own paper," said Lexa.

Persephone shook her head. "How?"

Lexa shrugged. "I don't know, but how hard could it be? Just do what you already do—give a voice to the oppressed."

Persephone tapped her nails against the countertop, considering Lexa's proposal. It was something she'd joked about before, but this didn't seem funny. It felt like a real possibility. She thought of all the reasons journalism had appealed to her—she'd wanted to find the truth, serve justice, speak for the voiceless—all things she could do on her own with no Demetri and no Kal.

"Thanks, Lex. You're amazing. I hope you know that."

Lexa smiled, and she focused on the counter for a moment before suggesting, "Maybe...we could go out sometime. Like...before. It'll take your mind off everything."

Persephone smiled.

"I'd like that."

For the first time in a long time, Persephone felt like she might be able to heal the guilt she felt over this whole ordeal.

"I'm sorry, Lex," Persephone said. She'd never actually apologized to her for what she'd done—for the deal she'd struck with Apollo.

"I know," Lexa said. "But I forgive you."

When Persephone arrived home from work, she found Sybil getting ready in her room. Her hair was curled, her makeup done, and she wore a pretty floral dress.

"I hope you don't mind," Sybil said. "I needed a place to get ready, and Lexa's in the shower."

"No, of course not," Persephone said. "I just came home to check on her. How's she doing?"

Sybil nodded. "Better."

"Are you...going out?"

The oracle blushed. "I have a date."

Persephone grinned, excited for her. "With who?"

"Aro," Sybil said quietly.

Before she became an official oracle, Sybil, Aro, and Xerxes had been inseparable. Persephone was glad they had reunited.

"When did this start?"

Sybil shrugged. "We've always been friends, and after Apollo fired me...we started talking again."

Persephone smiled. "Oh, girl. I'm so happy for you."

"Thanks, Seph."

Persephone felt bad for not saying goodbye to Lexa, but she sent a text to let her know she'd be back in the morning, then teleported to the Underworld, appearing in the library. She'd had the intention of curling up by the fireplace and reading. Instead, she found Hades waiting.

"What are you wearing?" Persephone giggled.

He had on a black shirt, pants, and what looked like black rain boots. She had only seen him this casual once, and that was when he came to her house to bake cookies.

"I have a surprise for you."

"Those pants are definitely a surprise."

He smirked. "Come."

He held out his hand, and she took it, fingers tangling with his as he led her outside. At the front of the palace, two large black horses waited. They were majestic, their coats glistening, their manes braided.

"Oh!" Persephone clasped a hand to her mouth. "They're beautiful."

The horses snorted and pawed the ground. Hades chuckled. "They say thank you. Would you like to ride?"

"Yes," she answered immediately. "But...I've never..."

"I'll teach you," he said.

Hades guided her toward the horse.

"This is Alastor," he said.

"Alastor," she whispered his name, caressing his muzzle. "You are magnificent."

The other horse neighed.

"Careful, Aethon will be jealous."

Persephone laughed. "Oh, you are both magnificent."

"Careful," Hades said. "I might get jealous."

Hades handed Persephone the reins and instructed her to put her foot in the stirrup and sit on the saddle as gently as possible. He gave more direction—*sink your weight, lean back, firm up your legs.*

"My steeds will listen if you speak. Tell them to stop, they will stop. Tell them to slow down, they will slow down."

"You taught them?" she asked.

"Yes," he said while mounting Aethon. "Don't worry. Alastor knows what he carries. He will take care of you."

They started at a snail's pace, but Persephone didn't mind. They'd often gone on walks, but those were limited to the gardens and her grove, and there was something refreshing about seeing the Underworld this way. Alastor and Aethon trotted side by side, and Hades took her into new territory—through fields of purple and pink lupin, rimmed by dark mountains.

"How often do you…change the Underworld?" she asked.

One corner of Hades's mouth rose. "I wondered when you'd ask me that question."

"Well?"

"Whenever I feel like it," he said.

She laughed.

"Perhaps when my magic isn't so terrifying, I will try."

"Darling, there is nothing I'd like more."

They came to the end of the lupin field and continued down a narrow path between the mountains. On the other side, an emerald forest bloomed. Hades kept close to the rocky wall of the mountain. The sound of running water piqued Persephone's interest. That was when Hades stopped and dismounted.

He approached her and helped her down, his hands lingering on her waist.

"You look beautiful today," he said. "Have I told you?"

She grinned. "Not yet. Tell me again."

He smiled and kissed her. "You're beautiful, my darling."

He took her hand and led her through a line of trees. On the other side was a waterfall that poured off the mountainous rocks into a shimmering lake. It was a million shades of blue and clear as crystal.

"Hades," she whispered. "How gorgeous."

When she looked at him, his gaze singed, aroused and intense. Awareness shuddered through her, and she turned to him.

They didn't speak, just came together beneath the trees.

Hades was unhurried in his exploration, and Persephone soaked up each second. Everything was slow—the kisses languid, the caresses dreamy. When he entered her, he paused and brought his lips to hers. There was something extremely raw about this kiss, though it was light and lingering. When she opened her eyes, she found him staring at her, still and swollen inside her.

She reached up and touched his face.

"Marry me," he said.

She smiled. "Yes."

Then he moved inside her, the friction built as slowly as he moved, and despite the pace he set, her breath came faster. She gripped his shoulders, nails digging into his skin, lost in the sensations he elicited all over her body.

She loved it, loved him.

She came hard but quietly.

"My darling," Hades whispered. He kissed her face, brushing away tears. "Why are you crying?"

She shook her head. "I don't know."

She just felt everything so keenly—every emotion was like a spear inside her. Her love for Hades was almost unbearable, her happiness near painful.

Hades lifted her and carried her into the lake where they showered beneath the waterfall.

After, they returned to the palace.

On the inside, Persephone was still struggling with her feelings. They were so powerful, so heightened. She was so deeply in love, it hurt.

It was a new level of love—one she had entered as his fiancée, as his soon-to-be wife and queen.

The thought made her chest feel warm—a sensation that didn't last when she saw Thanatos waiting for their arrival. She glanced at Hades. His face had turned stony, lips tight, eyes hard.

Something's wrong.

She tried to keep from jumping to conclusions, but it was difficult given the last few weeks.

Hades dismounted and helped Persephone down.

"Thanatos," Hades said.

"My lord," he nodded, and his blue eyes met Persephone's. "My lady."

The God of Death opened his mouth to speak, but no words came out. He tried again.

"I don't know how to tell you this."

Persephone swore her heartbeat slowed, and it suddenly felt really hard to breathe. Unlike before, Thanatos didn't even try to calm her with his magic.

"It's Lexa," he said.

Persephone was already crying. Hades's arms tightened around her as if preparing for her collapse.

"She's gone."

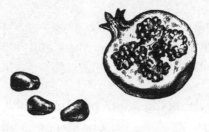

CHAPTER XXVII
Empowerment

There was a strange ringing in Persephone's ears, and she suddenly felt distant from the world around her—as if she were watching things from inside a globe. She couldn't feel anything, a terrible contrast to the earlier intensity of her emotions. Even Hades's touch was numb against her skin.

"Persephone." Hades said her name, but it sounded so far away. She couldn't look at him because her eyes wouldn't focus. "Persephone."

Finally, Hades placed his hands on her face and forced her to meet his gaze. When she stared into those black eyes, she burst into tears.

Hades pulled her against him as she shook and sobbed.

"My darling," Hades soothed, rubbing her back. "We don't have much time."

She barely heard him but felt his magic cradling her. They teleported, and she found herself on the bank of the Styx. She pulled away. Her face was soaked, and the pressure that had built in her nose and behind her eyes made her head hurt.

"Hades, what are we—?"

Her question died on her lips when she spotted Charon's ferry crossing the black river. The daimon was ignited like a torch against the muted landscape. Behind him, sitting with her knees drawn to her chest, was Lexa.

She looked pale but unafraid, and when Persephone spotted her, a raw sob escaped her. She clasped a hand over her mouth to suppress it.

Charon docked and helped Lexa to her feet. As she stepped onto the pier, Lexa embraced Persephone so tightly, she thought her bones would break.

They cried together.

"I'm sorry, Seph," Lexa whispered.

Persephone pulled away and met her gaze. It was strange to see her blue eyes in the Underworld. Beneath the muted sky, they were bright and...lively.

"I don't understand," Persephone said. "I thought you were...better."

Pain erupted in Lexa's eyes. "I...tried."

Persephone swallowed a thick lump in her throat, and then a horrifying thought occurred to her. She turned to Hades, alarmed and afraid.

"Where is she going?"

Hades looked just as distressed as Lexa.

"Seph," Lexa whispered, drawing her attention. "It's going to be okay."

But it wasn't going to be okay.

Persephone understood what had happened now.

Lexa had taken her own life. She was a suicide. She

was going to drink from the Lethe, which meant she would forget everything, including their friendship.

"Why?" Persephone's voice quaked; her mouth quivered.

Lexa just shook her head, as if she couldn't explain.

Your actions have condemned Lexa to a fate worse than death.

"I did this," Persephone wailed.

She'd bargained to heal Lexa, brought her broken soul back to occupy a body it didn't want, to a life it had finished. In doing so, she'd set her best friend up for another devastating end.

"Persephone," Lexa said, taking her shaking hands. "This was my choice. I am sorry it had to be this way, but my time in the Upperworld was over. I accomplished what I needed to."

"What was that?"

She smiled. "To empower you."

That made Persephone cry harder, and they embraced again.

They didn't part until Thanatos arrived, marking an end to their reunion.

"Are you ready?" he asked. His magic was calming, comforting, and for the first time in a long time, Persephone was thankful for it.

"Wh-where am I going?" It was the first time Lexa had looked uncertain since she arrived.

Thanatos looked to Hades, who explained, "You will drink from the Lethe," he said. "And then Thanatos will take you to Elysium to heal."

For so long, Persephone had tried to imagine a world where Lexa didn't exist, and now she realized this was it; this was the beginning of that world.

407

"I will visit you every day," she promised. "Until we are best friends again."

"I know." Lexa's voice cracked.

Persephone closed her eyes, trying to memorize the feel of her best friend's hugs, the warmth of her, the feel of her hands digging into her back.

"I love you," Persephone whispered.

"I love you too."

When they parted, Thanatos took Lexa's hand, and Persephone watched as they walked the stone path toward the Lethe. At some point, she and Hades returned to the palace. He encouraged her to rest, and she did, falling into the comfort of Hades's bed.

When she woke, she didn't remember falling asleep. She rose, exhausted, and went in search of Hades. She found him standing in front of the fire in his study. He stood with his hands behind his back, the firelight reflecting off his face, making him look serious and severe. He seemed deep in thought, but as she entered the room, he stiffened.

Guilt slammed into her, and she knew he was waiting for her anger, for her blame.

"Are you well?" she asked when he didn't turn to her.

"Yes," he said. "And you?"

"Yes," she said, and it was true. She was better, despite knowing that Lexa was dead, despite knowing that she had drunk from the Lethe.

Persephone stepped closer to him.

"Hades." She waited for him to face her. "Thank you for today."

He offered a small smile and returned his gaze to the fire. "It was nothing."

She reached for him, placing her hand on his arm. His gaze fell there first and then met hers. "It was everything."

He turned to her fully, and their lips collided. They kissed for a while, and soon, Hades drew her to the floor, entering her in one, smooth, purposeful movement.

"You were right," Persephone whispered. She was referring to Lexa's end. Her breath caught in her throat; her fingers twined into his hair.

"I did not want to be right."

"I should have listened," she said and moaned as a wave of pleasure rocked through her.

"Shh," Hades quieted her. "No more talk of what you should have done. What is, is. There is nothing else to be done but move forward."

As the first orgasm shook her body, Hades gripped her hard. "My queen," he hissed.

"*Hades,*" she moaned his name.

They reveled in the feel of each other, deepening their connection before collapsing together in a heap of skin and sweat and sex.

At some point, Hades rose with Persephone and moved her before the fire. She rested on her back, Hades on his side.

"I'm going to quit *New Athens News,*" she said.

The god lifted a brow. "Oh?"

"I want to start an online community and blog. I'm going to call it *The Advocate*—it will be a place for the voiceless."

"It sounds like you have thought about this a lot."

She smiled. She was taking Hecate's and Lexa's advice. She was crafting her own life, taking control.

"I have."

He placed his fingers beneath her chin. "What do you need from me?"

"Your support," she said.

"You have it."

"And I'd like to hire Leuce as an assistant."

"I'm sure she'd be pleased."

"And...I need your permission," she added sheepishly.

"Oh?"

"I want the first story to be our story. I want to tell the world how I fell in love with you. I want to be the first to announce our engagement."

Kal and Demetri had tried to take that away from her, but now she saw it as a path toward empowerment.

"Hmm." Hades feigned considering this. She could tell because of the look in his eyes. He was part amused, part admiring. "I will agree under one condition."

"And that is?"

"I too wish to tell the world how I fell in love with you."

He kissed her slowly at first, his tongue sweeping sweetly over hers, and then deepened the kiss.

They spiraled and lost themselves in the heat of one another again.

———

Lexa's funeral was scheduled three days after her death.

Persephone hadn't been able to visit Lexa in Elysium since the day she arrived in the Underworld, so seeing her body, anointed and pale, adorned with a wreath and coins, brought her to tears.

Hades attended and kept a protective arm around

her. It was one of the first times they had appeared in public, and his presence had not only drawn a crowd but also inspired many feelings in the room. She could feel them, teasing like wisps—curiosity and anger and sadness. These mortals obviously wondered why Hades had let Lexa die, wondered how Persephone could stand beside him. Once, she had wondered the same thing, and now that thought brought her immense pain.

Hades looked down at her, touching her cheek.

"You could never make them understand," he said, guessing her thoughts.

She frowned. "I do not want them to think poorly of you."

He offered her a small, sad smile. "I hate that it bothers you. Does it help if I tell you the only opinion I value is yours?"

"No."

After Lexa's funeral, they spent the next few days cleaning out her room and packing items into boxes for her parents to store. It was a strange day and left Sybil, Zofie, and Persephone feeling unsettled in their own apartment.

"I think we should move," Sybil said.

"Yes," Zofie said. "This home, it…smells of death."

The two looked at the Amazon.

"Persephone?" Sybil said. "What do you think?"

She opened her mouth and then closed it.

"I'm…engaged," she blurted.

Sybil and Zofie shrieked in excitement, and Persephone laughed.

Over the weekend, Persephone recruited Leuce to help with her new business. They met at the Coffee House and worked together over vanilla lattes.

411

"I've called every news outlet on your list," Leuce said. "They've all agreed to run your story. The *Divine* said it would be front-page news."

"Excellent," Persephone smiled.

She'd asked Leuce to cold-call several newspapers and magazines to announce her new business venture—and her engagement to Hades. It was a strategic move that would automatically guarantee she had a readership for her blog, where she would share the story of how she met and fell in love with the God of the Dead.

It would also enrage her mother. Persephone knew Demeter paid attention to the news from all the instances she'd scolded her daughter for writing about gods.

"Several have requested interviews," Leuce continued. "I said you wouldn't be available for them for another two weeks. I've put them in a spreadsheet. It took me forever. How do you use this…keyboard…so easily?"

Persephone laughed. "You'll learn, Leuce."

Sybil joined them later. Persephone had tasked her with creating a website that communicated simplicity and power, and the results were stunning. *The Advocate* was scrawled across the top of the page in a rich shade of purple.

Sybil also showed her a timeline for how the website would evolve as they added content—pages for health of all kinds and arts and culture.

Seeing the site fueled Persephone's excitement. Now all she had to do was focus on her welcome article.

It was strange to revisit the start of her relationship with Hades, because her mindset had been so different then. She'd been insecure and suspicious, and yet she'd wanted adventure. Little did she know her yearning would lead to an inescapable contract with the God of the Dead—a bargain that became love.

He helped me understand that power comes from confidence, from belief in your own worth. I am a goddess.

She felt those words deep in her soul.

———

On Monday morning, Persephone sat between Leuce and Sybil at the Coffee House as she pressed Publish on her article. She smiled when she read the bold lettering on the landing page of her website:

My Journey Toward Loving the God of the Dead

The two squealed and hugged Persephone.

"This is just the beginning," she said. She felt proud, she felt empowered, and she felt free.

Persephone left Leuce with a to-do list while she and Sybil gathered their things and headed to their respective workplaces. For Persephone, it was the most excited she'd been in a long time to return to the Acropolis, because she would never be going there again.

"Good morning, Helen!"

The young woman seemed surprised and stammered. "Good morning, Persephone!"

The goddess walked straight into Demetri's office. He looked up at her; his tablet glared off his glasses, obscuring his expression.

For a moment, neither spoke.

"You quit."

"I quit."

They spoke at the same time.

Demetri smiled, and that alarmed her.

"Can't say that I am surprised. I saw your announcement. You recruited every single news outlet," he offered a wry smile. "Well, with the exception of *New Athens News*." He sat back in his chair, and seemed sincere when he said, "Congrats."

"Thank you," she replied.

"*The Advocate*," he said. "Fitting. Will you continue to write about gods?"

She lifted her chin. She knew what he wanted to ask: *Will you write about me?*

"If it's an injustice, I will expose it," she said. She had promised she would dismantle Kal and unravel *New Athens News*, and gods were bound to keep promises.

He nodded. "Then I wish you all the best."

Persephone left Demetri's office and returned to her desk, emptying everything she'd brought into a box. It was a strange process, considering it felt as though she had just made this space her home. Now she was leaving, but for better things.

"Where are you going?" Helen asked, looking up from the desk as Persephone headed to the elevator.

She smiled at the young blond. "I quit, Helen."

"Take me with you."

Persephone's eyes widened. "Helen—"

"I'll work for you for free," she said. "Please, Persephone. I don't want to stay without you."

When the elevator doors opened, Persephone smiled. "Come on."

Helen squealed, grabbed her purse, and joined Persephone in the elevator. When they made it to the first floor, Persephone handed the box to Helen.

"Will you wait for me? I have to say goodbye to someone."

"Oh, sure," Helen said.

Persephone headed to the basement in search of Pirithous. She found his office empty. Glancing over his desk, amid stacks of work orders and tools, she spotted a notebook. She recalled the day she'd startled him in his office to ask if he could help her escape again and how protective he'd seemed of the information inside, and yet it lay open, tiny handwriting scribbled across the pages.

She might have left it unread had she not spotted her name on the page.

Curiosity overwhelmed her, and she began to read.

Date: 7/2

> *She wore a white shirt and a black-and-white-striped skirt today. Hair up. The shirt was cut low, and I could see the swell of her breasts as she breathed.*

Persephone's blood ran cold.

What the fuck is this?

She turned a page. There was a new description of her outfit for the next day—a pink, fitted dress and white heels.

> *Her legs are shapely. I found myself wanting to lift her skirt, spread her wide, and fuck her. She would let me.*

Further down, he wrote:

There was another report about her and Hades in the news today. Every single fucking day, someone is reminding me she is with him. She won't love him long. He is a god, and they destroy everything they love. I will make sure of that.

Then she found the list:

Duct tape, rope, sleeping pills, condoms.

Persephone felt something sour in the back of her throat. That day she'd interrupted Pirithous, when he'd seemed so nervous, he'd been working on a list.

"What are you doing?"

Persephone jerked her hand away from the journal. Her head snapped toward the door, where Pirithous now stood, blocking her exit. His eyes were steely and made her blood run cold.

She opened her mouth to speak but couldn't find words. Her heart was beating out of her chest, and a thin sheen of sweat beaded on her forehead.

"Pirithous," she breathed. "I came to say goodbye."

"Really?" he asked. "Because it looked like you were snooping."

"No," she whispered, shaking her head. There was a brief moment when neither of them spoke, and then Persephone reached for the closest, heaviest object—a flashlight sitting on Pirithous's desk. She threw it at his head, and as he dodged the blow, she attempted to rush past him, but he reached for her, his nails digging into her skin.

"Let me go!" she screamed. Her magic rushed forth, and vines sprouted around them.

Persephone barely had time to register her shock before Pirithous spoke. "Sleep!"

Persephone obeyed, falling into darkness.

———

When Persephone woke, she felt as if she'd been drugged. Her vision was blurry, her head and neck hurt, and her mouth was stuffed with a cloth and taped shut. Her hands were bound behind her back, and she sat in a hard wooden chair that cut into her arms.

Persephone began to struggle, wriggling her wrists and legs, but the ropes grew tighter. She expected her magic to rise to the surface in response to her hysteria, but it remained at a distance, just as foggy as her head, which made her even more frantic. Soon, she was rocking the chair back and forth in an attempt to free herself.

Then she caught sight of her surroundings and froze. There were pictures and newspaper clippings of *her* everywhere. Photos taken as she walked down the street, ran errands, and had lunch with her friends. Photos of her at her home, in her pajamas, and sleeping. The images were a log of her daily life. She felt sick and panicked.

"You're awake."

Pirithous came into view.

Persephone screamed, though her cries were muffled, and tears spilled down her cheeks.

"Stop, stop, stop!" he commanded. He reached forward and pulled the tape and gag from her mouth. "It is alright, my love. I won't hurt you."

"Don't call me that!" she snapped.

Pirithous's jaw tightened. "It is no matter," he said. "You will love me."

"Fuck you," Persephone spat.

The man shot forward, twining his fingers into her hair and pulling her head back. When she met his gaze, she noticed the color of his irises had changed from black to gold.

"You're...a demigod?"

A wicked smile cut across his face. "Son of Zeus."

"Oh gods, no wonder you're such a fucking creep."

He jerked her hair harder, and Persephone yelped, arching to lessen the tension. She reached for her magic again, and while it felt closer, she still could not summon it.

What did he do to me? she thought. Her head swam and nausea turned her stomach.

"Ungrateful," he hissed. "I've been *protecting* you."

"You're *hurting* me."

"You think this is pain?" he asked, but he released her. "Pain is watching the woman you love fall for someone else."

Persephone concentrated on her magic. It welled inside her, slow and steady.

"Pirithous, you don't know me. How could you love me?" she asked.

"I love you! Haven't I shown it? The hearts, the notes, the flower?"

"That's not love. If you loved me, you wouldn't have brought me here."

"I brought you here because I love you, don't you see? There are people who want to tear us apart."

"Like Hades? I assure you he will tear you apart."

"Don't say his name!"

"Hades will find me."

Pirithous moved toward her threateningly, and she squeezed her eyes shut. When he didn't touch her, she opened her eyes and found him glaring down at her. "Why him?"

Persephone searched for an answer—one that would appease him, that would make him go away.

"Because the Fates command it," she answered.

He paled, and for a moment, she thought she might have succeeded, but then he gritted his teeth and hissed, "You're lying!"

He knelt before her.

"Why him? Is it the sex?"

Persephone tensed, squeezing her legs together as Pirithous placed his hands on either side of the chair.

"Tell me what he does that you like. I can do better."

"Don't fucking touch me!" Persephone screamed and tried to shuffle away from him, but her heels wouldn't grip the floor. Pirithous's fingers dug into her skin, and he pried her legs apart. She reached for her magic again—it was close, so close.

"No!"

"You'll like it. I promise. You won't even think about him when I am finished."

No, she would only wish to die.

"I said no!"

She screamed, and her magic finally surfaced, breaking through the strange barrier that had clouded her mind. Thorns erupted around her from the ground. They created a cage, protecting Persephone from Pirithous's advances, cutting him in the process.

He screamed.

"You won't keep me from you!"

At first, he clawed at the wood, trying to break the branches with his bare hands. When that didn't work, he disappeared and returned with a knife, driving it through the thorn barrier.

Persephone screamed, and the thorns thickened until they exploded in shards and splinters.

Pirithous was blown back. He landed against the wall, his body sagging to the ground; a massive stake speared his chest.

He was dead.

There was a beat where Persephone sat quiet, breathing slow. Then, all of a sudden, she was slammed with an unspeakable feeling. It was a combination of shock and horror.

She had killed someone.

She screamed.

"Help! Somebody help me please!" she sobbed. "Hades!"

She struggled to free herself until her gaze caught something looming overhead.

"Furies," Persephone whispered, breathing hard from her frantic effort.

The goddesses floated; their pale bodies seemed to glow in the dark.

"Bride of Hades," their voices echoed. "You are safe now."

Smoke coiled in the air, and all at once, Hades appeared in his Divine form. Huge and imposing, he towered over her, a void of black. His eyes, fierce and furious, met hers and he froze. Persephone didn't think that anyone else would perceive the strange stillness that overcame him when he beheld her, but she saw it. She could feel it, and she knew that beneath those robes, every single muscle was rigid and ripped. He seemed to hesitate, and she felt that he was torn between going to her and taking care of Pirithous.

In the end, he turned to the mortal who had abducted her.

Suddenly, there was a gasping sound as he brought the demigod back to life.

Pirithous began to breathe hard, a strange whining coming from his throat. He didn't speak, but his eyes grew wide when he saw Hades.

"I brought you back to life," Hades said. "So I can tell you that I will enjoy torturing you for the rest of your eternal life."

Pirithous didn't seem lucid enough to register what Hades was saying, but the god continued anyway.

"In fact, I think I will keep you alive so you can ruminate in your pain."

He snapped his fingers, and a pit opened beneath Pirithous's feet. His screams were shrill as he fell into the Underworld.

Hades turned to Persephone, and with a wave of his hand, her bonds were broken. She fell into Hades as he approached, and he gathered her into his arms and turned to the Furies.

"Alecto, Megaera, Tisiphone, see to Pirithous."

They bowed their heads.

The Furies vanished, and Hades teleported to the Underworld. It was in his bedchamber that she fell apart. Hades sat with her cradled against him, soothing her with whispered words until her tears were dry, until she no longer felt like she was imploding on the inside. Finally, she pulled away.

"Bath," she said. "I need to scrub him from my skin."

Hades's mouth hardened, and Persephone felt as though she could see his mind working, deciding on the torture he would inflict upon Pirithous. Despite this, his voice was calm when he spoke.

"Of course."

Hades walked her to the baths, and she shed her clothes and entered the hot water. Steam curled around her, and she inhaled the scent of vanilla and lavender. She scrubbed her skin until it was red and raw. When she was finished, she left the water, wrapping herself in a fluffy, white robe.

Hades hadn't joined her. He sat some distance from the pool, watching her. She went to him and sat on his lap, wrapping her arms around his neck. She needed his comfort, his nearness.

"How did you know I was missing?" she asked, burrowing as close to him as she could.

"Your coworker, Helen, got worried when you didn't come back from the basement," he said. "She went to search for you and found the journals."

Hades's grip tightened, and the words came out from between his teeth.

"She didn't know who to tell. For better or worse, she told a security guard. Zofie had been patrolling outside when she was notified, and she realized she'd watched Pirithous leave with you—in a tilt truck. When she told me, I sent the Furies. You had already been gone so long…" His voice trailed away, and then he swallowed. "I wasn't sure what I would find."

"He was a demigod," she said. "He had power."

Hades nodded. "Demigods are dangerous, mostly because we do not know what power they will inherit from their Divine parent. What was Pirithous able to use against you?"

"He put me to sleep," she said. "And when I woke, I couldn't use my magic. I couldn't focus. My head…my mind was in turmoil."

Hades frowned. "Compulsion," he answered. "It can have that affect."

They were quiet for a moment, and then Hades spoke.

"Tell me what happened?" There was an edge to his voice that told her he wasn't ready, that if she spoke of her abduction, she would release the violence within him.

"I will tell you if you will promise me one thing," she said.

He raised a brow, waiting, and her eyes fell to his lips.

"When you torture him, I get to join you."

"That is a promise I can keep."

CHAPTER XXVIII
A Touch of Ruin

Thanatos accompanied Persephone on her first visit to Elysium.

"You won't be able to talk to her today," he said. "She must become comfortable with Elysium, or she will become overwhelmed."

Persephone had a feeling she knew what that meant—Lexa would have to drink from the Lethe again. That was the last thing she wanted.

"When will she be ready?" Persephone asked.

Thanatos shrugged. "It is hard to say."

She knew what Thanatos didn't say. *It depends on how much her soul has to heal.*

The thought pained her, but she pushed that away. She couldn't think of what she should have done. All she could do was learn from her mistakes.

They stopped at the top of a hill in Elysium. Here, Hades's sky was so bright, it was almost blinding. Beside her, Thanatos pointed to a figure in the distance. A woman whose black hair ignited like a torch against her white dress.

It was Lexa.

Tears pricked Persephone's eyes as she watched her best friend traverse the field, holding her hand aloft, touching blades of tall grass, and while Persephone couldn't see her face, she knew Lexa felt peace here.

Weeks went by, and Persephone visited Elysium every day, watching Lexa from afar, until one day, Thanatos approached and said, "It's time."

Persephone thought she'd be ready, that she would jump at the chance to be reunited with Lexa, but when Thanatos gave his permission, she suddenly felt nervous and more uncertain than ever.

"What if she doesn't like me?" she asked.

"Lexa is the same soul you found in the Upperworld. She is caring and loving and kind. She is ready for a friend."

Persephone nodded and took a breath. Preparing to approach was like preparing for a public speech. Anxiety whirled within her, making her stomach feel unsettled and tightening her chest.

She marched toward Lexa, who sat beneath a tree that was so full of pomegranates, it looked like it was on fire. Lexa wore a white dress, and her long, black hair spilled over her shoulders. Her head rested on the trunk, and her eyes were closed, as if she were sleeping.

She looked beautiful and rested, and Persephone was almost afraid to disturb her, afraid that when Lexa opened her eyes, she might not recognize the person behind them.

She took a breath. "Hi."

Persephone didn't use Lexa's name—Thanatos said she wouldn't remember it anyway.

Lexa opened her familiar, blinding blue eyes and met Persephone's gaze. Persephone thought her chest might explode when Lexa smiled at her.

"Hi."

"Can I sit with you for a little while?" Persephone asked.

"Yes." Lexa moved over a little so that Persephone could be seated and use the trunk to lean against. "You're not dead," Lexa said.

The observation surprised Persephone, and she shook her head. "No, I am not."

"Then why are you here?"

"I am Hades's fiancée," she said. "I visit Elysium often."

Lexa giggled. "I've noticed."

That also surprised her. "Have you?"

"I always notice Thanatos," Lexa said, blushing.

Suddenly, Persephone wondered if souls could have crushes.

"If you are Lord Hades's fiancée, then you will be queen."

"I suppose I will."

"Then you will have a crown and a throne," Lexa said. Persephone laughed. It was such a Lexa thing to say.

"I already have two crowns."

Lexa's eyes widened a little. "You must bring them," she said. "I have always wanted to wear a crown."

Persephone's brows knitted together. "Since when?"

Lexa shrugged. "Since…I came here. Will there be a wedding?"

Persephone sighed. "Yes, but I must admit, I haven't thought much about planning."

Between Lexa's death and her abduction, things had been a little hectic.

"You will be a beautiful bride," Lexa said. "A beautiful queen."

Persephone blushed. "Thank you."

Their conversation continued well into the afternoon. She probably would have stayed longer, but Hecate appeared and summoned her away.

"I must go," Persephone said, rising to her feet. "I have to get ready."

"Ready for what?"

"There is a gala in the Upperworld tonight," she said and then grinned. "You would love it. There will be gods and goddesses, pretty dresses, and dancing."

Lexa would love it because it was the event she'd been working on before her accident. An advocacy dinner for the Halcyon Project, and it was being hosted at the Olympian, one of Hera's hotels, a building Lexa had always admired for its beauty and architecture.

And because it was where most gods stayed when they visited New Athens.

"You must come back and tell me all about it," Lexa answered.

Persephone smiled. "Of course. I'll be back tomorrow."

When Persephone returned to the palace, Hecate and the lampades helped her dress.

Hecate had chosen a red, off-the-shoulder gown. The top was lace, and the skirt was full and made of layers and layers of tulle. Persephone loved the silhouette. It made her feel like a queen. The lampades smoothed her hair into soft, glamorous curls and applied natural makeup.

"We will let your beauty speak for itself," Hecate said, looking at Persephone's reflection as the goddess helped her accessorize with gold jewels and shoes.

Persephone smiled. "Thank you, Hecate."

"Of course, my dear."

Hecate left when Hades appeared. He stayed near the door, admiring her from afar. He was dressed in a tailored black suit—his signature color. His hair was slicked back, and his beard shaved close. He was handsome and regal, and he belonged to her.

That thought sent a wave of warmth through her.

"You look lovely," he said.

"Thank you," she said, smiling. "So do you. I mean… you look handsome."

He chuckled and extended his hand. "Shall we?"

He drew her against him, wrapping a hand around her waist as he teleported to the surface where Antoni waited for them outside Nevernight.

As Persephone slid into the back seat of Hades's limo, she laughed.

"And what is so amusing?"

"You know we could just teleport to the Olympian."

"I thought you wanted to live a mortal existence when in the Upperworld," Hades countered.

"Perhaps I am only eager to begin our night together," she said, looking at him through her lashes. The tension in the cabin thickened, and Hades's eyes glittered.

"Why wait?" he asked.

She moved first, grabbing layers of her dress so she could straddle him.

"Who chose this dress?" Hades asked, pushing aside the mountain of tulle that bloomed between them.

"You don't like it?" she pouted.

"I'd really rather have access to your body," Hades said.

"Are you asking me to dress for sex?"

Hades smirked. "It will be our secret."

They kissed, and Persephone's hands drifted down Hades's chest to the waistband of his slacks. She unbuttoned them and freed his sex, stroking him as her tongue explored his mouth.

He groaned, and Persephone's lips left his to trail down his jaw and neck.

"I need you," he growled. "*Now.*"

He was hard as a rock, and Persephone's breath caught in her throat, anticipating how he would feel inside her. She lifted herself, guiding his cock to her entrance, and sank onto him.

They groaned and rocked together in the dark of the limo.

"You have ruined me," Hades said. "This is all I ever think about."

"Sex?" She laughed, holding him close, loving the feel of his breath on her skin as he spoke.

"You," he said. His hands moved up beneath her dress until he held her hips. "Being inside you, the feel of you gripping my cock, the way you tighten around me just before you come."

She shivered. "You just described sex, Hades."

"I described sex with you," he said. "There is a difference."

She melted against him, and their lips slammed together, tongues stroking. Pleasure rippled through her, and she held Hades as if she might fall apart, rising and falling on him.

"Fuck, fuck, fuck," Hades cursed as she moved, and the sounds of their lovemaking filled the small space.

Hades's hips thrust upward, meeting her movements with furious speed. She gave a guttural cry, her fingers twisting into his hair.

"Come for me," Persephone whispered.

"My darling," Hades said, his fingers pressed into her skin hard, and he came inside her in a gush of warmth.

Persephone collapsed against him, breathing hard, their skin slick with sweat. Her legs shook, and she felt like she was floating.

He groaned.

"Fuck me," he muttered. "I'm like a fucking teenager."

She laughed. "Do you even know what it's like to be a teenager?"

"No," he answered. "But I imagine they are always horny and never quite sated."

Hades was still inside her—hard, wet, and ready for more.

"Perhaps I can help," she said and lifted herself from him. She started to slide to her knees, intending to take him into her mouth when he stopped her.

"No, darling."

Persephone frowned. "But—"

"Trust that there is nothing I would love more than for you to go down on me, but for now, we must attend this gods-forsaken dinner."

"Must we?" she asked.

"Yes," he said, pressing his finger beneath her chin. "Trust me, you will not want to miss it."

She wasn't so sure, but she held his gaze as she rose and sat beside him, adjusting the layers of her skirt. She watched as Hades tried to hide his aroused flesh. It almost made her laugh. Until he glanced at her, and a sound erupted from somewhere deep in his chest.

"*Goddess.*"

It was a warning, and her whole body began to feel warm again. She smiled and looked out the window, immediately jolted from her reverie when she noticed the sea of mortals outside the car. The crowd seemed to go on for miles, and they were packed together, standing as close to the car as possible.

It probably shouldn't have surprised her, given her experience at the Olympian Gala, but she had attended as a journalist then. This time, she was Hades's fiancée.

She inhaled sharply; anxiety gripped her. She wasn't sure she'd ever get used to this.

The car came to a stop, and the door opened. Immediately her vision was filled with flashing lights. Hades exited the car to a roar of adoration. They called his name, begged him to take them to the Underworld, begged to see him in Divine form.

He ignored the cries and turned, holding out his hand for her. She took a deep breath, steeling herself.

"Darling?"

The word comforted her, and she slipped her fingers into his palm. When he closed his strong hand around hers, it gave her the reassurance she needed to leave the cabin of the limo. When she rose to her full height beside Hades, there was chaos—the lights flashed faster, a machine gun of white light blasting her vision.

With their fingers laced, they began their walk

down the swath of red carpet that led to the front of the Olympian—a grand hotel that looked like a golden wall of reflective metal. Persephone was surprised when Zofie joined them, dressed in the blue gown Persephone had forced her aegis to buy for events like tonight.

"Zofie." Persephone pulled the Amazon in for a hug. She stiffened.

"Persephone, are you well?"

"Yes," she answered. "Just happy to see you."

The Amazon smiled.

Now and then, they were directed to a spot to pose for pictures. Hades obliged, pulling Persephone against him and slipping an arm around her. At one point, she swore she felt his lips touch her hair.

They were funneled into a reception hall with a ceiling made of glass-blown flowers. Persephone spent several minutes with her neck craned, staring at the display, but she was soon interrupted by numerous people who approached to greet her. Some were strangers, some were high-ranking criminals and members of Iniquity, but a few were Persephone's friends.

"Sybil!"

She hadn't seen her friend and ex-roommate since they'd moved out of their apartment a week ago. She hugged the oracle tight. The blond wore a sparkling, champagne-colored gown.

"You look beautiful!"

"Thank you. As do you," Sybil said. "How are you doing?"

"Good. Great," Persephone said. She couldn't stop smiling. "How's Aro?"

Sybil blushed. "Good. We're…good."

Persephone let out a small yelp when Hermes appeared, scooping her up into a tight hug. When he set her on her feet, it was in front of Apollo, who smirked when he saw her.

"So, Sephy," Hermes said, wagging his brows. "I hear Hades put a ring on it."

She laughed. "Well, not...literally."

The God of Trickery gasped. "What the fuck? You can't be engaged without a ring, Sephy."

"That's not true at all, Hermes."

"Says who? I wouldn't have said yes until I saw the rock."

She rolled her eyes.

"Congrats, Seph," Apollo said, and Persephone grinned at him.

They were directed into the dining room shortly after, and Persephone sat at a table at the front of the room between Hades and Sybil. Despite the excitement of the evening and seeing her friends again, Persephone couldn't help thinking about Lexa. She could see her in parts of the event—in the wine lists, the music, the decor. Everything was glamorous and dramatic, just the way she liked it.

She felt her friend's absence acutely.

Well into dinner, Katerina, the director of the Cypress Foundation, stood and welcomed the crowd. She offered an overview of the Halcyon Project and then turned over the remainder of the presentation to Sybil.

"I am new to the Cypress Foundation," she said. "But I fill a very special position. One that was once occupied by my friend, Lexa Sideris. Lexa was a beautiful person, a bright spirit, a light to all. She lived the values of the Halcyon Project, which is why we at the Cypress Foundation have decided to immortalize her. Introducing…the Lexa Sideris Memorial Garden."

Persephone gasped, and Hades gripped her hand beneath the table.

On the screen behind Sybil were sketches of the garden—a beautifully landscaped oasis.

"The Lexa Sideris Memorial Garden will be a therapy garden for residents of Halcyon," Sybil explained, jumping into an overview of the meaning behind each part of the garden, explaining that the nightshades paid homage to her love of Hecate, and the gorgeous glass-like sculpture at the garden's center represented Lexa's soul—a bright and burning torch that kept everyone going.

Persephone's heart was so full.

Hades leaned in and whispered against her ear, "Are you well?"

"Yes," she whispered, swallowing hard. "Perfect."

After dinner, they gathered in the ballroom. Hades pulled Persephone onto the dance floor, drawing her close. One hand rested on the curve of her back; the other held her hand. He guided her along the floor with grace and confidence, and though he was a perfect gentleman, there was something sensual in the way their bodies formed to one another.

Warmth swelled in the bottom of Persephone's stomach, and she couldn't take her eyes from his.

"When did you plan the garden?" she asked.

"The night Lexa died."

Persephone shook her head, biting her lip.

"What are you thinking?" Hades asked.

"I am thinking about how much I love you," she answered.

Hades grinned. It was a beautiful smile, and she felt it deep in her chest.

After that, the music spiraled into something more electronic, and Hades took his leave, encouraging her to dance with Sybil, glowering when Hermes and Apollo joined in. She spent a while with them, laughing and joking and feeling better than she had in a long time. At some point, she went in search of Hades and found herself outside on a balcony that overlooked the whole of New Athens. From here, she could see all the places that had changed her life over the last four years—the university, the Acropolis, Nevernight.

She wasn't there long when Hades approached.

"There you are." He drew his arms around her waist and pulled her against him. "What are you doing out here?"

"Breathing," she said.

He chuckled, and the sound sent shivers down her spine. He pressed a kiss to her cheek, squeezing her tight.

"I have something for you," Hades said, and Persephone turned in his arms.

"What is it?" she asked, a smile on her face. She had never been so happy.

Hades studied her for a moment, and she wondered if he was thinking the same thing. Then he reached into his pocket and knelt before her.

"Hades—" She wanted to protest. They had already done this. They were engaged—she didn't need a ring or a formal proposal.

"Just…let me do this," he said, and the smile on his face made her chest swell. "Please."

Hades opened a small black box, revealing a gold ring. It was both ridiculous and beautiful, encrusted with diamonds and gold flowers. It matched the crown Ian had made for her.

She gaped at it for a moment before shifting her gaze to Hades's.

"Persephone. I would have chosen you a thousand times over, the Fates be damned," he said, laughing. "Please…become my wife, rule beside me, let me love you forever."

Tears sprang to her eyes, and she offered a shaky smile.

"Of course," she whispered. "Forever."

Hades's smile grew, showing his teeth. It was one of her favorite smiles—the one she liked to imagine was only for her. He slipped the ring on her finger and rose to his feet, capturing her mouth in a kiss that she felt in her soul.

"You wouldn't have happened to overhear Hermes demand a rock, would you?" she asked when he pulled away.

Hades chuckled. "He might have been talking loud enough for me to hear," he said. "But if you must know, I have had that ring for a while."

"How long?" she demanded.

"Embarrassingly long," he said and then admitted, "Since the night of the Olympian Gala."

Persephone swallowed a lump that had risen in her throat.

How had she gotten so lucky?

"I love you," he said, pressing his forehead to hers.

"I love you too."

They kissed again, and when he pulled away, she

noticed something white swirling around them. It took her a moment to realize that it was *snow.*

Despite its beauty, there was something sinister to the way it fell from the sky.

Not to mention it was August.

Persephone looked at Hades. The happiness that had lit his face a moment before was suddenly gone. Now he looked concerned, his dark brows drawing together over severe eyes.

"Hades, why is it snowing?" Persephone whispered.

He looked down at her, his eyes an endless void, and answered in a solemn tone, "It's the start of a war."

Author's Note

First, THANK YOU to all my wonderful readers. I am so thankful for each and every one of you.

When I wrote *A Touch of Darkness,* I wrote the book of my heart. *A Touch of Ruin* is no different. Writing this sequel was just as difficult as writing the first book, but I knew there were a few things I wanted to touch on in ATOR, namely myths surrounding Apollo and his lovers.

I looked at several myths but settled on highlighting Apollo x Daphne, Apollo x Cassandra, and Apollo x Hyacinth. Obviously, these are the most well-known, and two really illustrate Apollo's horrible treatment of his lovers. He relentlessly pursued Daphne until she begged to be turned into a tree and cursed Cassandra when she wouldn't sleep with him. This is a modern problem, and so I wanted to challenge Persephone to handle it.

The other myth I knew I wanted to use was the myth of Apollo and Marsyas (another common and similar myth is Apollo and Pan). Marsyas was a satyr who challenged Apollo to a musical competition. There are several versions of this myth that have Marsyas and Apollo winning; however, it ends in the satyr's death. I thought this was important because it shows just how unstable Apollo can be—how he is tied to antiquity and how it conflicts with the modern world.

Now I'll touch on the myth of Pirithous.

I know in mythology, Pirithous and Theseus are bros (trust me, Theseus is coming *eyeroll*). The two decide they will wed daughters of Zeus. Theseus steals Helen of Troy (yes, Helen the assistant is Helen of Troy). Well, Pirithous decides he wants Persephone. Together, the two head to the Underworld in an attempt to abduct her. Exhausted, they sit for a while to rest and are unable to get back up. Later, Hercules will rescue Theseus, but Pirithous will remain. I wanted to include this myth because, to me, Pirithous is just a really creepy fan, and so, in the modern world, that's exactly what he is.

Maybe I watch too much true crime. Ha!

Last, I'll touch on the most heartbreaking part of the book—Lexa.

When I start writing a character, I make a list of "the worst things that can happen."

Well, number one for Persephone was losing Lexa, but I couldn't imagine Persephone understanding the mortal condition of grief unless she lost someone close to her. She'd also need to lose Lexa in the worst possible way (a.k.a., bringing Lexa back, seeing her suffer, then having her return to the Underworld with no memory of her) in order to understand why Hades cannot help everyone. It's a huge part of Persephone's growth, because up until this point, she takes Hades at face value. By the end of ATOR, she can speak from experience, as much as that sucks.

Finally, I got to highlight the thing that sparked this whole idea in the first place: Hades's club, Iniquity.

From the very beginning, I wrote these notes: *Gods in Modern Society, Hades rules the underworld—gambling dens, mafia,* and while I only scratched the surface of the world Hades rules in the Upperworld, I know it will be influential in *A Touch of Malice*.

About the Author

Scarlett St. Clair lives in Oklahoma with her excellent dog. She has a master's degree in library science and information studies. She is obsessed with Greek mythology, murder mysteries, love, and the afterlife. For information on books, tour dates, and content, please visit scarlettstclair.com.